MW01005594

The Last Pomegranate Tree

BACHTYAR ALI

Translated from the Kurdish
by Kareem Abdulrahman

with Melanie Moore

archipelago books

Archipelago Books
232 3rd Street #A111
Brooklyn, NY 11215
www.archipelagobooks.org

Distributed by Penguin Random House
www.penguinrandomhouse.com

Library of Congress cataloging data available upon request
ISBN: 978-1-953861-40-5

Cover art: Rostam Aghala
Book design: Zoe Guttenplan

This book was made possible by the New York State Council on the Arts
with the support of the Office of the Governor and the New York State
Legislature. Funding for this book was provided by a grant from the Carl Lesnor
Family Foundation. Archipelago Books also gratefully acknowledges the
generous support of the City of Literature, Jan Michalski Foundation,
the Nimick Forbesway Foundation, Lannan Foundation, the National
Endowment for the Arts, and the New York City Department of Cultural Affairs.

PRINTED IN CANADA

THE LAST POMEGRANATE TREE

I

From early that first morning, I knew he was keeping me locked in. He told me that a fatal disease, a plague of some sort, had spread outside. Whenever he told lies, the birds would fly away. It had been that way since he was a child. Whenever he told a lie, something strange would happen. Either a sudden downpour would begin, trees would fall down, or a flock of birds would soar above our heads.

I was being held prisoner inside a large green mansion within a sequestered forest. He brought me a stack of books and told me to read them.

"Let me out" was all I said in response.

"There is disease and corruption everywhere, Muzafar-i Subhdam," he said. "Stay here in this beautiful world. This is the mansion I built for myself. For myself and my angels. For myself and my devils. Stay here and be patient. What's mine is yours. There's a disease out there, and you need to stay away from it. You understand?"

True, I was far away from the plague there.

It was how we'd been since we were kids, he leaving his duties to me, I leaving mine to him, to Yaqub-i Snawbar, the man whose glance towards the sky could make things happen: a cloud might suddenly appear, a star might shoot across the sky, a light might suddenly enter our hearts, or night fall before its due. The world felt different by his side. I often went on walks with him and felt as if I were under a spell. He could drag you along the roads for many days and nights and you wouldn't even feel hungry.

I was his only childhood friend. Our fellow Peshmergas were all younger. Later on, one half would become his enemies and the other his servants. I don't know when my story with Yaqub started. Twenty-one years of imprisonment had left me with nothing but a poor memory, had made me a willing slave. In those years, he was the only one who sent me letters. He would write on a small piece of paper, "When you come out, it will be a new era. You will live in the loveliest mansion in the world." He sent that message year in, year out. He never signed his name. He'd either write "a friend who misses you" or draw a bird at the bottom, like in the old days. From one year to the next, I could tell from his handwriting that something was happening. In those twenty-one years, I received nothing from outside through which to interpret the world except for his messages; his short notes were my only window to the changes in the world. For twenty-one years, I received the same line from the outside world, but each time it had a different meaning for me.

My first night in the mansion was cold, quiet, and creepy. I had spent twenty-one years alone. I had been silent for twenty-one years. In all that time, I had made a huge effort not to forget language. During all those long years of incarceration, I had the time to create my own language, a language of poetry.

When I came out of prison, I could express anything, but in a way that others couldn't always understand. When I came out, I smelled of the desert. Every desert has its own smell. Only those who have spent a long time in the desert can distinguish these smells.

The only time they took me out of prison was when they'd hoped to swap me for a state prisoner. But it never worked out. After ten days in another prison, I was taken back to the desert. For twenty-one years, I listened to the sand. My prison cell was far away from the entire world, a cell in the middle of a sea of sand, a tiny room besieged by sky.

For a while, I was deemed the country's most dangerous prisoner. Cut off from the world, I was left at the far end of the country in a place where man is forsaken even by God, a place where life ends and death begins, a place like an empty planet. In those twenty-one years, I learned to talk to the sand. Don't be surprised if I tell you the desert is full of voices humans will never quite understand. I listened to the desert for twenty-one years and gradually began to decipher the hieroglyphs of its various sounds. If you are in a prison cell for that long, you learn how to fill your life, how to keep yourself busy. The most important thing is not to think about time. Once you can stop thinking about the passage of time, you can stop thinking about place also. Dwelling constantly on other times and other places can kill a prisoner. Until the seventh year of my captivity, I counted the hours day after day. At first, you count exactly, second by second, but one day you wake up and see that everything has gotten mixed up. You don't know if you've been there for a year or a century. You don't know what the outside world looks like.

The most dangerous thing is knowing someone is waiting for you. Once you are sure that no one is waiting for you and the world has forgotten all about you, only then can you start thinking about yourself, although after twenty-one years of life in the desert, all you can think about is sand. Some nights the desert calls your name, but the biggest problem is not knowing how to answer. I saw the spirits of the desert, apparitions made of sand, created and scattered by the wind. It takes a long time to learn to talk to sand. In those twenty-one years, I came to see that there is an art to doing so. It means learning never to expect a reply, learning to talk and then to listen to your own echoes, to echoes that fade away and are buried beneath hundreds and thousands of others.

Once a month, I was let out into the desert. Accompanied by a guard, I would walk across the sand for several hundred meters. Those were the best days. I always looked forward to them for a whole week, so that when I stepped onto the sand, I was thrilled. For twenty-one years, the sand was my only friend. When I dipped my feet in it, I felt life, I felt the earth, I felt my unbounded being, condemned to die in that prison cell.

I gradually forgot about people. The universe was my only companion. Twenty-one years is a long time to think about the universe. I would wash myself with sand and I would be filled with life again. Eventually, a day comes when you think of nothing but the freedom bestowed upon you by the endless sea of sand. A few years into my prison term – I don't know exactly when – I stopped thinking about politics. One night I was awoken by the moonlight. It had brightened my cell so much that I could see everything as if it were daylight. That light gave me the energy to think of nothing but the universe. I had died a long time ago. No one knew I was alive except for Yaqub-i Snawbar. Plus, no one was looking for me. I had come from nothing and to nothing I had returned.

Year by year, all my memories turned to sand.

I didn't know where I was being held. The desert remained nameless to me. My captors had blindfolded me to take me there. We were on the road for many days in the back of a ZiL military truck. I could tell from the smell of the road that we had driven through the desert for a long time. They held me for twenty-one years in order to swap me, one day, for a senior figure.

One dark night, they released me. When you leave prison after twenty-one years, you can see nothing but sand. You can think of nothing but sand. When I was brought to this mansion, I neither understood anything nor wanted to. It was so dark everywhere that I didn't have a clue what was going on. From the moment I left prison to the moment I opened my eyes in the mansion, I saw no light at all. One pair of hands passed me on to another in the dark, hands quieter than the night, quieter than the walls, quieter than an old prisoner's closed cell door. A man took my wrist and put me on board another vehicle. He said nothing. I didn't even hear him breathe. Until then I had heard only the cries of the sand. I didn't know where they were taking me, nor did I care. Thinking about the universe makes you unafraid.

I was twenty-two when I was arrested. I was forty-three when I was released. One dark night, they came, blindfolded me, and took me out.

"Are you leading me to my execution?" I asked the guard.

"No, to set you free," he said. I didn't know what he meant by "free." Nothing is more meaningless than talking about freedom after twenty-one years behind bars. My only real freedom was to be left alone to live in the desert. I was certain I wouldn't understand anything about the world; I had a great fear of cities and people. After years of imprisonment, you can no longer distinguish between a human being and sand. Throughout my prison sentence, I had seen no one but my guards. And they were quieter and stranger than the desert. During those twenty-one years, they rarely exchanged even a few words with me. They seemed to have been born and bred in the desert, to have seen nothing but the desert all their lives.

We drove through some tough terrain before we got to the mansion. I could tell from all the bumps and jolts of the ride that we were heading for a mountainous region.

In the morning when I looked out the window, I was terrified of all the leaves. There were thousands of leaves stirring in the morning breeze, and the view overwhelmed me. I saw all sorts of winged monsters in the trees. Green monsters, monsters with eyes that shone like dewdrops. When I awoke that first morning, I saw nothing but windows and horrors. There were no sounds and no people, not even the trace of another human being. All the windows were shut too. I was all alone in a huge mansion, and all the gates were locked. Nor could I find any sign of a human being outside. I hadn't realized I had been set free until I saw the brutal greenery of those leaves. But a bright ray of sunlight danced in the trees, just like the constant brilliant glare of the desert. After twenty-one years, it was the first time I had opened my eyes and not seen the desert, the old friend that had entered my soul. I knew *he* had brought me here. In the mansion I could see something that reminded me of him, of Yaqub-i Snawbar.

I started walking through the rooms of the mansion. My body couldn't get used to this new geography. It was a strange night that I would never forget. The desert still had me in its grip. I could barely believe I was free.

I don't know what time they brought me from the car, but it felt like early morning. I can recognize early morning by its smell. Soil, wherever it is, has its own perfume. When I stepped onto the earth after twenty-one years, I was still living in a sea of sand and my country had slowly become an illusion. Although I could smell the morning air, although I could smell the perfume of the trees and the cool breeze of the surrounding valleys, all these scents were mixed in with a strong awareness of the endless power of sand. When I walked on the soil, I feared the ground's precariousness, feared its giving way and sinking down. I saw nobody, sensed nobody.

When I opened my eyes, it was night. I knew I was inside a large house. It was dark, but a candle glimmered faintly in a corner. It was fresh; someone had lit it before my arrival and had just left.

I shouted into the mansion, "Hey, whoever lit the candle, where are you?" But all I heard back was a deep echo, an echo that traveled through the dark in layers and returned faintly. An echo that opened the door of another world for me. An echo whose ring was different from the sound of the sand. That night I saw nobody; there was nobody in the house. Someone had brought me here and left me. In the distance, I heard the sound of a vehicle pulling away.

The mansion was lavishly furnished. It was like a king's country retreat, but there was no sign of any other human being. I was exhausted. I wanted to sleep – or to die. Through the big windows, I could see the silhouette of a dense forest. The sky, as if about to assault me, hovered above my head. There was something in its blackness that was different from the desert night. In the desert, night always has a bronze glow. The sky's movement is similar to the sand's, and the sand's blackness resembles the darkness of embers that could be rekindled with a single puff of breath. That morning, however, the movement of the leaves scared me. For twenty-one years I had watched the world move a certain way; now I had gone from an orderly, familiar, law-governed universe to an entirely different one. I slept so as not to think. Rather than exploring the mansion, I lay down in the first corner I came across and slept. Something made me fear the beds. It was not just that I had been sleeping on the floor instead of in a proper bed for so long, but also that I was becoming suspicious of the place.

Before, I had known where I was, who I was, and why I was imprisoned in the desert, but that night I had no idea what I was doing in the mansion. The place was bigger than my imagination. My body was no longer used to moving from one room to another. All the things in the mansion were killing my solitude. I belonged in an undecorated world, a world where your only possession was your shadow, a world where the universe itself was an extension of man, where the sand and the sky were the only extensions of the soul. I thought that emptiness, desolation, and absence of ornamentation were tantamount to the most beautiful life. The sand helps us see man in his authentic image, as he is without any additions or artificial extensions. I was a stranger to everything, and everything frightened me immensely. At that moment, I was looking for an empty life, a life devoid of all shadows.

I don't want you to think I'm telling you all this for no reason. Saryas-i Subhdam was only a few days old when I left him. I didn't know then that after my first Saryas, a second and a third would enter my life. You shouldn't think I hadn't thought about Saryas during my time in prison. You shouldn't think I was a bad father and thought only about the sand. But when you look at nothing but sand for twenty-one years, one day you wake up and everything is mixed up. You wake up and all the other images in your memory have disappeared. Oh, nothing eats away at our memories like sand. Every day, you realize you've forgotten part of the past again. But I never forgot Saryas-i Subhdam, oh, no. I forgot the whole world, but not Saryas-i Subhdam. He was the only thing that didn't become sand, the only thing that remained evergreen in my mind. For many years, I would see him every morning. Every day, I would imagine him at different ages. I created thousands of faces for him, went through all the possibilities of what he might look like. Every day, I looked into the desert and thought about him.

I suppose the bizarre events surrounding Saryas-i Subhdam started during those strange desert mornings and evenings when I gave him more than one appearance. Year after year, I thought about him less because I no longer knew what I was thinking about: my thoughts had no form or direction. What stopped me worrying about the one person I had left behind was the thought of my own death. I was sure I had died during that lengthy period of time and that the whole world had forgotten about me. The thought that you have died and that others are living on without you, their lives taking their own courses and shapes, is extremely comforting. That nobody expects you to return is sheer bliss.

After the sixth year, I became absolutely convinced that, no matter what had happened, Saryas-i Subhdam had now grown accustomed to my death. Like prison, death is something to which you become accustomed. People must have first taken up a space for their absence to be felt later on. Like anything else – a vase on a table, the sound of a radio from an open window – they must first have a place before they disappear. But if there is nothing from the outset – if there is no sound, no physical presence – we don't feel their absence and loss. At one moment I felt my life in the desert had reached perfection when I had no need of anyone else. Myself and the infinite emptiness of the universe – that was perfection.

I felt that the outside world had its own kind of perfection too. I hadn't occupied an important place in the world: life was going on perfectly well without me; things had their own lives and meanings. I didn't feel my absence had left a hole in anyone's life. After twenty-one years, I was sure Saryas-i Subhdam was living his own life as well. I was sure Saryas-i Subhdam too, just like all the others, felt I was dead. Until the tenth year of my imprisonment, I had only one hope: to see Saryas-i Subhdam for a few minutes and then die. But then one morning, I woke up and abandoned that hope too. After ten years of separation, every reunion is another loss. Saryas and I had become an imaginary father and son.

One morning when I was looking at the sand, when I was looking at the aging of the desert, it dawned on me that I would never become a father. I knew I'd return like a block of sand, like someone who'd turn anything he touched into dust. Fatherhood is an embrace, but I was a fistful of black earth. On my return, I would only ever see life through images of the desert.

The night I was released, I didn't know where Saryas-i Subhdam was. I didn't know we would both eventually get lost in a desert that was neither mine nor his.

2

One evening a few years ago, Muhammad-i Dilshusha, Muhammad the Glass-Hearted, who is obsessed with discovering secrets, sets off for a meeting with an antique dealer. Not your usual sort of meeting where you casually drop in on someone either, but an important one that might unravel a mystery. It's a rainy evening, full of unusual and fantastical cloud formations. Without thinking about the clouds, he walks calmly south from the city's northern alleyways, singing. As well as the key ring he's playing with, he has a glass pomegranate in his pocket. He tosses the key ring into the air and catches it. Attached are glass keys that open imaginary doors for the young man who that evening considers himself the happiest person in the world.

Everybody knows him. Everybody has heard the story of the glass-hearted teenager who saw his own death in a dream, a death he keeps recounting, day in, day out. A dream of dropping his heart, of it breaking and shattering just like the glass antiques he has on display in the cupboards and on the long, tall shelves at home.

It starts to rain. Muhammad the Glass-Hearted looks up at the sky and realizes he has never seen such menacing clouds, but, unperturbed, he plays with the keys to the imaginary doors and carries on singing. It's a happy evening for Muhammad the Glass-Hearted; after all, he believes that one of his keys will only open doors when it's raining.

I have never seen him, but I can imagine him walking south through the alleys as he plays with his key ring, tossing it from one hand to another, passing it under his thigh and snatching it out of the air. I see a joyful young man who laughs as he looks at the sky rather than being afraid of it, a young man who has only recently created a life for himself out of glass, a life that only he knows to be so fragile and brittle. But there he is, nonchalantly walking along, singing.

His room is full of unusual vases, teapots with Chinese designs, glasses with etchings of birds, chinaware adorned with strange pictures of dragons, tigers, and fiery-colored doves. His cupboard, bookshelf, desk, and chest of drawers are all made of glass. Sitting atop one of the cupboards is a blue glass globe showing all the countries of the world.

When Muhammad the Glass-Hearted leaves home, he is confident about his chances in life. As rain begins to pour down stronger and harder, he keeps right on playing with his keys while people around him run off under umbrellas. He doesn't look at the sky or pay any attention to the rain, which steadily increases, eventually causing a massive flood. The streets and sidewalks now look deserted. People head into the tall buildings, looking down from the rooftops. They perch on the minarets, the blue domes, the hotel rooftops, the tops of the eucalyptus and pine trees. Only Muhammad the Glass-Hearted is being swept away by the water as the flood carries him from one neighborhood to another.

He's floating as if aboard a small but invisible boat. He's sitting cross-legged on the floodwater, looking on with a big smile. The flood is sweeping away cars, household items, chairs, whirling them all around Muhammad the Glass-Hearted, who is looking on. The floodwater is filled with unexpected items from the city: tires, piles of unread books, trays of food, household equipment, drowned women in their black cloaks, dead men whose hands still clutch their cash to keep it from getting wet. The water carries Muhammad the Glass-Hearted along with the objects, but he's sitting on the water as if on a prayer mat, grinning at the onlookers watching from the rooftops of houses and the balconies of two-story shopping malls.

He lifts his hands and waves to them, blowing them kisses. The waves propel him rapidly along, but he gets to his feet on the water, as if he's about to give some kind of performance, and returns the greetings of people on both sides of the street. He laughs as the water sweeps him away. Throwing his keys up into the air and catching them, he glides down the alleyways, the water sweeping him through the streets. Everyone sees the miracle; everyone sees Muhammad the Glass-Hearted playing among the dead as he walks on top of cars being carried away by the water and, from there, jumps back onto its surface. He catches drifting apples and oranges as they float by on the floodwater, juggling them as if he were a circus performer.

He picks up jewelry boxes swept away from goldsmith shops by the flood, throwing their shining contents to the people. The sight of him amid all that tragedy prompts laughter from the onlookers.

It's pouring down, but he moves through the streets as if helped by an imaginary oar or driven in a boat steered by God himself. He moves through the main roads, through the *qaysaris** that are now completely submerged. He sails through the butchers' sector of the bazaar, putting his arms around the floating carcasses, dancing with lambs that have been slaughtered and flayed. He passes through the shoe shops, and in the antique sellers' sector, he catches a floating silver vase and lays it on his lap.

He gives himself over to the course of the flood. Slowly it sweeps him away from the bazaars, alleyways, and streets to quieter places. The waves, now calm, are taking him to increasingly closed-off areas, to narrow and winding alleys in the south where the tops of the building are submerged in water and from which no voice can be heard.

Finally, as the rain begins to let up and darkness falls, at the end of his long journey, the water pushes him outside the gate of a two-story house in a cul-de-sac. He wants to turn back but cannot; he wants to stand up and walk across the waves and abandon himself to the course of the flood in another alleyway but cannot. An unknown force from within the waves propels him toward that gate. He stops and sits on the water, seized by a

* A *qaysari* is a covered labyrinthine bazaar typical of Kurdistan and Iraq. It is entered through the numerous alleyways that surround it and, normally located in the oldest sector of the marketplace. (Translator's note)

deep fear. Night falls. Slowly the clouds disperse, the moon emerging quietly and shyly.

Suddenly, an unknown cry from inside Muhammad's heart tells him, "This evening is the evening of love!" He reaches into his pocket and takes out his keys. One of them is the key of love, the key of his unrequited loves. He opens the gate with trepidation. When it springs open, the water carries him into the large courtyard of an old and stately home. As if circling an ancient temple, he circumnavigates the house and then does so again. He looks at the windows, listens to the profound silence of the walls. He circles one more time.

In one of the windows, two girls appear, both wearing white, both letting their long hair down into the water, and looking at him from above. One of them is Lawlaw-i Spi, the other her elder sister, Shadarya-i Spi. He passes by their window, borne by the water.

"Good evening. My name is Muhammad the Glass-Hearted. The flood has brought me here. Can you let me in your window?"

Lawlaw opens it, saying, "Please, come in." Little does she know that by opening the window, she has flung open the gates to a great storm in her life. Muhammad goes in, and all he takes with him are the glass pomegranate in his pocket and the ring of keys. At first breath, Muhammad the Glass-Hearted is certain he is entangled in an intricate and complex love. He looks at the girls, their hair unfurling onto the carpet, tangling around objects, forming waves, then straightening out.

He is the son of one of the city's famous men, Sulaiman the Great, who, since the success of the revolution, has been in charge of the city's most dangerous secrets. In the past six years, he has never seen such beauties anywhere. He is the key maker for all the impossible doors, and his bundle of keys has opened them all. He is a master of uncovering secrets. But still, he has not seen such a sight before.

That evening sees the start of a story of unrequited love. Friendly and open-minded, the two sisters open the window of their lives to Muhammad the Glass-Hearted, because they can see that he is an innocent and jovial young man. But Lawlaw-i Spi tells him, right from that very first evening, "Don't forget that you didn't come in through the door." That evening the two sisters look after him with great devotion, drying his hair and clothes and making him tea. "Consider us your own sisters. We are your sisters."

Muhammad the Glass-Hearted protests, laughing, "No way. You're not my sisters. I've come all the way through the storm to fall in love with one of you. The rain has sent me here to fall in love with Lawlaw." There's a strange ring in Muhammad's voice, a softness that blends the dance of sadness with the cry of happiness. His eyes, too, are full of laughter and weeping, shyness and audacity, the echoes of the wind and the ringing of glass. As Shadarya-i Spi looks into the young man's eyes, she knows the flood has brought him for an unknown reason and that, from this moment on, her life will take a strange turn.

"Muhammad the Glass-Hearted, we don't know you. Whether it was the storm that brought you or the wind, we must get to know you first," Shadarya-i Spi says.

"The most important thing is that my heart is made of glass, a very delicate glass, and the tiniest heartbreak will kill me. I am made of glass. If I break, I'll be shattered, and leave behind splinters, and my death and these splinters will bring nothing but bad luck. No one will know that it's my splinters small as dust that are the cause of all the misfortune in their life. So, don't break my heart." His words are a mixture of threat and plea, supplication and intimidation.

The evening passes peacefully. The two sisters ask him to give them the glass pomegranate. "It's not my pomegranate. It belongs to the secrets," he says bashfully. He leaves the silver vase with them as a souvenir instead; the pomegranate would come to the sisters in white in a different way. Years later, the vase would come into my possession, and I now have it with me on this sea crossing.

The two sisters in white listen attentively to Muhammad the Glass-Hearted until late into the night. He leaves their house in great distress, more afraid than he has ever been. He forgets, once and for all, to go to Sayyid Muzhda-i Shams, the antique dealer who has known some of this story's secrets since its inception, secrets that Muhammad the Glass-Hearted was also once keen to know. That evening, an unknown hand changes the direction of his journey, a journey that I must continue years later. It is as if that evening a force tells him that this is not his path, and his fears and sufferings confuse the way and take him somewhere else.

Outside, the icy night air stings his lungs, and he understands that he has not survived the flood because of his extraordinary fortune. No, his death has only been postponed. A death that will cause chaos among his friends, that some see as a divine curse and a punishment for he who reveals secrets.

That night when he leaves the sisters in white, he doesn't know where to go. For the first time, he feels a deep pain in his glass heart. The flood has left a trail of destruction all around. It appears to have wrecked half the city. Together with hundreds of other people, he walks up to the northern part of the city, splashing as he trudges through the puddles in the streets. It's horrifying, the city plunged into darkness. People are walking with torches. The rain has exposed half the city's secrets, tossing them around on the streets. Some alleyways are no longer passable because of the items that have piled up. It's like a ghost night. A cold wind is blowing as he walks among hundreds of strangers home to his glass room. An unusual shiver runs through him. "It's love . . . I am sure it's love," he says to himself as he walks. When he arrives at his room, a storm stirs inside him, a curious flood, more powerful than the previous evening's, sweeps him along, teeming with images. That night, Muhammad the Glass-Hearted dreams he is swept away by a white flood, a milk-white flood, seething with white boats and white creatures. In that flood, everyone can cross the water but him. Some people are sitting cross-legged on the water, others are walking upon it, while he, half-drowned, is carried away by the storm. In his dream, he goes to the doorstep of a white palace surrounded by a white sea. He takes out his key to open the door, but unlike the previous evening, he cannot open it. He tries all the keys, one by one, but still cannot open it. His hands begin to shake. Again and again he changes the keys, faster and faster, but still the door will not open. The water gradually pulls him into its white depths. He starts shouting. When he wakes up, he sees the universe in the form of a white fog and feels an excruciating pain in his heart, a pain that makes him scream.

That dream is the first appearance of the first crack in the young man's glass heart. The events of our story occur amid the wreckage of his love.

3

It was around noon when he arrived. Yaqub-i Snawbar entered the room alone. If he hadn't introduced himself, I might not have recognized him. There was still a huskiness to his voice, however, and he still cut an imposing figure. There was a certain coldness, indifference, in his welcome. I had expected that at the moment we saw each other again, we'd embrace one another and weep together. But we did not.

As if sensing my fears, he opened with strange words: "You're finally here, among us. You've become one of us again. In the desert, the earth is poor and barren so you have a lot of time to think about the universe. You have endless time to think about the sky, the stars, the sun, and God, to take an infinite look at the sand. Here though, among these dense forests and the rich earth, where each tree is a miracle; where each bird is an occasion for reflection, where each of us requires a whole lifetime just to think, the earth has made us its prisoners. We will become the property of the earth, of small, temporary, ephemeral things. Here you get lost among the details and forget the larger meanings. You're lucky to have come from a place where you could dedicate your thinking time to the larger meanings of life and the universe."

He took my hand and led me to a big room with sumptuous furniture. "Things have changed," he said. "We're in power now." The word *power* had a magical ring on his lips. He knew I didn't know anything about the new world. He had been the only one who knew I was alive and in prison. He knew everything about my imprisonment and living conditions. "I've thought about you a lot. Really, a lot," he said with the melancholy of a man talking about a deep sadness. "It wasn't easy to find you. I had to spend a lot of money, astronomical amounts, to send you those short messages. But you needed to know that I knew you were alive. You needed to know I hadn't forgotten about you, that I would prove my loyalty to you."

Yaqub-i Snawbar didn't know that, after twenty-one years, any talk of loyalty or disloyalty was meaningless.

He took a deep breath, the deepest I'd ever witnessed. He said, "I know you don't want to think about *that* night. I don't either. And nobody knows the story of that night apart from you and me. Nobody. I've kept it secret for twenty-one years."

For the first time in ages, I heard myself laughing. "My dear Yaqub, there are no secrets between us. None. Things had to go that way. You were the leader. You were more important than me."

He forced out a small laugh and said, "Nobody has called me 'my dear Yaqub' in ages. Absolute ages. How long has it been?"

I put my hand on his and said, "Twenty-one years. Yes, twenty-one."

He took a deep breath and said, "Yes. Twenty-one years. Twenty-one."

He wanted to talk about the night I was captured. We were holed up inside a small house, under siege. Either we would both be captured, or one of us could stay at the front and put up a defense while the other broke away from the ambush at the rear to escape. That night I hugged him and said, "I'll stay. I'll distract them until you get away. We won't meet again. Look after Saryas-i Subhdam." It was the last thing I said, and for years it echoed in my ears. I could have escaped. I had more chance of escaping than he did, but he was the leader and I was one of his closest aides. Ultimately, it was my duty to sacrifice everything so that he could live.

He had not come to embrace me. He was there to tell me to stay in the mansion. He said, "Nobody can live outside. Innocent and principled people simply can't survive. A terrible disease has broken out everywhere. It has no name or description. Call it a plague. Call it whatever you like, but you have to stay here. Stay here as long as you can. It's safer here than anywhere else." He looked at me for a while, deep in thought. "Forgive me for saying that you're one of us. You're not. You still smell of innocence. If you come out, if you mingle in our world, God knows what will become of you. You're just yourself. You're not one of us or one of them. You're just you. You are Muzafar-i Subhdam. Besides, you're dead. Apart from me, nobody knows you're alive. Your name has been scrubbed from everything for a long time now. I erased it myself, everywhere. I cleared you of any debts, any liability. Your name doesn't appear in any book, not even the history books. I've protected you from all the filth. You don't exist. Muzafar-i Subhdam, there is no life in the outside world for you. Nobody will believe you. Nobody. Nobody knows you were my friend that night and sacrificed your life for me. Those who knew the story have either died, migrated, or been forgotten. Nobody knows anything about it."

I didn't know exactly what he was trying to say, but it had always been that way. You never knew for sure what he was talking about. He was able to camouflage his sins as generosity and greatness. As always, wherever he appeared, he inspired a deep silence, an odd calm and melancholy. His departure always left you thinking. He made everybody think, even the flowers, birds, and trees. His serenity and deep voice would create such a tangle that it was like he had ensnared you in the web of his beguiling language. When he spoke, I always felt as if I was lost, walking through gardens, fountains, and rosewater ponds. There was a strange gentleness in his words, as if you were standing near a waterfall and the wind was spraying the water towards you, or you were asleep under a tree and the breeze had awoken you with a kiss. But there was also a dark tone to his words that somehow made you lose yourself. He always left you divided. Something emanated quietly from him to dwell inside your being, something that initially appeared delicate and normal, like the flight and descent of a bulbul from one garden to another, or the fall of a leaf from a high branch to the ground. When he left, however, he would leave behind a piercing pain, the source of which you couldn't trace, the pain of people who do not understand one another, the pain of wavering, hesitation, and complication. Wherever he went, nothing in that place would be able to sleep for days afterward. I noticed that, after his departure, even the birds, trees, and flowers wouldn't sleep for many nights.

He had confused me in this way for many years. That morning when

I saw him again, he was his old self, although he seemed more powerful, cruel, and indifferent than before. I didn't understand what he wanted from a defeated man like myself without a future, or why he might want to keep me in a mansion.

"My dear Yaqub, I am good for nothing," I told him. "I too am in search of a great forgetting. For twenty-one years in the sand, I was busy day and night wiping out my memories. For twenty-one years, the night, the wind, the sand, the sun, and I wiped out the memories and images of *that* night bit by bit. I am too weak to use my past. Don't be afraid of me. The desert teaches you not to ask for anything, not anything at all. I've had the soul of a mystic for a long time now, a mystic who's satisfied by merely watching the sand."

His life as a leader had not altered all his ordinary ways. He could mock without being condescending. He put his hand on his forehead and said, "You've always been a mystic. Always. I've considered you a dervish for a very long time."

This was an immense truth, the most bitter and complex truth of that time in my life. I had survived in the desert alone. The desert had been enough for me, but now I was too far away from it. I didn't know what to do with the sudden freedom they had offered me, that I had not asked for.

Yaqub-i Snawbar knew what I was going through. He said calmly in his deep voice, "Freedom will kill us if we're not careful. It will kill us." At one point, it occurred to me that he wanted to protect me from freedom, that he didn't want freedom to lead me astray. He didn't say anything directly, but every now and then he would take a deep breath in the middle of a sentence and I would catch a certain coldness in his eyes. Perhaps he too was lost in the beguiling labyrinth of words he had created. I was somehow living in an illusion that I was free of the past.

"I'm glad nobody knows I'm alive," I said. "I don't have any expectations of anything. No one owes me anything. But tell me why you brought me here, to this house. Why am I not allowed to see anyone? Who brought me all the way here?"

"Why did I bring you to this remote guesthouse, tucked away in a forest?" he said after a moment's reflection. "It's difficult to give you an answer."

I looked at his hands and knew he was telling the truth. It had always been that way. When he talked, I didn't look at his face, but at his hands or the things around him. Others focused all their attention on his face, and as a result, they could never be sure if he was telling the truth. I was the only one who knew what to look at when he was talking. "There is a plague," he kept repeating. "Or some other fatal disease that you can't escape."

I watched him pace up and down the room and knew he was happy. With me, he didn't have to forget all his old memories. But he was also indifferent to my freedom. In a way, we were similar. He had fulfilled all his dreams, the strange old dreams of our youth. I, on the other hand, had fulfilled mine by wiping out my entire inner world. We had gone in two different directions – I through a huge desert, he through a rich and busy life – but we had come together in the same place in the end.

When I saw him again after a while, in a different setting and in another emotional state, I became even more aware of how much we resembled each other. I was the dormant part of him but I had woken up and I didn't want to sleep anymore. "Sometimes success and death are the same thing," he said, as if reading my mind. I thought he considered me an apparition, a dead person. He had killed me everywhere except in his own memory.

He looked at me with kindness and said, "I'd like to talk to you about death."

"I haven't come back from the dead," I said reluctantly.

He took out a cigarette, lit it, and left it on a silver ashtray without taking a single puff. As if to comfort me, he said, "In a sense, we have both come back from the dead. The desert and politics are the same thing. They are both lands where nothing grows." As he talked, he walked over to the windows. I felt as if he were talking to something farther away than me. He spoke with a degree of agitation and impatience, as if suffering from a serious wound: "Muzafar-i Subhdam, my friend, I can't let you go back to that filthy life. I can't see you there. You're not one of us."

He had always imagined me outside of time and place, putting me into a world different from all the others. Now he had brought me to this mansion so that I would remain inside his imaginary kingdom forever. He had created a world for me that fit his memories. Lost in thought, he said, "We will grow old here, you and I. We will grow old here as we look out at the world from these windows and think. It'll be our place. We'll look at the universe from these windows. Together we'll give up everything; we'll become two mystics. Day and night, we'll talk about the stars, trees, and birds. A day will come when we will speak their languages. We'll dedicate our lives to understanding the flowers, to the strange light that comes from afar at night. We will look after our souls again. You'll keep yours as pure as it is, and I'll do all I can to cleanse mine."

For the first time since he had been talking, the curtains swayed, the leaves floating outside changed direction, the birds flew away, and a sudden silence prevailed. Tired, he dropped his head and said with a mocking smile, "My friend, do you remember we used to say that after the success of the revolution, we'd create a retreat, a neat and cozy life, that we'd dedicate all our energy to enjoying the beauties of nature? Yes, yes. All our energy to enjoying the beauty of the flowers, the beauty of the night, the beauty of the things that go unnoticed by everyone. Do you remember? Do you, my friend?"

"I don't remember a thing, nothing at all," I said. "I've worked very hard to wipe everything from my life. If I hadn't killed everything in my mind, the desert would've killed me. The desert puts a high price on even the smallest and most insignificant memories, my dear Yaqub. It took a long time to extricate myself from the past. Night after night I sat and calmly removed all those things from my head as if I were operating on the heart of a sparrow. Those things wouldn't let me sleep. They wouldn't let me think; they wiped out any glimmer of hope in my tears. I killed all the things that had filled my tears with memories. If you are imprisoned in the sand, you can't miss anything. Do you understand? You can't. The sand won't let you. Do you understand? It won't."

I cried as I said that. Just as I had in the cold nights of the desert. I put my head in my hands and cried. He too, although he didn't understand the depth of my pain, put his head in his hands and cried.

We didn't know why we were crying. We slowly wiped away our tears and glared at one another. My eyes were like those of a bird that had been burned by looking at the distant horizon of the barren yellow desert. His were those of a wolf sated with play.

For a moment, I thought perhaps he didn't know why he'd come to see me, that he didn't know where we should take up the thread again, but he made me understand in his circumspect and cunning way that I was indeed a prisoner. Calmly but sternly he said, "You will stay here. This place will become home to our fantasies. It's the place that we dreamed about for many years." Then he looked at me and added, "If you get out of here, you'll spend your whole life chasing after something you won't find. The desert has offered you something. Solitude has given you something more profound and meaningful than we've earned from the revolution and politics. If you go outside, you'll find nothing, nothing at all. You've attained greatness. You've lived in a deep retreat. Don't go outside, my friend, please. Things have been so badly broken that no one can put them together again." He took a breath and repeated, "Don't come out to look for things you won't find."

He spoke and wanted to leave, but I kept him near the door and said, "My dear Yaqub, he who can bear the fate of imprisonment must bear the burden of freedom too. I am not dead. I have to come to terms with this and truly know that I live. I fought for my life every day, year in, year out. Each night, I saw the ghosts, the apparitions, and shouted, 'I am still alive. I am still living!' No, Yaqub, my dear friend, my leader. There is no unfinished business or dream between us, bar one. Just one. Tell me: where is Saryas-i Subhdam?"

And with that, I opened the floodgates.

4

Long ago, Lawlaw and Shadarya made an eternal oath to each other. Neither would ever marry, cut their hair, sing without the other, nor wear anything but white. The agreement went back to the time a war of songs broke out at the two sisters' house, four years before the evening that the raging storms delivered Muhammad the Glass-Hearted.

They were fourteen and fifteen years old respectively back then, both of them secretly, childishly in love, and each singing to herself day and night. The main problem was that they always sang together, but each would sing a different song. This battle of songs lasted a long time. Some nights, just to rile one another, they both sang until morning when their throats began to bleed. They would be singing as the last light faded, then dawn would break and they would still be singing face to face. The sun would come up, and the pair of them would be as exhausted as two stubborn, merciless warriors. Suddenly, at the same time, they would stop singing, neither conceding defeat, and flop down on their beds half dead. No one knows how long this war lasted, how many seasons the sisters spent fighting.

One evening during this argument, Shadarya-i Spi fell ill with a sickness that took her to the brink of death. Only Lawlaw-i Spi knew why she was dying: an unrequited love was to blame. It was late spring when Shadarya was placed on a stretcher to undergo major surgery. The morning was engulfed in darkness. Sand had been raining down all night. Before Shadarya-i Spi went into the operating room with doctors who could promise her neither life nor death, Lawlaw-i Spi simply had to see her, to apologize and to weep over her. After a completely sleepless night, she arrived with tears in her eyes and a voice full of sorrow.

Shadarya was waiting. In a ritual of weeping and sobbing, of embraces and laments, of mutual forgiveness and the taking of oaths, the two sisters vowed to live together until death came between them, to wear matching clothes, never to cut their hair, and whenever they sang, to do so together. Their reconciliation was so intense that, had the nurses not taken Shadarya-i Spi away right there and then, the vows might have been much longer and more elaborate. As the nurses led Shadarya away, Lawlaw held her hand until they reached the operating room. Before Shadarya went in to submit to the surgeon's knife, she said to Lawlaw, "Swear to me you won't go back on your vows, ever."

In a whirl of tumultuous emotion, Lawlaw said tearfully, "I hereby swear to you that I shall never ever get married, nor sing without you, nor cut my hair, nor wear anything but white." Such was the beginning of the indissoluble oath that joined the sisters together.

They had a complicated life, riddled with secrets. Once Shadarya was discharged from the hospital, they renewed their vows during a summer night's sandstorm. They wrote an eternal pledge the way lovers of the time did, signing it with their blood, placing it inside a black glass bottle, and hiding it under a pomegranate tree known only to them – the mirror image of another tree that a man named Nasim-i Shazada had planted elsewhere.

Things took a dangerous turn from then on. One would have thought the two sisters were bewitched. They didn't look like other girls; there was a strange mystery in their cold, calm, and fixed gazes. When they looked at something, they hardly took their eyes off it, and even though they were not unkind, their intense gazes could make anyone uncomfortable. Their eyes seemed too big for their bodies. If they wished, they could fill them with coldness and indifference, but they could just as easily fill them with innocence. Their white garments and identical height, together with their long, wild hair, which grew at an extraordinary rate, made them look like a pair of enchantresses, their magic a mystery. They were the only two girls who didn't go to school in uniform and who wore white to funerals. At wedding parties, it was hard to distinguish their white dresses from the bride's. There was something in them that was hard to see through, a strange, unfathomable silence.

In truth, Lawlaw-i Spi and Shadarya-i Spi were neither cruel nor enchantresses. It was just that their expressions and their appearance created superstitions about them, myths they weren't disturbed by, but that they embellished and multiplied. For a while, they became obsessed with reading about and understanding horoscopes. They started learning the art of palmistry, poring over people's hands at parties and funerals. They would often stand back without a word. Their silence, the result of their ignorance of both astrology and palmistry, was presumed to be the silence of two girls who had seen the black fate awaiting the palms' owners. They displeased and unsettled, sowing doubt, hesitation, and unease.

They became genuine outsiders because their clothes and behavior were unlike everyone else's. They grew up isolated and avoided by men, not because they were not beautiful but because there was a force in their eyes that men feared. Their strong voices did not sit well with the desires of men who were only interested in conquering women like soldiers invading another country. This weakness meant no man had approached the two sisters until the arrival of Muhammad the Glass-Hearted. But their strange and complicated relationship, the only thing they had, took the place of everything else. When they woke up in the morning, they would sing a new song even before breakfast. Songs in their lives acted as prayers. They were daughters of an unusual era. They didn't believe in God, but had a profound belief in singing.

No one knows exactly how Muhammad the Glass-Hearted fell in love. The girls' lives were radically different from his. He hated complexities and mysteries on principle and yearned for transparency. His world could not have been further apart from that of the two sisters. Had the storms not betrayed him, they never would have met, but he believed in the storms. This belief would carry him to his dark fate.

Muhammad the Glass-Hearted lived in his fantasies with the many keys he had made himself: keys to life and death, love and solitude, secrets and silence, friendship and hatred, dreams and truth. He had grown up like an orphan in the city after his father went off to join the freedom fighters in the mountains. Then one day, he opened his eyes and found himself the fortunate child of a successful revolution. After its triumph and the revolutionaries' return to the towns, he was for a while the happiest of young men. He was one of those giving out flowers at official ceremonies. He always had a bright smile on his face and a glimmer in his eyes. His gaze was too clear to hold secrets; his face resembled a spring, the bottom plainly visible. In his eyes, everything was simple, and this made him unusual, alien in a world built upon secrets.

When his father returned to the city after a lengthy absence – triumphant, armed, and wrapped in the smell of sweat from climbing the mountains – he embraced him for the first time, met his gaze, and said, "There is a clarity in your eyes that is whiter and stranger than anything I have ever seen." This was the beginning of the era he spent in a crystal mansion made of a fragile glass, a kingdom with walls of thin, colorless, transparent bubbles.

Muhammad grew up at a time when everything happened covertly. He was born in the dark years of the revolution: the era of walls, sandbags, fortified basements, and closed doors. The state beheaded its opponents in secret, and its opponents lived and moved around in secret. Everyone was busy building walls between houses, alleyways, and people, between people and the sky, people and flowers, people and the moon, people and the night, people and the morning sparrows. Everything became a barrier, and life was lived behind it. People could only think behind walls.

Muhammad spent his childhood in the arms of a frightened mother, secretly shuttled from one house to another. He and his mother lived in constant fear of being arrested by the state and banished to the southern deserts. He became a secret child from then on. He did not use his real name outside. No one was allowed to see him in the clear light of day. They frequently changed houses, streets, and cities.

Muhammad the Glass-Hearted grew up in a world full of secrets and concealment, and he had a secret desire to explore. He wanted to learn to see the world, and yet he felt he could not see anything, that there was nothing to see but walls. One day he arrived at the sad truth that would determine the path and the meaning of his life: that his life should be as transparent as glass, should be seen from all sides and have nothing in common with that world of darkness. He would find a key to open all doors, and the world would become transparent, its walls hiding nothing because people would have nothing to hide.

Despite the harrowing nightmares of his childhood, Muhammad remained a cheerful young man, his eyes shining with small and simple truths. A year after the Kurds rebelled against Saddam, Muhammad's father, Sulaiman the Great, returned and became one of the mighty barons of politics. To make up for their long years of separation, he wanted to reward his son generously, to do something that would make him happy forever. One moonlit night, he said, "Ask for something, anything a man can do. Say it and I will treat it as an order."

After lengthy reflection, Muhammad the Glass-Hearted went to Sulaiman the Great one sunny afternoon and told him, "I have one wish, a small wish. I want a house made of glass. It doesn't have to be completely made of glass, but it must be built in such a way that you can see all the other sides when looking at just one."

That night, the design for a small and unusual house was born. It would be built in one of the city's quiet northern neighborhoods and be made of glass thinner than that of a wineglass, purer and more fragile than that of a tea glass. The house sat on a small hill among a number of tall buildings, its columns made of iron and most of its walls of glass. From whichever angle you looked at it, you could see all its nooks and crannies. You could see Muhammad sitting on his chair, the partridges' empty cage, the painting of a wild dance, flowers in bowls of water, vases of colorful sand, a blue silk carpet teeming with underwater images so that, from a distance, the house looked like a pond. In the mornings everyone could see Muhammad behind his glass walls, preparing breakfast, singing aloud, or sitting like a fish in a tank, leading a transparent life.

His deep desire to see and understand everything led him to seek out and examine people's inner lives. He wanted to learn their deepest and most private secrets. His desire for transparency and light led him to secrets larger than himself, and his talk abounded in strange stories about life and truth. And yet, apart from his friends – the few youngsters he knew here and there in the bowels of the bazaar – no one considered him a seeker of truth, but merely a young man greedy for knowledge. His desire for transparency and exploration created an extreme honesty in him, but he did not understand that the truth could be fatal, that something always remained unexplained, that there would always be secrets he couldn't fathom.

The morning after his return from the sisters' house, Muhammad woke up with an ache in his chest. He felt as if bright blood was dripping from a small hole in his heart, one drop at a time. In pain, he took off his shirt before a large mirror and looked at the blood seeping slowly onto his clothes. The strange wound neither grew nor healed. From that morning on, Muhammad always had a bloodstain on his chest, the wet blood regularly seeping through, drop by drop, in agonizing bouts, onto his shirt. A shirt, incidentally, that one of the Saryases had bought for him. The bleeding was inexplicable. No matter how much cotton or gauze he used, the blood would gather patiently and soak through the dressing, forming a large stain on his chest.

On the evening of that same day, he returned, bloodied, to the two sisters' house. They were both waiting at the same window as if they had been notified of his return. They had opened the window and were hanging half out, their hair streaming far out on the wind. To Muhammad the Glass-Hearted, it appeared as if their hair was mixed with the clouds, that he could see sparrows and flocks of doves flying through it.

"Lawlaw-i Spi, I would like to ask for your hand in marriage . . . Do you accept?" he shouted from outside the door.

Both sisters looked on with their cold stares. They calmly reeled in their bewitching hair: it was as though the clouds had cleared. They closed the windows and drew the curtains. Without a word, they looked at Muhammad the Glass-Hearted from behind their thick curtains as he showed them the bloodstain on his heart, saying, "This wound is your doing."

That evening, ruffled by a damp breeze from wandering clouds pregnant with rain, Muhammad again returned home defeated.

At home, Muhammad watches the relentless rain through the windows. He can tell another crack has appeared in his heart, in another, more delicate spot this time. He can feel more blood, now even brighter, seeping from the small wounds created by an invisible lancet, and he knows they are caused by heartbreak. The later it gets, the greater his agony. All alone, he places his hand on his heart and walks back through the rain, the lightning, and the dark, to the two sisters who once again keep their cold gazes on him from their windows.

Muhammad the Glass-Hearted counts the small cracks in his heart and realizes time and death are fighting over his life. Hand on heart, he stands outside the gate, blood dripping from his fingers as it mixes with the rain. He bangs on the door with his bloodied hands and calls out to the sisters. He can see their shadows and the sway of their hair behind the curtain: two people looking silently at the rain and Muhammad the Glass-Hearted as he says, "Lawlaw-i Spi, I will die if you don't love me." Soaked to the bone, he drips with rain like a small bird. The drops of water shine on his face like a thousand droplets of gold. The two girls do nothing but look at him calmly from behind the curtains. Muhammad the Glass-Hearted wants to unlock the doors, but they won't budge. In the rain, with bloodied hands, he tries all the keys but none of them work. He wants to climb the walls but he can't. He climbs the nearby trees and shouts but hears nothing apart from the rain and sees nothing except the light glimmering on his tears.

The night fades. Covered in mud, rain, and blood, Muhammad returns to his room. With each passing moment, he feels more heartbroken, the cracks in his glass heart widening. At daybreak, he falls asleep amid blood, rain, and tears. He dreams about a tree known as "the last pomegranate tree in the world."

In the evening as the rain resumes, he quietly returns to the sisters' neighborhood. They have waited for him around the clock, behind their windows. He steps into their large yard and quietly circles the house several times.

The bleeding never stops. He does not go home that night, and instead, despite his chest wounds, he goes to one of Sulaiman the Great's large gatherings. The gathering of a mighty politician, it is crawling with ministers, directors general, and the new barons of the market. At first the guards do not recognize him, but he tells them, "I am *his* son, the son of Sulaiman the Great." The young man is covered in blood, soaked, and exhausted. He has acquired a deathly pallor. When Sulaiman the Great finally invites him in, he doesn't recognize him. The young man looks nothing like his glass-hearted son. This is a sick, weak boy, with sunken eyes, trailing water and blood in his wake, leaving red footprints on the carpets and tiles.

Inside the room, Muhammad the Glass-Hearted stands up and quietly says, "Have you seen anyone die like this?" Everyone there knows the story of the secrets-obsessed boy who lives inside two small glass rooms like a winter plant in a greenhouse. But that night he is too wounded, too broken, to instill fear in them. They remove his clothes and change them as he sits on a chair, they apply a fresh cotton dressing to the small wound in his heart, they dry him off. Throughout it all, he recounts the fatal love story triggered by the storm. He mentions the names of two girls none of the men at the gathering has heard of. It is the sort of unusual night you come across in stories.

Ikram-i Kew is also there – a tall man who wears an army officer's jacket despite having no rank of his own, a quiet but energetic man. He is the only person who stays with Muhammad the Glass-Hearted and his father until morning. At dawn but before sunrise, in the short interval between the morning call to prayer and the muezzin going back to sleep, Muhammad the Glass-Hearted's father, Sulaiman, and Ikram-i Kew set out in a small blue car to ask for the girl's hand in marriage. It must be the earliest in the morning that anyone has ever asked for a girl's hand!

The girls' mother opens the door, a petite and frightened woman completely under her daughters' control. Sulaiman the Great and his companion enter the house quietly and sit on two small chairs. Someone had evidently put the oil heater on moments ago; its first smoke is still in the room. The two girls, their eyes tired, enter, both in white with a shawl over their shoulders as if they've just returned from a secret party. Something mysterious – almost magical – seems to hang in the air as they coldly welcome the guests.

Sulaiman the Great begins to speak softly. "I am Muhammad the Glass-Hearted's father. I've come to tell you Muhammad is dying. And he is dying not of hatred nor disloyalty but of love. Personally, I don't think love's worth dying for. I'm not used to seeing anyone dying of love. All my life I've dealt with death and worked with people who one way or another were doing the same. But now I think the reason my son is dying is a strange one. I never imagined it causing death. I'd like to know which one of you is Lawlaw-i Spi."

"I am," Lawlaw-i Spi says, standing up.

"There is no doubt you are a beautiful girl, but I don't like to see anyone dying like this, being humiliated like this. I want you to marry my son so he doesn't die."

Lawlaw-i Spi calmly takes her seat and says in a low but steady tone, "I am sorry, but I won't get married."

With a sudden sadness in his voice, Sulaiman the Great stands up and says, "If someone's life wasn't at stake, no one would visit a family so early in the morning to ask for a girl's hand. You have every right to say no. You do. And I have no power over you, nor can I impose this upon you. I know this is a strange offer of marriage. It defies all logic! If you don't accept whole-heartedly, my coming here is meaningless because I know that if you cannot clasp the bird of love he is throwing with all your heart, it's all in vain. Oh, my daughter, I am powerless. If it were anything else, of course, I could've done something. If it were an advancing army, I could have stopped it with the help of a few capable young fighters. If it were the peak of a mountain, I would have climbed it. But it is none of these things. All I can tell you is that he is my only son and he is dying because of you. Think about it. You do understand that we don't have much time? This is an unfair fight against time, unfair and ugly, evil and unjust."

He stands up and signals to Ikram-i Kew, who, giant that he is, also rises. "All we can do is implore you. Yes, ladies, that's all we can do."

Lawlaw-i Spi, in a low, barely audible voice repeats, "I won't get married . . . I won't ever get married."

It's a very cold morning. When the men leave the house, they are both in tears. Sulaiman the Great hasn't cried in a long time, but he's certain his son is dying a meaningless death. The more time passes the more Muhammad's heart breaks. That morning, they take him back to his glass house. The doctors don't know what's wrong with him. He falls asleep in his bed as the bleeding continues. He dreams of a pomegranate tree on top of a distant peak. Late in the evening, he dismisses his guests and caretakers, telling them that he is feeling better and doesn't need to be looked after anymore. As night falls, he wants to understand everything before his death. He wants to unlock the secret of his unrequited love. As he raises his head, he realizes that even in his final moments he is drawn by a deep desire to understand things.

That night, he returns to the girls' doorstep like a pale ghost. As always, he enters their yard with ease. He sees them by the windows, looks at their sad, pale gazes as they look at him coldly from behind the windows. He begs them to open the window and talk to him. And they do. Lawlaw-i Spi says in a sad voice, "Muhammad the Glass-Hearted, forgive me. There's a piece of paper under that pomegranate tree. Take it and go. Take it. Leave us alone and go away."

Under the pomegranate tree, Muhammad raises his head and sees the moon. In the moonlight, he realizes he is standing under the tree from his dream. At the same time, he hears the distant and divine music that is the music of the stars and their light, the same music that has accompanied his dreams since childhood. He closes his eyes and understands that the pomegranate tree is nothing but the mirror image of another tree. There he finds the letter, a copy of the ancient vows between the sisters, hellish vows, vows no force can break. As he reads the lines, Muhammad collapses completely, the cracks in his heart widening with each word, his heart turning to a handful of dust with each sentence, his glass world breaking, the glass walls of his house cracking.

As he rereads the vows, the stream of blood spurting from his heart increases. He bleeds more and more as he walks through the alleyways.

People see him, like a ghost, walking the streets, one hand on his heart, the other gripping the vows. People have never seen a man with blood bubbling from his chest like water from a spring and yet still walking as he reads. With each step, his glass house falls piece by piece, his glass objects collapsing and crumbling to dust. When he arrives outside his house, he finds himself in the dust of its collapse. With each spurt of blood and falling fragment of his heart, big chunks of the walls peel away and shatter. The keys in his hands turn into a soft white powder, and the box of his secrets turns to dust. He gets into bed and holds his heart. Above him he sees the branches of a pomegranate tree. He hears the shattering of the objects and is aware of the lethal glass dust being carried away on the night wind. He closes his eyes and hears the last roar of the glass sky as it too collapses above him, turning into a thick dust that is carried along by the wind before falling to the ground.

He raises his head again and sees the branches of the pomegranate tree, the one he had wanted to die beneath. He reaches out and touches the imaginary branches at the top, branches he sees growing in his dying dream. In the distance, an angel descends from the depths of the sky. Before the angel reaches him and takes his hand, he manages to touch the blood gushing from his heart one last time. In the ruin of his house, the vows fall from his hand and are carried away on the wind. At that same moment, the smiling angel takes his hand and says, "How are you, Muhammad the Glass-Hearted? It's all over. It's all over now. Stand up. Let's go."

He stands up quietly and says, "Yes, it's all over . . . Hold my hand. Let's go." The angel does as he asks, and like two doves driven from a forest by fierce winds, they fly toward the unknown through the dust of a glass death, a death in whose cold dust we shall all later be lost. A death, a part of which will always remain unknown and hidden, that blends dangerously with some of this story's other bitter truths.

5

When I asked him where Saryas-i Subhdam was, he replied quietly, "He's dead . . . Saryas-i Subhdam is dead."

I said, "I want to know how he died. I'm entitled to know." He did not answer other than to say he would be back and we would have time to talk about everything then.

I had not expected to see Saryas-i Subhdam since I never thought I'd leave the desert. I knew nothing about the outside world, but an instinct told me that an endless number of wars had broken out since my capture, that an endless number of people had died. And it was unlikely that a child who had no mother or father would have survived in such a tough world.

After I first brought up Saryas-i Subhdam, Yaqub-i Snawbar left me on my own for a few long days. Apart from several short walks around the guesthouse, I didn't do much. I had no desire to wander far and no idea where I would go. On a few evenings, I walked through the trees, around ponds, and across streams but got nowhere. Oddly, nature scared me. I couldn't bear the noise of the birds and missed the echo of the desert. The cries that rose from the sand felt more familiar. I summoned my strength and went deeper into the forest each time, but it seemed never ending, as if one tree were constantly passing me on to another. I imagined the house had been built in the middle of a massive maze, governed by such elaborate geometry that no one who ended up there could escape. One day I decided to set out and investigate, but I merely wandered in vain through a copse. I felt I had given up my own freedom.

There are two situations in which human beings do not require guards: when freedom in the outside world no longer has meaning and when a person in prison feels free. I had experienced both these conditions. At one point I had felt that freedom outside was worth nothing to me, while at another I felt I had absolute freedom in prison. I had the same feeling on the days I walked through the trees near the guesthouse. To me, freedom no longer meant going out and seeing other towns, people, or countries. Twenty-one years of imprisonment had killed that type of freedom within me. In my cell, in my retreat, I thought about all kinds of lightness and darkness and talked to myself out loud. The only voice I was familiar with was my own. I think people who talk to themselves slowly become prisoners of their own voices. Later, only Saryas-i Subhdam's story would free me from those fetters.

Yaqub-i Snawbar returned after a few days. (You have to forgive me: I had lost all sense of time and did not count the days and nights.) When he finally returned, he had aged compared to his previous visit. We resumed where we had left off.

After a brief exchange of greetings, he said, "Saryas-i Subhdam has died.

I don't know exactly how, but he has. I am sorry that his death, too, is complex and inexplicable." He placed a hand on one of the room's shiny crystal objects. "I don't know when or where he died. The period in which he died cannot be explained. You could put all the twenty-one years you spent in prison in a coffin and throw them away. There was nothing in them but death. I can't explain any of the deaths, I can't explain any of the births, there was no logic to any of them. But I can assure you he didn't live or die alone. He was with other people – but you shouldn't think that makes it easier. It doesn't. I don't know exactly who they were or what they looked like, but they nearly all died. I'm not really sure of anything because I can't be, it's not possible. Things become so entangled that no one can be sure of anything, like a chess game, except you don't know exactly which pieces belong to you because all the pieces have suddenly become white or black, so you can't tell which of them you should move. But Muzafar-i Subhdam, don't look for answers. I am the only one who knows most of the truths, and yet even I can't tell you. I don't have any explanation, and you may be certain I can't forgive myself for that. Muzafar-i Subhdam, my friend, you and I are deeply mired in the sin of those days. But rest assured, he's dead. When, where, and how? Don't ask me, please don't. I don't know."

All this talk sounded like an intricate puzzle. I asked him, "Who are *they*? Who did he die with?"

"With those who were like him, his friends. With those who died at that time." He paused, and a rueful smile appeared on his face. "I can't tell you any more than that. I don't have any more to give you. To understand it all, you would have had to be there with me. Plus, whether or not you know doesn't change a thing, nothing at all. But you mustn't take that path.

You're here so that that doesn't happen. Let's have a different old age, you and me, the old age of two men devoting themselves to reflection and wisdom. I brought you here so you could reenter life from a different place, one that isn't related to that past, that isn't connected to the present, to daily life, death, revolution, and politics. Listen to me, Muzafar-i Subhdam, my friend, I want us to pass through another gate, both of us. You are the only person to have been preserved outside of our time. You weren't imprisoned; you were kept unsullied by the filth of those ugly days, like something frozen in snow, like a hidden box of gold. I could've released you ten years ago, I could've swapped you for a senior army officer. There was a time when we had hundreds of officers at our disposal. After the success of the revolution, I held thousands of soldiers, ranking officers, and senior commanders prisoner. Back then I could've easily swapped you, but I would've had to bring you back to this place, to politics, to the quagmire of daily life. I would've had to bring you back to look at the filth of life, and you'd have had to forget what you'd learned in the desert. I spent a lot of money before I learned that you lived like a hermit in the desert. There would have been no place for you if I'd had you released. I would have had to sell you too cheaply – you, a precious gem. I would have had to put you back into the midst of all the fighting, the fights I and others had started, had to start. You're a rare piece of gold from the days of innocence. You are the only one who has done no wrong, hasn't hurt so much as a bird, hasn't taken part in any conflict. Fighting turned us into a group of monsters. Fighting, fighting, and more fighting. Fighting in the mornings, fighting at midday, fighting in the evenings. No, don't imagine that during those days I didn't consider having you released. Even once everything was arranged, the night I needed to sign the papers to exchange you, my entire body was shaking. There was nowhere at the time that could preserve your innocence. Like a child, you know nothing of your own purity. Even if I had brought you back then the same thing that happened to others would have happened to you and you'd have strayed just like them."

I was disappointed. "So that's it! You could have saved me but you did nothing. You could have prevented me rotting in the desert for twenty-one years, but you abandoned me. The desert turned me into sand, pure sand, and nothing can put me back together again."

He said, "No, I couldn't have saved you then. Saving someone is one thing, releasing them from prison is another. I could've released you and helped you get back here, but you're not one of us. It wouldn't have done you any good to return to our fold. You had to be alone. I don't know whether you understand me or not, but you need to be alone. I know this is a harsh sentence. It's a steep price for freedom, but if you're not kept apart, we lose everything."

In short, Yaqub-i Snawbar wanted us both to live in the green mansion, to dedicate ourselves to wisdom, to spend thousands of hours talking about the universe, the sky, death, and God. Even during the years of the revolution, he was selfish enough to have devoted a lot of time to himself, and he had tasted all the world's pleasures since the uprising. He had dedicated his life to ruling the world to such an extent that he had no time left to think about its essence. He felt that he had grasped all the superficial things in life but failed to penetrate its essence.

In the period when I lived in the green house, I didn't feel free. He would come over on many evenings and we would move the chairs under the trees.

Even though I was still scared of the greenery, I enjoyed being with him. In the desert, I had become used to a sort of certainty. Despite all his despotism, despite his many faces, despite all the confusion he caused, he gave me a degree of certainty, although I could not pinpoint its source. He instilled in me the belief that I was somehow pure, that being away from the disasters and the wars had preserved my innocence. He wanted to make it last forever, to create a retreat that would inspire us both.

The mansion was a haven for reflection. I know that after the uprising, the president, the ministers, the politicians, the members of the Party politburos all created their own private spaces, all had guesthouses of their own, homes of their own inside and outside the cities. This house just happened to be one of his special, peaceful residences. Only later did I find out he had dozens of others. Like all officials of the post-uprising era, he lived like a king, but on some nights a sudden fear, an unanswered question, an agonizing stab to his conscience, would leave him restless and bring him to me in a state of confusion. He had put me there so that when the sound of his body, his wants and desires, calmed down, whenever his soul opened up to talk, he could come and learn something from me.

As far as he was concerned, I had something no one else had, neither his politician friends nor his enemies. Here was someone unaware of what had happened during those years, and when I opened my mouth, I spoke about the sand, stars, wind, and silence. He wanted to usurp not only power, authority, and pleasures, but also beauty, purity, and wisdom. I realized too late that he wanted everything for himself. Anything that didn't become his, he'd ignore. He bought fighters, ministers, plots of land, streets, and beautiful houses. Throughout the years following the triumph of the revolution, he took everything for himself and for his friends. He even bought poets, sculptors and painters, engineers, and the mullahs at the mosques. He had orchards exclusively for bulbuls and separate ones for other types of birds. He had vineyards where he made wine and others where he indulged in pleasures of the flesh. He had mansions for himself and his friends, for sumptuous banquets offering all the world's rarest foodstuffs. In the midst of it all, there would be moments when he became bored of everything. It was then that he'd get in his car and come to me. The night I told him I wanted to go and see the world, he said calmly, "You can't. You and I shall grow old and die here."

I lived in that house from early spring to the end of a very hot summer. There were hundreds of video cassettes, thousands of books, and everyday I prepared colorful foods. But I wanted to go out. One night I repeatedly told Yaqub about my desire to be free. He said, "Do you believe in this tranquility? Tell me, do you think you'd find this tranquility, the music of nature, this stability, everywhere in the world? Here you are in this room listening to the sound of bulbuls. Do you think anyone else can live like this, like a king?"

"My friend, Yaqub," I interrupted him, "I've spent twenty-one years living in peace and silence. Don't tell me I live like a king. I am a prisoner as long as there is silence – as long as I am engulfed in this infinite, universal, and restless silence. Yaqub-i Snawbar, they imprisoned me in silence. I've thought about this a great deal. They didn't torture me or hold me accountable. Their punishment was that I would live in silence forever."

Abruptly and as if he were telling me a truth I did not want to understand, he raised his voice and said, "But of what were you a prisoner? Of the night, of the desert, of the universe, of stars you always had time to look at? Muzafar-i Subhdam, one night at the height of a bloody battle, I was moving my forces up a steep slope. At that moment, I looked up and saw the sky. I saw millions of stars. I saw my smallness compared to the universe, I saw myself within that world. Then it occurred me to that I hadn't had time to think about the sky, to look at the moon. At that very moment, I understood that I'd lost half the world. My life was passing, and I didn't have time to look beyond war. That night, I banged my head against a rock and shouted, 'What a fake, meaningless, and deceitful word *world* is.' Muzafar-i Subhdam, we won the battle that night, but I was defeated, a kind of defeat I had never experienced before. It wasn't that I wanted to lose, but one night I thought about creating a retreat. A retreat to someplace where I could forget about everything, could dedicate myself to enjoying the night, silence, and nature, someplace that could restore me to my rightful place as a small human being in a vast universe. You are fortunate. We were all prisoners but you were the luckiest of us all. Muzafar-i Subhdam, you don't understand how hard it is for me to become a small human being in a vast universe again. Teach me how to become small, how to go back to where I belong."

I will never forget his words. He wanted to go back to certain roots that he felt had been taken away from him, but at the same time, they were the one thing he didn't know how to regain. He could have everything – absolutely everything – but didn't know how to regain what he had lost within himself.

Right now, as I'm telling you this story on this starry night, as we listen to the sound of the sea, I swear by its waves that Yaqub-i Snawbar had wanted to free himself from everything right from the start of our meeting in the mansion, to live like a hermit – but he didn't know how.

One day he asked me in a defeated tone, "Muzafar-i Subhdam, teach me how to live like a prisoner, how to live like a desert-dwelling dervish. Teach me how to be able to live far from power, wealth, pleasure, women. Please." I swear to you he bowed quietly and kissed my hands, his warm tears dripping on to them as he said, "My friend, teach me. Please."

In all the years I had been his friend, I had never seen him being so honest. I told him, "Yaqub, I can't teach you anything. Only years of solitude, not me, can teach you that. I did not learn it of my own accord either and for a long time I fought it with all my might. This isn't what I wanted to become. For years, desires and pleasures were killing me inwardly. Yaqub-i Snawbar, you don't understand the immense torment of thinking year after year about being able to see a flower. You sit in an infinite sea of sand and live off your imagination. You imagine eating apples, you imagine holding a pomegranate. There are nights when you'd give your life for the smell of a pomegranate or when you wake up and find your cell full of the scent of pears. You talk about water in your sleep. The strangest thing in the desert is the bottle of water they bring you. Through that water, you can tell that the world is still alive. Through that water, you know that somewhere far away are seas and waves. Yaqub, just imagine: every day before I had even a sip of water, I had smelled it for hours. Who says water has no smell? What idiot says such a thing? Through the water, I could smell the whole world. I smelled fish. I smelled so deeply that I encountered the most hidden scents of the sea. For years, your desires kill you, and then a day comes when you realize that you need nothing. You understand that everything you desire is a mirage, that its importance is buried deep inside yourself. That is the moment that you can stop thinking about your desires, that you can reconstruct your fantasies. Yaqub, there comes a moment – I don't know exactly when it is – but it's a moment when prison and retreat become so merged that they cannot be separated. You no longer know if you are a prisoner or a dervish. You are suddenly free of everything, all weight except the weight of life itself. I can't teach anyone. I don't know what that moment is or how it occurs. It's a moment at which language doesn't function. It defies description. It shines, like light, from the inside."

While I was talking, he held my hands and wept. He was on his knees, his head laid upon my hands, tears coursing down his white beard, saying, "Teach me, please." I was surprised that he preferred my imprisonment to his freedom. At the time, I didn't know what on earth it could mean. He hadn't told me much about himself or his secrets. I didn't know his post in the Party. I was sure he was profoundly unhappy. I don't want to swear to it, but I can assure you that Yaqub-i Snawbar wanted to create something else for himself, something that would free him from all his burdens. He was like a star bearing a weight heavier than its own, a star prevented from shining by the objects littering its surface. When I saw him, he believed in nothing. He wanted to simplify his life, one piece at a time, and to allow the light inside him to shine.

He bowed and kissed my hands, and I told him, "Life is a light, but it's in a closed box, and that box may be contained in many other boxes. Whenever you want life to show through, you must take it out of the dark and strip it of all its skins. Yaqub, I don't know what you are or what is wrong with you, but make yourself lighter. Put down your heavy burdens. Throw away the huge amount of gold you carry on your back, and swim away."

He gripped my hands tightly for a long time as he wept. I believed his tears. At last he said, "I want to start all over again, but in a different way and from a different place. But that's a myth, a futile fantasy. Isn't it? A pointless and futile fantasy. We can't start over again. Can we, Muzafar-i Subhdam? Can we start all over again?"

He expected me to say yes, but with the coldness of someone intent on breaking his heart, I said, "I don't know what you are running away from. I really don't. But no one can start all over again. No amount of seclusion can free anyone from the world. I was engulfed by the sand for twenty-one years, and yet the world was always in pursuit of me." I laughed impassively and said, more cruelly still, "There's always something that takes you back to the past, something greater than an individual's ability. My Yaqub, I learned one thing in the desert, which is that people are creatures who should not forget about the big things."

In great agony, he said, "You haven't run away from yourself. You haven't fled from yourself. You have swum out of a shallow place, a small muddy part of life, to deeper water."

I had long known that prison and the desert had made me a great swimmer, but now that I was free, I didn't know what to do. Should I stay at the bottom of the sea forever, or should I come to the surface? Yaqub wanted to join me in the water. He wanted me to stay and lead him by the hand into its restless, boundless depths. But despite my deep desire for silence, loneliness, and tranquility, an inner voice was calling me back into the world. There was one question that I had never managed to run away from, a question that always brought me back to the world: Where was Saryas-i Subhdam? Where was he?

If it were not for Saryas-i Subhdam, my life would have taken a different course. I could hear a cry, a loud cry, from the deepest and darkest place in my life, the sound of weeping, begging, and death. In my dreams, it summoned me in a different way each time I heard it. Sometimes I felt as if someone was calling me from the middle of a remote wind or a merciless rainstorm. At others, I felt the call came from a whirlwind of sand. I felt it was the voice of someone being swept away by the storms or dying of thirst. It was someone whose face I never saw, like a silhouette standing behind a curtain in the dark, the voice more remote than the image. Some nights the voices sounded as if they were shrieking from the very pit of hell, and sometimes instead of one person, I saw hundreds. I smelled blood. I smelled a sigh of deep sorrow. And every time I woke up, I remembered Saryas-i Subhdam.

Saryas-i Subhdam's death stirred the desire to lift my head above that sea of sand. So one night I told Yaqub-i Snawbar that I was going to leave, that I wanted to see the world.

6

From the day Muhammad the Glass-Hearted's body was found in the wreckage of his glass house, the sisters' fame spread far and wide and their lives completely changed. As they had few genuine friends, it was a week before they heard the news of his death. It was a rainy noon when Sulaiman the Great arrived, accompanied by his guards. The sisters had not seen him since the bizarre early-morning marriage request. The girls had not made much of Muhammad's sudden disappearance. Both of them thought that men who appeared suddenly would disappear just as suddenly and that those carried in by storms would be swept away by storms as well.

Sulaiman the Great, who would never forget his son's death, arrived in his blue turban, with his hooked nose, silver teeth, long white sideburns, and yellowing Kurdish felt coat. He asked to be admitted, sat on the same chair in the same cold living room as on the morning he had asked for Lawlaw-i Spi's hand for his son. She could tell just from his expression that Muhammad the Glass-Hearted had died. Years later, sitting in front of a small blackboard beside a blazing fireplace, she cried when she spoke about that moment. But back then when she read from the man's gaze and breathing that his son had died, she stood perplexed and motionless. Sulaiman the Great looked like a wild god who had recently come down from the mountains. He was covered in hair. His face could barely be seen behind his beard, and even the inside of his ears and the top of his nose were covered in thick black hair. It was apparent he hadn't showered, shaved, or laughed for several days.

He had come with an unprecedented proposal. He calmly told the sisters the news of Muhammad's death. He did not expect them to shiver, weep, or mourn manically for him. He had understood that morning that the two sisters had eyes as indifferent as birds'. Sulaiman the Great had come to tell Lawlaw-i Spi that he was ready to make her a monthly payment, provided she visit Muhammad's grave once a week. His final wish for his son was that he be at peace in his grave.

He told Lawlaw-i Spi, "True, Muhammad the Glass-Hearted has died – and no, you shouldn't think I gave him that name. I knew him less than anyone. We were strangers to one another. In these unusual times, fathers have become estranged from their sons. His death was peculiar, too. He had the most delicate heart in the country. Everyone is saying it's all your fault, that his death was a heinous crime by Lawlaw-i Spi, but I don't blame you. He had a heart that couldn't bear anything at all. He was destined to die so prematurely, so fast, so futilely. He had a heart clearer than any mirror, smoother and more transparent than any glass, like a thin and delicate goblet in the hand of a drunkard in an alleyway full of potholes. When I saw him for the last time, he had the look of a barman holding a glass of wine, his hands and feet chained. I knew he would fall. What strange times when children do not grow up to be like their parents: from the seeds of one flower grows another kind of flower; from the egg of one bird, another kind of chick is hatched. I won't hide it from you: I was a killer, an expert in death. I never suspected that a child would grow up in my shadow who would not pass any of the tests set by death.

"Anyway, I couldn't fulfill his last wish. He wanted me to tell him a secret that I could not reveal. I couldn't say anything as this secret was connected to a matter of life and death. He's in the next world now. People will never understand or forgive you. I am not used to begging for mercy. I grew old in the mountains, taking part in one revolution after another, one battle after another. But now nothing is going smoothly. For the past few days, I have still been able to see his clear eyes – just as they were on the stormy night when he barged into my room not long before he died. That night, his eyes told me: *You are a pitiless father. My heart is made of glass, but yours is made of stone.* His chest was completely covered in blood; his hair was wet, like that of an itinerant dervish who has witnessed all the storms of the world, who has crossed a huge river, bigger than any I've ever seen. He was asking for a precious gem beyond human control, a gem I couldn't find.

"Lawlaw-i Spi, I've always believed there is another world after death. Despite all my wrongdoings, I still believe in an afterlife. Such a belief brings murderers peace. After each killing, I used to go out to the mountains like a man crazed. Nothing is worse than thinking you have put an end to some-one's life – even the word *end* is repulsive. I came to believe in another world so as to feel that those who had died right in front of me would nevertheless be resurrected. I came to believe I'd meet my victims in another life. It was not over, nothing was. Lawlaw-i Spi, you too will meet Muhammad the Glass-Hearted again in the next life. I am sure he is there now, waiting. I feel the dead do more waiting than us. They live with the same passion they took with them. Lawlaw-i Spi, I'll give you a monthly payment. Just visit his grave one hour a week. One hour, nothing more."

Throughout the conversation, the two sisters were all ears but said nothing. When he finished, Shadarya-i Spi said sadly, "We didn't know that Muhammad the Glass-Hearted had died. Our condolences. May God forgive him and grant you patience. But he only came here one night, called out to us a few times, and never returned. He entered the yard, but we didn't open the door to him because women aren't supposed to open the door to a stranger late in the evening. He first appeared here on the day of the flood. Even then, had it not been for the flood, we wouldn't have opened the door. But during a flood people are supposed to help one another. We are two girls who will not marry, not ever. If the heavens were about to fall upon the earth and could be stopped by our getting married, we still wouldn't do it. Nonetheless, I'd say to Lawlaw-i Spi, if her visit to the grave can put him at peace, go. Do it. I won't get in the way."

Lawlaw-i Spi said fearfully, "As long as you come with me. I won't go without you. I have never been to a graveyard. You must come with me."

The two sisters were not the demons the gossips described. When they began talking, their inner beauty came to light. That day, Sulaiman the Great left the house feeling fairly content. Some people found it odd that a father treated the apparent killer of his son in this way, but he did not think Lawlaw-i Spi had killed his son. His delicate glass world, which could not tolerate the lightest of winds, had killed him.

It was a windy day. The sisters dressed in their finest white and set out for Muhammad's grave. Their hair stretched out along the wind. When they reached the middle of the graveyard, all was deserted and completely silent. The cemetery, with its thousands of tombstones, sat on top of a hill. The wind toyed violently with everything. The smell of death wafted in the air, a death the wind had stripped of its great peace. The wind was moving the dead.

No one else was at the cemetery. The two sisters in white stood quietly beside the grave and said to the deceased in low, barely audible voices, "Forgive us." In the cold parts of their souls, they both considered themselves innocent, but in the corners where their emotions and compassions stirred, they felt great guilt. They began singing at the grave. The sky darkened, and the graves calmed with their echoing voices. It seemed no one had sung in that graveyard for a long time. When they finished, they felt deeply at peace. They felt the wind dying down, the evening becoming tranquil, and the trees intoxicated. Something changed in the air of the graveyard.

After a brief pause, a young man behind a tombstone rose suddenly to his feet, and said, "Ladies, what beautiful, enchanting voices you have! I've never heard such beautiful and magical voices. What voices and what delivery!" The man's odd, abrupt appearance came as something of a shock to the sisters.

It took a while for them to calm down, and then they looked at one another and said, "Thank you, but we don't feel we have such beautiful voices."

The young man calmly approached the sisters in white and said, "My name is Saryas-i Subhdam. I've been listening to your voices since you began singing just now. I'm not going to comment on them as I've rarely heard women's voices before. But it's great that, as well as the mullahs' recitals, two girls like you are singing for the dead. Do you think singing will make the dead happy?"

Shadarya said, "I don't know if it will or not. Anyway, this is the grave of Muhammad the Glass-Hearted. He died two weeks ago. Love killed him. We are here now to apologize to him and to offer him a little comfort."

And this is how Saryas-i Subhdam and the sisters in white became acquainted – next to a grave, among thousands of tombstones. It was an evening just like this one: wet and windy, the sound of the sea so loud it might cut our conversation short. I don't want to talk about that encounter at length right now. Suffice it to say the day passed very quickly. Lest the story of Muhammad be repeated, the two sisters did not allow the young man to speak to them for long. They walked rapidly down the hill and disappeared. That day the two sisters were running away from the inevitable. But what is created by chance, if it is part of an inevitable story sown by fate, will be repeated in the form of other chance incidents, however hard you try to fend it off. That evening, Saryas-i Subhdam stood among the tombstones and smiled at the sisters, who hurried down the hill as if running away from fate.

The encounter between Saryas-i Subhdam and the two sisters was only partly a coincidence. He had been one of Muhammad's closest friends, but it was by chance that his visit on that windy evening coincided with the appearance of the tall girls in white. At the time, Saryas had many friends in the graveyard. Right from his youth, friends of his had been laid to rest there. Some of them were killed before the uprising; others were killed in the daily clashes and battles after it.

Saryas and Muhammad the Glass-Hearted were on the cusp of revealing the biggest secret of their lives. And what a secret it was! Indeed. I implore you not to ask me about it, just don't. No, sadness won't allow me to say anything tonight. Look, even the heavens are crying as if they were inside my heart. In any case, tonight the storms won't allow us to talk. Even the sea isn't itself tonight. Right now, I'd like to look at the sea's infinite darkness. Let me be. I have no desire to carry on tonight. As for the secret of Saryas-i Subhdam and Muhammad, that's for another night. Let me look at the sprawling sea and weep.

7

One dark night, a stranger found me in the remote and abandoned guest-house. I heard the sudden opening of a window and the sound of things breaking. The light from a flashlight somewhere below fell onto my curtain, and I could see the shadow of a big man in the trees at the back. He knew his way around and was clearly familiar with the place. I had thought the green mansion was beyond anyone's reach, but the man's appearance filled me with sudden fear and doubt. He was a giant of a man. I'd never seen anyone so big.

Sensing my presence, he whispered, "Who are you?"

I stood facing him and said, "I am no one. Who are you? This is my place. I've been living here for six months. Who are you? A guest, or are you lost? Are you a friend or are you looking for something?"

The man and his flashlight came closer. I had been sleeping in semi-dark-ness in a second-floor room but had now come out and was standing at the top of the staircase. He was on the first step on the ground floor, carrying a strange weapon I'd never seen before. Despite his giant stature, he had a childish face. He was wearing an army officer's uniform, the shoulder straps adorned with various insignia. I felt that he was unsure how to respond, that he didn't want to give anything away.

In a slightly frightened but cold voice, he asked, "Who are you? A guard or a guest? But a guest wouldn't stay in this unoccupied mansion for six months. I was in charge of building this residence. It's a secret place built for the distant future. What are you doing here?"

Seeing me there seemed to have thrown him. He had never seen a creature like me before. He had not expected that on a night like this he would come across someone whose beard had grown down to his feet, whose hair fell to his waist, here in this strange location, wearing the Arabic robe he had worn for years in the desert.

Unperturbed, I said, "I am a prisoner. I have been for twenty-one years. I am not a real person. I am an apparition. I both do and don't exist."

He looked around and said cautiously, "Can I sit while we talk?"

He had no idea how glad I was to see another human being. He did not know that for twenty-one years I had seen no one but Yaqub-i Snawbar and the desert guards. He did not understand what I was talking about. At first, he looked at me with great suspicion, as if I were a madman, as if I were merely confused and just playing with words. We both switched on separate lights and sat opposite each other on two black sofas.

He looked around the room and said, "Everything is as it was, exactly as I left it five years ago when I handed the keys to Yaqub-i Snawbar. Back then, we were afraid that Saddam would invade our region again. We were worried that one day we'd lose everything and have to start all over again."

As if suddenly remembering something, he looked at me hesitantly and said, "What are *you* doing here? For God's sake, no one knows about this place except Yaqub-i Snawbar and I. Only the two of us."

It was night. I didn't want to give away my secrets too quickly. Dodging the question, I said, "You have the look of a child, and yet your body is like an old devil's. You look too young to be friends with the leaders. Don't hold it against me if I'm suspicious of you."

He paused for a bit and said, "I turn thirty-five soon. The face is the most deceptive part of a person."

"What are you doing here?" I asked. "Who sent you? Why have you come to this cruel forest in the middle of a pitch-black night? What do you want? What are you looking for?"

He lowered his head sadly and said, "My name is Ikram-i Kew. I am here to try to find a friend of mine." He looked me in the eyes and without a trace of fear said, "I am trying to find a friend of mine – I've looked everywhere for him but to no avail. I am looking for a childhood friend who disappeared suddenly one night and was never seen again. And I know *he* is behind his disappearance. *He* is."

"Who is *he*?" I asked in astonishment.

"Yaqub-i Snawbar. The leader," he replied.

I swear by the pure stars that guide us on this sea, I swear to you by this ferryboat, knowing as I do that our survival hinges on the skill of its captain, that this was one of the bitterest moments of my life. Something from inside me – in the place where conscience and truth meet – cried out to me in a voice like that of a wounded person, weeping in the wind. I didn't know who had disappeared or who had made it happen. Suddenly I could see and hear the victims. The night was filling up with distant cries, with the groans of the desert's dead, voices tormented by the sand and the stars.

As if he read my mind, he said hesitantly, "You don't believe me because you are his friend. *He* has given you the key to this place. You're his friend, but you don't know him."

Back then, the whole world, life in its entirety, seemed like a big puzzle to me. I said, "You are his enemy. You wish the worst on him. Listen to me, I am neither his friend nor yours. I was in a dangerous, remote, and scorching prison in the desert for twenty-one years. I am outside everything. I do not exist. I didn't then. I know neither your world nor his, and neither of you know mine. I am a prisoner and have nothing to do with your conflicts."

As if Ikram-i Kew did not understand what I was talking about, he said, "I am looking for a friend of mine. I've looked everywhere for him. I've secretly visited anywhere I suspected he might be. This mansion is the last of these places, but there's only you here. The years come and go and with them my friends. Isn't each of us entitled to have a friend who is still alive? Don't assume I am a bad person or that I want to hurt someone. Even during the revolution, I saved as many souls as I could."

Calmly, I asked him, "So, can you save mine?"

He was a strange sight, like someone back from hunting or who'd been chasing imaginary prey in the mountains but stopped to drink tea with a shepherd.

He looked at me astonished and said, "What shall I save you from? From whom?"

From the very first moment, I had felt some affinity with him. This was someone with purity and strength. His weapon, military uniform, and giant stature did not make him menacing; rather, he looked like a playful child. We were two very different people. His face was broad and white. He was so clean-shaven there was no trace of hair on his face. His eyebrows were black and thin. He had incredibly rich, full lips. He was so huge he could easily have lifted me onto his shoulders as if I were a bundle of twigs and taken me wherever he wanted. I looked at him more than he looked at me, and it was such an awkward look that later on I'd feel embarrassed about it. At that point, I was still unaccustomed to feeling affinity with people. His strange, secret-revealing looks sharpened my memory so much that I'm able to look at the water on a night like this and tell you the story of those days.

That night when I asked whether Ikram-i Kew could save my soul too, the question came from the bottom of my heart. Earlier I had been thinking that some day or night someone would surely pass through the forest, spot the house, and come ask who I was. I had wondered whether I could put my destiny in a stranger's hands, whether I might one day call out to a stranger passing the gate and say, "Hey brother, passerby, traveler friend, come and save me." I had slowly lost hope that Yaqub-i Snawbar would come and hold my hand and eventually return me to the world as a human being. I had become certain that he wanted me there forever. Somehow, I had become the prisoner of his philosophical obsessions. That night when I asked Ikram-i Kew to save me, I was firmly committed to going out into the great wide world to discover Saryas-i Subhdam's fate, to understanding what had happened in the twenty-one years I had been away. You mustn't think that I reentered the world because I was after something, out of greed. I wanted to go to lessen the burden of the long desert years on my shoulders. I had returned as a spectator, someone intent on making one final trip and then dying, or an ex-gardener aiming to take one last look at a garden he has not seen for a long time. That night I said to Ikram, "Save me from the sand, from the desert. Please." I was certain he didn't understand.

With his childlike appearance, he asked me, "And what will you do to Yaqub-i Snawbar?"

Rather than answering, I said, "My name is Muzafar-i Subhdam. I want to be saved from the silence."

When I said that, he put down his weapon and said, "Oh God, Muzafar-i Subhdam was one of the earliest martyrs of the revolution. What are you saying? Muzafar-i Subhdam died a long time ago."

"That's true," I said, "I did die a long time ago. But don't we have the right to live again?"

I had to explain everything to him. And you mustn't assume I had any bad intentions or any specific wish. I simply felt that he did not understand me, that he did not know what I was talking about. He listened to me until dawn, and I listened to him. It wasn't easy for him to understand what I had to say. Muzafar-i Subhdam was an ancient name. It seemed like one of those names you hear once and never again. He had evidently heard a story about me a long while ago but could not pin it down. He didn't find it surprising that I had been imprisoned in that mansion after twenty-one years in the desert, but he was surprised I was not aware of anything. He talked about a number of battles I hadn't heard about; he talked about towns that didn't use to exist; and I talked about towns and villages whose names he'd never heard before. During my imprisonment, hundreds of towns and villages had been destroyed. When he mentioned the destruction of certain places,

I'd jump up and beat my head with my hands; when he talked about the complete and sudden annihilation of all the residents of somewhere else, I would start beating myself like a madman. He didn't understand why I was so moved by the destruction and collective deaths of people I didn't know personally.

And no, my friends, don't assume Ikram-i Kew was a cruel man. He was an incredibly warm and friendly person, a truly compassionate man. I swear by this water that you couldn't fault him as a human being, but he had grown up in an age in which people had lost their sense of shock at disasters. Throughout the night, he recounted his stories of destruction, deaths, and wars, and I rocked to and fro to soothe my pain, as if I were an old boat being rolled from side to side, oscillating between life and death. He was talking about a world that had nothing in common with the one I had left behind. I had been looking at that world as if it were paradise. Although year after year I had tossed sand over its colors in order to forget it and prevent its beauty from hurting me, what he was talking about now was hell itself.

All through the night, he related one story of destruction after another, moving from one tale of the sudden deaths of tens of thousands of people to yet another. He spoke until sunrise, telling stories of collapsing cities; stories of cholera and plagues; stories of the obliteration of many tribes and clans; the extinction of birds; the demise of hundreds of types of flowers; the fall and death of stars; the birth of towns from the ashes of others. Morning came, and I was still involuntarily rocking to and fro, while he kept talking in his cold, deep, calm voice. He was neither scared nor indifferent. He had witnessed all these disasters, and his innocent and childish appearance did not match his eyes, in which I saw the shadow of them all. At first light, he gathered his things together and left quickly, like a frightened ghost.

Pleadingly, I said, "Don't leave me. Take me with you. Save me. Didn't you say you save people? Save me. I have a lot to do. I need to know so many things."

He didn't wait for me. From the doorstep, with the panic of a large bird taking flight to dodge a bullet, he said, "Muzafar-i Subhdam, no one must know I've been here. It could cost me my life. I will visit you again. Now it is very late. I must go." And with that he disappeared through the gate.

Initially he seemed like an apparition to me. In my long years in the desert, I had experienced many such incidents. Many a night, I had woken to see creatures looming over me and talking, or humans in the form of water, whirlwinds, black crystal, white foam. They had come to talk to me about the wind, the moon, the Day of Judgment, about the dirt and the rain. So when he left, I thought the whole night had been nothing but a hallucination, a dark fantasy. But to my astonishment, as darkness fell the following night, he returned.

He was wearing the same clothes, the same green cap, and carrying the same weapon. At the door, he said, "What do you need freedom for? What do you want from it? What has freedom brought us? What do you expect of it?" It seemed as though he'd been thinking about me all day long.

I told him, "I want to look for Saryas-i Subhdam. You know everything. You've searched every corner of this country. Tell me, have you never come across the name Saryas-i Subhdam? Didn't you say that each of us is entitled to have a close friend who is still alive? Haven't you yourself come to this forest looking for a friend? Saryas-i Subhdam was my son."

When I mentioned Saryas-i Subhdam, the color drained from his face. He said broodingly, "Was Saryas-i Subhdam your son? Was he really?"

I said, "If I am to return to the world, if I'd like to mingle with the living again, it is because of Saryas. Saryas-i Subhdam was my son. You know him, don't you? Don't you?"

He said sadly, "No, I don't know him. I've never known him nor met him, but I do know he's dead. Saryas-i Subhdam was killed a while ago. I don't know his full story, but I know people who do."

It was my first clue. I said, "Ikram-i Kew, take me away from here. I want to visit his grave. I need to get out of here. Help me."

He was a strange man. He said, "But where do you want to go? After all, you don't know anyone in this world or have any home to return to, no friend to put you up; your name doesn't exist anywhere in this world. You may be sure the world thinks you are dead. Besides, if Yaqub-i Snawbar finds you anywhere, he'll make your life hell. And I don't have a place I can take you to."

Like an angry dervish, I shouted, "But I have the earth, the night, the day, the shade, and the light. The world in all its vastness is before me. There are thousands of fields to feed me, thousands of trees to hide me, thousands of winds to conceal me. I am a friend of the universe, the mighty heavens, the moonlight, the wind."

He said, "You don't get it. He'll find you. He has people everywhere. It's futile."

I shouted into the night with all my strength, "True, I don't have friends or places to go, but there will be trees or water to adopt me, a cave to welcome me. I am only dead in the official records. I am only dead in the laws that govern the world. I am not dead to the treasure house of nature; water, birds, trees, and clouds remember me. I have a place in this universe. In the wheat that is growing right now, I have a share. In the water, which nourishes the flies and the wolves, I have a share. I am not as destitute as all that. There'll be something to act as cover, as a hideout, something to share its food with me."

Ikram-i Kew listened with composure and said, "Well, you must know that the day you leave here, things will change. You'll be entering a major conflict. To enter a war, you must have prepared a shelter beforehand. Listen to me, Muzafar-i Subhdam, I do want to help you, but you'd need a roof and four walls, you'd need a room. Nature gives everything to human beings: the wind, the night, the garden. It gives you everything except a room. A human being without a room is lower than a stray dog. After all, everything nature gives to human beings is so that they can build themselves a room."

I said, "Who says I need a room? I have been in one for twenty-one years. I want to live in the rain and moonlight forever and to talk to nothing but the universe."

He paused for a moment. There was a bead of sweat, the sweat of weariness, on his forehead. He looked like a large, placid horse on a hot evening, stooping to look at the darkness from the window as if he were saying goodbye to something. He felt hot and stifled, but I felt cold. When he looked back, I realized he was deep in thought. And whenever he was thinking, he'd close his eyes and sweat.

He said, "Tonight is not the night. It's too early to interpret your freedom. People are always in such a hurry to do so."

And so I fell again into the sins Yaqub-i Snawbar had wanted to keep me from. Ikram was innocent. All his years of involvement in the wars had not wiped out an incredible purity in his heart. His giantlike figure, his calm, which suddenly turned to panic, are always in my mind's eye. Wherever I went, I would think about him before I went to sleep. In the morning, before I got up, I would see his image. Wherever I saw crystal clear water, I'd say it reminded me of him. You got the sense he was someone whose soul God had made a special effort to create.

Finally, with a soft laugh, like that of someone passing along a street only to disappear in the dark, he said, "I am not bothered about freedom. But if I took you out and you couldn't bear the night, the wind, and the storms – if no tree sheltered you, no moonlight hid you, then what? Where would you go then?"

I shouted back at once, "I'd go back to the desert . . . to the sand . . . or to any eternal retreat . . . Listen, Ikram-i Kew, I have a journey, and I need to make it. I have a mission, and I need to accomplish it. That's just how things are. There's some reason I haven't died in the past twenty-one years. There's a wisdom in the fact that you and I have met in this place. This is not fate; it's stranger than fate. More mathematical and calculated. Even if it's not you, some other night, some other year, another person will pass by here. A lost hunter will pass by, and I'll call out, 'Hey friend, take me with you.'"

Untroubled, he said, "Don't indulge in these fantasies. Only he and I know how to get here. Whoever comes here will get lost among the trees. There's no such thing as fate. This house is his most secret and strangest refuge. For a brief time, I was the only person he trusted. He treated me like a complete fool that he could punish over feeding the wrong fodder to his horses, millet to his bulbuls, or lettuce to his rabbits. Many years ago, and shortly after the success of the revolution, I became his bodyguard. I didn't think anyone wanted to kill him since he had good relations with all the leaders of the world. Well, they all wanted to kill him. One night he punished me so severely over the death of one of his rabbits that I cried. I hadn't cried before. In none of the fierce battles, gas attacks, or armed fights that turned into hand-to-hand conflict had my humanity been hurt so much. I hate him. He and his friends took everything, absolutely everything. Only one secret has been left us, the one thing they can't reach: our hearts, our inner worlds. Don't think nature can hide you – he is more powerful than nature. The rulers, the parties, they're all more powerful than nature."

At the time I didn't know what he was talking about. I thought some inner torment, something that didn't go with his bright face and sharp gaze, was making him speak so hopelessly. He held no grudge; his grief was as clear as a fish's. In a way, we were both reborn that night. He used to say, "In this country, no war is left that could be entered with a clear conscience."

Later, I felt that, in his support for me, he was revisiting his old fantasies about a world in which wars could still be beautiful. He was from one of the demolished towns. During the armed revolution, he had worked for a while at a secret printing press in the mountains where he met youths who then died, disappeared, or deliberately got lost one way or another. But a guardian angel had given him an enchanting way of talking. He had decided to focus on smaller causes. He was a simple man who had concluded after long reflection that he couldn't create an army or an armed force. His close relationship with the leaders had offered him the chance to support some tormented souls. Like any unhappy traveler, he sought people he could comfort with a small gesture. Just as he dispassionately told me stories of wreckage and destruction, so without a shred of pride he told me stories of the people he had saved from storms, hunger, prison, and attack. When he spoke, his sad eyes twinkled with the traces of a secret deeper than he realized.

Ikram-i Kew did not allow me to escape from the house that night. To him, nothing was more dangerous than not having a house. It was in complete contrast to my own attitude, since I liked nothing more than fields and walking, being at the mercy of the rain and lightning. Of course I had fears of my own; I was afraid of everything. When I told Ikram-i Kew that I would like to live naked in an orchard where the rain never let up, I was shaking inside. But I was someone who could tolerate fear. Bravery is not being unafraid; it is being able to tolerate our fears.

Ikram-i Kew took his gun and left before dawn. He told me, "I won't return until I find you a place where you can rest." I just had to wait, which reminded me of the beginning of my time in prison, the years when I was inexperienced, counting the weeks and months and fantasizing about freedom. Nothing is harder than teaching oneself not to wait. Oh God, people are so weak, constantly waiting for something, waiting until the Day of Judgment for some alluring good news that will never arrive. Tonight I tell you that if you strip human beings of waiting, there will be nothing left of them. Stripped of waiting, they collapse. Stripped of waiting, they are finished forever.

8

Now let's go back to the sisters in white, these sisters who were extremely beautiful yet disliked. They were not ordinary people, and many strange stories were told of them, stranger than any others, especially after the death of Muhammad the Glass-Hearted. They repeated the song once sung at Muhammad's grave in the days that followed, and more loudly too, singing it not only at his grave but in other places when they shouldn't have.

The strange stories spread about the sisters in white are intrinsically linked to my own. Those stories were responsible for their resulting loneliness, a loneliness so deep and so crushing that it eventually gave rise to their obsession with creating an imaginary brother. You can all remember the earthquakes, the two weeks of fear, sleeplessness, and death when the ground trembled several times a night as if it were being shaken by the angry dead beneath. You can remember the nights of doubt and anguish when hundreds of thousands of people made their beds in the streets, on the sidewalks, looking up at the stars, the moon, and the listless patches of cloud, which were alienated and sickly and swept away into the unknown as if by a wind from hell.

Those earthquakes that played hide and seek with life disappeared, letting the world regain its composure, silenced the nights, soothed hearts, and granted a mysterious peace of mind to people who slowly, slowly began to trust the walls of their houses again. Those nights of calm made people stop fearing the earth, the heavens, and the cracks in the Kingdom and prompted them to go back under their roofs. And as soon as they went back to their homes, reassured and at peace, the earthquakes returned, rocking the world again like a cunning snake playing a devilish game.

I wasn't there, so I don't know the exact interval between the tremors, but those who were always trying to find demonic qualities in Shadarya and Lawlaw thought it odd that the two sisters always left home minutes before the earthquakes, as if they knew the times they would occur, as if they had a magical internal clock that whispered the time of the earthquakes to them. After the fortieth tremor, a story was born. It traveled from one street to another, spread from one bazaar to the next. It was the story of two sisters with connections to ghosts and devils. Two sisters whose voices could numb birds, butterflies, and people alike, whose voices could shatter hearts, who walked around the graveyards and sang. That story turned them into two lonely people. One day they looked back and realized they had no friends in that land. They were like two sparrows who had found themselves flying through large swathes of mist only to land in a garden full of plants that were hostile to them. It was as if the morning and the stars were their enemies. They did not understand the secret of their loneliness.

Lawlaw and Shadarya were like two friendless birds, and what kept the stories about them fresh was that they were always being seen. They were not the kind of girls who were content to keep to the house. The deeper their loneliness and the more unpopular they were, the more they went out, as if looking for something. They would take endless walks through the dark alleys and quiet streets, so they would be seen at odd hours. At night they appeared next to graves, and in the early morning on the empty streets, like two quiet souls, forever bound together.

When they were most afflicted with loneliness, Saryas-i Subhdam reappeared. Now, please, don't jump to conclusions. I want to reassure you from the very start that Saryas-i Subhdam and the two girls were never in love. I can assure you that this tale is devoid of all love stories. And no, don't assume that I – a man who has come from the desert and been aged by the sand – have become like the operators on the top floors of the movie theaters, who censor the films as they please, cutting out the scenes of kisses and enchanting, beautiful bodies. No, my friends, I assure you this is not a love story. When Saryas-i Subhdam appeared again, both sisters were certain they had no need to worry about falling in love: the youth was covered in dust and grime. And don't tell me you, Muzafar-i Subhdam, lived in the sand for twenty-one years so could not understand it all, or that he was blind to love. In our world of meaningless, wounded men like you and me, people realize early on if they are any good at love. Saryas-i Subhdam was the type of man who was not inclined towards it.

The evening Saryas-i Subhdam visited Muhammad the Glass-Hearted's grave was an ordinary one. He had compartmentalized his life. He did not live in the city but rented a room from an ailing old couple in one of the state-built collective towns outside it.* He had divided the room into two with a wooden wall. On one side was an ordinary, bare room. It was carpeted and contained only a mattress, an oil stove, and a cupboard. On the other was the strangest room I had ever seen. Obviously I went in there many years after his death. Some of his things were missing, some stolen by poverty-driven thieves, while the old couple had sold the more valuable items for a song. And yet, when I entered the room, it smelled of his absence, of the life of a man who was killed while still young. What told me something about him, his character, and his behavior were the strange pictures he had hung on the walls. I was sorry that he had clearly been deeply obsessed with macho masculinity. The pictures were mostly of men on horses or motorbikes, or of astronomers looking through the windows of space rockets, as well as hundreds of pictures of karate fighters, Indian actors, and muscled bodybuilders. Only a few broken tapes were left in the box where he'd stored them.

No, give me a moment. Don't ask me to go on as if this were all just a story. It's night, and here we all are out on this vast sea. God, I feel as if

* The Iraqi army destroyed the Kurdish countryside in the late 1980s as part of a plan to deprive the Kurdish insurgency of a support base. These efforts peaked in the 1988 Anfal genocide campaign in which thousands of villages and small towns were destroyed and tens of thousands of civilians killed, wounded, imprisoned, or forced to flee their homes. These places were declared prohibited areas. The government then set up new "collective towns" near the major urban centers to house residents from the decimated areas. (Translator's note)

81

too much looking at the sea at night sickens the imagination. Where was I? What was I saying? Oh, yes – I was supposed to be telling you about the worlds Saryas-i Subhdam lived in, the two different worlds. He and his strange room that once housed a bizarre assortment of stuff – broken scales, weights, gloves, old magazines, pictures of imaginary creatures, and his incredibly patient attempts to write his name in different types of hand-writing. If I hadn't seen it myself, I might have doubted he lived there, but there was a huge piece of cardboard on the wall on which the letters had faded with the damp of successive cold winters. But you could still see that, hundreds of times over, a patient hand had written: Saryas-i Subhdam . . . Saryas-i Subhdam . . . Saryas-i Subhdam. As if he had been worried he might forget his name, or had somehow wanted to fix it in his sight and grant it respect. There in that place, he had dreamed about power, meaning, and beauty. From that room he had become "a great human being," and there too he had pondered the meaning of his life and his name.

Saryas and the sisters in white next came across one another on a battered bus, heading to a northern neighborhood. This time, the sisters greeted him amid the smell of passengers' sweat and fruits bought by cloaked women. He had had his hair cut in the style of the day, but he was so weak, emaci-ated, and burned by the sun that he did not attract any attention. As always, he was talking and laughing loudly. He wore a cream-colored shirt with a white collar and a pair of old, baggy trousers. He might look like a weakling dressed in rags, but those who knew him were aware that, poverty notwith-standing, he did not behave like the poor.

When they got off the bus, he said to the sisters in white, "It's no fun at all going to the lovely northern neighborhoods on the world's most dilapidated bus." He was a great fan of walking around the northern neighborhoods.

The two sisters said, "All the buses are dilapidated."

Laughing, he replied, "All the buses are the most useless things in the world."

That evening Saryas-i Subhdam and the sisters walked together for a short while. During that time, Saryas had the chance to answer the basic questions girls ask on such occasions, such as how many siblings you have, what grade you're in, what your father does. Saryas said that he had no brothers or sisters, father or mother, and he didn't go to school. And when Saryas asked them the same questions, they spoke about the death of their father and not having brothers and with some pride said, "We go to the Teacher Training Institute."

When they finished talking, he said, "I know you. You're the sisters in white. I'd like to hear you sing again."

In tones of ice, Shadarya and Lawlaw said, "No, don't. You can't want to hear our voices again. You simply can't."

When Saryas left, the two sisters regretted their rudeness. They rarely regretted anything. God, you don't know them. I am the only one who knew they had good hearts, hearts like white cotton. But when they did regret things, you can't imagine how bitterly they did. I am sure one of you is now going to ask, "So why did they regret this?" The two sisters' regret was rooted in a wretchedness, the shadows of which could be seen in Saryas's face from that evening on. There was something in him that was attractive to anyone after only a short conversation or interaction, something I'd call "life energy," the magic that eventually killed him. He called himself "the poorest boy in the world." He had known poverty that defied description. The only thing that saved him was his laughter, which knew neither day nor night and so was ever present.

That evening, the sisters were plagued by anxiety. Yes, I told you from the outset that two great womanly hearts, like two big diamonds, shone in their chests. Something happened, almost the opposite of what had happened in the case of Muhammad the Glass-Hearted, in the dust of whose death we shall have to live forever. No, they did not fall in love, but Saryas's shadow was gnawing at their consciences.

It was late at night when they left home again and embarked on a search for the sound of his laughter. It echoed constantly in their ears, but they could not find it. Wherever they went, they heard it, in every alley they visited, yet they did not see him anywhere. Eventually, they returned home with a heavy feeling in their chests. If it had not been for that night, this story would not have existed. Had it not been for that sorrow and unease, I would have nothing to recount, or maybe I would have recounted something that didn't feature the sisters in white, that cold night, their cold eyes, or their kind and tender hearts.

When Shadarya and Lawlaw were not at peace, they became very agitated, and when I got to know them later, they possessed that same excitability and restlessness. Whenever they were moved by something, they would panic, their cheeks flushing red. They would bite their nails, stare at each other, then plait their hair in hanging braids. In moments like these, their eyes would widen but still appear cold and unkind. In the days that followed, Shadarya and Lawlaw looked for Saryas-i Subhdam wherever they went. During lessons at the Teacher Training Institute, they heard the echo of his laughter in the empty corridors; when they went to the women's toilets, above the sound of flushing water, the whispers and laughter of the girls, they heard his sad guffaw from the hallways. They looked for him tirelessly for many days without knowing why. They had nothing to tell him, but they wanted to sing just once to make him happy.

A few weeks later in one of the city's big squares, they saw him pulling a cart that carried a few sacks of potatoes. He was trying to pull it up a sloping street to the gate of a mosque and park it somewhere near the fish sellers, exerting huge efforts to turn the cart out of a tight corner before it was balanced again and could be pushed forward. They both looked at him, astonished, as they heard someone calling, "Marshal . . . Marshal . . . You forgot the cigarettes." It was the first time they learned that Saryas was an ordinary seller among the army of street vendors. His friends called him "Marshal of the Cart Vendors." The sisters heard him angrily telling a water seller, "If I was thirsty for a hundred years, if your bucket of water was the last one on earth, I wouldn't drink it. Go away and leave me alone." They popped up in front of him and both said in a melodious tone, "Good afternoon, Marshal."

At that moment he was holding a rock, attempting to balance it against a five-kilogram weight that belonged to one of his friends to see if it could be used as an alternative. The day before, in one of the daily skirmishes between the cart owners, he had thrown his five-kilogram weight at someone, and it had traveled a long way. He spent ages looking for it but with no luck. His friends said, "You twerp, you threw it so hard it probably hasn't come down yet."

He was in such a state he could not see the sisters in white and did not reply. He said, "Shit . . . Shit . . . This is the most stupid rock in the world.

It's too light by half a kilo. What am I going to weigh things with?" As he spoke, he raised his head and noticed the two sisters. In a twinkling of an eye, all his cheerfulness and joy returned. "Ladies, what a pleasure! Forgive me. I wish you hadn't heard me swearing, but this is the bazaar. If you don't swear, you go mad. If you didn't swear during the day, they'd take you home dead in the evening."

The sisters, who were now filled with kindness, said, "Saryas-i Subhdam, we've been looking long and hard for you."

He was overwhelmed and stammered, "Thanks . . . I appreciate it . . . That's very kind."

For years, when the two sisters told the story, they would burst out laughing at this point, but, as for me, tears always rolled down my cheeks. I left prison too late to witness the world of the carts. However, I can picture a young man in the hubbub of a big bazaar, in the middle of the cacophony of masses of carts, engulfed in the clamor of hundreds of vendors extolling the virtues of their apples, onions, radishes, and tomatoes, descriptions that elevated their produce to the level of the divine. And right there and then, he sees two girls and greets them. He is the poorest boy in the world. No one knows where he came from; he doesn't know himself. He's a nobody. All he knows is that his name is Saryas-i Subhdam, a strange name in the merciless jungle of names.

Just as I am sitting now in the night breeze, the sea's cold air touching my face, so I have sat on hundreds of nights, thinking about these moments. When he saw two angels in the busy midday market, what must Saryas-i Subhdam have felt, wearing shabby clothes beside the smallest cart in the world? I am certain he expected nothing. Everything tells me he expected

86

nothing. The only thing he was sure of was that he wanted to become a great human being, and yet he was too simple and too young to know what *a great human being* was. I know that in the moment he saw the girls, he felt ashamed – ashamed of himself and of the world, ashamed that he was not one of the men who ruled the world, the world that was ever present in his sentences, the world that he called "the dingiest world of all the worlds."

Saryas-i Subhdam was the most lively, cunning, and jovial vendor among the army of cart vendors, yet he wasn't free of aggression. Three years before he was killed, his last aunty died. I say "last aunty," because he had had a whole series of aunties by then. As villages were destroyed one after the other and gradually evacuated, from those highest in the mountains to those in the hottest plains, he was taken in by many families. He called any woman who fed him or washed his clothes "aunty."

For a short while when he was ten, he lived in an orphanage. He learned to read and write from a mullah who was living in the mountains. When he finally wound up with the old couple in the hot and waterless collective town, he began his long journey with sundry menial tasks that didn't match his physical abilities. He did all sorts of work: waiter, car-repair assistant, construction worker in the newly-built collective towns, water seller at the border crossings. He loaded tires onto trucks to be smuggled out, washed cars at roadside restaurants, cleaned poop in the country's first private hospital, sold plastic bags in the grocery section of the bazaar. And all that before he bought the cart he called "Kazhal's Chest."

It was not Saryas himself who gave the cart that name, but another vendor, who was in love. The vendor had been infatuated with a certain Kazhal for years, but she had married a veteran Peshmerga fighter, who fancied another girl, who fancied another boy, who fancied another girl, who reportedly fancied a married man living in another country, who himself fancied a younger woman. As a result, all these unrequited loves were concentrated in that small cart. I looked for it for a while, but soon realized it had been smashed to pieces in the campaign to abolish the carts, to clear them off the streets.

Someone had written the words *Kazhal's Chest* in blue paint on the front of the cart. Below that, in the same handwriting, they had written: "If my love has a tongue, may my life end early." On the other side were the words "This love, dark fire, for no good reason burns the heart, a phoenix." The year Saryas-i Subhdam bought Kazhal's Chest, the deployment of the carts was at its peak. So much so that the first evening of Saryas's life as a street vendor was also the first of his battles with the police and municipal inspectors. He was one of the horde of vendors who flooded the town center with their carts early in the morning. His first day at work was a dark one: the vendors killed a policeman near the cooking-oil sellers. Saryas had already seen a large number of killings and deaths at close hand, but this was the first time he had touched the blood of a corpse. Three vendors beat the policeman to death with three steel pipes, and his brain eventually burst out onto the cans of milk, the loose washing powder, and the Turkish soaps. That day the bazaar was rife with rumors that the government would set fire to all the carts. After that, Saryas and a number of his fellow vendors parked the carts in an empty square and stood guard over them. Saryas would rarely return to his room then, and spent many a night in the square inside a makeshift room of tin.

The sisters in white stood by the carts for a long time, telling him how sorry they had felt after their last meeting. They both spoke sadly, but there was a hint of two coquettish girls in their voices. Some of the nearby vendors heard their comments. They had never heard such music in anyone's voice before. The two sisters told him they hoped he could treat them as sisters and that they could sing if he wished. Saryas got into such a panic that he didn't say a thing. When the sisters in white left, he was annoyed with himself. He threw down the weighing dishes and grumbled, "This miserable tongue of mine, this unfortunate mouth of mine, they have never been so useless."

He thought that his shyness, confusion, and sudden numbness had left a negative impression on the sisters, but on the contrary, they spent the whole night laughing, unusually amused by his embarrassment. They had never seen someone panic like that and found it very reassuring. After all, as they said, they were looking for a brother. At dawn, almost choking with laugher, Shadarya and Lawlaw decided to make Saryas-i Subhdam their brother and permanent friend. They embraced each other calmly and happily by the window, ran their fingers through each other's hair, and inhaled the dew-filled air carried on the morning wind. With smiles that were half human, half divine, they fell asleep, unaware of all the strange days that lay ahead.

9

Ikram-i Kew visited me again after three weeks.

I learned to wait during that time, and even now I do not regret accepting freedom with all its horrors. I do not regret that I opened my arms to the world and said that I was alive and could bear my own aliveness. I could have stayed in that quietness, like a hermit unaware of the world, like someone who has ceased to worry, but after twenty-one years I wanted to try everything. When Ikram-i Kew returned that night, he seemed even calmer and more jovial than before. Physically bigger, he filled up the room like a bear cub. At the same time, he had the appearance, movements, and attentiveness of a child looking at a group of other kids from the side of a playground.

Ikram-i Kew took me out on condition that I could protect myself. Back then, he was scared of something I couldn't pinpoint exactly. It was a dark night; the moon nowhere to be seen. He seemed to have chosen it on purpose. He paced the room, wearing a cap and carrying his gun. He said we had to wait until late at night. At the time, he did not tell me anything, he just talked about himself.

"I served the revolution for many years," he said. "I've done everything except kill for it. I often regret it, and often I don't. Muzafar-i Subhdam, innocence creates two feelings in us: on the one hand, you feel you're nothing, you're weak, and your innocence is like a rabbit's in the middle of a pack of wolves. At other times, you have the opposite feeling – that you have encountered every kind of war and filth but retained your innocence. You tell yourself: that's good, that's beautiful, it's a great achievement. Muzafar-i Subhdam, the revolution is a great big lie. You're fortunate – you're a revolutionary without having been in the revolution. And that's divine grace. I had thought that the success of the revolution would automatically bring about paradise on earth. And yet, from the next day, the very next morning, when you opened your eyes and washed your face, you could see that everything was starting all over again. I saw that devil being reborn day after day, a devil that was only small to begin with. At first you say, So what? That devil is part of all of us, it's only small, a natural part of any human being. But you can see it gradually grow bigger, sweeping everything away. Everything."

At that point, he paused and looked out of the window. His eyes were so wide open, you felt he could be gazing at a vast sea.

I sensed that the revolution had robbed him of something great. "Ikram-i Kew," I said. "You don't want to tell me anything. I laid my story bare for you, but you don't want to tell me a thing. There's something missing in your life, and you're hiding it from me."

"No, there was nothing valuable in my life that they could usurp. I'm not talking about myself but other people I came across. Muzafar-i Subhdam, I was inside the Party, but people don't see anything if they don't look carefully. I saw certain things by chance. People are free not to notice. They can pass by and not look. That's how I've maintained my dreams for many a year. I'd free a prisoner, secure a pension for an old woman, find a way out for a youth who wanted to leave the country, hide a person who belonged to a different party. I'd do anything that meant something, things that could help me not to be lonely on these long, dark nights, things that were helpful for me, that made me feel alive. I've been very lonely since the uprising."

He came to a halt in front of me. God, his eyes were full of tears. He looked like a mythical creature unable to walk after being shot in the middle of a clump of trees. The tears I saw in Ikram-i Kew's eyes were different from Yaqub-i Snawbar's. Ikram's tears were for the whole world, but Yaqub's were the tears of someone who had destroyed everything around him but still couldn't find what he desperately desired. Ikram's tears were like those of someone standing outside a garden, watching the flowers wither, but Yaqub's were those of a man who tramples on all the flowers in his search for an imaginary bud.

Ikram faced me. "I've felt useless ever since the uprising. At first, I wanted to study, to start anew, but it's difficult to start again from scratch. Muzafar-i Subhdam, nothing is harder than starting all over again. I slept on the roof at night, and all night long the old nightmares would return – I always had images of ruined trees, houses, and towns here. Yes, here," he said, pointing to his head with his fingers, which were several times bigger than mine. There was some madness in him, but it was internal, invisible, and unaggressive. He always spoke in the same manner and the same tone, his voice the same whether he was crying or laughing, his eternal essence unchanging. There was a hoarseness to his voice akin to the sound of a fire being rekindled by the wind. He too was running from the past.

Yes, my friends, companions on this journey through the night and across the sea, since the day I left the desert, I have met one person after another who is running away. Look at yourselves: what are you but a group of ghosts on a ferryboat, running away from something, from something that has no name or color, that cannot be caught or tamed? Ikram-i Kew was also running away from something but did not know where to run. He had tried to start over again in a different way, but the smell of gunpowder and death prevented him. When he slept at night, he was not the calm person he was during the day. He shouted all night long, his throat closing up as if he were being strangled. He would wash his face frequently and say, "Oh God, oh God. What a night this is!"

That night, before we left, he helped me get changed. It was the first time in many years I had worn anything other than my prison dishdasha. That night, I didn't want him to shave my beard. I said, "Ikram-i Kew, let me go back to the world wearing my prison face." The moment he took me out, his eyes filled with tears and his face took on a divine brightness and beauty. In the dark, he seemed even bigger and more imposing. It was a cold night. For the first time, I was wearing a white shirt, a dark gray sharwal,* an old checkered Kurdish headscarf around my neck, and a small traditional hat. Don't forget I hadn't walked across hard terrain for twenty-one

* Kurdish baggy trousers

years or seen any steep slopes. The night was similar to the one when I was captured. The moment Ikram took my arm and led me through the trees was like the moment the green-uniformed commandos apprehended me and took me away. Walking through the trees, I could feel the same cold air, the same twinkling of the stars, the same fear. That night was similarly moonless yet full of the cries of the stars.

Don't forget that in those six months I had tried several times to find an escape route, exploring all the gates and paths, but had always ended up at mountain peaks, clumps of trees, or precipices, which forced me to retrace my steps before losing my way back. That night the world appeared smaller than before. In the desert I had been used to vastness, to an infinite openness, but that night as we walked, I felt that at some point the world itself would come to an end. It didn't occur to me then that the ground I was walking on in the dark was connected to other lands and worlds. I didn't know that much later, one night on a ferry out at sea – on water you say is not faithful to anyone – I would raise my head and understand the enormity of the truth I had learned in the desert, that the earth and life are a single interconnected whole. I would then understand that the great universal aspects of being human, which the desert had revived in me, would help me feel at peace. They help me not to be scared in the middle of these waves, not to fear death, to look at the sea as a friend, to touch its infinity and shout, "Oh, sea, guide us." Who among you has come out here one dark night and shouted from the deck, "Oh sea, save us"? I shouted thousands of times from the window of my prison, "Oh desert, save me. Oh sand, save me." I was sure something in the desert could hear me, something that isn't like you and me. You feel it in the air, coming towards you with the daylight. You feel its coolness in the evening shade. It's invisible, but you can see it with your eyes closed.

That night when I left the house, I felt I was standing on ground that was not on this planet, our Earth. People often forget they live on a planet. They forget that their house, their field, their garden is part of the universe. I too had forgotten that when I went out that night.

I asked Ikram-i Kew, "My friend, why is the world so small?"

As if he could not see me in the dark, he stopped and looked back. He said, "Because we look at it from the wrong angle." That night Ikram did not let me dwell on my fantasies, he didn't want me to feel too safe. "Confidence kills you," he said. "Muzafar-i Subhdam, it lulls you to sleep, just as it blinds a house sparrow so it no longer sees the cats. Well, I have never felt safe. Never."

When we passed the trees, he stood on a rock and prayed. I hadn't known until then that he did pray, and his method was unusual. All of a sudden, he would stop walking and start praying, with no concern for the set times or places of prayer. After that, I wanted to discuss God with him, but he categorically refused. He never talked about God, not even once. He'd start praying as if he had suddenly been woken from ignorance of God. As I got to know him more, I noticed that on some nights he would start praying for no reason, without performing ablution, without a prayer mat – in the dirt, on the ground, amid hard rocks.

After he finished his prayer, he asked me, "Muzafar-i Subhdam, are you sure Saryas, I mean Saryas-i Subhdam, is your son?"

"And do you think the person exists who can create an imaginary child for himself? Who could make a child their son by the sheer force of their imagination?"

After a pause he said, "I'll take you someplace where they'll tell you the whole story of Saryas's death. It will be painful for you, but after all it's what you're searching the world for."

We walked until dawn. Not a bird flew, not a wolf howled, not a mosquito whined. I was engulfed in a silence more menacing than the desert's. Ikram-i Kew and I did not break that silence. I looked at the stars, and in my heart I said, "I am free. I am free. I am free." I greatly enjoyed the walk, the air, and the darkness, but there was also a fear in my heart, the fear of a duck flying through the crack of bullets for the very first time.

Every now and then, we took a short break and sat quietly. He didn't say anything but wiped the sweat from his brow with his handkerchief. I didn't need to talk; I felt like a fish that has leapt back into the water from a fisherman's net, its heart still filled with the recent shock of its probable death. I knew the stars were watching me, looking at the freedom of a man summoning all his strength to achieve a distant goal.

In the morning, we arrived at a house on the outskirts of a peaceful village. A girl dressed in white and wearing a neckerchief, the most beautiful being I had ever seen, opened the door to us. Ikram-i Kew broke our long night of silence. "Good morning, Shadarya-i Spi. We've finally arrived. This is Muzafar-i Subhdam, the man who has been imprisoned for over twenty-one years, and this is his first morning of freedom."

I looked more beast than human. Shadarya had never seen anyone whose beard had grown to his feet, with white hair to his waist and eyes full of the desert's copper tones. I bowed before the beauty and purity of the first woman I had seen in so long and said, "May your life be filled with light. I am Muzafar-i Subhdam. And here I am, dragging all the darkness of the world behind me."

With that, I pointed to the last dusting of darkness in the sky and looked at the space in front of her, which was bathed in light. This was my first encounter with one of the two girls who was to fill my life with light forever, just as they had illuminated the end of Saryas's.

10

They called Saryas-i Subhdam "Marshal of the Cart Vendors." His was the young mind that guided hundreds of youthful street vendors through the complex and intricate geometry of the bazaar. He would tie a red handkerchief around his forehead and carry a Turkish cigarette in one hand and a small walking stick in the other.

He was the person who relocated the children who sold milk, putting them behind the blacksmiths' section, and moved the oil sellers outside the mosque nearer to the section where chickens were sold. He placed the mirror vendors close to the qaysaris and transferred the medicine vendors from the smelly puddles of the bazaar to the clean sidewalks of the city center, a move that made them neighbors to the book and picture sellers. It was he who would conjure exits out of nowhere to allow vendors and their carts to flee and he who converted dozens of vacant lots, unused warehouses, and abandoned yards into safe places for the vendors, even installing night guards. He dreamed about drafting a law for the bazaar and drawing up a plan for a different city, a different world.

Those who knew him intimately said he could be highly persuasive. There were hundreds of children out there who, had it not been for the carts, would have been forced to take up arms, return to their dark and dirty villages, or leave the country with one of the many groups of migrants. Saryas knew more than anyone else that their lives depended on the strange game they played in the city's convoluted geometry. His conversation skills were beyond his years. One dark night, after a lengthy argument, he convinced a journalist that no one on earth had the right to force these children back to their villages. When the journalist arrived, Saryas and his friends were sitting around a teapot and the glowing coals of a brazier. The journalist, slender, with straight hair and white-framed glasses, was a likable young man but overflowed with the arrogance of people who regard villagers as worse than dogs. His father was a school principal and his mother an officer in the budget administration; he had worn clean shirts all his life and spent his time in university cafés and newspaper offices. One of his cousins regularly sent him perfumes from a L'Oréal warehouse in Freiburg. He had gone to the bazaar that night to write a lengthy dispatch about "the animals who, rather than polluting the city, should be plowing the abandoned fields of Kurdistan."

Saryas-i Subhdam was the only street vendor who read the newspapers. When the journalist showed up, Saryas was crouching down next to the brazier. The journalist, who was wearing tight jeans and a white shirt, saw himself as a great investigative reporter whose work forced him to frequent unusual places and talk to strange people. He considered his visit to the cart vendors that night extraordinary.

That night by the fire, the journalist spoke about the wealth of agriculture and the yield of livestock, but Saryas spoke about the neglected and forgotten wealth of the thousands of abandoned children who found themselves on the streets from the age of four. The journalist talked about the charm of the cities, of clean sidewalks, and of the right of drivers to sufficient space for cars, but Saryas talked about the lost beauty of those children, himself included, who were forced to wash in filthy swamps because they had no access to clean water. The journalist argued for the return of the villagers to the countryside, Saryas for the return of people to a decent life. The journalist mourned the devastated fields awaiting the plow, Saryas spoke about the tens of thousands of children and adolescents who could never live happily again, in the cities or the villages. When I think about it now, these children were lost in a geography, just as we have been lost on this sea for ten days.

The night when Saryas defeated the journalist, as the young street vendors put it, was one of the most important of his life. The following day, a photo of him standing next to Kazhal's Chest was published in the newspaper's features section. He looked like a knight of old with his steed. In the picture, a long More cigarette dangles from the corner of his mouth and he's holding a big walking stick, beaming at the camera. It's the clearest picture of him I have ever seen. Oddly, Saryas-i Subhdam's name wasn't mentioned in either the caption or the rest of the report. Nowadays I think that if his name had not been left out, the truth might have come out faster.

From that night on, his friends called him Marshal of the Cart Vendors. Saryas was not like some of the youths who went looking for clashes with the police and inspectors. After all, just like everyone else, police officers have to take a decent meal home to their children in the evening. Each of the vendors could have paid the officers a small sum to win over their hearts and ward off their cruel behavior. Everyone knows that Saryas was the architect of the secret agreement between the police and the children who would all spend a good deal of their lives on the sidewalks and in the filthy puddles of the bazaar.

Weren't the policemen of those days young men just like Saryas and his friends? They were youths who wanted to provide for their wives as best they could lest they end up on the streets and at the mercy of the rich merchants, people who wanted to get engaged as soon as possible lest someone from afar come and spirit their intended away, never to be seen again. If things had not got out of hand as they did, Saryas-i Subhdam could have become friends with the people who, one wretched evening, would go on to kill him.

It was thanks to the agreement between Saryas and the young policemen that the army of carts managed to survive for as long as it did with its remarkable strategy of hide and seek.

This was a show in its own right: whenever the police came and hit the carts with their sticks, the vendors would create a collective commotion and begin shouting, before dodging into side streets and alleys. It was a remarkably clever performance, this combination of truths and lies, this game whose rules always contained a loophole enabling two groups of downtrodden people to keep earning a living. Saryas-i Subhdam knew better than anyone that they had to play the game carefully or else the broken geometry and narrow paths of the city could easily become a dangerous trap. But the market is a jungle and always will be.

In those days, he stood with his cart, his youthful voice inviting customers to buy the nicest turnips on earth, to eat peppers sweeter than baklava. Playing with his voice, he would summon them to look at the largest chard on earth, at cucumbers that melted into Zamzam holy water in the mouth. He'd shout out that the plums had come from God's own beloved orchard in paradise, a pear had been planted by the angel Gabriel, and the pomegranates – oh, lady pomegranate – would heal the blind.

Here, you should pay attention, my friends. When Saryas cried out about his pomegranates like that, he was not merely talking about some imaginary fruit. No, he was also referring to the story that is at the heart of everything, the story of a pomegranate that could heal a blind boy.

No, tonight I'm not going to tell you about Muhammad the Glass-Hearted, Saryas-i Subhdam, Nadim-i Shazada, and their connection to a pomegranate tree that heals the blind. It's too early to reach the heart of our story. It seems as if we'll be out at sea for many more nights. And if God comes to our help and our story is cut short because we've reached some country's shores, if the coast guards detain and separate us, don't worry that you haven't heard the end of the story. You are right there at its end. This ferry marks the very end of the story. And if it sank tomorrow and one of the passengers managed to swim to shore, he could resume where I have left off. I could stop now and any one of you could carry on the story provided that your version too ends on this ferry. This ferry that is lost at sea, this ferry whose fate and direction are unknown. The ferry – since we have no idea where it will deposit us – is the only way this story ends.

Anyway. Friends, Saryas-i Subhdam's life in the bazaar was part pain, part game. He assumed responsibility for organizing hundreds of kids, and eventually they created a small council. He made a number of loyal friends on that council, who gave him their support and stood guard over the carts with him on many a night. Zhino-i Makhmali sold fish and Adam Marjan lamp chimneys. They were less hotheaded and less well-known than Saryas, but they were wiser and more patient when it came to keeping the peace between and organizing the cart vendors. Saryas would sometimes act out of character, a strange aggressive desire bubbling up within him. He would take part in most of the fights without really thinking about it. One of the most fatal of these was the fight between the tomato-paste vendors and the cigarette vendors, in which even pistols were used when the cigarette vendors shot dead three of their rivals inside the toilets of a mosque in the bazaar. That evening, fighting between the various groups spread from the tail end of the qaysaris to the toffee vendors outside the hospital. It was one of those fierce fights where reason deserted them all. Saryas-i Subhdam got involved as well, using his scales, the beam of a steelyard, and ropes with hooks. Every time, he would reach for his weights and throw them randomly over the brawlers' heads. One day in one of those fights, someone sliced his cheek open with the edge of a plastering trowel.

At the peak of the fighting, Zhino-i Makhmali sat Saryas down on two concrete blocks, placing one cloth after another on his wound. At precisely that moment, the sisters in white popped up before them, as suddenly as the landing of two angels, as abruptly as the descent of two fairies. The arrival of Shadarya-i Spi and Lawlaw-i Spi was so unexpected, it brought back memories of the earthquakes. Both of them arrived beside Saryas-i Subhdam a few minutes after he was wounded, as if an internal clock had told them about the timing of his injury. Zhino-i Makhmali kept on applying a red medicinal powder to the wound, saying, "Last night I saw this wound in a dream. But it wasn't on your face. It was on my right hand." Saryas-i Subhdam, who was unable to smile, said, "It's the stupidest wound in the world. My face will still have this scar when I'm old, a sign of this terrible day, the day a monkey shat on my face."

The fight forced everyone to leave, and the bazaar was engulfed in an eerie silence. The streets and alleyways were littered with broken carts, spilled baskets, plastic bags, and boxes of fruit. Flour and tomato paste mixed with the blood of crushed hens, doves, and ducks, while rabbits roamed free among the scattered chard and spinach. Children howled behind the closed shutters of the stores.

The arrival of the sisters in white made the destruction look different, as if two angels were surveying the devastation of a battle scene from heaven. That evening, they took Saryas-i Subhdam to the hospital where a young Arab doctor, wearing a pair of shiny glasses, stitched the wound. While treating him, she kept saying in broken Kurdish, "Why the carts doing this? Why is the poor fight? I sewn five stitches. You be back on feet after three weeks."

When the two sisters left the hospital with Saryas, they put their hands in his for the first time, and told him, "We are your sisters. From this day forward, you are our brother forever. So, get used to it. Who would a brother turn to if he had a problem? His sisters. And you too should come to us."

Not even in his wildest dreams had Saryas ever imagined such a bizarre day; he was so used to being an orphan. But the sisters had one condition. That night, before they took him home, they told him that their relationship must always be that of siblings. They told him that they were not like those girls who told guys they were like their brothers but secretly harbored and cultivated other desires, girls who would call men their older brothers, and yet when they were in bed at night, fantasize about kissing them, embracing them, and all the rest. These two sisters said that for them a vow meant something, that their word of honor was more important than anything else, and that they would never accept betrayal.

The anesthetics given to Saryas hadn't completely worn off, and when he exhaled, he still smelled of medicine. Scenes from the evening's fights were replaying in his head. In a dusty southern neighborhood of the city, two months after the death of Muhammad the Glass-Hearted, exhausted by the day's turmoil, Saryas-i Subhdam, who I am sure had always wanted to have a family, told the sisters, "Don't you worry about me. My life is too short to upset people."

It was Saryas's first night with the sisters. They sang for him until late, let down and retied their hair in front of him, frequently offered him water, laid their hands on his forehead, reminded him when it was time to take his medicine, and washed his socks. Saryas was astonished by their world. He had always imagined that the delicate world of girls was the loveliest of lives.

Theirs was an agreement based on fairness, two lonely sisters making a kinless boy their brother. Late that night Shadarya and Lawlaw-i Spi told Saryas the great secrets of their lives: that they would never get married, cut their hair, sing without one another, or wear anything but white. That same night, the trio drew up a contract of their own and signed it in blood. They vowed that Saryas was their brother forever and that no one else would ever become so. That delicate agreement which Shadarya-i Spi had written down, which was stamped by three small fingers at the bottom of the page, still lies beneath the same pomegranate tree, and always will.

When Lawlaw-i Spi told Saryas to join them and place the agreement under the pomegranate tree, he looked at both of them, rather bemused. A few years earlier, he had hidden another oath under another pomegranate tree. The tree stood at the other end of the world and bore a remarkable similarity to the one in their front yard. It was the mirror image of a pomegranate tree that, on a bright morning years later, would come to be called "the last pomegranate tree in the world." But no, it's still not time to tell you about that other oath.

Saryas said nothing about his first agreement that night. He did not know how to explain this bizarre repetition. What did it mean that he took a second oath, which would bind him forever to two girls he hardly knew yet? Do people need oaths and written promises in this cruel jungle of life in order to trust each other?

When I think about it now, there was a touch of the philosophical about the three teenagers' relationship. The sisters in white later told me that they were acting in defiance of an uncertainty and a weakness in their own characters, but I think this was typical of the whole era: people felt they needed to tie their fellow human beings down, to tie themselves down. When the sisters in white and Saryas put the oath in a tin and buried it, they were taming an unknown force inside themselves, they were killing off a potential betrayal.

When Saryas opened his eyes the following morning, he had a fresh wound on his cheek and two sisters in white.

When he returned to the bazaar, Zhino-i Makhmali and Adam Marjan were expecting to hear a very different story. You know perfectly well the fantasies of sixteen- and seventeen-year-old boys, constantly dreaming about being kidnapped by two women who would spend the night romping around with them, acting out all the fantasies they had ever harbored. What man has not dreamed about a woman kidnapping him and then begging him to sleep with her? Even the boys in the world of the carts were not exempt from these fantasies; both thought two white angels had come and kidnapped Saryas and had sex with him all night long.

That day Saryas took the big knife Zhino used to cut up fish, still covered in scales and slime, held it right under their noses, and said, "I'll kill anyone who says even one word against Lawlaw and Shadarya. It would be the last hour of his life because I'd skin him like a dog. They are my sisters." This was the first time Saryas had thought about honor in those terms.

Until the evening of his death, no one believed in the white-clad girls' sisterhood with Saryas. But at the moment that Saryas was vomiting blood into Zhino's lap, surrounded by hundreds of weeping cart-vendor friends, he said, "Take me to my sisters' home. Take me to my sisters in white. I want to die there." Only then did his friends believe what an innocent agreement existed between him and the girls.

Before I bid you goodnight this evening, I want to tell you a little bit about some things that will play an important role later on in this tale. You mustn't forget that during that period Lawlaw and Shadarya were visiting the grave of Muhammad the Glass-Hearted once a week to sing to him. Meanwhile, Sulaiman the Great, the sad, bearded man from the mountains, whose black hair was as tangled as the fur of a sick animal, was also visiting his son's grave every week. One evening Sulaiman the Great invited the two sisters in white and their mother for dinner at his house, that is, the home of a dejected senior official of the era after the 1991 uprising.

There were few officials in the post-uprising era who had a sad soul, but Sulaiman was one of them. Nonetheless, his life, just like those of all the politicians of the post-revolution era, had a royal air about it. At night his gatherings crawled with men who ran the world, and yet day after day he was increasingly drawn to solitude. After the death of Muhammad the Glass-Hearted's mother, he hadn't even thought about re-marrying. He had grown used to living without a wife. That evening when he saw those two beautiful girls at the dinner table, their hair black curtains spreading over the back of their chairs and down onto the Persian carpets, he felt that life had treated him very unfairly. He spent all his time among his guards, wrapped in the stinking breath and sweat of politicians, with secret briefcases, murder plans, and reports being written for the Party. Unlike his colleagues, he did not have a coterie of lovers. He was still his old self, a wild man, in a new guise.

When the sisters in white accepted Sulaiman the Great's invitation, they did so in the hope of finding out more about Muhammad the Glass-Hearted. But that evening they returned home with a glass pomegranate which a stranger had given to Sulaiman after his son's death. The pomegranate was the only item from Muhammad's glass world that was not broken; a secret was buried deep inside the pomegranate that Muhammad the Glass-Hearted had failed to crack. Since the pomegranate had not become part of his glass world, it was the sole item that remained intact even when that world collapsed.

When the sisters in white took the pomegranate home, they had completely forgotten what Muhammad the Glass-Hearted had said on the eve of the storm. "It's not my pomegranate. It belongs to the secrets."

And then one day Saryas-i Subhdam came and saw the glass pomegranate inside Lawlaw's bookcase and shouted, "Almighty God, what is this I see! That's my glass pomegranate."

Only then did the two sisters remember Muhammad's strange words. This was the moment they asked Saryas for the first time, "How do you know Muhammad the Glass-Hearted? What secret binds the two of you together? If this is your pomegranate, why isn't it in your possession? And if it wasn't his pomegranate, why did he have it?"

And so the sisters in white entered the serpentine stories of Saryas-i Subhdam, oblivious to the fact that there was not only one Saryas but a second and a third.

II

Now the time has come to tell you how Saryas-i Subhdam and Muhammad the Glass-Hearted met.

On that night in March 1991, when everyone in the villages and towns north of Iraq's deserts left their homes, fled to the mountains, and gathered at the Iranian and Turkish borders, Saryas-i Subhdam was only eleven years old. In the period between the uprising earlier in the month and the crushing defeat of the popular forces, which enabled the return of the Iraqi Army's tanks and the Republican Guards, he had been living in a state-funded orphanage. During the few weeks when the state disappeared, warehouses were looted, safes were broken, and he and his fellow orphans begged for bread in the city's alleyways and streets. On the night that the uprising was crushed, Saryas had no one to worry about; he was completely alone in the world. Even the friends he had made during his three weeks at the orphanage were now so scattered that he had no idea where any of them were. That night, he might well have been the only person not trying to find a relative, but also the only person no one else was looking for. No, not a single soul among the hundreds of thousands of rain-soaked individuals trekking the mountains, valleys, and rivers was thinking about Saryas-i Subhdam.

When I picture it now, I see a small, dark-skinned child with a glass pomegranate, a few flatbreads, and a bagful of dates, who has realized for the first time how acutely alone he is. But he is also glad that, unlike other youngsters, he does not have a mother he could lose in the crowd, or a father who might be searching for him, and that he can walk to the end of the world and back undisturbed.

It rains all night long. At every fork in the road, he stops to ask for directions. The villages remind him of the ruined villages he grew up in. As he walks, he looks at the thousands of families who have packed lorries, pickup trucks, and small cars with TV sets, fridges, provisions, and utensils. Barefoot children walk at the side of the roads, some stepping on landmines that explode under their feet. He watches old women walking in the rain, unveiled, weeping, and venting their fury at God. He sees mothers and daughters lose and find one another, and old men who sit down on the rocks and die.

That night, another boy, the same age as Saryas, flees from another part of the city. He can't find his parents. As he walks through the rain, he plays with a few keys on a key ring. Singing aloud, he tosses the key ring into the air and catches it. He doesn't seem to care that he has lost his parents, in fact he is glad he's alone. He has neither money nor food, but he does have a happy, smooth glass heart inside his chest. It is none other than our old friend and the first character in our story, Muhammad the Glass-Hearted. He is the only child who's singing and dancing. This is one of the happiest nights of his life, because he can see people outside their homes and hidden residences, and he is elated that he can see the naked world.

Now, it so happens that a blind child who is the same age comes to a stop in the dark and the rain. No one knows where this boy has come from, or how he ended up in the middle of these roads. He stands there shouting, "Who will help me? Who will take my hand? Who wants to save me and be saved by me? Who will give me their sight so that I can give them mine?" The blind boy is Nadim-i Shazada, Nadim the Prince, who, despite his name, is the poorest blind person in the world.

Thousands of people pass him, but no one stops. Furious, he cries on the side of the road, shouting at passersby, "You are a nation of dogs. You are the shit of this earth, a tribe of bastards and cowards." Nadim-i Shazada, who grew up among beggars, knows all the crudest insults. One minute he is pleading for help, the next he is hurling abuse. Wearing only a shar-wal, he covers his head with a rain-soaked blanket, yelling, "The door to enlightenment will open to whoever helps me, and whoever has the door to enlightenment open to them can see their own destiny, and whoever sees their destiny can avoid misfortunes." He has learned these words, which are at odds with his childish appearance and voice, from his fellow beggars.

Among those thousands of people, only two listen to the cries of the blind boy. "Come and help a blind boy reach his destination. If one of you changes your path and takes my hand, God will remember that act of charity forever. Whoever guides the helpless will have God as their guide on Judgment Day." These two people are, of course, the young vagabonds, Saryas-i Subhdam and Muhammad the Glass-Hearted. As if their hopelessness had a similar schedule, they arrive in front of Nadim-i Shazada at the very same time.

And so Saryas-i Subhdam and Muhammad the Glass-Hearted meet each other in a torrential downpour, among hundreds of broken-down lorries and trucks, amid the shrieking of women and girls and the screaming of men, all terrified of daybreak and the soldiers it will bring.

Nadim-i Shazada begs the two boys to help him reach a pomegranate tree on a nearby mountain peak, a tree he must sleep under in order to regain his sight.

If the souls of the two boys had not been rich in imagination on a night when reality was sinking its ugly teeth into people's bodies, if their attraction to secrets and adventure had not been greater than anything else, they would hardly have set out in search of a mythical tree, a tree that Saryas would later call "the last pomegranate tree in the world."

While everyone else is busy saving their belongings, the three youngsters start looking for a mythical tree. The blind child has an ancient but clear map in his mind but cannot reach the tree without a sighted person's help. He says to Saryas and Muhammad, "From this place where we're standing, we must take one thousand steps. We will then come to a fork in the road. One path is a paved road; the other is a muddy track. Anyone else would take the paved road, but we have to follow the other one. After four hundred steps, the road slopes down to a stream. We have to cross it – the stream's sluggish, it doesn't rise even in winter. We must then resume our journey and it should take us twenty minutes to reach a ruined village. Then we have to pass through a small graveyard. My father, may he be immersed in the mercy of God, is buried there. We will say the Al-Fatiha at his grave and resume walking. Then we have to climb a mountain path behind the graveyard. Once we reach the summit, there should be a tree. It must have grown bigger by now. If the tree is there and has grown, I'll sleep under it and when I wake up, my blindness will be healed."

And so, on that night of terror and rain, Saryas-i Subhdam and his two friends set out to find the last pomegranate tree in the world.

The tree stands on the very top of a mountain with a summit that, unlike most others, flattens out like a vast sports pitch. On this flat expanse, from which you can see nothing but stars, Nasim-i Shazada, Nadim's father, planted the tree for his son. Nadim says his father took the sapling from a magical garden. One day, years later, he was out looking for healing herbs for his blind son when he was captured and killed by two state intelligence agents, bounty hunters who were paid handsomely for each head. They decapitated him, shaved off his mustache, bagged the head, and sold it to the state for the price of an Iranian soldier's.* Later on, his brothers found the head, now without ears, among hundreds of others in the backyard of a small burned-down state security building. After the uprising, and a long time after the night when the three children had gone in search of the last

* This is a reference to a practice of Saddam Hussein's Iraq in the 1980s whereby people received rewards for capturing Iranian intruders in the border areas. The border areas, mostly mountainous in the Kurdish region in northern Iraq, were declared a prohibited area, so civilians and villagers were not allowed there. (Translator's note)

pomegranate tree, the head was reunited with its body and they now lie together, peacefully buried in a new grave.

Before the boys go to the summit, Nadim-i Shazada visits his father's original burial site, and addresses him: "Nasim, I know you don't have a head, but I know you can hear me because I know people can hear sometimes even if they don't have ears, just as I can often see without eyes. I am now going to lie under the sapling you planted years ago. You told me to lie under it when I grew up and to sleep for a while and that then, when I opened my eyes, I would be able to see. Nasim, if you lied to me, I will lose all faith in you. You mustn't tell me lies. The pomegranate tree must have grown now. I've been trying to visit it for two years, but I can't because you planted it in a prohibited zone. Couldn't you have planted it in an ordinary field? Did you forget that I'm blind?"

As they listen to Nadim, Saryas-i Subhdam and Muhammad the Glass-Hearted start cackling. Nadim ignores their laughter and goes on to say, "I was born blind. My uncles and the beggars say someone born blind knows nothing about sight, but I know that's not true. I know all about it because the blind also dream. People see things in dreams, but not with their actual eyes, with another eye that is deep inside us, so deep inside that only the person dreaming knows it's there."

Along the way, Nadim recounts his entire story, the story of a child born blind and constantly crying for the light. As a young child he cried so much that his father was forced to search high and low for a magical cure, restlessly carrying him on his back from city to city and from village to village, visiting doctors, herbalists, magicians, and shrines.

Nadim says, "I've tried all the drugs in the world, applied every ointment made by man to my eyes. All the money I made from begging, I spent on medicines. I won't hide that I envy anyone who can see." Nadim covers his head with the blanket, then continues, saying, "We, the blind, feel the rain and cold more on our skin. When I heard that the tanks had already reached the outskirts of the city, I had no time to go home to put on thicker clothes. I'd heard that, in villages off the beaten track, the army had gouged out the eyes of the sighted and slaughtered the blind. I didn't dare go back for warmer clothes. I was wearing a jacket, but it was so soaked that I threw it away en route. A young man hurled the blanket onto my head, and said, 'Fucking blind man! You'll die like a dog from the cold tonight. Take it. I can't be bothered to carry all these blankets. Give it back when we meet again in Iran.'"

Saryas-i Subhdam and Muhammad the Glass-Hearted have never met anyone who talks so much, moving relentlessly from one story to the next. Every now and then he stops, banging his stick against a rock to knock off the mud. He talks so much that they forget the effort of walking. His knowledge of the area is astounding, and he says something new at every turn. At one point he says, "We should now be nearing an oak tree with purple galls, if you can see through the darkness and rain, that is. It's an amazing tree. It's said to have been used in the olden days to make the drug that cured the piles of the Iranian king and queen." Or again, "From here on, it's the flank of the mountain. Every three years, a cloud descends, wrapping itself around the mountain as if it were a belt. That's what I've heard. I don't know exactly what clouds look like or how they can wrap themselves around a mountain. We should be near the belt about now."

He is a child who knows all the stories of the area, filling the gap left by his loss of sight with words.

Muhammad the Glass-Hearted and Saryas-i Subhdam talk to Nadim-i Shazada so much that night that they end up talking very little to each other. At around dawn, they reach the summit, which rises up above the clouds like an island surrounded by silver waves. The day's first rays hit them as they look out of the clouds, and the boundless sea of white is the most beautiful thing they have ever seen. The air is clear and fresh, the sun so warm and soothing on this stirring spring day, it's as though the children have flown to a different planet. The dreary world below the clouds has nothing in common with this light-flooded expanse. Even the rocks seem softened by their eternal proximity to the clouds, sky, and sun. The summit appears untouched by humans, as though it is where earth ends and the heavens begin, created by God as a resting place for the angels on their journeys between the two.

The rocks have a divine fragrance, unlike anything anywhere else. It is the delicate mixture of the earth with moonlight, sun, and clouds. Nadim-i Shazada uses this scent to find the summit. When they arrive, he cannot see the beauty of the vast silver sea, but with his first step, he shouts, "This is it! This is the one fragment of paradise on earth." He has been here only once, four years before, but the smell is unforgettable.

Right in the middle stands the enchanted pomegranate tree. Saryas-i Subhdam is the first to see it. "God Almighty, guys, look. This has got to be the last pomegranate tree in the world. No other pomegranate tree can have ever grown so tall, in such a remote location, at the end of the world." And yes, indeed, it is the last pomegranate tree in the world, on a mountain peak where the world ends and the vast and mythical realm of God begins. This is a place where one feels a strange sense both of the world's limits and of infinity. The pomegranate tree has grown on the border of two kingdoms, the realm of reality and the realm of dreams.

They look like three children who have fled this day of defeat and climbed a mountain leading to another world. Under the sun that shines with the power of all the seasons, Nadim-i Shazada sleeps beneath the last pomegranate tree in the world in the hope of healing. Facing the endless sea of clouds, Saryas-i Subhdam and Muhammad the Glass-Hearted sit on the summit, telling each other their stories. It is here that Saryas takes the glass pomegranate from his pocket and tells Muhammad the Glass-Hearted that he has carried it since childhood. He does not know what it is or what it signifies, but as a child he learned not to lose it. It is a crystal-clear, sparkling pomegranate. That morning when the sun's rays hit the glass, a small rainbow appears around it. Muhammad the Glass-Hearted's hands become so red in the pomegranate's glow, it's as though he has washed his hands in bird's blood. From that moment on, Muhammad the Glass-Hearted becomes obsessed with discovering the story behind the glass pomegranate. When he picks it up, he can feel that there is a deep secret behind this man-made fruit. He looks at the rise and fall of the undulating clouds, then at the magic of the glass pomegranate. "Only death," he tells Saryas-i Subhdam, "will prevent me from discovering the secret of this pomegranate."

While it pours below, and hundreds of thousands of refugees drift through mud and slush, Saryas-i Subhdam and Muhammad the Glass-Hearted sit above the clouds discussing the pros and cons of uncovering secrets. Yes, my friends, in those hours that you were lost in the rain, only those two children were out in the sun. While the rest of the world was lost in a bloody reality, they were opening the door of a myth.

Over and over again that day, Saryas said, "This is the last pomegranate tree in the world. There is no other pomegranate tree in such a high, remote spot." The summit seemed like the edge of the world. The two children felt a profound peacefulness under the tree, a sense of calm they would never experience again. It may have been because of their proximity to God, or because they were far away from earthly perils, or because they were both children who knew that they would die prematurely, that they did not belong to the Earth. Rather, they were two angels, temporary guests upon Earth who would soon take their leave.

But the great happiness the two boys experienced up on that light-drenched summit was fleeting. Don't forget that day was the day of blindness, when hundreds of thousands of people had to leave everything behind and flee towards an uncertain future. No one knew if they would survive even the next few hours of their lives.

When Nadim-i Shazada wakes up after a long sleep he is as blind as ever, but there is a sense of peace in his expression. "No, I can't see anything," he says. "I am still the same, as blind as I've always been. But I could talk to my father in my sleep, and he explained everything."

The other two boys expect him to cry, bang his head against the rocks, or break branches off the tree, to throw stones at the sky, utter blasphemies, or injure his chest. But Nadim-i Shazada gently kisses the trunk and says, "You are a blessed tree."

When the boys descend through the clouds, Nadim-i Shazada recounts his dream to Muhammad the Glass-Hearted and Saryas-i Subhdam, all the while walking through a thick fog that he cannot see. In his dream, his father stood beneath the pomegranate tree and said, "Nadim-i Shazada, my little son, the sweetest boy in the world, I know how much you have suffered in the years since my death. It pains me that you are forced to stretch out your hand to survive, to sleep on sidewalks or mosque verandas or in vacant lots. You are the most beloved child in the world. From now on, you must be braver. You will wake up and your eyes will be the same. No, Nadim, I didn't lie to you. One day you will have a pair of eyes better than anyone else's, but those who want to regain their sight must work very hard. To really see, people have to learn to understand many things and endure great hardship. But one day, you will have two clear eyes. Your eyes will be different from the eyes of other people. No, my little Nadim, all people are born blind, every single person on this planet. Do not assume that those who have healthy eyes are able to see. Nothing in the world is harder. A person may have two clear, bright eyes and still see nothing. Nadim, my little Prince, I can't help you but this pomegranate tree can. You mustn't be afraid of the darkness around you. Day after day, a light will grow inside you, until the day comes when you will be able to tell rotting and sweet fruit apart just by smell, identify the secret desires of others by the sound of their whispers, and intuitively know how to navigate every road. Then, my dear son, you will never be lost again. One day you will be able to see, but before that, you must understand the meaning of seeing. Nadim, those who killed me had eyes, but they couldn't see me. Whenever you feel tired, come to this tree. It is the tree of sight, and it belongs to you and me because we planted it together. Go and travel the world. Search field after field for a medicinal herb. Never let yourself lose hope that one day you too will be able to see. You may go now, little Nadim. Whenever you need me, come here and summon me. Don't worry, I shall always be close to you."

When blind Nadim reaches this point, his heart fills with tears. "He is with me. He is near me," he says.

A slight boy with straight hair, two white eyes, and full lips, he climbs over the rocks and down the rough terrain of the mountain as well as any sighted person. "No, the tree didn't lie to me. Now I can see two things I couldn't see before: I can see you and my father."

At the foot of the mountain, they swore an oath to visit the tree again, although at the time none of them knew when, how, or on what extraordinary occasion this might occur. I have no words to describe to you the happiness the three children felt.

The three boys lived together for a few weeks that would see them become friends for life. I don't know exactly how long they spent together but I do know that, unlike hundreds of thousands of others, they did not cross the border. Instead, they stayed in the ruins and vacant lots of a destroyed town, where a man selling copper goods gave them work. Constantly engaged in his search for copper and aluminum, he was utterly uninterested in what was going on in the world around him. This small, blond man, with a nose like a big tomato and the eyes of someone who has spent a week in hell, is Abbas the Aluminum.

When he first meets the children, he tells them that if they help him, they'll make a lot of money in a month. He takes them to a vast field that no one has stepped in for three years, and says, "A war raged here for eight long years. This area is full of thousands of artillery shell casings. The defeated had no time to collect them, and the victorious never arrived here. Do you have any idea what kind of fortune lies in the ground? Well? If we can manage to collect a few thousand shells, all four of us will be rich."

Abbas knows the area is riddled with hundreds of thousands of land-mines. He himself would never go anywhere near it, but the unsuspecting children will search every inch without fear.

Nadim-i Shazada accompanies one or other of the boys every day. All he can do to help is to carry the shell casings. During those three weeks, they enter many areas that no one has ventured into since the end of the Iran-Iraq war in 1988. They can see that the mountains and valleys are strewn with soldiers' corpses, their bones left behind in their military uniforms and boots, bodies staring up at the sky open-mouthed, pleading with God.

Saryas-i Subhdam and Muhammad the Glass-Hearted work among the dead bodies for a while. Every day they load hundreds of shell casings onto a small, ailing donkey, and lead it to a main road. There, Abbas the Aluminum piles the metal into a tractor and pulls it away. The three children live in a small tent, unaware that they are in the Region of Death. Among the rubble and ruins of a lengthy war, they become lifelong friends.

At night, Saryas tells them of his childhood in the villages, on the border crossings, in the vacant lots of the new collective towns, among the drivers, servants, and mule owners. It is here that they develop a strong hatred of war. Here too that Muhammad the Glass-Hearted says, "I will die of love," words that sound ridiculous and meaningless at the time, prompting his two friends to laugh hysterically. He tells them about the divine music he hears constantly, and shows them his key ring, saying that each key belongs to an imaginary door. He tells them the names of each key, and about a door he will unlock with one of them in the rain.

In the tent, they come to understand that there is a great secret in Saryas-i Subhdam's life, and Muhammad the Glass-Hearted's obsession with understanding and cracking open secrets is born. One night, while they sit around a fire, Muhammad says, "I'd like to know everything about everything. I want to know who you are, and what that glass pomegranate is."

While Muhammad the Glass-Hearted, wrapped in the smell of death, was looking for artillery and mortar shells in the old military posts and rocky mountainous terrain, his parents searched for him everywhere – but to no avail. Day after day, Sulaiman the Great's bodyguards and *Peshmergas* scoured the borders in their Toyota pickup trucks and jeeps, announcing on loudspeakers that they were looking for a young boy they feared might have died in a ditch at the side of the road.

One day, in a field under the spring sun, Muhammad the Glass-Hearted and his blind friend are about to drag a huge shell casing to the side of a dirt road when an ash-gray American jeep pulls up. Someone leans out the window and shouts, "That's Muhammad the Glass-Hearted! That's him!" Two men jump out of the jeep, grab hold of him, throw him over their shoulders, and rush him into the vehicle without saying a single word. All Nadim-i Shazada can hear is Muhammad yelling, "Put me down! Let go of me! Let go!"

This is the first time the three children are separated. The next day,

Abbas the Aluminum tells the other two boys, "One of my sisters has drowned in a river. I'll be heading south. When I return, we'll settle our accounts."

None of them will ever see Abbas the Aluminum again. One hot summer a few years later, he will step on an old mine in a remote field. His body will be blown apart and scattered over the dirt, stones, and thorn bushes.

12

After Saryas-i Subhdam's death and the dispersal of the army of carts, the sisters in white withdrew into deep seclusion. When they graduated from the Teacher Training Institute, Ikram-i Kew helped them find jobs in a remote village. The school, founded by a humanitarian aid organization, was a remarkably large building. Ikram-i Kew and I arrived early in the morning, and knocked on the door. The complex included a clinic at the back, but for some reason it was still empty.

When the sisters opened the door, we saw a cozy, well-lit home. No one came to visit apart from Ikram-i Kew, and sometimes Sulaiman the Great, but the vast expanse of nature where they roamed hand in hand had granted them some calm and peace. Early in the morning, they would go to the bank of a stream and sit on the rocks or dew-drenched grass. When the wind played with their extraordinarily long hair, I couldn't take my eyes off them. It seemed like a flood that rose from their heads and flowed to the end of the world.

They also had a strange habit of going to the stream at night, no matter what the weather, to sit on the rocks and sing. They had a harmonious relationship with the villagers, who viewed them not as teachers, but as two angels sent by God. The sisters showed me the way back to the world.

Tomorrow night, I'll tell you about the two nights that marked both my return and the start of my downfall. I call the first the Night of Death and the second the Night of Resurrection. On the Night of Death, the sisters in white led me to Saryas-i Subhdam's grave. The next night, when they told me Saryas-i Subhdam was their brother and recounted those strange days and the oath they had stored far away under a pomegranate tree, I found my freedom again.

I could hardly believe that Saryas-i Subhdam was buried in a nearby plain, in a field of red soil where hunters set their traps for partridges, rabbits, and foxes. The sisters visited the solitary grave every week, indeed had become teachers in that particular village precisely because it was close to Saryas's final resting place. Their voices betrayed a great uncertainty when they talked about it, although no one would have guessed their secrets had they said nothing.

Since Saryas's death, they had both worn black neckerchiefs. On the day we first met, they put their arms around me and said, "He was our brother. If you want, as his father, you can live with us."

They found me strange. Just as I had never met anyone so suffused with mystery, so they had never met anyone so marked by long years of solitude. I had the smell of eternity, of someone from beyond time. And yet we did have something profound in common: they too wanted to live outside society with all its fights and politics. I was surprised that they didn't know the names of most of the political parties, that they did not listen to the radio or read the newspapers. They had built a wall of songs around themselves. I learned only later that the lyrics and melodies were their own.

They were not witches, but they could sense pain before it stung, a wound before it was inflicted. The day Saryas died they had given him many warnings, but to no avail. It was as if they were in touch with some unknown, ethereal natural force. They were so inseparable that they were free even from the world of men. Their vow not to marry did not weigh them down, but had steadily become a natural way of life.

The sisters lived modestly and had only small desires: to walk at night without fear, to feel no shame at singing outside. When I lived with them, I became intimately aware of all their strange habits. In the mornings, they washed their faces in the stream and their white dresses always seemed to be filled with dewdrops. Like everyone else, I was scared of their cold, glowing gaze at first. No, they were not easy to understand, and they could not be pigeonholed into the hackneyed stories and fantasies of the local men. In relocating to the village and living among children, they were not running away: they were protecting and strengthening themselves against some unknown fear.

Every night, when they went out hand in hand, they seemed to be answering a distant call that only they could hear. They may not have been seeking a specific place or creature, but when they set out, they were looking for something. I had heard the same inescapable cry in the desert. Maybe it was from a wildflower or a deadly wound in a bird's chest. Perhaps I was hearing the golden breath of a sparrow, the whisper of a stone, or the sigh of earth that wants to escape for fear of the spirits of its own trees. How can we know who is calling us? We can only be open and attuned to nature's whispers, servants of the universe. We must listen to recognize the course of the world; the two sisters listened, and they understood.

They had lived in the same way in the city, strolling from one neighborhood to another in the middle of the night in their white clothes and neckerchiefs. That city had tried to protect its honor behind locked gates and bolted doors. How strange that in a city ruled by greedy and merciless politicians, two girls should wander the streets after dark, their eyes shining with a light that scared the police and night watchmen. Their appearance was regarded as a sign of bad luck. The clicking of their heels on the quiet roads and concrete sidewalks encouraged the sisters to keep walking. Sometimes they would stop on a street corner to breathe in the beauty of the night. In the city's silent alleys that the sisters were so fond of they heard, through the restless rustle of the wind, the voice of the night itself. The girls had found the same beauty that I had discovered in the desert.

Apart from the young cart vendors to whom Saryas had introduced them, the sisters knew no one. They sensed the hatred towards them at school, in the bazaars, and in the eyes of their neighbors. Some shopkeepers spat at them, and they were conscious of the fear that made young men keep their distance. After the death of the Marshal of the Carts, everyone avoided them except the young boys who were fighting a losing battle for the empire of their carts.

When I returned, the sisters in white took me to where they used to sing in the bazaar before and after Saryas died. The army of carts had completely disintegrated, and the world was utterly changed. Even so, it was still unusual – considered inappropriate – for two young women to be singing late at night in a place full of young men. The melodies of their songs still ring in the ears of those young cart owners, and all of them knew that the two girls were purer than the morning dew.

In the bleak summer before Saryas was killed, Shadarya and Lawlaw would go to the bazaar at night. When they first came to the bazaar in search of the Marshal, a young man with enormous cucumbers under his arm went running to tell him, "Marshal, two angels are here to see you! Really, two girls who seem to have fallen straight from the sky."

Saryas knew immediately who they were. He was cheerful and full of boisterous joy that night. Even in hard times, Saryas always had a laugh ready. He built a huge fire out of leftover wood and old cardboard, made a pot of tea and called out with a laugh so loud it echoed across the square, "Shadarya, Lawlaw, if you truly love me and regard me as your brother, sing to us tonight!" He knew that in the early hours of the morning, the children and youths who slept in the area would wake up to their miserable lives once more and have to race after pickup trucks and lorries in the wholesale fruit and vegetable market. He knew that from dawn to dusk their lives consisted of endless brawls with drivers, shopkeepers, customers, police, and even each other. Sometimes he would shake his head and say to Zhi-no-i Makhmali, "This is the most miserable life in the world." That evening gave the poor young men, most of whom had never heard a girl sing before, a chance to listen to the golden voices of Shadarya and Lawlaw.

That night, Shadarya and Lawlaw went on singing until late. And no, you mustn't assume that this so much as dented the high regard in which the young vendors held them. On the contrary, it was then that they began to love the two sisters. Only housewives who sit and gossip on their doorsteps, jealous, two-faced girls, and malicious men sullied their beautiful story.

When Shadarya and Lawlaw left, Saryas walked them home. Of course, he knew his friends harbored dirty fantasies, but he was certain the songs had a magical power that would force the youngsters to respect the two angels.

After that first night, the sisters went back to the bazaar several times to sing to the young men and children. They met Zhino-i Makhmali and Adam Marjan, whom Saryas jokingly introduced as "two jewels in a dung heap." It was in that period that Saryas started talking about becoming "a great human being" and calligraphy became an important part of his life. No one knows what sort of life he would be leading today had he lived. Adam Marjan once told me, "He was a young man of great promise. He wanted to sell his cart in a few years' time and become a calligrapher or else cross over to the other side of the bazaar and become a bookseller. That was the job he fancied most. He also dreamed of owning a video-cassette player one day to watch the latest films."

I wouldn't have come across Zhino-i Makhmali and Adam Marjan had it not been for the sisters in white. Every time they talked about Saryas, tears filled their eyes. One day we found Zhino-i Makhmali at work. The girls called him down from a building where he was painting a railing high above. He climbed down from the scaffold, washed his face in an old rusty barrel, and embraced me. "Almighty God, Glory to God, Saryas didn't even know he had a father. He thought his father had died before he was born," he said. Right there in the scorching sun, he put his arms around me and said, "No one calls me Zhino-i Makhmali nowadays. It was a name Saryas came up with. I'm now plain Zhino Faizullah Sofi." Adam Marjan and Zhino-i Makhmali knew everything about Saryas's last day. They had been with him from morning until he took his last breath.

When Saryas died, the two timid young men were a great solace to Shadarya and Lawlaw. For a long time, the sisters would go to the square every night and sing for the young men who all gathered around them, some crying, others dropping their heads in their laps as they sang along.

The two sisters met Zhino-i Makhmali and Adam Marjan only a few times after the area with the carts was demolished and the young men dispersed. Once they became teachers in the remote village, the city – which had never been able to understand their presence or their gaze – forgot about them for a while.

The Marshal's death, a senseless, unnecessary murder, appeared to be connected to the daily clashes that occurred in the cart bazaar. It was pointless, like all the killings, imprisonments, and suffering in our country. I can assure you that had Saryas not been so passionate, he would have survived. Although he wasn't at heart an aggressive person, his fiery temper proved fatal. His dream of becoming a great human being also played a role. Later, when I went to his room and saw the dumbbells, I understood that he believed in muscle power and the strength of delivering a blow. He lived at a time when physical strength was considered crucial.

The days leading up to his death were filled with clashes. His role supervising that complicated world got him into frequent trouble with other street vendors, shopkeepers, and passersby. He would get into fights as he made his way from one end of the bazaar, only to engage in more brawls as he left at the other. And yet, he would be all smiles afterward and put his arms around the shoulders of his opponents. These minor scuffles, squabbles, and upsets were simply part of the daily hubbub of the bazaar.

In the week before he died, he visited the sisters in white every night, sitting on their lawn, telling them stories of the bazaar and the fights and commotion between shopkeepers and cart owners, his voice so loud it echoed through the courtyard. The sisters sat next to him and affectionately called him "kaka" – older brother. They giggled when he laughed, engrossed in his stories, occasionally interrupting to ask him questions.

The day before he died, they implored him not to go to the bazaar. They begged him to sit with them and tell them stories of his childhood, but Saryas laughed at his innocent sisters. "The day will never come when I don't go to the bazaar," he said.

Just before he died, life in the bazaar took a turn for the worse. The policemen were replaced every day, and each was crueler and more violent than the last. That morning, as usual, Saryas sold his cartload of tomatoes early and started pushing the empty cart through the bazaar.

Zhino had been waiting for a fresh batch of fish since early morning, but the fishermen had never arrived. At nine o'clock, bored, he gave up and went to find Saryas, who seemed restless and anxious. "What if the fishermen are dead?" he asked Zhino. "What if, one night, all the fishermen died, turned into fish, or drowned in the water?"

Saryas was full of these strange questions that day. He passed the water sellers and said, "If one morning people wake up and are no longer thirsty, what will the water sellers do? Or if they wake up and never feel hungry again, what will the chicken sellers do? Or if the earth goes on strike and never produces another apple, what will the apple sellers do?"

"What you're talking about is never going to happen in this life, especially not in this city," Zhino replied. "People are always thirsty, always hungry, and always like eating apples."

Then Saryas asked Zhino whether he has seen the last pomegranate tree in the world. It was the first time Zhino had ever heard of it. Saryas laughed, saying, "When I die, put me under the last pomegranate tree in the world. I would be at peace there."

"So where is this last pomegranate tree in the world? Is it in paradise or what?" Zhino asked.

"No, not in paradise but not very far from it."

"Saryas, if something isn't in paradise, it is very, very far away from it."

"You're right," Saryas said wistfully. "Everything not in paradise is indeed very, very, very far away from it."

At ten o'clock the two met Adam Marjan, who was unpacking some newly delivered glass cylinders for kerosene lamps. Around eleven o'clock, they made fun of the new Iranian wicks he was selling for the price of English ones.

At quarter past eleven, Malik Dulbar made his first appearance of the day, accompanied by three other policemen. He was one of the harshest and most brutal policemen, but also one of those whom only Saryas could tame. Dulbar received a special payment from the street vendors at the end of each month, and Saryas was the only one who spoke his language. Malik Dulbar's real name was Abdulmalik Shamurad Harun and he was a hot-headed man from Garmiyan, the warmer region at the foot of the plains, who considered himself king of the bazaar. Everyone knew he lent his wife, Dulbar, out to a high-ranking official at the politburo and to another senior politician at a ministry.

Four days earlier, the Marshal had given the first half of the bribe to Malik Dulbar and promised he would get the rest soon. At twenty minutes past eleven, an angry Malik Dulbar stormed into the bazaar, planted himself in front of Saryas's cart, and said, "Marshal, you've developed a knack for lying recently."

Unfazed by both the policemen and the scorching summer sun, Saryas looked at him and said, "That's not true, Malik Dulbar. It isn't. You'll receive your money by evening at the latest."

Malik Dulbar left, beating a few street vendors with his stick and overturning some baskets. At half past one, Malik Dulbar and his colleagues returned. This time they drank water from the water sellers, took two apples from a child's basket, and walked away quietly. At half past two they reappeared at the other end of the bazaar and dumped the contents of a child's tomato crate onto the street. The child ran crying to the Council of the Carts. The Marshal didn't seem to be up for a fight that day, however, telling the child, "There's nothing we can do. Drop it so we can go home safely today."

Around half past three, Malik Dulbar came back again, armed with a long stick, and beat up a group of watch sellers and a number of cooking oil vendors near the mosque. At four o'clock, several cart owners gathered around the Marshal and threatened to give Malik a thrashing if he hurt them again. At half past four, accompanied by several policemen, Malik

Dulbar appeared again, armed with a baton. Starting from the entrance to the bazaar, they began destroying everything. They smashed Adam Marjan's new glass cylinders right in front of Saryas-i Subhdam. Adam burst into tears, hunched over his wares as if to protect them, then fell onto the shattered glass as Malik Dulbar and the police beat him ruthlessly.

At that moment, a voice rose from the crowd of angry vendors, saying, "Leave him alone, you husband of a whore." From every nook and cranny of the bazaar, from its quiet and neglected corners, from its sweaty heart, from behind the tired and rusty carts, a chorus of voices cried out: "Stop, you whore's husband! Stop!"

Many years later, when Zhino-i Makhmali recounted that moment, he said, "God Almighty, it was as if the whole world was on our side. All the things that had seen our sweat, our tiredness, our thirst; the stones that we walked over that felt our pain; every stretch of road that was familiar with our breath and filth; even the bent and twisted electricity pylons – it was as if they all recognized our suffering and were on our side.

"The Marshal hadn't done anything yet. The younger vendors, who had complete confidence in him, were saying, 'Marshal, Marshal, why aren't you doing anything?' But it was as if he couldn't hear them.

"When Malik Dulbar heard the insults, he seethed with uncontrollable rage. He brutally attacked Adam Marjan, whose body was already bathed in his own blood. Saryas and I stepped back, watching. Saryas, who was biting his nails like a child, was thinking. Twice he reached into the pocket of his sharwal – I knew he had a new knife, a knife with a yellow handle that I'd bought for him myself. Saint of Baghdad, without saying a word, he suddenly lunged at a young policeman, stabbing him in the shoulder.

Whenever the vendors saw Saryas attack someone, they knew it marked the start of a big fight. God Almighty, in no time at all it turned into a massive commotion. I was trying to drag Adam Marjan over to a shady spot when I heard the first shots. Children, cart owners, and customers fled into the alleys. When I turned around, I saw Saryas gripping Malik Dulbar by the collar. From a nearby street, above the commotion of the carts, someone shouted, 'Kill him, Marshal! Kill him!'

"It was a cry that could be heard throughout the seven heavens. Even today I don't think Saryas would have been killed had it not been for those shouted words. God Almighty, that shriek left Saryas no choice. I yelled at the top of my voice, 'Run away, Professor, run away.' He recognized my voice and looked at me, but the time for running was past. Everyone else kept shouting 'Kill him, Marshal! Kill him!' I can still see him raising his hand to plunge the knife into Malik Dulbar's heart. We were all watching. The handle of his knife shone in the sun. He hesitated, holding his knife in the air for a long time, but the vendors were all shouting, 'Kill him, Marshal, kill him!' Suddenly he lowered his hand. I'm sure it wasn't to kill him. No, he lowered his hand to drop the knife and spit on the floor, as he always did, and to hang his head and say: 'This is the stupidest day in the world.' At that very moment, a second volley was fired.

"To this day, no one knows who shot. The police say it was a street vendor from among the commotion of the carts. By all that's holy, I don't know what to say. I wasn't looking at anyone except Saryas. Dear Lord, it felt like I saw every bullet that hit him, all four of them. Two went into his left shoulder, one into the right, and the last lodged somewhere between his stomach and his chest. The vendors say a police officer fired the shots, but nobody knows which one. Saryas screamed as he fell to the ground, 'Oh God, they've got me.' I was the first to reach him, to draw his head onto my lap. The police fired volley after volley into the air as they tried to make their way through the carts and vendors surrounding him. Adam, covered in his own blood, couldn't believe Saryas had been wounded.

"'Come on, someone help me get him to hospital, quickly,' I yelled. Smiling, Saryas looked at me and said, 'No, no, don't take me to the hospital. I'm begging you.' Almighty God, he looked so beautiful! Most of the vendors were still shouting in panic, but some came over to Saryas and couldn't believe how badly he was wounded. Tears streaming down my face, I kept on shouting for help. Adam Marjan, unable to stand, shouted with me, and soon every single person gathered around us was yelling too. Finally, Saryas took my hand and said, 'Take me to the sisters in white.'

"'We're taking you to a doctor,' I yelled in return.

"Three of the street vendors extricated Kazhal's Chest from the rubble and said, 'We have to take him to the hospital. The taxis can't get through. It's jam-packed.'

"I felt as if he had already died. He looked at us one last time and said, 'Take me to my sisters' house.' When we put him on the cart and pushed it along, over two hundred street vendors walked on either side, shouting 'The Marshal's been killed. The Marshal's dead.' Lord of the Earth and the Heavens, lying there on the cart, he really did look like a great man. There was something about him that wasn't like the old Saryas, as if his last hour had transformed him into a being that neither the earth nor the sky felt worthy to claim."

Zhino paused frequently as he told the story, saying, "Please, God, don't blame me. God, have mercy on me." He believed it was a great sin to recount someone's death and the passing of their soul. After Saryas died Zhino became deeply religious. Eyes brimming with tears, he'd interrupt his tale to say, "May God have mercy upon him. If he were still alive now, he would laugh at me for crying."

Zhino continued, "When we arrived at the hospital, we thought he was already dead. They quickly took him away and rushed him into a dark corridor. Hundreds of street vendors gathered outside the hospital, all of them in tears. No one had ever been so dearly loved. We'd all forgotten that he was a poor street vendor just like us. I don't know how to put it, but from the very first day, we'd seen him as someone special. As if, God forgive me, he could change the world for us, or something like that. After two hours or so, a young nurse came out and said, 'Who are his relatives? They must come and take him.' I said, 'I am. I'm all he has. Give him to me.' Subhanallah, God decides the precise moment of death. When we retrieved him, he was assumed to be dead, but he wasn't. Either the doctors had made a mistake or they didn't want to treat him. Outside the hospital, he opened his eyes once more and said, 'I told you, take me to the sisters in white.' I kissed him on the forehead and told him we would.

"We carried him southwards through the city, thousands of us, vendors with our carts, filling the streets with noise. People would ask who had died, and we would reply, 'Saryas-i Subhdam, the Marshal of the Carts, the Professor of our Dark Nights, has been killed.' No one in the city knew him except us. When we arrived at the sisters' house, we saw them leaning out of a window on the top floor, their hair falling all the way to the ground. Almighty God, He who answers our calls, their eyes were full of madness, a blinding sorrow, something none of us would ever forget. You can't imagine such sad eyes. When they put their arms and tangled hair around Saryas, he whispered, 'I'm not dead. Take me inside before it's completely dark.' Adam Marjan and I told the vendors, 'Saryas-i Subhdam is still alive. Good news, good news! Let's give him some space and let him rest. May God grant him recovery.'

"The vendors began to disperse. Many of them spread through the narrow alleys nearby, some sat on the side of the road. Finally, the sisters in white, Adam, and I carried him inside. He had lost a lot of blood. As if talking to us from the brink of death, he said, 'When darkness falls, all five of us will go.' I thought he was hallucinating at first, but after a short while he opened his eyes with difficulty, clutched his chest, and said, 'I don't know what it is – but there's a strange pain in my heart.' He was quiet for a moment, then said with a smile, 'Zhino, tonight we'll go to the last pomegranate tree in the world. I want to die there. Forgive me for not telling any of you about it. But tonight you must take me there and bury me beneath it. I can see everything from there.' That night Saryas rested in a warm bed, opening his eyes now and then and saying, 'Let me know when darkness falls. The five of us will go to the last pomegranate tree together.'

"Dear friends, I know this is an old story. Everyone imagines their own burial place under a tree, at the foot of a mountain, on the bank of a stream, or in a corner of a garden. Some people don't see their death coming and have no time to think about where they will die, while others may not believe they're going to die until their last breath. I think it's a beautiful thing to think about your final resting place, to have the right to choose where you will be buried, and not just rest in a graveyard with hundreds of thousands of other people. I believe Saryas had thought about his own death on many a long night; he lived at a time when death was everywhere. When the bullets hit him that day, he didn't think about his death, only about where he wanted it to happen. I'm sure he saw his life as if it were a short film, like the ones he used to see in the video stores or the old, dilapidated cinemas he went to with his friends. The polite group of youngsters would sit in the middle of the cinema with a pack of sunflower seeds and wipe their tears away at the end of the films."

When Zhino talked about Saryas's death, in his paint-covered clothes and hands speckled with white, he felt that Saryas had wanted it to be beautiful, to be worthy of a great man.

Zhino continued, "When darkness fell, Saryas summoned the strength to stand. We kept telling him he needed to rest, but he wouldn't listen. Tired and weak, struggling to keep his eyes open, he said, 'If you're not coming with me, I'll go alone.' It was his last wish. Hour after hour he defied death to be sure of getting there. I tried to hire a jeep, but no drivers were willing to take us once they found out that the wounded person was at the house of the sisters in white. Some of them would spit on the ground or swear crudely before they left. In the end, an elderly driver in a traditional turban came with us, torn between the fee I was offering and the risk of the journey.

"Right from the start, he was shaking, his hands barely able to clutch the wheel. The sisters had their doubts about him from the outset, but we had no choice. No one else would venture into the mountains and wilderness on such a miserable night. With great difficulty, we placed Saryas between the two sisters in the back and covered him with a blanket; Adam Marjan and I sat in the front. Adam was crying and blaspheming nonstop. From that night on, our lives took two different routes: he became a communist, while God's light settled in my heart. Adam was in agony and had lost his patience because of the pain. However, he was adamant that he would stay with Saryas until he breathed his last. Adam's weeping frightened the driver even more.

"When we got in the vehicle, Saryas's eyes were closed, his lips a frightening blue, and his hands, neck, and eyelids darkened. He told the driver, 'Take us to the road near Sewaze, the foot of the mountain at Shekhali Harme Sheen.' I knew what a dangerous area that was, full of night bandits and solitary gunmen from villages rife with tribal feuds. We made somewhat hesitant progress, but the driver's concerns only seemed to grow. He used to raise horses and mules in this area and knew it well. After an hour, he stopped right in the middle of the road as if he'd seen a ghost. Shaking with fear, he said, 'I'll take you back to the city if you like. Otherwise, wait here, and in an hour you'll be able to hitch a lift from one of the smugglers who bring their tractors up here to pick up their stuff.'

"My God, how the sisters showered him with abuse. Adam Marjan was weeping; I had my arms around Saryas, pleading with the driver not to abandon us in that godforsaken place, especially when we were accompanied by two women. But it was no use. Something stronger than greed was eating away at the driver's soul. He had been terrified of everything right from the start: the white clothes of the sisters, who looked like two fallen angels; the large flashlights they held; the blood on Saryas's body; Adam's howling; and my blind despair. He dumped us at the side of the road.

"God knows, we didn't want to go back to the city. I kissed Saryas time and again, saying, 'I will take you to the last pomegranate tree even if I have to carry you on my shoulders.' Blood was oozing from his wounds when he coughed. He opened his eyes and said, 'Just tell me, can you see any stars or not?'

""The stars are out, Saryas,' we said.

"That was the dark night of people's indifference and mercilessness. I felt as if God had deserted us, as if we, his creatures, had strayed so far that He was ignoring us. Adam, covered in wounds, paced up and down, saying, 'Who benefits from this injustice, who?'

"Finally, a tractor appeared, driven by a young man with tattoos covering his hands and wrists – a clear sign he wasn't religious. When he stopped alongside us, he laughed loudly in the quiet of the night, and said, 'Is that a dead body you've got there? Is he a snakebite victim, or did his appendix burst?' He assumed we were going to the city. We had a hard time explaining that we were carrying a wounded man who wanted to die in the mountains. 'If you're going to die, get on with it. Why cause so much trouble for everyone else in the middle of the night?' he said to Saryas. 'I'm not going as far as the Sewaze path,' he added, 'but I will take you to another path, and from there you can cross a plain and after an hour you will reach the stream and climb up to Shekhali Harme Sheen from there.' He let us get in the back of the tractor as he began singing in the front. As we set off, he turned around again and said, 'It's a good night for dying. It's not raining. My biggest fear is dying when it's raining. Nobody in this country hates the rain as much as tractor drivers. Thank God, at least it's not raining.'

"None of us knew where to find the last pomegranate tree in the world. Saryas just asked us to let him know once we reached the foot of the mountain. He lost a lot of blood in the tractor trailer, his condition deteriorating rapidly. The sisters in white started to cry again. I felt Saryas wanted to tell us something, but we could barely hear his voice over the tractor's roar and the driver's singing. Eventually, we clambered down beside a large field and Shadarya and Lawlaw took out their flashlights. The driver said, 'I charge double for transporting the dead. I've been working this route for four years and that's the rule. Most tractor drivers wouldn't even take them. I'm no Azrael to be taking the dead to heaven for free.'

"Oh, that night changed me. It woke me to the fact that we humans live in a jungle of tyranny. We made a makeshift stretcher from the blanket, put Saryas in it, and set off through the desolate plains in the dark. None of us knew which summit this tree was on. Again and again we had to put Saryas down and ask him where we should go. He'd open his eyes with difficulty, emitting a deep groan of pain, but he could no longer speak. We kept going, but we got nowhere. The two girls wept continuously as they walked, their white dresses in tatters from the thorn bushes. I don't know exactly when his soul left his body, but it was as if he knew he wouldn't reach the last pomegranate tree in the world, the tree he wished to die beneath. We took it as a sign that none of our wishes, great or small, would ever come true. All four of us were blind, walking in circles around ourselves, with no light, enlightenment, or divine inspiration to come to our rescue.

"He died in the blanket, and we were hopeless and lost. We laid Saryas on the ground in the middle of the plain, bursting into tears as we sat around his body. We opened our arms to him, kissed him, and appealed to God, but nothing answered our cries except a murder of crows and scourges of ruthless mosquitoes. Finally, our tears dried up.

"We couldn't take him back to the city; we didn't want to kill him twice.

We knew we would never find the last pomegranate tree in the world, so we thought it best to bury him on the way to it, rather than in a graveyard he would not have wanted.

"I walked through a sea of mosquitoes and chirping crickets before I came across a village where I could borrow a pickax and a shovel. The night grew darker and darker. I don't know how I found my way back through that empty plain without even a tree to use as a marker. But from that night on, God settled in my heart and guided me. He held my hands all the way to the village and back. I could feel His presence in my heart. I am sure God loved Saryas, a boy who, despite a touch of aggression, had a good and innocent heart. And only I know the divine respect he had for women. God be merciful to him, according to his purity, together with all believers and all the followers of the Prophet.

"Subhanallah, Subhanallah, when I returned, the sisters in white were singing songs that would draw tears from stone. I put my arms around them and said, 'Sisters, don't cry. God will forgive him his sins. I know it. God was with me all the way. He loves Saryas-i Subhdam, the Professor of our Dark Nights.'

"Despite his wounds, Adam Marjan was the first to swing the pickax. I took it from him, crying as I struck the ground, and he took it back, crying, and dealt his blow. The grave was not worthy of Saryas. Without tombstones or marker, it matched his strange and senseless death. We covered him with earth and returned to the city.

"We decided that the following day we would get the tombstones and hire a couple of buses to transport the street vendors. We would visit his grave and cover it in flowers. We reached the city weeping, bid each other goodbye, and slept. But I assure you, that night, the longest of my life, never ended. It never would."

13

On my second night of freedom, the sisters in white took me to Saryas-i Subhdam's grave. I was not yet aware that there was not just one Saryas on this earth, but a second and a third as well.

It was so bright that we walked through the slumbering farms without so much as a flashlight. There's no need to ask how I felt. My grief was not only that of a father visiting his son's grave after twenty-one years of imprisonment, but also that of a farmer returning to burnt fields after much toil. The moon rose above my futile life and his futile death. The stars twinkled above his unfulfilled life and my own. Neither his death nor my long incarceration seemed to have had any impact on the world. Everything seemed to have died in those fields, as if life, like a barren seed, had never taken root there.

What caught my attention was the silence; man had left no mark there. The place was as remote as the glaring desert where I spent my exile. But you mustn't think that I'm caught up in delusions, that those dark years constantly prey on my mind. It was a small grave, like a bird's. The wasteland around it was so vast that the shadows of the stones at the head and foot of the grave seemed to extend forever. I felt that the endless horizon gave Saryas a huge amount of space for contemplating the universe.

In recent years, nobody but Shadarya and Lawlaw had been to visit the grave. I bent down and kissed the gravestone. "Saryas-i Subhdam," I called, "It's your father. Can you hear me? When I was taken prisoner twenty-one years ago, you were only few days old. You've never seen me, or even thought about me and yet, tonight you must listen to me."

The two sisters were sitting quietly on the thorny ground near the grave. I had been with them for two days, but for most of that time I had been immersed in my own solitude. It wasn't easy for me to open up. When they saw me in this inconsolable state, they became frightened.

I calmed them and said, "No, no, my dear girls, this is not the wailing of grief. No, my dears, there's something I need to tell my dead son, something he has to know. I'm sure he can hear me, that he's waiting for something in this vast plain where every single human sound and whisper has a value of its own. He may not recognize me, but through my cries he will understand that someone has been trying to reach him for a long time. He has to understand that man is not alone in the universe, that the cold and silence of this plain need not scare him. He needs to know that I have been making my way toward him, running from my prison to find him for twenty-one years. He needs to know how desperately unfair it is that we are only meeting now, here in this desolate field."

I put my ear to the grave and said, "Almighty God, he can hear me, I know he can. Come and touch the grave: it's moving." I could feel the grave moving. A soul was yearning to be free of its shackles; a choked cry, a stifled fervor inside the grave was longing to break out. I screamed and the force inside the grave intensified.

The sisters tried to restrain me, saying, "Muzafar-i Subhdam, you're torturing him. Your shouting's waking him up. His wounds will really hurt if he wakes. Hush, Muzafar-i Subhdam, be quiet."

Slightly calmer, I said, "An empty-handed father and a son who died a futile death are reunited in this plain with its thistles, thorns, and dirt. Look, as far as the eye can see, a dome of meaninglessness stretches above us, a great vault of absurdity, a massive canopy of futility." I was scared by the infinite desolation, the soulless light in which we met. What could we say to each other? We had each lived and died in different ways. We had no words to exchange. Instead, the silence and dust that blew from all directions spoke for us.

That night I understood what disasters a person's absence leaves behind, what an important place each human being occupies on this earth. Once someone is born, they leave a mark on other people's lives. They become a link in an infinite chain, and if one link breaks, other links break with it, and the whole chain disintegrates. A person's absence or death reshapes the whole of life on earth.

Had I been present, had the desert not shrouded me as though I were dead, the whole of life might have unfolded differently. A person is a star that does not fall alone. Who knows where the echo will reverberate when we leave this earth? Perhaps someone will rise from our ashes in another time and realize they have been burned by the flame of our fall.

That night I understood that that grave had been born of my absence.

Listen to me when I tell you that a person's death disturbs all the equations of life on earth. I myself have left a sequence of lives disturbed in my wake.

Late into the night, the sisters in white tried to calm me down, to convince me that I too was a victim who had experienced disaster. But I ran barefoot through the fields like an animal, beating my chest and throwing fistfuls of dust over myself. I ran across thorns and stones, leaping over weeds and the dry, tired earth until the sisters in white lost sight of me.

Tonight I can admit to you that I couldn't accept Saryas-i Subhdam's death. He had been the only thing I lived for. I circled the grave, crying like a madman, like an injured sparrow hawk. I couldn't believe he was dead. I covered myself with earth and shouted to the vastness of the plains, "This is not your grave! You're not dead! I will search for you and find you."

The following night my life changed completely. Now I call that night the Night of Life and Resurrection. It was then that I grasped that a second and a third Saryas were still in the world. The origins of that night go back several years.

On one of his cheerful evenings, Muhammad the Glass-Hearted is listening to song requests on a radio station owned by one of the political parties. In affectedly genteel tones, the presenter says, "Saryas-i Subhdam dedicates this song to Wasta Majid, his wife Bahe, their daughter Shilan; Ghafour and Rehanah on the occasion of their marriage; all the Peshmergas of Battalion 21; and Mam Abdullah at the secondhand clothes market." Muhammad the Glass-Hearted is sure he has just heard the name Saryas-i Subhdam in a request for a Kamkars song. But since he's known him, Saryas hasn't had any friends or relatives or anyone he'd want to dedicate songs to.

It is here that the mysteries begin. Muhammad the Glass-Hearted knows that Saryas-i Subhdam is such an unusual name that it's unlikely to belong to more than one person. Given Muhammad's obsession with secrets, this fleeting mention is enough to catch his attention. He is pushed towards the sea of mysteries, which would eventually engulf him and, indeed, all of us.

That evening Muhammad the Glass-Hearted, jingling his key ring cheerfully, makes his way to the cart vendors' part of the bazaar. Over the evening hubbub of the fruit sellers, he asks Saryas if he had requested a song on the radio. Since he has never owned a radio set, Saryas says in astonishment that it's been a long time since he even listened to such shows. When he hears Muhammad the Glass-Hearted's strange tale, Saryas laughs and replies, "It can't be. There aren't any other Subhdams in the world. I'm the only person with the name Saryas-i Subhdam."

Now Muhammad the Glass-Hearted is convinced that a big secret lurks behind that name. Let's not forget his obsession with secrets. He looks for them everywhere, even venturing into danger to find an unsolved mystery behind every curtain. He tells Saryas-i Subhdam, "There is someone else with the same name as you, and your secret is tied to his." I'm sure that Muhammad the Glass-Hearted had no proof, and only said this to provoke Saryas.

That evening, they visit the radio station together and urge the presenter to show them Saryas-i Subhdam's letter. With her usual airs and graces, she finds a colorful piece of paper sent by a certain person of that name. But apart from what she said on air, the letter contains no information. Muhammad the Glass-Hearted does not give up and, with the help of his father, finds Battalion 21's military base in a small settlement outside the city.

Late in the evening a cold wind blows outside that old military base. In a small room full of metal bowls, trowels, and open bags of gypsum, a strange thing happens. Saryas-i Subhdam meets Saryas-i Subhdam, an event that will shake my life to its foundations.

You will notice that from this point onward, the entire direction of our story changes and our dependable world comes to an end as we lose ourselves among people and mirrors. From here on, in order to tell the various Saryases apart, we shall call the first one in our story the First Saryas, and the other the Second Saryas.

It is a strange and dangerous night in the lives of the two boys who bear no physical resemblance to one another but have the same name. They are both kinless, have both been shunted from one family to another as they grew up, and have both been carrying a glass pomegranate since childhood.

Muhammad the Glass-Hearted, who is the architect of all these discoveries, wakes the Second Saryas, who is still in bed, and asks, "Why did you send that letter to the radio? Who are you and where have you come from? How did you grow up? What did you do before? What do you do now?"

The Second Saryas, a fair-skinned boy with honey-colored eyes and an aggressive, furtive gaze, is suspicious of everyone. To begin with, he has no idea what's going on. He splashes some water from an old barrel onto his face, then says, "This doesn't feel like evening. It's like some awful morning. No, nothing about it makes you think of an evening. There are many days I can't really get a handle on. Some mornings seem like afternoons, evenings like mornings, or mornings like midnight. I don't get that. Today is one of those days."

With a thoughtful smile, the First Saryas says, "It's a strange evening, isn't it? And here we are, bringing you the strangest mystery in the world."

"I don't know what you're talking about," says the Second Saryas, who seems somewhat indifferent, yet still attentive.

"There's someone else, another person, called Saryas-i Subhdam, just like you. A rare name that wouldn't be repeated unless there was something behind it, right? Still, if you know exactly who you are, everything will end here. We'll say goodbye and go. But if you don't, it means the start of something new. It could all just as well be a fantasy, a myth that's planted itself in my mind for no reason," Muhammad the Glass-Hearted says, calmly relating the whole story.

Now rather thoughtful, the Second Saryas asks, "If you're Saryas-i Subhdam as well, who am I?" It all seems very peculiar, the two of them somehow connected. And then this strange bond becomes even more obvious.

Muhammad the Glass-Hearted puts a glass pomegranate on a table and asks the Second Saryas if he has ever seen one like it, if it means anything to him. The Second Saryas looks at them for the first time, completely befuddled, and says, "Today isn't like any other day, it really isn't. Today's a terrible day." He takes the glass pomegranate and says, "This is the pomegranate I've been carrying since my childhood, although I don't know if it means happiness or unhappiness, fortune or misfortune. Who are you? What a day. A shit of a day, shitty as a dog's arse. It's shite, complete and utter shite. If you're me, then who am I? Just another Saryas-i Subhdam! Another one who grew up without a family, who also has a glass pomegranate that's as precious to him as the apple of his eye. I don't know whether I'm meant to give you a hug or tell you to go to hell, whoever you are."

He has two bright eyes that would have been stunning in a smooth face, but his rough voice and rudeness don't match them. He looks older than the other two, older than his years.

The Second Saryas can't wait much longer. He has to accompany a patrol going out on inspection. He tells his visitors, "You've picked a really bad time to see me. I feel like you've stabbed me, opened my heart up for surgery, then gone off and left me. If you have the slightest idea what's going on, please tell me, but quickly. I haven't got a clue. I don't like being in the dark either, but as you can see, I'm at work right now and duty calls. Whether my name is Saryas-i Subhdam or Shitty Subhdam, I have to take my gun and go. It will do the thinking for me. The mountain is waiting, my guests, I'm sorry. It's a strange story, but the bosses and the officers on the night shift don't care about such things. I still have to go and keep watch up on one of those cold peaks tonight."

As he puts on his gun and equipment in front of them, he says, "You've unsettled me. I didn't know requesting a song would create all this hassle for me. I'm Saryas-i Subhdam and there is only one. If you're Saryas-i Subhdam as well, who am I? And if I am, who are you? Which fucker's been messing around with this stuff? How is it even possible?! I have to go now. I have to guard the country without even knowing who this person is that's off to keep watch over the ever-increasing bullshit. There is so much chaos around. My brothers, listen up. It's a shitty time, it reeks of a donkey's ass." Holding his gun, he continues, "I'll see you out of this ruin of a place. We must meet again. Something's up. I'm not sure what. We need to talk about it another time."

"We're not taught to ask who we are," replies Muhammad the Glass-Hearted. "And when we do face that question, it throws our whole life out of sync. But, in the end, we each need to understand the meaning of our own life."

On their way to the gate, they pass through a large yard that smells of autumnal sadness, lonely and withered grass. A place that belongs neither completely to nature nor to man, torn between the kingdom of people and the kingdom of animals and wild birds. As the Second Saryas-i Subhdam gets in his vehicle that night, he salutes from the window. "Till I see you again, my friends. This is the first night I've been worried about myself. Look at the sky, full of bullshit stars. My dears, only things that are bullshit things look alike."

When the two young men return home, the road seems endless. Muhammad the Glass-Hearted is in a reflective mood, which always means he is filled with passion. "Saryas," he says, "it's a lie that people don't resemble each other, a lie. We grew up together and our lives are like mirror images, as if someone far away is holding a copy of the perfect life of each one of us. Anything that happens in our life has already happened at his end, as if our suffering comes from that of a greater person, someone whose life none of us embodies alone. Instead, we are each a small part of his suffering. So it isn't bullshit that things look like one another."

Saryas, visibly confused, pushes his unkempt hair off his tired, sun-burned face, pausing now and then to tie the laces of his tattered white trainers. "Why do flowers have the right to be different, and every bird is allowed to have a unique song, but I have to ask who Saryas-i Subhdam is? Which of us is the reflection of the other's life?"

Muhammad quietly lowers his head and says, "People are entitled to be unique. But suffering makes our lives essentially the same. There's something that brings us together, despite our differences."

"I worry that I may be someone else's shadow. I worry that I, Saryas-i Subhdam with my glass globe, am the shadow of someone who lives somewhere else."

Muhammad stops and says, "I'm talking about thousands, millions of souls, none of us knowing where we came from or where we're going. I'm talking about secrets, a great lock, a wall that blocks our view of the meaning behind it. Ever since I heard your name on the radio, I've been thinking about the secrets that have besieged us. They might be small, but they act like a huge lock on our lives. I am talking about the biggest misfortune of all – that we know nothing about ourselves. Neither you nor I. Who says Muhammad the Glass-Hearted can't be repeated? Who says I won't wake up one day and find a replica of myself looming over me? Who says we're not a group of people who keep on replicating each other?"

14

That evening's meeting between the two Saryases was too brief and hasty for them to take in anything about one another. However, recounting the story to you now, I am sure that the meeting disturbed both of them greatly.

Later on, when the Second Saryas sent me recorded tapes from a dark and remote prison hemmed in by mountains, he told me about the confusion and pain he felt the next day. And no, don't just assume that the Second Saryas, unlike the first, was a lucky young man. His only fortune in life was being alive. Life is a bundle of happiness, which when opened is full of suffering, a paradise made from little hells, a boundless beauty woven from a thread of horrors. I spent many long years in prison considering these great issues, dedicating much of my time to ruminating about them. I have never believed the notion that if small fragments come together to form a larger whole, the new entity will have the same properties as the tiny pieces. A shower of sparks is different from fire. And that's what life's like, great swells of beauty, composed of thousands of small waves of suffering. Look, my friends and travel companions, look at the sea beneath us. Should you confuse the essence of a wave with that of the sea? We understand a single wave, where it comes from and where it dies, but which of us can tell where the ocean begins or where water ends?

So it is with life. The living are always happier than the dead, even if they have painful memories, even if they're on a burning field where the wind beats them like scarecrows. We are afloat on this gigantic, ungraspable sea, but we live! The dead are exiled from that sea. We are lucky as long as we are alive. And please, don't tell me you're fed up with this sea or ask how long we'll be drifting in it. Don't ask me, even though I have now become the Prophet of Suffering. We must not tie our small destinies to the magical music of the universe. Even if our life's melody is full of dissonance, great power and beauty can still exist in the depths of the laws of being. I didn't listen to the unpleasant melody of my life in prison, but to the profound harmonies that sprang from every corner of the universe.

I know how desperately heartbreaking it is to have boarded a ferry to the West, to paradise, only for the wind to whisk you away one night, to be lost in an infinite sea by a captain who knows nothing of its ways. Don't just think about this miserable time in our lives when we're lost at sea, think instead about the hidden melody in this infinite order where everything comes together to create great harmony.

More than anyone, it was Muhammad the Glass-Hearted who used to look for the fine, invisible thread connecting all things. He could see the whole of the sea, the whole picture. His search for small secrets was designed to find something bigger, something I'd call "the meaning of our era," of the times, the century we lived in. Muhammad the Glass-Hearted was already familiar with many secrets. After the Kurdish uprising, he knew more than anyone else what was behind the dignity, honor, and respect that everyone used to decorate their lives. He got to know the leading smugglers, saw the fake honor of their wives and daughters, learned the lies politicians told, and stumbled on their plots to kill one another. But he knew that he was too delicate to get involved in warfare, that he was made of glass, that his obsession with finding the truth must not become an obsession with going to war in the hope of change.

One night, Saryas asked, "What's the point of learning and knowing these secrets if you can't reveal them or use them? Why don't you write them all down in a big book, publish it, and give everyone a real shock?"

"But I'm not sure of anything, so what would I put in the book? I'm not even sure about your secret, or mine. Plus, there are some secrets that simply shouldn't be written down, that would torment people to death. I'm scared of secrets like that," Muhammad the Glass-Hearted replied. "There are two types of secrets: those that make the world darker and render us blind, and the others that take us deeper and further. Saryas-i Subhdam, on their own, small secrets have no value. What does have value is the meaning we obtain by putting all the secrets together."

I feel that Muhammad the Glass-Hearted was the only person who wanted to fully understand everything, that he had a certain unquenchable excitability. When he was searching for the truth, nothing could keep him from his path. But then he came across a door he could not open. The minute he realized that love might remain elusive and riddled with secrets forever, all the dreams he had built his life upon collapsed. Just as I have thought about the destiny of my sons, I have thought about his too. Right now on this ferry, which may be the ship that determines whether we survive or perish, I can say that I am indebted to him. He, too, deserved to be one of my sons. Many of the things I learned later were in some way related to his life and death.

On the night I boarded the ferry in Patras, I could see the shadow of a storm in the distance and smell a wind carrying the glass dust of the ocean. I became sure I had inhabited his death for a long time. It's as though I'm completing the story he couldn't finish, as though I am Muhammed the Glass-Hearted but, having cast off my desert shroud, I have a heart made of sand instead of glass. It is unbreakable although the sand is leaking out, steadily, grain by grain. Even now I am amazed at the fragility of the youths who died so prematurely, so naturally. In the desert I had a certain image of human beings as strong and thick-skinned, capable of enduring anything. But it was shattered by that weakness, that profound and eager readiness to die.

Before leaving Kurdistan, I went to Muhammad the Glass-Hearted's grave – and no, you mustn't think it was my first visit. Back then, I used to wander among graves and the vestiges of other lives like an itinerant dervish, long bearded and obsessive. On this visit, I kissed the grave's headstone. I wanted to bid him goodbye, to thank him because I owed him everything. It was his love that introduced me to the sisters in white, and without him, no one would have uncovered the mystery of the Saryases. No sailor but him would have seen the pearls of meaning behind the glass pomegranates, and it was because of him the last pomegranate tree in the world acquired the meaning it did. I was indebted to him – and even now, like everyone else, I am walking in the dust of his death.

But let's go back to our story. I've told you that my entire life changed on my second night of freedom after being released from Yaqub-i Snawbar's mansion. It was the night of my resurrection, of my real rebirth but, at the same time, of confusion, disappointment, and loss. You all remember the pact the sisters in white and Saryas-i Subhdam signed in blood and buried under a pomegranate tree in the courtyard, the tree mirroring another somewhere else and the two of them unknowingly connecting the protagonists of this story.

You may also remember that the sisters in white promised they would not regard anyone but Saryas as their brother. After that meeting on the military base, Saryas didn't tell them about his namesake and new friend straight away. The first days of the new trio passed without any problems. But a few weeks before he died, he returned exhausted one evening from a long day in the turmoil of the bazaar, sat down guiltily, and told them he wanted to divulge a secret. The sisters in white never forgot his tired, sad face, nor his wounded voice, as he told them the story. He could no longer stay silent, and they deserved the real story, the one about the glass pomegranate that they'd brought from the house of Sulaiman the Great and that Saryas-i Subhdam said was his.

"My dear sisters, dear Shadarya, dear Lawlaw, I know you've accepted me as your only brother, and for that I am forever grateful. But there's a secret you must know, as it's become an important part of my life. I don't want the strange truth to come out later and you to blame me for having kept it from you. You need to know there is someone else besides me named

Saryas-i Subhdam, a person just like me in every respect except physically. His life has been similar to mine, and, like me, he has a glass pomegranate. We have been close friends for a long time now," Saryas said. "There's a secret that binds his life to mine. It brings us closer together, but neither of us knows what it is."

That night, Saryas told them the entire story of Muhammad the Glass-Hearted, Nadim-i Shazada, the Second Saryas, and himself. He recounted the stories of their lives in so much detail, it was as though he wanted the sisters to bear witness to something he wouldn't be able to share with anyone ever again. And so the sisters in white became the chief witnesses of a story that, in a different way, they would later feature in themselves.

When Saryas had finished, they said, "We have one brother, and that's you. No one could ever replace you. As far as we're concerned, there is only one Saryas-i Subhdam, and we don't want to get to know anyone else who shares that name. No one can steal your name, your memories, and your life for themselves."

Saryas laughed and said, "I'm nothing but an unhappy man from the world of the carts. No one wants to steal my life. He's an unhappy person too, and thinks I want to steal his life. Each of us is stupidly scared of losing our useless lives."

"You're Marshal of the Carts and Professor of our Dark Nights for the children who have no one but you to help them put their lives in order, explain things to them, share news about the world with them, or read them newspapers. The entire army of the cart vendors has only you."

To the sisters in white, there was only one Saryas, and they were concerned that the appearance of another might undermine the oath they had with the first. They feared they might weaken and relent one day, that someone else with the same name and story would enter their lives, and that their extraordinary mental image of Saryas might fade and lose its magic if repeated. After Saryas's death, they would not allow another man called Saryas-i Subhdam to come and offer his condolences. And even later on, they declined to receive this Second Saryas. For them, the whole story ended with the death of the first.

My return disturbed the sisters' peace. On the night that Ikram-i Kew told them my story, that Saryas-i Subhdam's father had returned from the desert after twenty-one years and wished to visit the grave of his son, their peace and assurance were thrown off balance, their life lost its rhythm and harmony. At that moment, they were forced to confront the story they had been running from ever since Saryas died. They didn't know whether they should tell me the secret of the Second Saryas; whether they should take me to the grave of the first and let me live with my disappointment, or tell me there was another Saryas who was alive and well somewhere else.

Shadarya believed they shouldn't talk about the other Saryas, for to do so was a betrayal of an irreplaceable brother who had died young. But Lawlaw-i Spi spoke about the misery of a father returning after twenty-one years, dying to hug and kiss someone and call him "my son." Shadarya said, "As a father he needs to accept the death of his son and become the custodian of his grave." To this, Lawlaw retorted, "But he could equally well be the father of the young man who's alive, of the Saryas who's alive. How can we deprive a father of his son? What gives us the right to hide the truth from him?" Shadarya replied irritably, as if she were walking through fire,

"And what if Muzafar-i Subhdam is the real father of our one and only brother? What will we achieve then except for depriving him of his past?"

One night they walked by the stream into the small hours, thinking and singing their sad songs, their hair loosened against the night chill. Finally, they resolved to lay all their information before me. They took me to Saryas's grave that night so I could see and understand that he was dead with my own eyes. The two sisters wanted the whole world to care about Saryas, but once the army of the cart vendors disappeared and the children of the streets and alleys were scattered, they could not find anyone with treasured memories of Saryas-i Subhdam. They wanted to find someone else, a companion, who would share their grief and understand their sorrow.

But when they saw how devastated I was, they realized that I refused to believe he was dead. The following night, Lawlaw-i Spi came to my room alone and said, "Muzafar-i Subhdam, our unfortunate old man, there's still a lot you don't know." From that night on, they addressed me as "unfortunate old man," "father of suffering," or "sheikh of sadness."

Wearing her black neckerchief, Lawlaw-i Spi told me the whole story herself. It could not be done in one night, but throughout my time with the sisters in white they continued telling me the tale, some nights in my room and some beside the blackboards in their school classrooms. I engraved it in my mind, letter by letter, line by line. I can remember every word. The long years of imprisonment had emptied my memory, and when I re-entered the world, my memory was a white page with very little on it. The sisters in white handed me the beginnings of threads so that I might track down the secrets.

"Saryas is worth all your grief and all your tears, but there is a truth you must know," Lawlaw began that night. "Neither I, nor Shadarya, nor anyone in this world, can guarantee that the grave you wept by so uncontrollably is that of your son. Muzafar-i Subhdam, as well as the boy who sleeps there till the Day of Judgment, there is another boy still living who shares his name, another Saryas-i Subhdam. Let me be clear from the start, however, that no one knows which of the two is your son."

These were no ordinary words. It was as if they took me out of the roiling pit of hell and raised me to the heights of heaven, tossing me ashore as I was close to drowning, freeing me like a fish from a deadly hook. And so I learned there was another Saryas who might be my son, the child who I had awaited for twenty-one years. And no, you mustn't think I was blinded by happiness or that my renewed hope numbed the pain in my heart. Later, as the night passed and I pondered everything by the window, it dawned on me that my despair would be as great as my hope for as long as I lived. There and then, I vowed never to ask which was my son. There was no other solution, and it was a decision I never regretted. The fact that there might be more than one Saryas gave me a broader outlook on life. I could be a father to all those who were lost on the streets, killed in vain, or still unaccounted for. I was a man who had come from the past to say something about those who had no future.

Tell me, what would you have done if you'd been in my shoes? Would you have chosen one and renounced the other? No, my friends, you too would have embraced both sons. Now I know that I lost a great deal, but I gained a great deal as well. All my life, I have had the strange idea, which I am not ashamed to share with you, that if you feel as if you're suffering for the world, you will be immersed in an unmatched happiness. That night

164

when Lawlaw-i Spi embraced me and said, "Oh, unfortunate old man, you will lose yourself between your sons and still won't find the truth." I replied, saying, "No. God has sent me on a mission of fatherhood unlike any other."

I didn't know just then what kind of father I was. I don't really know even now, but the feeling I had was without limits. On the night I visited Saryas's grave, what hurt me wasn't his death itself, but the deep silence that separated me from the grave. It was a silence between two souls that became a silence between me and all living beings. Learning that there was a Saryas alive somewhere turned everything on its head. I once again found a language through which to talk to the universe and all its creatures.

That night I embraced Lawlaw like a madman and said, "Saryas is not dead, he didn't die a senseless death, he's here, he can talk, he can tell his story! He can throw pebbles in the ponds, revel at the water's edge, and curl up and sleep in the leaves. There is someone to whom I can tell everything from beginning to end. I've come back to do just that, to talk to someone I can be sure will hear me. So, a Saryas is living, somewhere on this earth, who will listen to me. Do you know what it means to have someone to listen?"

Lawlaw-i Spi said in astonishment, "No, no, Saryas is dead. He was killed by a stupid policeman in the middle of the bazaar. And yet, there's a second boy who is also called Saryas-i Subhdam. He doesn't have a father either, and his life has been similar to that of Saryas, except he's still alive."

I shouted aloud, "The one who is still alive can listen to me on behalf of all the dead and speak for everyone. The living must have the strength to shout on behalf of the dead."

Lawlaw said angrily, "Nobody can shout on Saryas's behalf. Wherever he is, you mustn't mix up his voice with someone else's."

I said excitedly, "My daughter, my Lawlaw, just as a part of our life is to be found within all other lives, so a part of them can be found in ours. Just as our deaths contain a part of all other deaths, so a fraction of ours is to be found, one way or another, inside all the rest."

These few sad days of freedom had exhausted me as much as years of imprisonment. I said, "My Lawlaw, sweet Lawlaw, my daughter. I was in the desert for twenty-one years. There I came to understand that nothing can separate human beings from this world. No matter how much you banish, expel, even kill someone, they remain part of the world's great cycle. I've thought like that for twenty-one years, I can't change my mind now. You have to understand that he lives through you and me, just as I lived through all of you during my years in prison, as I lived through the sand, the desert, the sky, and the night. No, don't treat me like a crazy old man – with my white beard and tangled dervish hair – speaking about the laws of the universe as if hallucinating. I speak from a place you don't know. I am here to live part of the life he didn't live. Lawlaw-i Spi, don't deny me the feeling of living on his behalf. Ultimately, I see the two Saryases as one human being, one son, one beautiful creature cruelly divided by fate."

The night we had this conversation, I didn't yet know anything about the life of the Second Saryas. I still didn't know what I was talking about. Lawlaw-i Spi told me that they knew nothing about the Second Saryas, had never met him, and had no idea where he lived or what he was doing.

After so many years of waiting, I found it hard to wait any longer.

15

When I was freed, it was a long time since anyone had heard anything about the Second Saryas. The last person to have seen him was Adam Marjan, who spotted him one day among a group of tired Peshmergas outside a senior official's house, carrying an old Soviet machine gun and laughing. That must have been during the third phase of the Kurdish Civil War, when it was normal for the doorsteps of the Party's military officials to look like a battleground. Armed forces would gather in the street, outside politicians' houses, hotels, bars, and sometimes even the homes of prostitutes rather than at a military base or camp. In other words, they could be found in close proximity to wherever their commander happened to be sleeping.

Adam Marjan had no idea what the Second Saryas was doing, nor what subsequently became of him. Speaking as a communist, he said, "I took his hand and told him not to get involved in the war. 'It isn't your war,' I said. 'It's a bourgeois war to seize the bread that feeds us. The working class must take a different stance.'"

The Second Saryas laughed, "I'd like to take part in every war, but right now this is the only one on. If you know of any others, tell me, and I'll go off to those as well."

Disappointed, Adam Marjan said farewell. "I hope you don't get killed, my friend."

But Saryas scoffed, "Ah, but I hope I do. I really hope I do."

That was the last thing any of Saryas's friends heard him utter.

One day, after revealing the mystery of the Saryases to me, the sisters in white put me in a car and took me to the city. There we came across Zhino-i Makhmali and Adam Marjan, but neither of them had much idea about where the Second Saryas might be.

Then, one night, Ikram-i Kew came to see me again. He was unhappy with everything and uncomfortable about me going out so carelessly, with my beard and hair long. Nevertheless, he radiated peace and forgiveness, as he always did. Ikram knew nothing about the Second Saryas either.

He paced my room, his body big and calm. "I'll do anything, search everywhere to find him," he promised. "I'll check the records of all the bases until we turn something up." He took incredible pleasure in doing something that would bolster my belief in life.

He came back another evening, put his hands on my shoulders, and said, "The Second Saryas isn't in this city. He's been in enemy hands for over eight months."

It was the first time I'd heard the word *enemy* used like this, by one warring Kurdish party referring to another. Only then did I understand how serious and widespread the civil war had become.

Ikram-i Kew said, "Muzafar-i Subhdam, I am sorry but there are some secrets I can't say anything about. As far as I know, he can't come back to our side anyway because he faces serious charges here too."

Those things didn't matter to me at all. What mattered was that I had a son who was imprisoned somewhere on this earth and I needed to find him.

Despite the pain caused by the death of the First Saryas and then the beginning of the Second Saryas's story, the house of the sisters in white was the most peaceful and beautiful home I had ever seen. Truth be told, I had never experienced a peaceful and happy home and knew very little about the lives of happy families. My room might have been a long way from theirs but they never treated me like a stranger or made me feel unwelcome.

After a month, I told Ikram-i Kew I would like to build myself a small hut, rent a patch of land, and become a farmer. Even though you see me on this cursed ferry of yours constantly gazing at the sea, I am also a great lover of the earth.

One evening Ikram-i Kew brought me stacks of money in a black bag and said, "This is all I have, dear friend. I've been saving up for years, but this is all I have to show for it. I own nothing except a small jeep and this bagful of money. Take as much as you like and rent whichever patch of land you want." A wide smile appeared on his face as he spoke, as if he was embarrassed by his vast bulk and the fact that he couldn't produce a smaller, more delicate smile.

Despite feeling old and vulnerable, I bowed and kissed his hands. "My Ikram," I said. "My giant sparrow, I'll start again from scratch with a small plot of land and young animals. I'll dedicate myself to a different life. I only need a small sum, just enough to help me start over."

We went together to a fertile plot of land owned by a farmer who had migrated to the West, leaving everything behind. The plot could be irrigated, and his relatives rented it out so that it didn't go to waste. Standing there, amid streams and the sounds of water, Ikram and I looked at each other. The smell of the village, of fresh grass and cow manure, wafted over us both. Ikram was suspicious of everything and was convinced Yaqub-i Snawbar was bound to find me. But despite all our fears, we only had one real wish at the time: to find the Second Saryas.

After the death of Muhammad the Glass-Hearted, Sulaiman the Great assigned his close friend Ikram-i Kew to cater to the needs of the sisters in white. In reality, the sisters didn't really need much help once they left the city. They had moved into the village of their own volition, although some people thought they were fleeing the stories that had plagued them in the city.

They had dedicated their life to something strange at that time, a task that was simultaneously too intimate and too alien. They made white wedding dresses on a pair of old Singer sewing machines. What surprised me was that they made nothing else. They stored large rolls of fabric in a room in the school they had set aside for sewing. When a dress was finished, it would be exquisitely wrapped in a special bag. At the end of each month, the sisters drove into the city to visit the grave of Muhammad the Glass-Hearted and deliver their dresses to selected stores. It puzzled me that two women who had vowed never to get married should devote themselves to making wedding dresses for other women. But Shadarya-i Spi said, "Each person chooses the happiness or misfortune they create." They were in love with the whiteness of the dresses. When they finished one, they would put it on just once before wrapping it up. Many a time I would catch sight of them at the crack of dawn returning home from the plains in their wedding dresses.

Ikram-i Kew visited me once a week. I never got a full picture of his life. Even now, I don't know where or how he grew up, though he insisted he was no vagabond. And it was true. He especially liked furnishing homes and provided everything for the small hut all on his own. Back then, I was still incapable of such things; I still looked at life like a prisoner of the desert. When I stepped out of my hut at night, my eyes reflected the line of the desert horizon rather than the shadow of the high mountains.

Every Friday, we donned the appropriate clothing and walked through the open plains to visit the grave of the First Saryas. Our visits passed with great respect and in silence. The sisters in white always burned a large number of candles and various types of incense on the grave and the scent hung over the plains late into the night. The girls knew that grief would haunt me forever. They knew that at night, I would take to the mountains, thinking only about Saryas-i Subhdam, and that when I went inside and turned the lock, I had nothing on my mind but my sons.

I was jealous of the noble missions the sisters in white had found for themselves in the village. They and dozens of other young, sweet-natured teachers with a genuine love of children, were fighting for the neglected offspring of the local villages. Sometimes I felt that they regarded me as one of the village kids. Their love for me was not like a daughter's for her father but like a mother's for her child. Their long interactions with children had turned them into mothers.

My life was empty by comparison. I dreaded becoming an old man with no war to wage – no causes, no issues. The empty nights of waiting in the village scared me. A person never has more profound meaning in their life than when they are imprisoned or enslaved, because that's when they are fighting a great battle for their freedom. Nothing threatens the meaning of life like freedom. People lose their purpose and their interest in searching for the meaning of life when they are free, and yet only then does the search for meaning reveal a person's greatness. On some nights I shouted like a madman, "God, please tell me where to turn!" I was too weak to unravel mysteries; the universe was too cruel to support me; and God was too silent to expect anything from. Despite all the problems and questions that I had, I felt I was gradually beginning to experience a freedom without any meaning at all. I had an infinitely dangerous sense of being old and abandoned in my hut.

Ikram-i Kew wanted to give me a realistic picture of the world we lived in. Most of the nights that we walked in the fields, he was busy explaining his image of the world. It was one that I didn't want to understand. Ikram, who would sometimes stoop slightly so that I could hear him clearly, said, "Muzafar-i Subhdam, imagine a city with thousands of narrow alleys, thousands of closed doors, and thousands of fortresses with people wandering around, unable to find the gates. A city completely made up of puzzles, its alleys and doorways changing places, its windows not where they are supposed to be. Imagine a city like that, teeming with millions of rooms, with millions of things in each of those rooms, and it's there that we're trying to find something incredibly small. There is no point railing against it: we live in an era where our people have not yet seen the truth, as if they were traveling around a new city with an old map. Many addresses may be suggested, but you won't find them because those providing them have the map of a different city in their heads. Muzafar-i Subhdam, the Second Saryas is imprisoned in a secret location. This country is full of secret prisons, secret forces, secret curses. Hate rules this country, and there is nothing that fortifies closed gates like hate. In this city of ours, no one loves anyone."

"But Ikram-i Kew," I said. "Since the night you rescued me, I've only come across good-hearted people."

He looked at me, filled with a fear so deep I wished I could take back my words. He trembled and mopped his brow. Even in the coldest seasons, he had to take out a handkerchief to do so after talking. In a voice that seemed to be trying to warn me of some great danger, he said, "No, Muzafar-i Subhdam, no. Wherever there are plenty of secrets, there is plenty of hate."

I didn't want to believe Ikram-i Kew. I still don't. I am not naïve; I knew what humans could do to their fellows, what pain they could inflict on each other. I know that all of you who are sitting opposite me as you listen to me recount this story drop by drop every night have run away from other people. All of us on this ferry, lost and probably drifting forever in vain, have run away from someone, not so dissimilar to us, who might at times have been more unfortunate, more wounded than you and me. But despite all the suffering that we inflict on our fellow humans, where could we turn if we stopped believing in them? What creatures are out there to trust? Even if we turned to nature and asked for its support, how could it help us? Through people, of course. If we turned to God and asked for His help, how would He provide it? Again, through human beings. To whom, apart from us, can nature say, 'Build me a city, play me a piece of music, read me a secret that is buried deep inside me, interpret the chemistry of these flowers, waters, and stars for me. Who else can do it? Only human beings."

Ikram-i Kew, who had lived through the revolution and the post-uprising world, had seen so much cruelty that he no longer believed in anything. That night, when I told him I had a profound belief in humanity, he said in his invariably deep and calm voice, "Well, I don't doubt their greatness, that we can expect great things of them. Let me explain myself better, Muzafar-i Subhdam." He was inhaling the steam rising from the fields. The nighttime murmur of water made us both feel content. "I've given this a lot of thought since the collapse of the uprising and the beginning of the civil war," Ikram said, raising his voice slightly. "I've read plenty of books about it. Sometimes, my beard, mustache, and hair grew out as I took to the plains like a huge elephant. I would stomp around with all my might, looking up at the sky, and ask, 'Why are people behaving like this? What's wrong with this nation? What's the matter with them all?' When the first phase of the civil war started, I was crushed. I realized that a bloodthirsty monster was hiding inside this country. The war didn't pit two peoples, or two religions, or two different types of politics against each other but two sets of impoverished people. Two groups of people were eating away at each other like monsters for no reason. Muzafar, being human is like being a light that switches on and off. The light in our souls might go out and never come back on again; it might glow for a while and then turn off. But I've never seen it burn and keep on shining."

I looked at him in the moonlight and the quiet of the night and found in him all the lost humanity about whose death he spoke. I saw in him the shadow of the kind of person he said was dying out.

The Second Saryas was imprisoned in a far-flung fortress, the sort of structure used to house prisoners in times gone by. It had been built a few years earlier by the state as a formidable base for its armed forces, and could instill a profound fear even at a distance. Buried among mountains, plains, and woodlands, it was surrounded by such a high, circular wall that those inside could see out only from the top of its round watchtowers. Something about the stronghold gave it the aura of a mythical monster made out of stone, iron, and steel.

Ikram and I approached it one evening, having surveyed it from afar. He knew the history of these fortresses built of modern materials but born of age-old fantasies, an engineer's imagination trying to link the prestige of the modern state with that of the ancient caliphs. This one had stood empty since it fell under the people's control during the uprising, when the resident soldiers and officers either killed themselves or surrendered to the people for fear of dying of starvation. After that, displaced families made it their refuge for a long time. When the civil war broke out, the warring parties encircled it with barbed wire, deployed forces around it, and turned it into a prison. Now only birds could get anywhere near it.

When I saw the fortress that day, I fell prey to abject terror. It was unlike any prison I had ever seen, so different from the one in which I had spent so many years. The worst prison is not the one with cruel jailers, but the one from which you can't see the surrounding land and sky. Hell is where nothing stimulates your imagination, nothing makes you think. A true prison not only keeps inmates apart but separates a person from all sources of life. The smallest cracks can whet one's appetite for life, but if the walls are completely blank, that's no longer a prison; it's hell. And Saryas was inside that old fortress.

Ikram-i Kew and I had left the village one night in his jeep, and set out on our journey to find Saryas. We traveled a long way.

First, we encountered a man, an ugly little monkey, whose life was a total mess. He was a security officer and indebted to Ikram on two counts: for saving his life during the bloody battles of the revolution, and for reconciling him with his wife and bringing her home when she ran off with another man. He came with us and showed us the fortress from a distance. He talked all the way.

"Kak Ikram, apple of my eyes, I am indebted to you twice over," he said. "I can deny you nothing. I could say no to Almighty God, but not to you, because you have been more use to me than all God's angels. Even so, what you want is impossible. It's not within my power. It's not within anyone's power. You haven't worked at the security agency; you don't know. The leader himself oversees everything directly and the Party is in charge of every little thing. I am a minor employee. That prison is teeming with secrets. It contains things that only the Party may know about. My colleague who works in the prison, I know this guy, he's my friend. He'd sacrifice his own son for me but there would come a point when even he would have to stop. People like you and me can't enter it just like that. It's impossible to get inside. Put it out of your heads. All my colleague can do is take a recorder and tapes, pass them on to Saryas, and bring his tapes out. The young man's in solitary. Record whatever you want to tell him on a cassette, and he'll do the same. Any more is simply not possible. Believe me, I have promised my friend the very best type of honey. He'd die without top-quality honey. Yes, of course, he's my friend, a very good friend, and he'd die if I asked him to, but he won't let us take a tape recorder in without giving him the honey, which cost me a lot of my own money. You can drop the idea of ever being able to see Saryas. It's not going to happen."

His name was Taifoor Pasha. He wore a hat like Atatürk's and a great many gold rings. He had run one of the Kurdish parties' prisons during the revolution. He later joined the security forces, only to be removed from his post because of his wife's frequent comings and goings and his family's bad reputation. I had no interest in listening to his constant chatter about the story of his wife, Skalla. He kept repeating that we wouldn't be able to see Saryas and that made me even more ill at ease. I had been an impatient listener ever since I was released.

Eventually, after sustained pressure from Ikram, he agreed to introduce us to the guard who might take us to meet Saryas. The young man was called Idris Honey, and he too had an interesting story. He had been a honey seeker for most of his life and had an exceptional ability to locate trees where bees made their nests. He would follow the music of the bees' wings from one mountain to another with the utmost delight, chasing them from one flower bed to another. Then one day he lost all his powers. He couldn't find a single bee. Only his unusual love of honey remained.

The security agency recruited him when they recognized that his former abilities were actually pretty useful for finding suspects and criminals, and shortly after that, he became a guard at the menacing fortress.

We met him for the first time on a dark night, at a bus station. He had chosen the venue, saying no one would suspect such a place. The young man wanted to give up his prison job and immigrate to the West. I couldn't see his face clearly in the dark, but there was something of the bees' wings in his voice so that, when he talked, it was as if a swarm of bees were flying overhead. He said, "I'm emigrating. I can't do much. If I am caught, I'll lose everything. But I am true to my word – I'll take a recorder in so he can listen to your tapes and record anything he has for you over them. Don't you go saying Idris Honey isn't a good man. I've not done this sort of thing for anyone before. But you should also know I expect something in return."

I wanted to see Saryas, to embrace him immediately, but he said, "Boss, let me kiss your hands. Do you hear me or not? It's not possible. I know Saryas-i Subhdam, I deliver his food. But what you're asking is not within my power. Visitors go through four checkpoints before they're admitted. If someone let you in, he'd be killed on the spot. Do you want me to be executed? There's only one thing I can offer you, and I've told you how much I charge. It's up to you. If I weren't planning to emigrate, God himself wouldn't have convinced me to take in so much as a needle. And remember, first things first, I need the agreed amount of honey up front. Otherwise, I'm not doing a thing. Got it?"

Idris Honey was our only hope. Unable to help me as he would like, Ikram-i Kew seemed sad and powerless. He kept raising his offer, but Idris grumbled louder and louder, buzzing like a swarm of bees. Saryas seemed to be a particularly valuable prisoner; he came with a large price tag, the kind of prisoner who might come in handy in certain circumstances.

We stood on the shiny patches of engine grease that had spilled from the buses, the smell from their old exhaust pipes all around us. Some of the drivers were calling out as they waited for the last passengers of the evening. A few faint yellow lights destroyed the beauty of the night.

"Your son is one of the prisoners who will be kept locked up – for one year, or ten, or fifty, I don't know," Idris said. "Some disaster might strike tonight and they would be released. Or he and the rest of the prisoners could be shot. My dear, that's how it is in this country of ours. These things happen every so often. An order arrives all of a sudden, and they release a whole group or make the prisoners dig their own graves in front of the fortress. I can't give you any guarantees. If you don't hear from him tomorrow, it's not my fault. I'm merely a guard. You could offer me ten thousand dinars, even a million, nay, all the wealth in the world, and I couldn't do what you ask. If it were possible, I'd happily have done it for free."

Ikram-i Kew was quiet when we returned that night. He wouldn't talk for a long time when he felt he had failed. I knew he was thinking nonstop because his facial expressions and gaze would freeze; he would sweat and sink into silence. Finally, I tried to console him. He looked at me silently, driving the jeep with the calm of a wrestler who has just lost a fight. "Be quiet, Muzafar-i Subhdam. Stop talking," he said. "I don't want you to say another word."

The next night, I started recording my tapes. I had to pay attention to every sentence, every word. I knew nothing about the Second Saryas. I still remember much of what I said on the first one. It was something along these lines: "I am Muzafar-i Subhdam, a man who has come from the desert. I might or might not be your father. It doesn't matter how you think of me, but I regard you as my son. I was twenty-two years old when I was arrested and left you behind. And now, after spending twenty-one years in a sea of sand, I have come looking for you. I've searched the whole country. But you are like a dream. Are you real? Do you want to see me or not? Yes, my Saryas, Saryas-i Subhdam, I've come back from the dead after all these years to find you inside a dark fortress that no-one can enter."

Thus I recorded my story for the Second Saryas on a cassette, on a new tape recorder expressly purchased by Ikram-i Kew. From that day on, my world changed, as Saryas and I talked to each other about life and the world. A father and a son who would never meet but continued talking to each other on tape.

Tomorrow night I will be quiet as we listen to some excerpts from Saryas's tapes. Here they are, you see. I am carrying them with me wherever I go. When they talk, I fall silent and am a listener just as you are now.

But it's getting late. Let's all stand up, look out at the sea, and sing for ourselves, for those who are lost on the waves. Stand up, and let's sing the songs of those on whom the earth and the sea have no pity.

16

My name is Saryas-i Subhdam. I don't know who'll end up with this tape or who'll listen to it but, yes, that's who I am – Saryas-i Subhdam. You call me the Second Saryas and you're worried I won't like that. Don't be. You didn't know the Marshal, the Professor of our Dark Nights, like I did. He'll always be the First Saryas. I'm not worthy of the name. Even now I want to cry when I think about it.

Even now, imprisoned in this fortress, I am reliving my memories of my time with them – Saryas-i Subhdam, Muhammad the Glass-Hearted, and Nadim-i Shazada. Listen, if you are the person closest to me, you must find Nadim. He'll tell you everything – every single thing.

Where should I begin? Like any child, I don't remember my early childhood, but I feel as if I'm forgetting more and more here in this darkness. Some of the inmates who've been here longer than me say that we wouldn't be able to stand being in daylight any more, that it would make us go blind. I don't know if it's true, but I do know that darkness makes you weak. I've been feeling really weak for several months now.

They might kill us in the next few months if peace isn't achieved. I'm not afraid of death, only that when it comes I'll have forgotten everything. Muzafar-i Subhdam . . . Please don't be upset that I've used your name like that. Something in your voice reminds me of Saryas-i Subhdam and Muhammad the Glass-Hearted. I'm glad you visited the grave of Saryas the Great. I was devastated when he died. I felt betrayed. I tell you, Nadim-i Shazada knows everything; he can tell it better.

What a shame you and I will never meet.

I wish I could tell you about them. I feel ashamed about my past. Everything changed when they all left me behind; I'll never forget that day. I cried when Muhammad the Glass-Hearted died. I just kept saying, "It's all bullshit. Life is nothing but bullshit." The Marshal placed his hands on my shoulders to console me. He was incredibly sad but he didn't cry. It was morning when we heard the news. We were having breakfast when Sharif-i Papula stormed in and said, "It's all over. Muhammad the Glass-Hearted is dead and his glass house has turned to dust." I was holding a kettle. I dropped it when he spoke.

But Saryas smiled at him and said, "You're lying. I don't believe you. You're the biggest liar in the world."

Sharif was wearing a small gold Koran on a chain around his neck. He took it off, placed a hand on it, and said, "I'm not lying. Muhammad the Glass-Hearted died last night." The Professor of our Dark Nights didn't believe it until he saw Muhammad's body with his own eyes. I was crying like a madman. No one's death had ever caused me such grief. Even though I'd done all sorts of terrible things since childhood, committed all sorts of evil crimes during my years as a bandit and a fighter, I cried more over him than anyone else did. They used to call me "the Filthy Saryas" or "Professor of the Dark Hearts" as a joke. In that innocent group I was the only one who had shed other people's blood, and yet that day I became convinced there was some light, some compassion, inside me too.

Don't be surprised that I am being so open with you. Something in your voice reminds me of them. They swore never to lie to each other. We signed the pledge under a remote tree that bears witness to the most wonderful memory of my life, the tree of our friendship, our loneliness, our honesty with one another. We called it "the last pomegranate tree in the world," but Nadim-i Shazada said it was "the tree of sight." The Marshal called it "the tree of the wretched of the earth," while for Muhammad the Glass-Hearted it was "the tree of inspiration, of our proximity to heaven." Muhammad believed there are certain places in the world from which people can see things more clearly, and that under the last pomegranate tree was one of them.

It was the tree of our hopes. We dreamed that one day we wouldn't need to work any more, and we'd be able to build a house next to the tree that bordered both heaven and earth, where we could enjoy life and our friendship in peace. Sorry. These are not my words. They're Muhammad the Glass-Hearted's. He was the one who used to talk about "the border between heaven and earth, between man and God, between reality and the imagination."

When we went there, we'd be cut off from our normal lives – we were either fantasizing, talking about the future, or trying to understand the mysteries of our lives. It was under the last pomegranate tree that we decided we wouldn't lie to one another. It was there that I recounted all my wicked deeds, one by one, and asked the tree to forgive me. I've been a murderer since an early age, but at that point, I wanted to be cleansed. I wanted to become one of them.

I am the corrupt side of Saryas, the side that couldn't stay innocent during the wars. That morning when Sharif-i Papula entered the room and said Muhammad the Glass-Hearted had died of love, I believed him instantly. I was convinced that people like Muhammad the Glass-Hearted could die of nothing else. When I dropped the kettle, I started frantically trying to find the key to my room, shouting at the Marshal, "It's all bullshit. What do you think people are? What do you think we are? What do you think Muhammad the Glass-Hearted is? We'll all die just as pointlessly. How did you think he'd die? In battle, in a holy war, for the homeland, the motherland which the patriots are fucking like a whore? Tell me, what did you want him to die for? He had to die of love – someone like that has to die in the full flush of youth and for love. Otherwise, his life would be meaningless."

When I got angry, the Professor of our Dark Nights would fall silent. I, the wicked Saryas, had told them under the last pomegranate tree to stay away from me when I'm angry.

When we reached Muhammad the Glass-Hearted's body, he was still sunk in the glass dust of his death, still in the clothes I had bought him at the secondhand market. He wore them for our sake so as not to appear different from the rest of us. We were the children of the flea market, raised in the sewage soup of the bazaars. He liked to be seen as one of us, felt he belonged in our world, even though we lacked his skills and gifts. When I saw him covered in blood and tiny shards of glass, I lost the plot, jumping up and down like a bird on fire, like a child seeing blood for the first time. I rolled around in the mud of the street, the First Saryas shook me manically and slapped me across the face. It was the first time I ever let someone slap me without objecting. Thousands of people had gathered around the body, watching us, all of them expecting us to get into a fight. I was sobbing bitterly. Saryas was stronger at times like this, acting like he could withstand any disaster.

I didn't go to the funeral. I was so restless that I followed the procession from afar, even though I knew I couldn't watch them lower him into the grave. He had a large procession, but it was still less than he deserved. All the people at the front were men he didn't like, his father's friends, the dirty politicians of the day. "They stand on our necks," he used to say. We, his genuine friends, had to be content with watching the funeral on TV at a tea-house. What infuriated me was the TV cameras surrounding the body. I knew that in the evening a news presenter would affect a hoarse, sad voice and say, "Muhammad Sulaiman Hussein, known as Muhammad the Glass-Hearted, died today in a tragic accident. It's worth noting that he is the son of our nation's famous freedom fighter, Sulaiman Hussein Karkhi, who, together with his family, has played a significant role in all our nation's revolutions. Our condolences to the family on the occasion of this young man's untimely demise. May Almighty God admit him to paradise." It was all bullshit, a massive lie made of pure bullshit. Watching it all on TV that evening, I was actually sick. I couldn't help it.

When the First Saryas slapped me and walked away, I knew he'd regret it. That's what he was like. It was the same with his fights at the bazaar. No sooner did he become angry than he regretted it. He would always come back, with his loud laughter, to make up and be friends. No one could refuse when he laughed.

That evening, I was sitting in the Buraq Teahouse, waiting for the news to come on. When he arrived, laughing, the whole mood of the place changed. I was surprised that he was laughing on a day like that. He sat quietly next to me and said, without looking at me, "Good for you. You've cleaned off the mud you were covered in this morning." He continued, even more quietly, "You were wise not to come to the funeral. It looked more like a whore's wedding." He put his arms around me. "You and I should organize our own service for Muhammad the Glass-Hearted."

"Listen to me, Saryas-i Subhdam," I said. I still resented him. "You who consider yourself superior to me, you who everyone calls the Professor of the Shitty Nights, the Minister of the Cart Vendors, the King of the Swiss Chard. I know you have a low opinion of me, but Muhammad the Glass-Hearted is dead and you're laughing. You're acting as if nothing happened."

The First Saryas smiled, like one brother sympathizing with another, and said, "You know my laughter has nothing to do with how I feel. I know that the dead will later reflect, look back, and see who is grieving for them. I'll visit him one day, but you won't. On that day it will become clear which of us loves Muhammad the Glass-Hearted more."

At the time, I didn't understand exactly what he meant. He had placed a number of newspapers on the table and was stirring his tea. I picked up the newspapers and said, "Everything you're saying is bullshit. I'm no angel, but you're just hard-hearted. Muhammad the Glass-Hearted's death is the end of the world. I know what I am saying is ridiculous, and I know you're not taking it seriously, you who consider yourself the philosopher of the street vendors and potato sellers. I know you think you're superior to me because you read these worthless newspapers and because the stupid zucchini sellers call you Marshal. But you and I are through for now. We'll never know who we are. Who'll help us with that? The eggplant sellers? The matchstick sellers? Come on, Marshal of the Shitty Days, tell me: Who's going to help us from now on?"

He always listened calmly at first and only made up his mind later. He kept stirring his tea without drinking it. He loved holding the glass cup in his hand and just looking at it. Even now when I think about his composure and his smile, but also his bouts of anger, I want to scream and beat myself about the head. He used to tell me repeatedly, "Saryas-i Subhdam, there are some limits you shouldn't overstep."

"Not for me there aren't. I piss on them," I'd reply.

But that day he just smiled at me and said, "I know. I've known for a long time that you and I would never understand each other." Muhammad the Glass-Hearted's death had changed everything about me. It had made me shaky, unable to hold a cup of tea, a glass of water, or a piece of bread. When the First Saryas said this, I became even more despondent. I thought it was ridiculous that both of us had the same life, the same name, and the same past without knowing why.

"If you and I don't know who we are or why we're alike, why should we be friends? And why did we sign an oath and bury it under the last pomegranate tree in the world? It's all bullshit," I said. "Fuck everything, our names, our glass pomegranates, even the tree."

He put his teaspoon down, took the newspapers, and left. There, in the crazy tea-house, I put my head on the table and started crying. The sad gypsum plasterers, the unemployed, and the students all laughed at me. I left the place in tears. That evening, I ran into the First Saryas again at Zhino-i Makhmali's. He said, "We didn't only lose Muhammad the Glass-Hearted. I lost my glass pomegranate too. Saryas, I'm sorry. When I saw Muhammad lying dead, I wanted to find my glass pomegranate. He'd had it since the day before the floods. I was trying to find it before anyone else could take it, but when I saw you drenched in the mud of the alley, I got confused. It's gone now. It's lost." I didn't know then why Saryas had given it to Muhammad the Glass Hearted in the first place.

Anyway, on the evening that Muhammad the Glass-Hearted left home and was caught up in the flood, he had been on his way to see Sayyid Muzhda-i Shams, the son of the antique dealer Sayyid Jalal Shams. He knows a thing or two about the secret of the pomegranates. Nadim-i Shazada knows more about that. You have to find him. From the day Saryas the Great died, I stopped caring about the story of who we were. That night, the First Saryas and I put our arms around each other's shoulders and made up, just as we always had. But it wasn't until he died that I went back to Buraq, the tea-house where we had drunk the first tea of our friendship.

On the whole, I had gone to Buraq less often than the others. I never really felt at home there, meaning I didn't know many of the people and they didn't know me either. It meant not hearing Saryas's stories of the bazaar and not being aware of goings-on at the market. The teahouse played an important role in the life of Saryas the Great. It was where the street vendors poured out their grief to him, where the cart vendors haggled to sell their carts before moving on to other jobs, and where lovers copied out other men's letters to send as their own. New street vendors went there to see the Marshal and the Cart Council and ask them for a place in the army of the carts. It was there that Saryas the Great made his deals with the police and municipal officials, paid the street sweepers a bit extra to clean places they might otherwise miss, and scolded children who didn't understand what it meant to be living among the army of the carts. But what astonished me most was his huge respect for women.

Hold on. Hold on. Hold on, Muzafar-i Subhdam, I need to pause here and think. The three of us were miserable guys who had no women in our lives. Forgive me, but I'm about to trample on father-son respect and say that none of us had fondled a breast, sucked a lip, or kneaded a thigh. Saryas the Great called it "honor", I called it "misfortune", and Muhammad the Glass-Hearted called it "patience." Who would have believed that a woman would kill Muhammad the Glass-Hearted?

Here in my prison I have just one hope, but even that is a lot for this country. My hope is to get out of prison and lose myself somewhere in the world, to assume a fake identity, change my name, and have a child who's never heard the name Saryas-i Subhdam.

Muzafar-i Subhdam, do you hear me? Sometimes I need to turn off the recorder and think. I am talking to you from complete darkness. I don't know what time it is. You were once imprisoned; you know how it is. Even though people don't need a clock in prison, they still like to know the time, what people are up to, what corner of the world is quiet and where it is always busy.

No matter what I talk about, I go back to my memories of them. My life was ruined when Sharif-i Papula entered the room with a bowl of yogurt and three naans and said, "Muhammad the Glass-Hearted died last night." The malicious version of myself resurfaced as if resurrected at that very moment. The truths about our lives died with Muhammad the Glass-Hearted. The cloud of dust in which he died still blinds me, still envelops you too. It's what he used to say himself, that we would be lost in the dust he'd leave behind when he died. You must know that if Muhammad the Glass-Hearted hadn't died as he did, we would all have led different lives. You'd have come back now and met me and the other Saryases and embraced us all. But he dragged us all to death. I remember one night he talked to me about his dying; he was certain he was going to die. He knew something would kill him but didn't know exactly what. He told everyone else that love would kill him, but he told me that he might be killed because of the secrets, that he might uncover a truth that no one should know. God, in this darkness with no beginning or end, I talk about his death nonstop, because it was the beginning of everything. It signified my death as well.

TAPE NO.2

Good evening, Muzafar-i Subhdam. It's always night where I am. I've listened to your second tape, the one where you talk about the universe and such. You said something about how our lives are fragments of your own, our voices fragments of yours, and that you will continue the story on our behalf, and so on and so forth. I'm sorry, but that bullshit makes me want to laugh. That you've come back from your imprisonment to try to understand my situation may be true, but it's a lie that you can do anything for us. Who are you? A dead man. What could you possibly do when you've emerged from the sand after twenty-one years? What do you think you are? Sand, just sand. I can tell by your voice. Muzafar-i Subhdam, I'm talking to myself here in the dark, just to myself, not to you.

Last night I started to worry and decided I wouldn't tell you anything anymore but then I changed my mind. You're asking me to tell you everything, all there is. I can't do that. Just as you say you freed yourself from your past drop by drop when you were in prison, so I wanted to do the same. Since starting to recount our story on the first tape, I've become dejected. Telling this story hurts more than being in prison and yet I can't stop. I feel a need to keep the memory of the dead alive and to unburden my pain. It feels like they died just yesterday.

Who are you, Muzafar-i Subhdam? You're not my father; that's who they were. One night I told the First Saryas exactly that. I can still remember him laughing out loud. Sharif-i Papula, our roommate, was washing the dishes, Saryas was sifting rice on a large tray, and I was lying on a flowery mattress listening to the Kamkars, as usual. I never did any chores. As I said, I am the Filthy Saryas. I would leave the table as soon as I finished eating, leave my teacup upside down on the TV table when I'd emptied it, and leave my socks in a jug to soak.

The TV set was mine, as was the stereo. The Great Saryas would stay over with us if it was raining and he wasn't going back to his own place in the collective town. When I said, "You're my father" to him, he thought it was funny. My face and build made me seem older than him, but no one respected me the way they respected the Professor of our Dark Nights.

I wasn't raised by anyone, yet then again, in all honesty, neither was he. But he had the ability to educate himself. Some people can, but not me. Saryas enjoyed being talked to like a real man, being asked for his advice or support. I made fun of him for it, for his life among the cart vendors. I'd tell him he was drowning in a sea of bullshit. And he'd tell me I didn't know what I was living for. Sometimes I would listen to his advice; but sometimes I would lie on my back and tell him I wouldn't give a faulty coin for what he had to say.

My job and my lifestyle meant I visited Buraq less frequently than the others. But once I got to know them, I decided to leave the ranks of the Peshmerga forces. One evening I barged into Buraq, kitted out with a weapon, military equipment, the lot. They all wanted to know the latest news of the war, what it was like at the front. I lied and told them the names of hundreds of mountains, peaks, and hills that our party had seized. Such lies made people happy. Muhammad the Glass-Hearted and Saryas the Great were the only two people to look at me sadly. I stood up in the middle of the tables and declared, "The Party is in danger. We need to get rid of the old mercenaries and spies and create another parliament. Understand? The Party is in danger!"

The Marshal was playing with the sugar cubes in front of him and said sadly, "Sit down, you idiot. No one except you is in any danger."

In the evening, they took me to a popular place, a small bar which almost didn't let us in. There, Muhammad the Glass-Hearted said, "Don't go to that war, Saryas-i Subhdam. You'll get killed and that'll be it. You'll get killed, and your body will be all that's left of you." They spent all night trying to persuade me. That night I understood why they called Saryas the Great the "Professor of our Dark Nights." Somehow, he spoke more beautifully in the dark. I swear, it was like the philosophers. I have no idea why was he less eloquent during the day. Perhaps because he was always exhausted then, tormented by the problems of the bazaar. He was always dreaming of establishing a new, different order. Muzafar-i Subhdam, something in his speech about life and death resembled the things you say. For example, he used to say, "Your life is worth more than the honor of a thousand political parties fighting over the spoils." Both of them loathed the war. I was different because I'd been a fighter from an early age. I was familiar with gunpowder, bullets, and gunfire. Fighting was in my blood.

They could be extremely persuasive. I'd listen to them gloomily and merely nod my head at their words. From that night on, I gradually withdrew from combat until one day I found myself completely cut off from my previous life. I can't talk to you about those days, Muzafar-i Subhdam. They were my only friends, even if we often got into arguments with each other. I knew they wanted to protect me from something. They acted like a father to me, constantly worrying about my life. After I left the Peshmergas' ranks, I didn't know where to go. They supported me all that time and their only condition was that I didn't take part in Kurdish infighting.

They gave me a room in a small house rented by students from outside the city. Sharif-i Papula was my roommate. Muhammad the Glass-Hearted paid my rent. He rarely invited us back to his glass mansion as he didn't want us to be envious of him or to compare our life to his and feel sad. Both of us had it easier than the First Saryas. Even on my worst days, I could still put some smart clothes on and stroll around the bazaar. But life was torment for Saryas. He had to wake up very early in the morning and he slept in awful places at night. Sometimes we'd go back to his small room in the collective town, filled with photos of race cars, karate fighters, and bizarre Arabic inscriptions that I couldn't read. At night, he'd lie on an old metal bed where he spent most of the time lost in thought. Every time he spoke, he'd start with loud laughter.

One night I asked him, "Saryas, do you think we're brothers?"

He looked at me sadly and said, "We are brothers, you and I. All the wretched of this world are."

"I don't mean brotherhood and shit in that sense," I scoffed. "I know that if the wretched of this world could, they'd piss on each other's faces. I mean real brothers, born from the same parents."

"There's only one type of brotherhood, the one that's created by life and love. All the rest is a lie."

"Do you think we'll ever untangle that secret?" I asked. "I mean, will we find out why we're both called Saryas-i Subhdam, why we don't have parents or relatives, why we're each carrying our own glass pomegranate?"

"No, Saryas, I don't think so," he said. "I can only speak for myself, but I am sure I'll die without an answer to that question. My life is like an arrow that has left the bow. It's moving fast, without a target, and ultimately, it will hit something and snap."

Muzafar-i Subhdam, don't be surprised that he and Muhammad the Glass-Hearted talked like that. They both used to say they would hit something and snap. While Saryas the Great compared himself to a swift arrow released from a bow, the direction of its flight impossible to alter, Muhammad compared himself to a delicate glass pomegranate, rolling down a stony slope, about to be smashed to smithereens. They were both certain they could do nothing about their own destinies, so instead they tried to improve other people's, as if they were responsible for the suffering and pain of others. That's what they were like, my fathers. Until one day they did indeed hit something and break.

Don't talk to me about the sisters in white, Muzafar-i Subhdam. If you send me tapes again, don't mention them. I'll consider them satanic till the day I die. They killed the Glass-Hearted and they are to blame for my relationship with the Professor of our Dark Nights turning sour. I hate them, Muzafar-i Subhdam.

One day, Sulaiman the Great brought all of Muhammad's true friends together and told us the whole story. He and the First Saryas insisted the sisters in white were blameless. Beating myself around the head, I said, "Blameless? How can they be? If that's the case, how come Muhammad the Glass-Hearted is dead and buried? What crime is greater than failing to return someone's profound love of you? Someone loves you with their life's blood only for you to look down at them coldly and say, 'I don't love you'? If you ask me, that's worse than gunning someone down, or cutting their head off."

I was at the center of the furor that followed the funeral – myself and three other people who wanted to understand the cause of his death. You shouldn't assume the story of Muhammad's death is a simple one. At the time, everyone at the bazaar was talking about it. They spoke of a secret gunshot being fired at Muhammad after the floods. Everyone was saying he had been about to discover a great secret and that was why he was killed, but who could really get to the bottom of it?

That evening we went to the house of Sulaiman the Great and said we wanted to see Muhammad's father, but the bodyguards wouldn't let us in. We started throwing stones at the windows. The bodyguards wanted to shoot us and chased us through the alleyways. We regrouped that same evening, only there were more of us this time. We all knew one another, the wretched youths who had become friendly with the Glass-Hearted in different places and at different times. I called out to Sulaiman the Great in a loud voice, "Hello, sir. Come out of your room and tell us why Muhammad the Glass-Hearted died. We were his closest friends. We would have died for him. We can't make head nor tail of it. Someone needs to come out here and explain to us instead of all this bullshit." I knew he didn't want to talk about the death of his son but he was worried we might harm the sisters in white. Back then, it was as clear as day to us that they'd killed Muhammad.

The next day, an even larger crowd gathered in front of his house. The city's street vendors who sold plastic-bags, water, sunflower-seeds – they were all there. But again, Sulaiman the Great did not come out, and the guards chased us off. When the Marshal finally appeared, I took a step back. He was the most skilled negotiator of all of us.

At first, he went in alone to talk to Muhammad's father, whose reputation meant he was highly respected. Since childhood, I knew the respect accorded to these people was completely misplaced. I had no respect for him at all but I pretended to hold him in high regard for the sake of Saryas the Great. Finally, the guards brought out a table and Sulaiman the Great came out of the house. He stood on the table to talk to us but there were so many people that he struggled to calm us all down. To protect him from our outbursts and violent reactions, Saryas stood next to him. Otherwise, things might have ended badly, but we – the kids who grew up in the streets and alleyways of the qaysaris of the bazaar – had more respect for Saryas, the Professor of our Dark Nights, than for any politician, revolutionary, writer, or artist. When we saw Saryas standing next to him – saying, "Shut up. What's wrong with you? Are you animals or what? Let the gentleman speak" – we all fell silent.

Sulaiman the Great told us he had done everything he could to prevent the Glass-Hearted's death. He told us how he and another person had gone at dawn to ask for a girl's hand in marriage because Muhammad the Glass-Hearted's sudden love for her would kill him. He said everything had moved so quickly that it was impossible to explain. "He had a heart that the wind carried away and broke."

I was the first to yell from the back, "Let's kill those two whores. Let's kill the two bitches."

"They are innocent," Sulaiman the Great said. "The only culprit is Almighty God above us, who gave Muhammad such a fragile heart."

Shouts rose from the crowd: "Let's attack the sisters in white. Let's storm their house."

Saryas the Great soothed us and said, "I have been the Glass-Hearted's friend since childhood. You all know how much I hate injustice. Like you, I also grew up in the bazaar. We need to be certain before making any accusations. I assure you, if they turn out to be guilty, even if you forgive them, I will not. But if they prove to be innocent, I won't let anyone touch them. You must believe me."

Almighty God, the day after Saryas met the two sisters, it was as if they had put him under a spell that remained in his blood until the night he died. When he returned and told me, "Their songs testify to their innocence," I went crazy. From that evening on, there was a deep rift between the two of us which would never heal.

That day Sulaiman the Great and Saryas the Great, one a tiger of the mountains, the other of the alleyways and the bazaar, calmed us down and dispersed us.

Muzafar-i Subhdam, who would have predicted that you'd come out of the desert and visit the house of the sisters in white? I've always hated them and always will. The evening when Saryas the Great came back from visiting Muhammad's grave, I realized the two sisters were two powerful witches, two evil souls who could entrap any man in their mystery. He stormed into the room I shared with Sharif-i Papula, talking loudly and laughing. He was recounting the events for Sharif, but he wanted me to hear too. Saryas, who always spoke of women's honor with ridiculous politeness anyway, talked about their voices, about the serenity and mystery in their eyes, as if he'd been bewitched. I hit the roof.

"You're not Saryas the Great," I said. "You're not. You're not the Professor of our Shitty Nights. You're not even the cow dung in the alleyways. You're nothing, nothing at all. Have you forgotten that those girls killed your closest friend? That they killed the Glass-Hearted? I won't hear this. I don't want you saying such things in my house."

It was a darker and more bitter night than the endless nights of this prison. Saryas the Great smiled and said, "Those sisters are two angels, two angels of Almighty God."

When I later found out that they had signed a pact of brotherhood with Saryas the Great as strong as the vows of love, it led to the complete collapse of my relationship with him.

In fact, one night I nearly shot him in an empty alleyway. That's what I'd decided to do. "You betrayed our oath, pissed on it. I'm going to kill you. Instead of avenging the Glass-Hearted, you've made his killers your sisters." I pulled out my new fourteen round handgun. "I'm ashamed to be called Saryas. The two girls have made you scum. You've become a joke in this city. That's it – it's you or me. Either I shoot you, or you shoot me."

He sat on the stoop of a house, leaned back, and said, "Kill me, Saryas-i Subhdam, go on. Kill me right here, like this: I'll sit back, spread my arms, and you fire one shot at my forehead. Or actually, hang on – let's go to the last pomegranate tree and you can kill me there. No one will witness you doing it." His sarcastic laughter echoed through the silent night. "Kill me. One of us really isn't needed anymore, it's true. Come on then. Why don't you do it?"

Until that moment, I too had thought there were no other Saryases apart from us. But hold on, hold on. I don't want to give anything away. Nadim-i Shazada knows everything. He's the only person who can help you. You must find Nadim-i Shazada, the blind boy who knows the secrets.

So it went on, back and forth between us in that alley. "You kill me or I kill you." I said it over and over again. One of us was no longer needed. We should never have found each other in the first place. I was afraid of him and he of me.

I had grown up among mercenaries, thieves, bandits, and the political party men. He had grown up in the bazaar, among smugglers on the borders. The best part of his life was the time he spent in an orphanage, while the happiest years of mine were when I was friends with Muhammad the Glass-Hearted. We didn't hate each other; you mustn't think that. We were very close. We loved each other, but we had a difficult friendship, a painful relationship. Whenever we saw each other, we could not escape the question of who we really were, and it angered us both.

Sometimes we would weep on each other's shoulders for hours before Sharif-i Papula managed to soothe us, but then one day Sharif left and never returned. He eventually sent me a letter from Damascus, in which he talked about the room he shared with a group of Shiites in the Sayyida Zainab district. That was the last I heard of him. Some people say he's smuggling Russian girls into Germany through Ukraine; others say he is at an Arab fighters' camp in Afghanistan. Sharif-i Papula was the only witness of the love between Saryas the Great and me, but who knows where he is now?

As long as I live I will remember the evening two strangers woke me up. I had a big picture of the Kamkars over my bed and pictures of the martyrs of the Kurdish national movement on the rest of the walls. Back then, I enjoyed collecting their names and pictures, creating fictional biographies for them the way the Party's radio stations did. I'd sit with the other Peshmergas, imitating the radio presenters. No, I will not forget the evening when Saryas the Great and Muhammad the Glass-Hearted appeared among the photos of the fallen. When I first opened my eyes, their faces appeared blurred among those of the martyrs. I splashed water on my face several times before I could see clearly. I had twenty minutes until my night shift. Those twenty minutes changed everything. That night I realized there was nothing worthwhile in my life except for the Kamkars' songs and my stupid interest in their music. I felt too ashamed to tell my story to the two young men. I wanted to kill myself. I would put the barrel of my gun into my mouth then take it out again; I would place it against my forehead or under my chin then move it away. Even when I took out my fourteen round pistol in the dark and told the Marshal, "Either you kill me, or I kill you," I was lying. I've always been afraid of death, but that night I felt so ashamed of my life that I genuinely did consider suicide. All night long, I contemplated inventing a fictional story about my life. I was so ashamed of everything that I'd become a master at this. Even the names I sent in to the radio request shows were lies, fictional people who existed only in my head. Sometimes I would ask for leave, saying I was going to visit Auntie Halim, but there was no one in my life with that name. I was living a lie.

Nowadays, I'd say how wonderful it was when I could do that. How wonderful, what bliss to be able to live on those simple lies of my youth forever, but the appearance of the Marshal and Muhammad the Glass-Hearted made me grow up.

Serene and full of confidence, I launched into a made-up story about my past life. I told them about the noble family who raised me and the very beautiful girl who fancied me and wanted me to marry her. I told them about the money I had converted into dollars, which I'd deposited at a friend's. I told them that I wanted to open a boutique shop. I even said, "I may go abroad soon. The Party will send me."

I was in the middle of my lies when Muhammad the Glass-Hearted looked at me and said with the gentleness of a friend, "Saryas-i Subhdam, you're lying."

I paused at that, looked at them both and started to cry. "Yes, I'm lying."

That was the moment when I had to reveal my whole life to them, absolutely everything. To calm me, they said, "No, Saryas Junior, keep your life story for under the pomegranate tree. Stories taste different there." And that's how I ended up telling them all about myself, under that tree on one of our picnics.

I can't be sure even now if it was the charm of Muhammad the Glass-Hearted, to whom everyone told their secrets, or the magic of the last pomegranate tree that loosened my tongue. Whatever it was, I told them the story of my entire life in all its filth.

TAPE #3

My first memories are of a village. A small village, really, really small. I hate the lot of them, even the most wonderful village in the world is hell to me. Saryas the Great was the same, and would get angry when the newspapers talked about people returning to villages that had been destroyed by the army. We might have started out in villages, but we grew up in the city, alongside cinemas, video stores, flea markets, and the carts of the watermelon and pomegranate sellers.

And so my memory goes back to the village. I must have been six or seven when one day everybody, the whole village, fled. I can remember the air strikes, livestock being hit, two girls being killed at the women's waterhole. The Jash* and all the other bullshit groups had launched an attack. Obviously, there are thousands of other examples of bullshit that I don't

* A derogatory term which literally means 'donkey foal'. It refers to a member of local pro-Hussein Kurdish paramilitary units officially known as National Defense Battalions. (Translator's note)

remember or want to talk about. A certain Mullah Habas and a Ms. Kharaman, who were supposedly my parents, were killed that day. They had raised me; I called them mom and dad and so on, although I don't remember it well. Apparently, before she was killed, Ms. Kharaman told everyone I wasn't their child, "My dears, he's the son of a martyred Peshmerga and we've been raising him. For the Kurdish cause, my dears. For the desperately unlucky Kurds." Apparently, Mullah Habas treated me appallingly, whipping me with switches and stuff. Of course, I was said to have been very naughty, but I can't remember that or anything else.

So, I can remember back to being in a small village, a village as puny as bird shit, completely abandoned. I remember being left behind all alone. I've been told that if I'd left with everyone else, I'd have been killed. Ms. Kharaman and Mullah Habas had climbed a mountain when enemy surveillance spotted them. From then on, the artillery bombardment pursued them. As they walked, an artillery shell – boom – landed right where they'd just been standing. They continued: walk – boom – walk – boom – walk – boom – walk – boom. Boom, boom, boom—until they walked no more. And that, supposedly, is how my first parents died.

I also remember the Jash militias entering the village and finding no one but a snot-nosed child named Saryas-i Subhdam carrying a glass pomegranate. They doused the village in kerosene, and I was excited to see the fire that followed. I even helped them. I recall those days as the happiest of my childhood, even though I can't remember any of it very well anymore. Don't think that I'd hated our homeland since childhood, or that I was "the most savage child in the world" as the Marshal put it. No, it was all just a big game to me.

I was rescued by a mercenary called Kaikhusraw Agha-i Sufian Agha-i Sadr Arhami. I have no idea why his full name was always used. I learned four important things while I lived with him: how to be a mercenary, a bandit, and a Peshmerga, and how to read and write. He had a bunch of beautiful wives and daughters but no sons. He never treated me as a son though. Obviously he could have adopted me in order to provide me with an ID, to settle properties on me, and the rest of these meaningless things, but he didn't. The only thing he liked about me was my name. Sometimes when we were alone, he would become lost in thought and say, "Saryas-i Subhdam . . . Saryas-i Subhdam . . . Saryas-i Subhdam . . . what a beautiful name! What does it mean?" I don't think he could bring himself to change it since he knew that if he did officially make me his son, he'd have to call me Saryas-i Kaikhusraw Agha-i Sadr Arhami, which he considered a huge injustice.

It's possible I was the youngest mercenary in this country. The first picture I have of myself is from those days: I am with a group of other mercenaries high on a mountaintop. It's a windy day. I am nine years old, carrying a Brno rifle three times my height. We are standing near an outpost, carrying a picture of Saddam the dictator, and making a V-for-Victory sign with our hands. Once, we and all the mercenaries' families were taken to see the dictator. All the way there, Kaikhusraw Agha kept telling his daughters, wives, and other bullshit people what a great day it was. After searching our asses dozens of times, they took us to a place called the president's Hall of Meetings. When he arrived, we all had to stand up and clap and other such bullshit for half an hour. I didn't clap. Panicked by my odd behavior, Kaikhusraw kept saying amid the applause and cheers, "Clap, Saryas-i

Subhdam. Clap, you son of a bitch." I didn't. We all lined up to take our turn kissing the president's hands. When it came to me, I was introduced as the country's youngest mercenary. He seemed very pleased to meet me. I was supposed to kiss his hands and so on, but I stood still and did nothing. They pushed me in front of him, and he put me between his legs. At that point, my head was at the same level as the president's testicles. The president's crotch gave off an awful stench. I pulled my head back and said in Kurdish, which neither Saddam nor his bodyguards understood, "President, don't you wash your ass?"

No one understood what I said except Kaikhusraw Agha and he fainted on the spot. I started crying when I saw him fall. I didn't know why, there was just an incredible fuss. The state newspapers later attributed Kaikhusraw's fainting to the ecstasy of seeing his son between the president's knees. The picture of me with the president went on to become very well known, although it angered me so much that I decided to give myself a different face year after year until the day came when the world no longer remembered seeing me right next to the President's crotch. It is a strange picture in any case, taken on a podium, beside two large wreaths of flowers. The President's mouth is open and laughing, while mine is open and crying. Kaikhusraw Agha never forgave me. From that day on, he banned me from joining his wives and daughters in their gatherings and sent me off on guard duty to remote military posts. Those three years put my ability and skills as the country's youngest mercenary to the test, and Kaikhusraw Agha obviously cursed the day he took me home. I was regularly pushed to the front so that I would be killed during heavy fighting, but as if all the devils were protecting me, it simply didn't happen. I would crawl into any dangerous hole without fear. During heavy fighting, I would go on the attack before anyone else. The other mercenaries called me "the midget." In two battles, our entire forces were obliterated except for me, and I returned, armed with my long rifle and the news that one of Kaikhusraw Agha's brothers, one of his uncles, and two of his cousins had perished. A force from the heavens protected me. A mine exploded beneath me once and I was unscathed. Another time, a Peshmerga shell fell inside our military post, killing all the other mercenaries, and yet I leapt like a lion and emerged from the smoke and gunpowder of the blast. I was one of the bravest mercenaries in the country.

When the Peshmerga forces were crushed in the late 1980s and our regiment was scaled down, Kaikhusraw Agha could no longer support his large family. No one knew the exact number of his wives and daughters. He couldn't earn all the money he needed as a Jash mercenary. That was when I and a number of his men became bandits. I would happily do anything I was asked. It was in that period that I killed for the first time. Obviously, I don't know if gunshots I'd fired had killed anyone in previous clashes, but the first person I killed at close range, face to face, was at that time. Along with dozens of Kaikhusraw Agha's armed men, I would set ambushes in every nook and cranny of our homeland, looting smugglers' convoys, halting vehicles, and stripping passengers naked.

The first person I killed was a gold dealer. One dark night, he was driving to the border alone in his white Mercedes, with three kilos of gold dust hidden under his seat. When Mamosta Khalil Hurmiz went to check beneath the seats, the trader attacked him from behind and nearly managed to grab his pistol. I fired out of fear, and I almost took out Mamosta Khalil too.

When I came to my senses and opened my eyes, the trader's head, with its surprised eyes, was resting on Mamosta Khalil's shoulder, vomiting blood. To stop me from feeling either scared or sorry, Mamosta Khalil remarked, "Good job you killed him. That motherfucker had lived long enough." His praise made me so happy that the following nights I couldn't sleep from joy and fear.

The day I saved Mamosta Khalil, he said, "I owe you one. I'll teach you something that will stand you in good stead for the rest of your life." He taught me to read and write. It was how we spent the days from then on. When the uprising took place in 1991, I had completely mastered basic literacy. But I had also grown used to life as a street bandit lying in wait for his prey. It was hard to give that up.

Things changed quickly after the uprising. Kaikhusraw Agha swiftly became a Peshmerga, hastily burning the pictures we took with the President and replacing them with photos taken with the new Kurdish leaders. The latter never tired of dinners, banquets, drinking, and traveling around. Plus, they loved songs, partying, women, and laughter. You would never guess they had returned from a long and bloody war. It was more like they were just back from one wedding party and were getting ready to go to another.

When I later became an active Peshmerga and took part in the civil war, I was shocked at the cheerfulness of the leaders and officials. They had something in their life that we lacked: they were constantly having fun. When we set out for battle, they would be telling jokes, and they would still be doing so when we returned. At funeral services, they would whisper jokes to each other in the intervals between the Koran recitals. In the trenches, they would tell each other jokes over the radio. When they created peace committees during the civil war, they would open the meetings with the latest jokes. All this helped me understand that everything is meaningless, that it's all bullshit, although I did eventually realize that in order to take part in armed conflict, you should be able to laugh a lot.

One evening, I visited Kaikhusraw Agha Sadr Arhami, kissed his hands, and said, "Sir, I've come to thank you. You've raised me for many years. I've been a heavy burden on your shoulders. I'm grown up now, and henceforthI will look after myself." I don't know why I did it but I think all the jokes I had heard in his guest wing had a great influence. Even then, something in my blood drew me to the dark side of life. I could no longer bear all the jokes I heard from Kaikhusraw Agha's guests.

When I left the house, I was very happy and felt incredibly free: I never went back. In my time as a bandit I had saved a small amount of money, which I quickly spent at the bazaar and the cinema, in the video stores and restaurants. When I had just enough left for a small sandwich, I enrolled with a Peshmerga force. That evening, I went back to the long hours of guard duty in the rain, snow, wind, and darkness as a Peshmerga.

My only real friend at the time was Mamosta Khalil Hurmiz. He was the first person to strike gold through currency conversion, open a store in the middle of the bazaar, and become very rich. "In the evening, when the stock market closes shop," he said, jokingly, "come over and we'll continue our classes." And that's what we'd do whenever I had a day off.

When the First Saryas and Muhammad the Glass-Hearted turned up, I was at a low point. To be honest, I had nothing to live for. I thought a lot about suicide and such bullshit. Our first meeting, at a small teahouse near the cinemas, opened the door of a new world to me. I had spoken to Muhammad the Glass-Hearted twice by phone. As I made my way to the teahouse that evening, I wasn't only struggling to understand myself, I also wanted to get to know these two strangers who had a different version of my life story. Right away, Muhammad the Glass-Hearted said, "What really matters is that the glass pomegranates are not lost. Nothing matters as much as them." It turned out they didn't know anything about me.

I'd never had any desire to look for secrets and such bullshit, and I didn't like getting to know people. People couldn't be trusted; I was suspicious of everyone. I'm just the same today. I don't buy what you say on your tape, that people are beautiful and good, or the other bullshit you said.

But the three of us immediately became friends. We agreed on names that very first evening. He was to be "Saryas the Great," and I would be "Saryas Junior," even though I was both bigger and taller than him. That day when I started crying, neither of them could believe the surly monster with such a stern expression was weeping so passionately. I cried twice that evening, first when I felt my life was so ugly I couldn't recount it truthfully. And again when Saryas the Great talked about his own childhood, growing up on the borders alongside the dung of the smugglers' mules. He talked about the nights of hunger when he was forced to beg for food at people's doors. I cried twice that night and Saryas comforted me each time.

If I hadn't, perhaps they wouldn't have called me Saryas Junior or "birdbrain." They both knew I still had some growing up to do. All three of us seemed to be around the same age, but I was less mature. They wanted to make an adult, a noble human, out of me, but they just couldn't.

I will remember the first time I saw the last pomegranate tree in the world until the day I die. Something always drew them to it. I can't describe it to you. It was a strange tree, not just the tree of our friendship and peace, but of our vision and dreams as well. Nadim-i Shazada's long journeys were inspired there; Muhammad the Glass-Hearted grasped some of the secrets there; Saryas the Great thought about a thousand things there.

He'd lie down under the last pomegranate tree in the world and say, "I'm thinking about things." None of us knew what these "things" were. When we returned from the pomegranate summit, Saryas would be talking and laughing nonstop. And some of his words were real gems. I remember now, Muzafar-i Subhdam, that he foresaw your return while lying under the last pomegranate tree in the world. One evening we were both gazing up at the sky, and he said, "One day a man will come from the desert. A very remote desert. A man without kin who doesn't know what to do or where to go. He will embrace us and say: 'I am your father. The father of you all.'"

Blind Nadim-i Shazada, who couldn't see this world's bullshit, would say, "Whatever we say under the last pomegranate tree in the world doesn't belong to you or to me or to anyone at all. The words we speak are God's words." He believed God would appear in his father's guise, bringing him inspiration and telling him to do this rather than that. They all three expected to receive a divine message beneath that tree, inspiration of some sort that would change their lives, although their imagination never ventured beyond the boundaries of their ordinary existence.

It was under that tree that Saryas decided to buy Kazhal's Chest. But hold on. Muzafar, do you even know what Kazhal's Chest is? It's the small cart that he pushed around the bazaar. It was also there that he decided to set up the Council of the Carts, to fight on behalf of all the young and deprived street vendors, to avoid party politics, and oppose all sides involved in the civil war. He drafted a document appealing to all the vendors not to increase their prices during tough times. He wrote to them all, advising them to boycott large-scale traders who did raise their prices. He told the milk vendors to set aside one can of milk of every fifty sold for the babies of displaced families. He established a cashbox to support street vendors who suffered sudden serious losses. He was also preoccupied with the idea of creating a syndicate for the street vendors and setting up an evening school for people forced out of education by poverty. I don't know, all sorts of things. He got the inspiration for all these and thousands of other things right there. He used to say, "Well, birdbrain, these are things you can't easily understand."

We always visited the last pomegranate tree in the world together. We would only be allowed to go alone if we were dying. Nadim-i Shazada couldn't get there without us because of his blindness and the tough mountainous terrain, and the rest of us agreed not to do so either. Visiting the tree strengthened our relationship. Nadim said it was a divine tree, then I'd pluck up the courage to add, "It's the tree of our earthly ambitions." They would all applaud me then, because I rarely said lovely things, I mainly talked bullshit.

Nadim dreamed about his father under that tree. When he woke up, he would tell us long stories of his father's journeys in the afterlife. He would get up and head towards strange places, returning with a number of bizarre words and stories about fantastical journeys in wonderful cities. None of us knew if they were real or not. Their names astonished us all – Lahore, Zanzibar, Yazd, Kerman, and Herat – and dozens of others that I've forgotten.

Nadim went looking for his sight all over the world. On one of those long journeys through the mountains of Kurdistan, deep in a remote area buried between the peaks, he became acquainted with Sayyid Jalal Shams beside a spring in a small village. This man holds an important part of the mystery of the Saryases.

Oh, I know you still don't know their full story. I don't want to hurt you. I don't want you to take to the mountains, but the Saryases don't end with Saryas the Great and me. Nadim-i Shazada knows everything. Absolutely everything. He can take you to Sayyid Jalal Shams, and he might help you.

Although I have forgotten much of life's bullshit, the last pomegranate tree in the world will stay with me forever. It was a spring evening when they first took me there. Nadim and I were the guests of Muhammad the Glass-Hearted and Saryas. They were able to buy the freshest fruits and best cuts of meat in the bazaar. They took a lot of pride in being well acquainted with the bazaar's best butchers and grocers.

When I arrived at that magical summit, however, I forgot everything. From there, the heavens and the earth were completely different. It was a place closer to dream than to truth. Do you know what I mean? After seeing it myself, I couldn't speak for a long time. As a bandit and mercenary, I had spent a great deal of time in the mountains, the boundless plains, and the natural world in general, but the beauty of that place took my breath away.

Muhammad the Glass-Hearted put his arms around me and said, "Subhdam Junior, do you know why this place astonishes people so much?"

"No," I said, "I don't. Believe me, I don't. All I know is that I am astonished. My mind doesn't work as well as yours."

The Glass-Hearted thought a little, lifted his head, and said, "It's because here we have a sense that life could be different. The last pomegranate tree tells us so, that we could live in a bright, transparent world. The tree is endlessly inspiring." He rose to his feet and, as if trying to reach someone far away, called out, "Inspiration! Inspiration! Inspiration!"

Saryas the Great was busy under the tree, chopping tomatoes, making tzatziki, dicing meat. Every now and then he would interrupt our conversation, hold up the meat, and announce, "Look, what a lovely piece of meat."

Nadim declared, "This is my tree, the tree of Nasim-i Shazada, whose father was a champion many times over at the Houses of Strength of the Pahlavis. The king of Iran gave him the title "prince," Shazada, and so my name is a gift from the Iranian king. He gave our whole family its name. It's said that since that day our crops have never been blighted by drought and our livestock have produced three times as much milk as any others."

I interrupted him. You had to on a regular basis, to prevent him blabbering away until he fell asleep. I said, "You cursed Blind Man, I don't have the energy to listen to your bullshit. But this guy's words make me happy."

Nadim-i Shazada was a thick-skinned boy. I don't remember him ever being upset with anyone, unlike Muhammad the Glass-Hearted, whose delicate nature drove me to distraction. Muhammad put his arms around Nadim and said, "Nadim is right. It is the tree of the princes – but it's not only your tree, Nadim. It belongs to all of us. Because when a father plants a tree, he doesn't plant it just for his own son. A real father plants for all the children in the world, for all those who come after him. And Nasim the Prince knew that you wouldn't reach this summit on your own, that someone else would have to lead you by the hand. And he would have known that whoever that was had a wish in their heart too. What mattered to Nasim-i Shazada was that someone would always take your hand. He planted the tree here so we would hold each other's hands and make the journeys easier for each other. He planted the tree for all of us. That's why I am telling you that this is the tree of inspiration, because only this tree could inspire us all to form an honest brotherhood."

The civil war hadn't even started yet, but like a fortune teller, he said, "Now is the end of the age of brotherhood. May all evil deeds come my way and may you be safe. Peace and all that stuff is a lie. We must truly become each other's brothers. This tree must be our witness. We must swear to support each other forever, to not let the war drive us apart—an oath that neither time nor place can undermine. Because soon we will live in an era when brothers will mangle each other like rabid dogs."

That night, the four of us drafted a pledge and signed it in blood: to be friends and brothers forever, to support each other until death, to hold each other's hands when times were tough, in war and times of hardship. God, he talked so beautifully about death. I had spent so many years at war and among fighters, people constantly close to death, yet I had never heard anyone talk about it, the sheer amazement of it, more beautifully.

Back then, we were all still young. We didn't know what would become of us. Today, in this dark hole of a prison, I tell you, Muzafar-i Subhdam, that tree was the world's last tree of brotherhood. And no, it's not bullshit. All my life has been bullshit except that tree, which will always be the most beautiful and sacred thing in my life. At that time, I didn't understand the profound meanings of the pledge that I signed with my three eternal brothers, placed inside a silver canister, and handed over to the earth under the tree for safekeeping.

On the day the civil war started, I entered Buraq equipped with all my military gear, feeling like the last lion of India, the last man standing. I still smelled of gunpowder from firing rocket-propelled grenades. In Buraq, I told all my stories of the war and even spiced them up. The Glass-Hearted looked at me with a degree of disappointment that I'll never forget. One night when we were drinking beer at the small bar, he said, "You broke our pledge. You have no regard for it at all. I mean it. If we want to be brothers, we must act as brothers to everyone else and not hurt anyone." It was the first time I had seen him so angry and dejected. I didn't know what I'd done at that point. Muhammad insisted, "How can someone who signs a pact of brotherhood go off to war? How can he hurt people he doesn't even know? On whose command does he act that way? The leaders'? Well, the leaders don't know what brotherhood is."

Stung by his words, I left the Party and returned my gun the next morning. In the first days of the civil war, when everyone was praying for it to end, we would often go to the last pomegranate tree and reflect on our lives. Back then, Saryas and I would put down the glass pomegranates and look at them. We would pick them up and say, "God, the lord of the earth and the heavens, for the sake of these beautiful pomegranates, end this civil war." A prayer that I now understand was an absurd wish but a great one.

TAPE #4

I renounced Saryas after he got to know the sisters in white. One evening, he put an arm around my neck and said, "I've signed a pact of brotherhood with those two girls." I went crazy. I hated the sisters in white, and the truths that I later discovered about Muhammad's death did nothing to change that. I saw them one summer night in the square where some of the street vendors slept. I was on my way to have a word with Saryas when I heard a lovely song in the distance. I saw the cart vendors sitting cross-legged on the floor, mesmerized. The sisters in white were sitting on a tea-house table, singing. When they finished, they slowly got to their feet and, their gazes cold, told the Professor of our Dark Nights to walk them home. The Marshal, diffident and respectful, like a brother with his sisters, said, "By my eyes, I'll take you right away."

I had gone there that night with a lot to say. "Don't go," I pleaded. "I've got over a thousand stories. What am I saying? A thousand? I have as many as a hundred thousand, new ones. I want to tell you a whole load of amazing stuff." I tried everything to make sure Saryas didn't go off with the sisters and leave me behind.

But he just laughed, "It's not the last night in the world, Saryas. Tell me another time."

It was the last night of our friendship. I didn't talk to him the following day. He came over quite a few times, embraced me and kissed me, but I said nothing. To be honest, I wanted to kill him, to put an end to the whole story, and to become the one remaining Saryas on earth. Back then, Nadim-i Shazada still hadn't returned so I knew nothing about him finding more clues in the mountains. It would be a long time before he came back, long after the deaths of Saryas and the Glass-Hearted, and by then what he'd learned would all be in vain.

In the meantime, Nadim interrupted his long journey east, when he should have been crossing the border in a Toyota pickup with some acquaintances, in order to tell us something after meeting Sayyid Jalal Shams. He scoured the city, trying but failing to find Saryas and me. Instead, he proudly told the whole story of the Saryases to Muhammad the Glass-Hearted.

A day before the floods, singing and playing with his keys, Muhammad set out to see the Professor of our Dark Nights, oblivious to the sudden death that lay in wait for him, the happiest man alive. Without divulging a thing, he asked to borrow the glass pomegranate for a day and said, "I'm about to uncover a deep secret. I'm not telling you anything until I'm sure." He was so happy, in such a good mood when he left, that the Marshal was quite taken aback. It was the last time they saw each other. When the Glass-Hearted set out the next evening, he was due to meet an antique dealer. That meeting would never take place.

Oh, what can I tell you, Muzafar-i Subhdam? I can't be of much help to you from here, from the dark night of this prison. Once I knew everything, I lost all desire to reflect on it. I cursed my name. After a very long time, Nadim-i Shazada returned. He found me on duty in a front-line trench. I told him, "I'm done with all that. I've erased it from my memory. I'll piss on you, the last pomegranate tree in the world, and the whole story too. My name's not Saryas-i Subhdam. I have no name. Look, I live only for the rifle on my shoulder. Go away, don't get me mixed up in all this bullshit. Go on, before I piss in your blind eyes. Get lost, and don't ever come and see me again."

Nadim knows everything. He can help you. He can.

Sometimes I have to turn off the recorder and cry, Muzafar-i Subhdam.

It was eleven in the morning when they told me Saryas-i Subhdam had died. I hadn't spoken to him for two months at the time.

There's a small tea-house in the middle of the square that's frequented by people who enjoy sitting out in the fall sunshine. I'm one of them. I remember a commotion starting up in the bazaar. I was sitting on a small chair on a balcony, eating ice cream after ice cream, completely carefree. I'd taken my jacket off as I watched the kerfuffle among the street vendors. When the shooting started, I was laughing at what I could see. By the time hundreds of vendors abandoned their carts and headed north towards the gunfire, I was tired and fed up so I left the balcony, leaving the uproar behind, and walked down to a video shop that played porn films. I stayed there, watching these films, till late in the evening. When I stepped out into the night, I understood that something terrible had happened. I reached for the glass pomegranate in my pocket and felt blood on it. I'm certain that's what it was. I looked at my hand in the starlight: it was covered in blood. The pomegranate was bloody too. When I went into the light, I could see nothing of the kind. But in the dark, it was as if my whole body were covered in blood.

By the time I was back in my room, I had the strange feeling that I was absolutely drenched in blood. There was no one else in my room. All that night, I was killed and brought back to life, losing blood and repeatedly being startled awake. I would turn the light on, look at my body, then go back to sleep. I left the house early in the morning, as if I were running away from the bloody nightmares. I left the glass pomegranate at home because I still felt as if it were oozing blood.

I bought a glass of Ayran from a vendor and asked him, "Why isn't it chilled?" He said, "We've only just started. We've been at the Marshal's grave since early morning. All the bazaar folk were there. He was killed by the police yesterday." I dropped my glass, just as I had dropped the kettle when I heard Muhammad the Glass-Hearted was dead. I didn't believe the Ayran seller at first, but all the others told me the story from the beginning.

I just kept saying, "It can't be true. It just can't." I asked the entire bazaar, the cigarette vendors, the milk vendors, the mirror vendors, the fishmongers. All of them told me the same story, down to the very last detail. They showed me the spot where he died, showed me his blood, which still hadn't been cleaned up. They had all known the Marshal, and they wept for him. Although they didn't know me, they hugged and kissed me in an attempt to soothe their own grief. I kept saying, "It's a lie, a lie. You're liars, all of you."

When I wanted to leave, someone took my hands and said, "Let me take you to the mosque where a service is being held for him." I didn't believe in funeral services and such things. I didn't believe the whole thing about sitting on cold chairs for two days, drinking water and what have you, and then moving on to someone's house where they'd eat apples and call it a service. It was all bullshit to me. What I did believe in was real crying, covering your body with mud, wounding and beating yourself.

That day, I went into an empty alleyway and burst out crying. Or rather, I didn't cry at first, I banged my head against the wall. I hit the stone wall of the house with all my strength until I really was drenched in blood, saying, "Why is it that a miserable guy like me doesn't die, but you do? Why doesn't a pathetic guy like me get killed, but you do?" I managed to walk home despite the pain, yelling like a madman as I went. I hit my head against any tree, any wall I came across. I put my hand in the dust of the alleyways and threw it into my face. I shouted, telling myself, "Saryas, you're the only one left. You son of a bitch, you've been left all alone. As if none of it ever happened. None of it at all." At home, I took the glass pomegranate and slammed it against the walls, tried to crush it with my feet, but it wouldn't break. It was the end of everything, the last day of my life. When Saryas-i Subhdam died, so did I.

Nadim-i Shazada came to me three times after that, and I kept chasing him away. But he just kept coming back, telling me part of the story each time. He always showed up when I was on duty. There I would be, at my post, guarding the night, the rain, and the wind, and the blind boy would show up with that damned stick of his. "Saryas," he said, "don't send me away. I have a big secret. It'll help you understand everything. You and I must solve the mystery they failed to clear up."

I hated him. I no longer wanted anyone to remind me of the past. One dark and rainy night, he came back with a big umbrella. "You blind bastard!" I said. "Why can't you leave me alone? Can't you see I'm on duty? Well? What do you fucking want? Why can't you leave me alone?"

"Saryas, birdbrain, you know absolutely nothing," he shouted. "You're not alone. There are others as well as the Marshal, other Saryases. Other stories. Other secrets. Who do you think you are? Do you think there's only you out there, that this story ends with the death of the Marshal? It's up to you – you can take your secret with you to the grave if you like. I don't care, go right on living like a mangy dog. You can rub your nose against the ass of a dog till your dying day, but all the same, I know there's a secret that has to be revealed to you. Not for your sake but for the two boys who wanted to make a man of you. For the sake of the two angels who will tell the boys who died young that Nadim-i Shazada hasn't given up on them. The man who knows the secrets wants proof which I don't have, but you do. Do you understand? Now can you see why I'm shouting like this in the rain?"

It was pouring so heavily we could hardly hear each other.

"You blind bastard! Don't come anywhere near me, or I'll shoot you. Do you hear? I don't care about anything, not my life or anyone else's. You blind devil, I piss on your angels. You don't have any angels; all you have are dogs. My name isn't Saryas anymore. Go and ask the devil to give you that proof. Ask your father's precious angels. Just leave me alone."

That night I sent him away many times only for him to return soon after, and all the while, the rain was getting worse. Each time he returned, he told me a fragment of the story. Good Lord, in the end I went crazy and started firing shots over his head. He took to his heels, I chased after him, and he fell in the mud. He got back on his feet and swore at me, and I shot at the night, at the air, at my own past. Like a madman, I cocked the rifle and continued to shoot, yelling after him: "Leave me alone, you son of a bitch. I told you to leave me alone!" He ran away and I sat in the mud and the pouring rain, weeping like a helpless orphan.

After Saryas's death, I went back to the last pomegranate tree in the world one final time. I stood on the summit, as if bidding farewell to the days when I'd had such dependable friends. I lifted the glass pomegranate and threw it from the peak with all my might. It's lying somewhere out there now, in some rocky valley no one can reach. I didn't understand what the pomegranate meant: my existence, my origins, my youth, and the pact I'd signed with my brothers.

With them dead, I felt as though the devil inside me had been liberated, that I wanted only to destroy myself and everything else. Their deaths drove me back to the war. My entire life was inside that glass pomegranate, and I had tossed it away with all my might and headed back into hell.

You know that there's plenty of time to think about things in solitary confinement. I think we both speak so sadly because we learned how to think in prison. I certainly have, Muzafar-i Subhdam. Everything I'd thought about before that was bullshit. When I returned from the last pomegranate tree in the world, I felt there was nowhere left for me on earth. I smashed all the mirrors in my room, gathered up all my photos, and burned them. The only one I couldn't bring myself to burn was the one of the crying child standing between the legs of the laughing dictator. It had been printed tens of thousands of times. I haven't looked at my face since that day. Listen to me, Muzafar-i Subhdam; anyone who doesn't look at their own face is dangerous. From the evening I tossed away my soul beneath the last pomegranate tree in the world, I could no longer contemplate the person known as Saryas-i Subhdam. Saryas-i Subhdam was a lie in every respect, not a human being, but an illusion created in those dark times. I had no way out. I took myself back to the one path that I knew I couldn't avoid.

Unshaven and unwashed, I returned to my old military base. As always, I was returning to the bosom of the Party with no money in my pocket and no food in my stomach. At that point, the civil war consisted of one wave of clashes after another. Fighting would flare up then go quiet over and over again. When I rejoined the fighting, there was a devilish aggression in my soul. Like every hopeless loser on earth, I wanted the world and all its gods destroyed. All that mattered to me was having the chance to shoot at the world from somewhere. I didn't know why I was fighting or for whom, who I was killing or who was trying to kill me. But none of it mattered.

I became absorbed in these bloody clashes. I rarely went to the city, keeping to the mountains, military posts, and front lines. I bowed to the officials and enjoyed the process of becoming a cruel servant. Like a dervish's, my beard grew longer and longer. Whether there was fighting or not, I was always in a state of alert. I wore full military gear for weeks on end, my fellow fighters sleeping as I kept watch on their behalf. Like a madman, I sat in the dark, listening to the sound of the wind and the whispers of wakeful night creatures. Even when there was a truce, I stayed with the units that lived in the mountains and caves, waiting for another bout of fighting.

I had become hideous, just like the wars I fought. I couldn't not become a servant of the war, of the officials who fed me and gave me orders: "Shoot, Saryas-i Subhdam. Shoot, you son of a bitch. Shoot, you motherfucker." My leaders loved me; they loved anyone who protected them like a guard dog. I was always way out in front in every battle. Whenever they wanted to take an inaccessible peak and couldn't find any volunteers, I was the first to go forward and say, "Send me." They called me "the tank."

Periods of truce were the unhappiest days of my life. All I did then was clean my gun twice over and sleep. When the other Peshmergas played the Kamkars' music, I would go off somewhere else. Anything related to the beautiful days of the past tormented me. If I could still hear the Kamkars, I would attach a seventy-five-round-magazine to my weapon and shoot at the sky. I would take a rocket-propelled grenade and fire it at the tired valleys and mountains. I wanted to do something to kill the memories. One evening, I was sitting on a rock on a high peak, when a Peshmerga called

to me, "Saryas-i Subhdam, the Kamkars are in town. They're actually here."
He called to me so loudly that his voice echoed through the mountains and
valleys. He knew my only wish had been to see them perform live. On the
night of their concert, I went to a valley, took out my pistol, and fired a shot
at my head. Don't worry. Don't worry. I didn't die. It was the biggest load
of bullshit. The bullet just scratched my forehead; it left a long scar, but it
didn't kill me.

Because I was injured, my commander had a special task for me. I was
to deliver a letter to a prostitute in the city for him. There were murmurs
that the fighting might resume, so he couldn't go down to the city himself,
and he couldn't find anyone more tight-lipped than me. At first he said
the letter was for his sister; then he paused for a bit and said, "No, it's not
actually. It's for a prostitute. She's driving me crazy – I'm mad about her."

I delivered the letter. The prostitute was a very beautiful, delicate
woman who worked in a tidy government office. She was so beautiful I
almost embraced life again. I nearly went down on my knees and asked her
to marry me. But when I gave her the letter, she said, clearly disgusted, "Not
that moron. I was hoping it might be a letter from Ihsan. But it's that fool.
And you, you ugly man with your big head, damn you for bringing it. Some
gift! Come back in an hour for my answer."

During that hour, I went to the bazaar and witnessed the end of the
army of the carts. It was the day that hundreds of policemen seized and
destroyed them. Countless broken carts lay in the streets and alleyways
and outside the main gates of some of the shopping centers and qaysaris.
When I arrived, the carnage had come to its conclusion. I stood in a sea of
wreckage, broken cartons and boxes scattered all over the streets. There

was something of the end of a war in the air. Here and there, the blood of street vendors spilled over fruit, fish, cigarettes, and Iranian shampoos. I saw police officers hosing down and beating vendors as they loaded them onto a green pickup. Like someone looking for the body of a friend on a vast battlefield, I went past the wreckage of the carts until I reached the spot where the Professor of our Dark Nights used to park his own. There, in that very place, I found bits of Kazhal's Chest, once the most beautiful cart in the world, now smashed to pieces. After Saryas's death, a young man took it over and sold Turkish and Persian cassettes in the same spot. A blue necklace sparkled on the front. I wanted to reach out and take it but didn't dare. I didn't have the courage to open the gates to all those memories. Instead, I stood there and burst into tears. The destruction of Kazhal's Chest marked the end of an era that no one talks about today except me. It was the beginning of the end of all the beauty in the world.

TAPE #5

I was the last to abandon the front-line trenches in every battle. Amid the whistle of the hand grenades, the dust of mortar shells, and the smoke from rocket launchers, I would scream so loudly my throat bled and the enemy could hear me. "Don't leaaaaaave the trenches, any of you!" Just as I was once known as the youngest mercenary in the country, after the uprising I became famous for fighting on every front of the civil war. Thinking back now, it's as though I was fighting in lots of different areas at once: one location in the morning, another in the evening, another again at night. Some people thought I was the bravest person in the country because I was always the last to clear the field. I decided that I wouldn't take my boots, backpack, or belt off until the war was over. Even when the commanders ordered a retreat, I would sometimes refuse to withdraw, keeping up my incessant cry of "Don't leaaaaaave the trenches, any of you!" But nobody understood why.

Muzafar-i Subhdam, no two things in this world are as closely linked as bravery and hopelessness. Do you understand? A brave person is without hope since hope makes cowards of us all. Why was I the last to abandon the trenches? Because I was the most hopeless person in the world. All my friends had dreams of their own: they were engaged, wanted to emigrate, or longed to become senior officials. I was the only one who had no dreams at all. Throughout the mountains of Kurdistan, wherever a gun was fired in battle, I was there, long beard, backpack, devilish gaze, and all. I carried a Kalashnikov, a rocket-propelled grenade, and like a devil escaped from hell, I would seek out the highest spot. Baring my chest to the wind and my own rage, I would roar so that my whole body trembled, "Don't leaaaaaave the trenches, any of you!" I'd pop up with a hand grenade and attack the enemy, screaming across minefields, jumping barbed wire as if it were childish non-sense. Among rattling machine guns, I would run through the hissing rain of bullets towards the enemy line and yell everything I had suppressed for so long. In the middle of bloody fields of battle and the firing of thousands of weapons, I would shout out, "Muhammad the Glass-Hearted, where are you? Marshal, where are you? Why can't I reach you?"

Our force was one of those that took no prisoners. There were twenty of us, a strapping lot with long beards and so on. We were up to our necks in the war. Our commander was the kind of guy who couldn't manage without women and alcohol. He was called Kareem-i Shirin, although not even the devil could have said how he came by a name that meant "sweet." There were hundreds of stories about it: that he'd worked at Gulala Sweet Store; that as a young man he had fallen for a prostitute called Shirin; that he would reply, "sweet, very sweet," when asked about the taste of a woman who had once entered his life. Lord, I've never seen anyone cry for women like that at night. It would start as soon as the trenches fell silent. He wasn't married, but he knew a woman in every nook and cranny of the country. If there was no fighting, I would lean against a rock or tree, sipping tea, my rucksack still on my back, and he would talk to me about the prostitutes who had been most important in his life. "Sanarya!" he would say. "Oh, Saryas-i Subhdam, you have no idea what she did to me. She devoured my soul. By the time I finally slept with her, I had lost my soul seven times over. Her sister, Kanaria, was even more beautiful. They didn't look alike, but just one glance and Kanaria was in your lap. But she didn't taste as good as Sanarya. Or Naghada. She was the wife of a goldsmith; she wanted for nothing. When her husband fell asleep at night, we would go at it in the backyard. I've never seen anyone so horny, not even in a film. She wore a perfume that her sister sent her from Austria; it would drive anyone wild. And Bafrin, the darkest skinned woman I've ever met. Don't be fooled by her name; she wasn't white or fair or anything like it. She had the finest ass I've seen, it smelled of petunia." The way he told the stories, no one doubted their truth.

He would tell us not to hold onto any prisoners of war: that was something the forces behind us, "the blind mice," would do. Initially, we used to take the occasional POW, until one day Kareem-i Shirin was summoned to the Party Leader and didn't return until late in the night. Rumor had it that the Leader wanted to teach him a lesson about his relationship with prostitutes, but that turned out to be complete bullshit: he had been sent for to receive great honors and to be rewarded for his so-called bravery. When he came back, he sat drinking tea until midnight and talked about how he had dined with the Leader, how they'd shaken hands, how the Leader had laughed. After that meeting, he ordered us not to take POWs under any circumstances. Some Peshmergas were afraid to kill the prisoners. I don't know when during the civil war the practice of killing POWs began, but every side did it. They all also kept a few alive to be proudly exchanged if a peace treaty was signed.

Unbeknownst to us, there were rules for killing POWs during the civil war, Muzafar-i Subhdam. You had to know about the prisoner: he couldn't be from an aristocratic or agha family; he couldn't be the son of a senior politician or have the backing of influential people who could easily avenge his death. Kareem-i Shirin either didn't know those rules or just ignored them. He would sigh for his prostitutes and order us to put the POWs to death.

Once, we captured a POW we really shouldn't have killed – a twelve-year-old boy whose father had brought him along to show him the trenches. He was the son of a close relative of our enemy's leader – one of the smartest, most delicate, and most beloved children in his family. One of those who would go on to head the Party's offices in Italistan, Francistan, Pig-stan, Camel-stan and other countries whose names I don't even know. He was incredibly polite, the epitome of good manners. When we took him into custody, he didn't think we'd kill him. It was all a game to him.

I told Kareem-i Shirin to let him go. "Send him back to his mother. He's no good for killing. Let him have his milk and chocolate at home."

Kareem-i Shirin was in a bad mood that day. He said, "I'll kill him if he's the son of Almighty God himself. He won't escape my clutches even if he's first cousin to Jesus Christ."

I pleaded again, "Let him go home and play hide and seek with his sisters. His mother must be waiting to give him a bath. Let him go back to do his homework."

"I never stopped badgering Chilura, whom they called the Virgin Mary of Kurdistan and had turned into such a paragon of virtue that they also called her Rabia al-Adawiyya. I gave her no peace until I slept with her still in full hijab. How can I leave him alone?" He didn't distinguish between killing someone and sleeping with a woman. Bloodshed gave him the same pleasure as a woman's kiss.

I had a terrifying sense that killing the child would lead to disaster. I stood in front of him, with my long beard and rucksack, and said, "If you want to kill him, you'll have to kill me too." I was lying. Deep down, I've always had a ridiculous fear of death. Otherwise, I would have killed myself after the death of Saryas-i Subhdam.

"I won't kill you, my own friend, someone I've shared all my precious memories with," Kareem replied. "But I am going to kill him."

Kareem-i Shirin only ever did what he wanted. He rarely behaved like our commander, but sometimes he could be very stubborn. He was in a terrible mood that day, and there was no persuading him. Samal-i Kunji, who had been a Peshmerga for a long time, talked to him the longest. He knew more than any of us what a grave mistake it was to kill the child. But when he realized that Kareem wasn't listening, he wandered off to sit quietly on a rock and just watched us from there. Later that evening, when we were all busy doing other things, Kareem seized the opportunity and killed the child at dinner. It was a strange scene – never in my life had I seen such a bloodstained tablecloth. The rice was full of blood, the bread soaked in it. The boy slumped, his small head in my lap – blood and tiny bones and all. It was as if he was hugging me.

I stood up and threw the rice away. To Kareem, I said, "You can't even let us eat a meal in peace." It was a stupid thing to say, I know, but I couldn't think of anything else. When I looked at Samal-i Kunji, I knew what he was thinking straightaway. Two hours later, while we were busy wrapping the body in a blanket for burial, Samal disappeared. I climbed up on a rock and announced, "Samal has gone over to the enemy. We've got to get out of here. Immediately."

Kareem-i Shirin, who was also known as the Rommel of the Mountains, had a different idea, a devilish plan. He too was sure Samal had run away to ingratiate himself with the other side, and he knew they would send a large force to attack us that night. Kareem laid an ambush for them close to their own peak. We advanced until we were right under the enemy's nose so that we could strike the moment they left their trenches. I knew nothing about strategy, tactics, or that kind of thing. All I knew was how to spot the enemy and open fire. Around midnight, the enemy's forces came down off their peaks singing the famous song, "It's Raining Again." When they were level with us, I shouted in my hoarse voice, "Get them. Fire!" Even before I stopped yelling some of their poor guys had already met their maker in heaven. Disaster struck when we took eleven of them alive. Knowing that

Kareem-i Shirin would toy with them until they were dead, I wished we had just killed them.

His devilish games were vicious.

We were as tired as dogs that night, our bodies covered in blood, gunpowder, and dust. My beard was soaked in blood. When we reached a pond, I jumped in the water. I remember the others building a fire. As I swam, still carrying my rucksack, the sound of the group making camp and the stray dogs barking in the distance stirred a feeling I hadn't had in a long time: an awareness of the beauty of nature, the beauty of the night, the beauty of life. When I got out of the water, I sat on a rock a little way off. I could hear Kareem-i Shirin beating the POWs. The night air was pleasantly cool, the air clear, the mountains wrapped in starlight and silence – as if nature were trying to show us the futility of fighting. I dried my beard with the sash I wore round my waist and stood still. I think that cool night changed me. Something in my heart had broken when the child was killed.

But it was too late now. Our Peshmergas were sounding the ululation of victory, dancing beside the fire. I could tell Kareem-i Shirin was starting to play his satanic games with the POWs. I was sure he was going to kill them by daybreak, but I didn't know how. I heard him bring out one of the prisoners and tell him, "We'll play a nice game tonight, a really nice game. I'm going to tie your friends to that tree – can you see it? It's not all that far – and you'll be aiming at their foreheads. Only the forehead counts. As long as you keep hitting foreheads, you'll keep the gun, but as soon as you miss, it'll be your turn to be tied to the tree. Understand? Only one of you will make it out alive. I'd like that person to be you."

He was a lanky young man, but I couldn't make him out fully by the light of the fire. My body felt cold from my wet clothes but I didn't want to move closer to the fire. From where I stood, I shouted, "Don't give him the gun. Don't . . . Don't do that." I knew perfectly well that once Kareem was buoyed up by the taste of victory, he would become careless. He laughed out loud and said, "Saryas-i Subhdam, don't you worry. Tonight is our night." It was the last time he ever laughed. I couldn't see clearly. It all happened in an instant. I was bending down to reach my bootlaces when I heard gunfire. Later I was told about the prisoner's lethal rebellion: instead of shooting at his own brothers-in-arms, he shot Kareem-i Shirin and a couple others. It was over in a second. I heard someone shouting near the fire, "They killed Kareem!" Then the sound of multiple rifles being cocked. Gunfire, cries of pain. My hair and beard still wet and my rucksack heavy with water, I went for my gun. Looking back, I saw the prisoners running into the night. The young man opened fire. Our Peshmergas scattered, dropping to the ground, cocking their own guns.

I released the catch and started shooting. I could hear someone crying in the darkness, "They got me! I'm done for." We fired wildly at the prisoners, chased them, and ripped them apart with bullets or daggers. Nobody knew who he was killing. We couldn't see the faces of the prisoners we set upon and beheaded in the grass, on rocky ground, or amid the tiny pebbles on the bank of a stream. I do remember that we kept on thrusting ahead, killing all but two of the prisoners, who escaped under cover of darkness. Our group was so widely scattered that we didn't all arrive back at our base until the early morning.

At the crack of dawn, I came across Kareem-i Shirin's body. You could still see a remnant of his last laugh on his face. I removed his watch and checked his pockets. All they contained was a blue bra – it must have belonged to someone with very small breasts – and a note written in clumsy, girly handwriting: "Dear Kareem, this is for you. In memory of the night in the bathroom." I threw away the bra and the piece of paper.

"I'm in charge till we reach the other forces," I said to the Peshmergas.

We were ordered back to our old position at midday. I tried to get them to understand over the radio that we were in great danger. But they said, "It's an order from the military bureau." I didn't understand such bullshit. I shouted into the radio, "Tell the military bureau to come and put their own asses on the line on this stupid peak. They're trying to get us killed!" I was certain we'd all be wiped out there, and I felt bad, not for myself but for the other youths who had only recently learned to dream.

An hour later, they told us, "If you don't go back to your positions, the Party will execute the lot of you." All the radio operators could hear my harsh and desperate voice as I shouted into the radio, "I piss on the Party."

With tears in my eyes, I said to my fellow Peshmergas, "Listen to me, the Party wants us all to die like dogs out here. Just as we cut off our opponents' heads last night, they'll do the same to us tonight. In this war, no one is more noble than anyone else, understand? You've all seen active combat. One night you attack, the next it's the other side. Tonight they'll kill the lot of you. Listen to me, I'll go back to the peak alone. I stopped caring about anything a long time ago. The Party has decided to create martyrs on this peak and then hold a special service for you forty days later and all that bullshit. I fear death like you all do, if not more, and I don't want any of you to be mowed down up there. Go back to your mothers. If you can afford to leave this war, go away and don't come back. If you have money and can

leave this country, go and never return. If you can find a different job, do it."
I'd never thought like that before, but the events of the past day had been so hideous I was fed up with this miserable life. At that moment I had the words of Saryas the Great on my mind. For the first time, I wanted to be the "great human" he was always talking about.

I was sure all the young men would be beheaded that night. I could already picture their bodies amid the rocks, the grass, and the hot summer dust. The two prisoners who had escaped in the dark knew everything about us, and our enemies in their trenches would have recognized my shrieks. I just wanted to surrender that stupid peak with as little bloodshed as possible.

All the Peshmergas headed out that night, bar two who insisted on dying with me. The three of us sat at our sad post waiting for the enemy. It was a hot night with swarms of mosquitoes everywhere. At around midnight, we sensed them approaching. Oh, yes, it was unmistakably our enemies, arriving heavily armed to avenge their martyrs. First, they pounded us with mortar shells, but we were unfazed. We sat at our machine guns motionless, lying in wait. At roughly one in the morning, they attacked. I had decided to fight my last battle honorably; not one of us left our position until we'd reached our last bullets. About two hours later, we ran out of ammunition. The three of us lay down, our arms around each other's necks, looking up at the stars.

About an hour passed; then Samal-i Kunji, who was now the enemy's guide, yelled at me from the shelter of a nearby rock, "Saryas-i Subhdam, I know you're out of bullets. Surrender. Come down, and I give you my word that they won't kill you." Lord, what an ugly practice of this country it was to say to prisoners, "I give you my word. We won't touch you."

I suggested to the others that we sing a Kamkars song. I hadn't done that in ages. I'd given all that up since Saryas-i Subhdam died. So the three of us sang one of their songs, and when the enemy arrived, we kept on singing. As they led us away, they put their arms around me and informed me that I was a special case. They gave me a can of Coke and I drank it happily, laughing even. They took my two friends over to a nearby rock and shot them. Everything was happening so fast.

Those were the last shots I heard in the battlefield. They weren't cold, cruel, and horrific like the others: they sounded like the singing of a wounded partridge. "Saryas-i Subhdam," they said, "you'll be dealt with differently. You're a special case." At that point, I knew they weren't going to kill me. They were keeping me for something harder to endure than death.

When they took my rucksack away, removed my army belt, sash, and shoes, I understood that, for me, the war was over for good. Obviously, war goes on in all sorts of ways, Muzafar-i Subhdam. Those who have experienced nothing but fighting in the trenches, with its shrieks and its escapes under showers of bullets, know nothing about the other types of warfare, which are even dirtier and more underhanded. Let me tell you, the wars of intelligent men are a thousand times dirtier than the fighting of wild, untamed men like ourselves. I'm telling you this so that you can take precautions.

They took me to a TV station to talk about my war secrets. I had never been on camera before in my life. All the same, they brought along a full film crew. I told everything I knew to the cameras. I gave details of the fighting, from the prisoners we'd killed to the sad prostitutes of Kareem-i Shirin. I told them everything coldly, just as I'm telling you now – absolutely everything: all the jokes and the bullshit; all the conversations I'd heard; the exchanges I'd witnessed at the guest house of Kaikhusraw Agha-i Sufian Agha-i Sadr Arhamai; the jokes told by the laborers in Buraq; the story of the Professor of our Dark Nights; the death of Muhammad the Glass-Hearted.

The journalist interviewing me was the type who made you wonder if he slept in his suit and tie. He was a sweet guy though. He told me to talk as I liked, they'd cut it later. Every time he used the word, I'd scratch my beard and ask him what it meant. He said it meant cutting out irrelevant comments, connecting the sections so there were no breaks or interruptions. So I told the whole story of my life. Sometimes he seemed to think I was mad. He kept asking me the same two questions. I'd be talking about the last pomegranate tree in the world, and he would ask, "But how were you linked to the mercenaries and traitors at that time?"

I would reply that I had no links. What links was he talking about? At the time, I was the Marshal's, the Professor of our Dark Nights' friend. What did the last pomegranate tree in the world have to do with mercenaries, traitors, and such bullshit?

The interviewer hadn't heard these names – the Marshal, the Professor of our Dark Nights – but he continued unperturbed, "And as far as you know, were they receiving weapons from the central government at the time?"

"No, at that time they were receiving potatoes, tomatoes, and stuff like that from the government. Saryas the Great got them at the wholesale fruit market in the morning and then sold them on."

No matter what I said, he signaled that I should keep going. "Don't worry," he'd say, "We'll edit it later." We took a tea break at the end of each tape. During the breaks, the whole crew would come over and kiss me, saying, "What you're saying is an important document for the Party. It will break the backs of those traitors."

I would scratch my beard and say, "What do you mean, a document?"

"Evidence," they'd reply, "so that if the mercenaries on the other side say they haven't done such things, we can present this and say: 'Look, this is what your own fighter says.' We'll pass the film on to everyone – the world outside, our neighboring countries, the UN, honorable presidents, international courts, the Islamic Conference, the Vatican."

When I was a child, the picture of me between the president's knees spread everywhere. And now these pictures too would be distributed around the world. To be honest, I didn't like recounting all that bullshit, and I didn't want it to be seen by all the mullahs and the Pope. Once I knew that the films would be shared with people much more important than you and me, I focused more on describing the battles. I relayed everything I knew about the savagery of war. Again and again, I turned to the interviewer and said, "We weren't the only ones doing this stuff. You lot were no better. In this war, no one is any more honorable than anyone else." I wanted to say something that would leave people horrified, even ashamed, of the war.

Later, I said to the young man, "When you show the interview, let me know so that I can watch it." That was clearly pointless. There was no more tea or Coke after the interview. That same night, they took me to a small prison. I was blindfolded, my hands tied, and the next night, they brought me here to this fortress, dark and quiet and remote.

I haven't seen anyone except the guards since. I don't know if the interviews I recorded have been broadcast or whether anyone has heard me speak about the deaths of Saryas and Muhammad the Glass-Hearted. It doesn't matter; I can't go back to my past life. If I am released one day, I'll go to another country, marry there, and change my name.

If I'm released, I'll make sure you can't find me. You think you'd put your arm around me and say, "Oh Saryas, my dear, my sweet son," or I'd put my arm around your neck and say, "Oh my dear father." I'd die of embarrassment and disgust. I think both our lives are too hideous for such a loving gesture. Isn't that so, Muzafar-i Subhdam? Both our lives are too ugly to be able to stand such love.

17

Saryas-i Subhdam and I exchanged tapes for a good long time. I sent my last one from Patras. There was a great deal of sadness, sarcasm, intelligence, and also naïveté in the boy's voice. Not even once did he ask what was going on in the outside world. In his dark and narrow prison, he had lost all interest in it and lived only in his own memories. I am sure that if he's ever released, he'll choose to live somewhere remote, somewhere his memories are his only connection with his previous life.

From his tapes I could tell there was yet another Saryas, as well as other people I knew nothing about. This gave me terrible anxiety and a restlessness even greater than I'd experienced during my search for the Second Saryas's shadow. At night I wondered, "Oh God, what is this strange world I've ended up in, where people are broken and fragmented, each one landing somewhere that can't be seen from anywhere else?"

On all the tapes, he kept saying, "Go and find Nadim-i Shazada. He knows the answer to the secrets." I looked for him everywhere and turned every corner upside down, but to no avail. It was as if Nadim was a mere fantasy, a fog produced by a story, which thinned and then dispersed. Finally, we learned that Nadim was away on a long trip and no one had seen him in months. I never did manage to meet him, and I know that leaving Kurdistan without doing so meant that a lot stayed hidden from me. A dark hand held me back from all the sources that could shine a light onto those bleak days in the children's lives. So, my friends, I had to choose a different route.

I needed to see Sayyid Jalal Shams.

When I first heard that name on Saryas's tapes, it sounded familiar, as if I'd heard it before, but it had then been burned in the hell of my memories. The name meant something to me but I didn't know what. Like anyone who ever needs to search through the debris of their memories, through the ashes of an era they once needed to un-remember, I had to peer into the furthest and darkest reaches of my mind.

Sometimes when Ikram-i Kew visited, he listened to the tapes with me. At other times he would disappear and I wouldn't see him again for many days. When he'd step through the door again, he'd resemble an angel commander, an archangel. Calm and quiet, he seemed like the chief of angels, the keeper of many people's conduct records, although his shyness and silence meant he went unrecognized in this hectic world. One of my greatest regrets is that I didn't see enough of Ikram-i Kew. When I finally left the country and we hugged each other farewell, I cried loudly while he wept with all the serenity of an angel.

"Where have you been, Ikram-i Kew," I often asked him. "Why don't you come to see me here more often?"

Almost ashamed, he would reply, "This country is full of vulnerable people, who can't treat their wounds alone. And no, of course, I can't do anything for them, but I feel that I should go and offer to help, even if only with a few words or a small gesture of support. I go to grieving mothers and sisters, bow to them, and ask them to accept me in place of their sons and brothers who have been killed. I have to be out there, in that jungle, waiting to see what wounded bird lands near me and requires my healing. I'm sorry. If there weren't so much misery, I'd be with you all the time."

One night, when we were listening to the tapes, I asked him if he knew Sayyid Jalal Shams.

"Of course. There isn't anyone who doesn't know him."

He reminded me who Shams was: a tribal leader and a walking contradiction. I had seen him once at the start of the armed revolution but then I'd forgotten him. He was one of those aghas who was everyone's friend, and he was also close to Yaqub-i Snawbar. In those early days of the revolution, when Yaqub was ill, he was cared for at Shams's house. He was well known from one end of the country to the other. The president, king, prince, and the main tribal leaders of the region all trusted him completely.

Sayyid Jalal Shams was living on a big farm in the mountains, away from the hubbub and sadness of the world. I found him reading in an extraordinary chair like a king's throne in a peaceful green meadow. A white-bearded old man, he was waited upon by an eighteen-year-old girl dressed as a palace cupbearer from an ancient court. In front of him sat a desk covered in books, papers, and large inkpots. A branching vine surrounded him, sagging with dozens of bunches of grapes.

He brought to mind the ancient poets, the likes of Khayyam and Ferdowsi, images of whom, surrounded by their mistresses, adorned the covers of their books. On the desk were a lamp with a painted butterfly and a jug of wine. I later found out that the young woman serving him was his most recent wife. He had married dozens of times.

I stood in the middle of his vineyard and said, "Sayyid Jalal Shams, I am Muzafar-i Subhdam, a confused man who has no one to seek help from but you."

He raised his head from his book, looked at me, and stood up. "So you are Muzafar-i Subhdam, are you?"

"Sir, guide me. I am the most confused man in the world, and I have no one else to turn to."

"Come, take a seat. If you are indeed Muzafar-i Subhdam, I will be able to discern it in your words and behavior. And if you are not, I won't let you drink my wine."

I stood opposite him and replied, "Look at me, Sayyid Jalal Shams. Look at me and in my face you will see the signs of a life no one else has lived. Smell me and you'll find traces of a great desert on my body. Look into my eyes and you'll see the shadow of that same vast desert. You can read it in my hands."

He didn't expect the feeble man in tattered farmer's clothes to talk like that. He looked at me calmly as he filled his own wineglass but not mine, sipped with the tranquility that is the sign of a peaceful life, and said, "Thanks be to God. I'll never forget that name, never. I may have forgotten the names of kings, princes, ministers, and walis, but I will not forget the name Muzafar-i Subhdam."

"I am Muzafar-i Subhdam. If you search this world end to end, you will find no other. I am the only father of the boys whose mystery you know."

Reclining, he said, "Talk to me, Muzafar-i Subhdam. Tell me your story."

And I did. I told him everything, my story that was a long wait for death, nothing but black hope from start to finish. When I spoke of "black hope," he got up and said, "It is you. It must be. Only someone who has lived for years in the dark with his hopes would know what black hope is. You were arrested twenty-one years ago. Like thousands of others, you sacrificed yourself for Yaqub-i Snawbar. You sank into the desert sand, and all your sacrifice was for nothing."

His long hair had come loose from under his big white turban. He took a great gulp of his wine and filled up my glass too. "Now you may drink from my wine, which is replete with divine light. Now I can drink with you in peace and tell you everything while I am intoxicated. I've been waiting for you for ages. I thought you were dead. After all, that's what was being said. Someone erased your name until the time came when no one remembered it, nor those of your friends. But I knew that people must have patience to wait for the dead. Life has taught me to do so. One day a blind boy visited me here in this bower and drank my wine. He said he knew two Saryas-i Subhdams, two boys, each carrying a glass pomegranate. I don't know how the blind boy got here, but once he was drunk, he started telling me his life story. He didn't seem to know what he was saying or who he was talking to but he still told the long story of the Saryases.

"I interrupted him, saying, 'Bring me proof, blind boy!'

"He said his proof was the glass pomegranates, the Saryases who didn't understand their own lives or the similarities between them.

"I said, 'Clueless and blind as you are, if you give me two Saryases, I'll give you a third.' He didn't know there was another one, and who knows? Maybe there are dozens of them that you and I don't know about. I kept plying him with wine and said, 'Go on, talk. Tell me where the Saryases are. Where are these lost sons of the revolution?' Late into the night, I continued topping up his glass while he drank and talked incessantly. He tried to make me reveal my secrets, but I could tell he couldn't keep his mouth shut. He was restless too. I didn't tell him anything, just said, 'Bring me the pomegranates. I won't tell you anything without them.'

"'I am on a long journey to the other end of the world,' the blind boy retorted. 'I may or may not return.'

"'Then send someone to show the glass pomegranates to my son, Sayyid Muzhda-i Shams, who is an antiques dealer in the city.' I've been waiting ever since, but no one has come until now. When the Civil War finally broke out and the leaders did not listen to me, I quit that world. Books, wine, and my beloved are my homeland now. I don't leave this orchard. I don't open my door to the leaders like I used to. I live right here in the divine beauty of wine, seclusion, and love."

As the old man spoke, he poured the wine so expertly that his hands betrayed no signs of age. He was immersed in light and his wife served us quietly like a houri in paradise. As the evening wore on, he became increasingly drunk, and she more beautiful. Although he was drinking a strong wine, his voice still had something like the tranquility of water.

Eventually he said, "I took the Saryases in. It was twenty-one years ago.

Three Saryases, three tiny, half-dead infants, along with three glass pomegranates. By the Lord who created wine and taverns, I remember Yaqub-i Snawbar himself bringing me the puny little things. He didn't want me to know anything about them. He put the wailing infants in front of me, all of them crying as if God had created them from the sperm of three sad angels. They were so ill that I said, 'What they need is the elixir of life. They really do.'

"Yaqub didn't enter my guest wing that night. He didn't approach the light of my candles which were constantly circled by moths. He said, 'I don't have the elixir of life. If you don't, no one does. Even if it's only a drop, give it to these infants so they survive.'

"'Who are they? Are they from angel's or devil's sperm, from your blood or other people's?'

"At first, he said nothing. He was worried his words would be revealed to the world by the trees, the air, and the birds. He had brought me the three infants secretly, his face so well hidden by a scarf that no one could recognize him. He said all three had to bear the same name. They were reminders of a loyal friend and faithful member of our revolution – Muzafar-i Subhdam. He asked me to give the infants to three unrelated families in three different regions, some in the hotter part of the country, some in the cooler highlands.

"'Sayyid Jalal,' he said, 'this is the biggest secret of my life. No one but you can save these children. I can't do anything for them.'

"My whole body trembled as I took the babies from him. I asked him once, twice, three times, 'Whose children are they, Yaqub-i Snawbar?'

"Every time he replied coyly, 'They're children, sons, of the revolution. Don't forget that all three must have the same name.' At this, the trees started moving, there was a strange stirring in the air, and the ground beneath us became restless. 'Don't ask me any more questions.' he continued. 'I need to go, I must. You are responsible for the lives of these children, Sayyid Jalal Shams.'"

I kept looking at Sayyid Jalal Shams as I put my hands on his.

The evening light broke through the gaps between the vines, wafting the scent of the heavenly grapes towards us. "When I was captured I had only one son," I said. "But what does that matter now. Now, I understand that one became three. They are all my sons. They all bear my name, after all. That night when we were under fire from all sides, I told Yaqub-i Snawbar to sneak out the back and escape while I distracted the enemy. But I also begged him to take care of Saryas-i Subhdam. It was my only request. Saryas was just a few days old at the time. His mother had died giving birth to him and Yaqub brought him to a friend. I had only set eyes on him once. I couldn't organize the funeral or see my son, but one dark night, unseen by spies and security forces, I visited a small village where I held Saryas-i Subhdam to my chest for a quarter of an hour. Those brief moments were my longest spell of fatherhood. I was at peace in prison, telling myself that Yaqub-i Snawbar and all the others at home would not neglect Saryas. I was certain they would keep their arms open to him. But now that I've returned, all I have is a handful of stories. Saryas after Saryas appears, and I see nothing but alienation, death, and loneliness in their lives. Almighty God, Sayyid Jalal Shams, tell me, whatever made this my sons' fate?"

Sayyid Jalal Shams refilled his glass. As if talking to himself, he said, "There were three of them. I took them to three far-flung areas, to three villages, in the east, west, and south. Three innocent babies, three scraps of flesh, all without sin. Each with a glass pomegranate. That night, I put each one in my car, driving hundreds of miles between stops to find three families to adopt them. Back then, I had blind faith in Yaqub-i Snawbar and men like him. Not like now. I hadn't yet become an old man who had withdrawn to a world of wine and flowers."

He suddenly lifted his head as if he just remembered I was there. In a sad voice that gradually turned to sobs, he said, "The three of them should have grown up together, but I separated them as if I was hacking someone to pieces. I placed them a hundred miles apart from one another and later I could only find one of them. Just the one. Oh Lord, two were lost amid the smell of gunpowder back then. The smoke took them away." Tears ran down his beard and dripped into the wineglass.

"I know the story of the other two," I said. "But tell me, Sayyid Jalal Shams, where is the third?"

The radiant Sayyid Jalal was weeping openly now as he carried on drinking. He put his head on his papers and muttered, "There were three of them, that's right. I lost two of them later on, when the war suddenly ravaged the country, death flooded in from all sides, and a black wind devastated towns and villages alike. Before food shortages set in under international sanctions, before the looting and the deaths that went unaccounted for, I used to check in on them discreetly once a season, without ever revealing myself to them. I did once call out to one of them, saying, 'Saryas-i Subhdam, come here. Come to your uncle.' He looked at me suspiciously and ran away. With the country destroyed, I could find only one of them who emerged, scarred, from the hellfire of those days. His face was deformed. He couldn't speak. There had been a war and he had lost everything he had in it."

I bowed and kissed his hands and the tears on his beard. He continued, as if talking to the trees, "I never did find the other two. When I lost them, I understood how vast God's earth and water are. In those days, everyone was fleeing. Within a few months, thousands of villages were wiped out; hundreds of tribes melted away like candles, leaving no trace."

With the clarity of a man who has experienced everything life has to offer, good and bad, he unfastened the top buttons of his white shirt, took off his jacket, put his hand on his heart, and said, "Lord, the heart of this slave no longer worships the divine. All it does is get drunk." The girl who looked like an angel brought us more wine every so often in ornamented goblets on silver trays. He looked at me and said, "The universe is an old witch."

I feigned patience although I felt like I was sitting on hot coals. I just wanted to get to the bottom of the Last Saryas's story. The vineyard, the orchard, the wine – none of it could calm me. I held his hand and said, "But where's Saryas-i Subhdam? Where is he?"

Now he stammered like an old fool searching for infinite worldly pleasures. "Drink up. Drink wine. Sing to the beauty of the vineyard. Sing." He wiped away his tears, refilled a silver goblet, and took a great gulp without closing his eyes, his head lifted to see the evening stars. "Which Saryas are you looking for? Hmm? How can you and I begin to know how many Saryases there are in this part of the world? How can we know whether there were other nights when other Sayyid Jalal Shamses distributed other babies across these areas? Who knows which is your son?"

"I am not looking for my own son. Do you understand, Sayyid Jalal Shams? I am looking for Saryas-i Subhdam."

"He was still a kid when his face was burned. An Iraqi-made bomb containing nitric acid landed in the house where I had taken him to be raised by a childless couple. Each of the three went to a different farming family. When the villages were destroyed and everything was being annihilated, I lost track of two of them. Just like a glass of wine that no one will ever drink, that won't be served at any table, that will never wet the lips of a beautiful woman, these children had no one to act as parents to them. Not a soul."

He tied the faqiyana, the long shirt sleeves of his traditional costume, at the wrists and reached for his cup. "You mustn't assume I was distracted by wine back then. I kept an eye on them, without needing to be asked by either God or man. They were too young to understand very much. I am the only person to have held each of those three sad babies in my arms. Masked and on horseback, I watched them until they reached the age of six.

"Two of them vanished in the great uproar, one when his parents died, the other when he disappeared in the woods and valleys during the mass exodus in 1991. My dear, look: can you see the border? Do you know the mountains and valleys that separate our country from the kings and mullahs of Iran? Tens of thousands of people were killed right there and never found.

"Once the dust settled and I, an old man, could start drinking again, once the vineyards came back to life, I started searching for them in the border regions and the plains. I heard that one of them was working for the traffickers on the border, helping them water and feed their mules, and organizing where to stay for the night. I set out there, only to be told that a child matching his description was now working with drivers on the southern roads.

"I had a feeling they were still alive, the way a drunken man intuitively knows how much wine is left in his pitcher. Alas, man cannot follow a cloud any more than the course of underground water."

"But the Last Saryas is with you," I said. "Isn't he?"

"I only know the whereabouts of one person called Saryas-i Subhdam, a wounded man whom I don't want you to see. I really don't," he said.

I lifted his hands, kissed them, and said, "You are a good man, but I want to see him."

Sayyid Jalal Shams was looking at a tray full of candles that his angel of a wife had quietly brought in. His face was shining in their light. Looking at me directly for the first time, he said, "Even I only visit him now and then, because it's too painful to see him. Listen to me! They were not just your sons. They were the sons of nature, of this land, this homeland. You can see the searing of this land in his burns. Why do you want to meet someone who can't speak to you? You've been thinking about your son for twenty-one years; you have an image of him in your mind. He is handsome, lively, and so on, right? Well, that's not the case. Your son lives in a home with other burned, wounded, and disturbed children. Some volunteers look after them. Muzafar-i Subhdam, you'd be devastated if you saw him. It would be the end of all your hopes. I've always cried for him and all the other kids as if I were their father. With each sip of wine, a drop of black sorrow for the children's distress has entered my soul and stayed there. Let him go. There's nothing you can do for him, nothing at all. Come on, join me and get yourself drunk like any failed father would."

I knew that his words stemmed from extreme unhappiness, that this great sadness had driven him towards a lonely indifference.

He started to speak again, almost in a whisper. "Once upon a time, there was a king who was in love with the image of a woman painted on a wall in a remote cave high in the mountains. Obsessed, he sets out to discover the woman's identity. He leaves the glory of the palace and the royal court in search of the painted woman. He throws away his crown and scepter, takes up a walking stick, and dons a dervish's cloak. For years, he travels from one end of the world to the other but cannot find the person in the picture and quench his heart's desire. Eventually, he is no longer young but so old he bends over his wine cup in the taverns. And yet, despite his great age, his bowed back, and his frailty, the fire in his heart does not subside. One day, a stranger approaches him with a message. 'Come and see me. I am your beloved, the person in the picture that you have been searching for the world over. Come and be my guest tonight.' That evening, the king, frail but adoring, looks at his reflection in the mirror and sees what old age has done to him. But it dawns on him that his beloved, too, is made by the Creator and so cannot escape the effects of Time. When he finally reaches his beloved's house, his knees weakened by old age, he hesitates at the door. Should he enter and see her time-ravaged face, or turn back and forever remember her as he imagined? As he reaches to knock on the door, his knees begin to shake, his whole body trembling and sweating. At that moment, he decides to continue living in a fantasy, just as he has all the years before, in love with the woman's image. He steps back from the door, gathers up his cloak, and takes to the mountains and wilderness once more. Never does the king return to the house of the beautiful lover of his imagination, for whom he had been searching his entire life."

I held his hands and said, "Wise old man, what do you mean by this story? What are you trying to tell me?"

He drank his wine and said, "You are too intelligent not to have understood. I'm telling you: it's best to hang on to the picture in your heart. The sweet wine of imagination is better than the bitter water of truth."

"No, sir. I prefer the bitterness of the water of truth. I'm not like the mystic who throws away his crown and scepter for imagination's sake. Nor am I the type of person whose knees would tremble before turning away from my beloved's door. Even if my sons are nothing but a bunch of charred sticks, I have to embrace them. After all they have endured, they deserve someone who loves them unconditionally. You don't know their full story. You might have the story of their beginnings and know where they came from, but I know how they lived, how they were lost on the sidewalks of the cities and amid the gunpowder dust of the wars. They are my sons, and I will carry the pain of their fate until my last breath."

He looked at me angrily and said, "They are not just your sons. They are the sons of us all. We should all carry their pain."

"Or they were no one's sons, no one's at all. Neither mine, nor yours, nor anyone else's."

As he shut his eyes, his image in the light of the candles seemed fantastical, like a soul appearing for a while but then lost and impossible to find.

The wine gave him a certain tranquility, and he muttered, "They were the sons of us all, they were. The sons of us all."

Kissing his hands again, I said, "Tell me, where is the Last Saryas? Please."

He took his hands away and said, "God, forgive my drunkenness. It's the one sin I can't give up. God, if you believe I am to blame for the fate of these young men, forgive me for that too since I don't know who's at fault. They were the sons of all of us and none of us, like the moon, like your divine power, like the wine in the grapes, which belong to all of us and to none. They were three infants, three tiny innocent boys, carried away by a wind stronger than the hands of a drunkard like me. Muzafar-i Subhdam, just as earthquakes can shatter jugs and overturn glasses full of wine, there are storms that can carry off our sons. These three saplings were uprooted and carried away. Each of them had a glass pomegranate as a keepsake so they would not forget the garden they came from, would recognize each other if they met by chance, and so we could find them if we searched the world for them."

"But no one, no one, has looked for them," I retorted angrily.

With great embarrassment, he laid his head on his books and papers. In a quiet, muffled voice, utterly unlike the one he had used all evening, he said, "That's because we didn't have time, my friend. We were carried away by wars and alcohol. By wine and war. Wine and war. Time and time again." He lifted his head and looked at me intently. "*He* didn't want it. *He* didn't want anyone to turn the pages of those stories."

"Who didn't? Tell me who you mean?"

Like someone afraid of the stars, the clouds, the trees, and even his own wineglass, he said quietly, "The leader. Our leader, Yaqub-i Snawbar."

I wanted to get more out of him, to understand the essence of the secret, but he gave nothing away. I had to get to the core of it before it was too late and he was so drunk he left the table and went to bed with the divine houri who had been serving us, fluttering around us like a butterfly. "Sayyid Jalal Shams, light the way for me," I said. "You believe in wine, candles, and love. Swear by all three and tell me where the Last Saryas is."

As if I had worn him out, as if he hadn't expected the story of the children to be so painful, as if the wine could no longer intoxicate him and he could no longer sleep, he stood up. He was tense. In the candlelight, he towered before me like an ancient statue. He said, "He's there. He's at the home for burned children with his brothers. Go, Muzafar-i Subhdam. Go and see my son Muzhda-i Shams – they also call him Sayyid Muzhda. He has an antique shop in the bazaar. He'll take you to Saryas-i Subhdam." He sat down again and wrote a letter in the most beautiful calligraphic script I had ever seen. "All you need to do is give him this letter, show him the glass pomegranate, and tell him who you are. But, Muzafar-i Subhdam, you should know one thing: you must know that love will no longer heal these children's wounds."

I shivered when I left his vineyard; it was the coldest night I could remember. I felt as if I were drowning in a bottomless secret. I was impatient for the morning that, lacking all mercy, would bring me to this ship.

18

The day Muhammad the Glass-Hearted was swept away in the floods, he was on his way to see Sayyid Muzhda-i Shams. That evening could have been an important day in the Saryases' search for one another had love not ambushed both him and the glass pomegranate, forcing a change of plan. When love broke Muhammad's heart, he didn't have time to resist the current and get to the bottom of their story.

And no, I am not sowing seeds of doubt in you as to whether Muhammad the Glass-Hearted was murdered, as the Second Saryas suggested, because I want to live amid the wreckage of his love, rather than the mystery of his death. It was that cold, strange evening of the storms that brought the Saryases' story to this ocean. You see, every story is like a small stream that eventually spills into the broad sea of thousands of other tales. And if a storyteller dies along the way, another must replace him and carry on the story from one river to the next and on out to sea. And that's what has happened with this story. I am completing the journey Muhammad the Glass-Hearted was unable to finish that stormy evening.

When I left Sayyid Jalal Shams, the night was so dark that life itself seemed to be in crisis. A voice at the other end of the world seemed to be shouting, "That's it; life has acquired its final form and there's no room left for comments, hesitation, or modification."

I headed back to the village, as if into nothingness, and was surprised to find the sisters in white waiting for me in the dark. The story of the Saryases was a great torment to them. They feared a day when hundreds of Saryases might emerge, an army of orphaned children with glass pomegranates pouring into my life. They feared that the country's towns and villages secretly harbored thousands of children whose stories were the same as the Saryases'. They feared I might lose the ground under my feet and sink into deadly quicksand.

They were waiting for me on a large rock at the side of the road like two mighty angels. I hugged them both. On the dark path home, I related my strange encounter with Sayyid Jalal, telling them that there was another Saryas, in a different body, somewhere else in the city. At that point, I didn't know anything about the Last Saryas except for Sayyid Jalal's few ambiguous sentences. And remember, "the Last Saryas" was the name I eventually gave to a child who had been to hell and back, although now I don't think of him as the last Saryas in the world but rather as the last to enter my life.

Agitated, I spoke to the sisters nonstop that night as if to ease my pain. I talked about the unity of man, saying that *Saryas* was just another word for human being. I told them no matter what form the story of the Saryases took, no matter how it unfolded, it wouldn't alter the fact that it was the story of numerous helpless people caught up in a storm. I had long since given up looking for just one person. His life had merged with thousands of other lives because I knew that separating the Saryases from each other was tantamount to killing them and rendering their lives meaningless.

Oh my friends, maybe you see it differently, given that you have always lived in the homeland. But for years in the desert I had looked upon only one scene, year in, year out. Just as the infinite sea of sand taught me about the inter-connectivity of nature and drew my attention to the link between man, animals, and God, so it had also taught me about the unity of all life. You might each look at your individual lives and say, "This is my life," but when someone returns after an absence of twenty-one years, when he pauses and looks around, he is unable to say to each of you, "This is your life." Life is one: your lives, our lives are one.

I couldn't single out just one Saryas. I will happily declare before you here tonight that in my long search for Saryas-i Subhdam, I never found the real Saryas, the boy whose image was imprinted in my mind. Instead, I saw the entire world in which he had been lost. When I returned from my visit to Sayyid Jalal Shams, I talked to the sisters in white late into the night with the enthusiasm of a dervish speaking of God. I told them that Saryas was another name for Adam, a Godless Adam burned and resurrected here on earth, constantly banished and constantly coming back. But the sisters in white showed signs of worry and desperation that I didn't understand.

I raised my hands in the dark and said, "My Lala, my Shasha, what will be will be, let things take their course. Let this search bear me along to storms and deserts, to dark ivory towers, to any door to which humans do not hold the keys. Why are you worried about me? I am here to comb the seas for him. I know you're going to ask me which Saryas I'm looking for, what is so special about him that I'm surrendering myself to the floods like a madman for his sake. I don't know – maybe they are a series of unfortunate souls connected by stories strung together by Satan, each one leading to the next. I will go as far as I can. I will follow this path for as long as my mind can cope with this holy mess, whether it's God or the devil who has me by the hand."

The following day I borrowed the glass pomegranate from the sisters in white and visited the young antique seller Sayyid Muzhda-i Shams. He looked nothing like the old man I'd seen in the mountains. Seated in a big office, he talked with a self-assuredness I had only seen in the politicians who occasionally spoke to local TV stations from behind their desks. There was a certain hoarse, nasal quality to his voice that made him sound like he was addressing a group of women and trying to impress them. I gave him his father's letter and the glass pomegranate. He reached over to a large safe next to his desk and took out another pomegranate that looked very much the same.

He quietly compared the two then said, "I am looking after him at my father's request. He's not a relative. A foreign organization takes care of them." He looked at me. "Do you know how he is? Have you seen him? Do you know what he looks like these days?"

"No," I replied, "how could I? I haven't seen him yet."

He reached for his car keys. "Let's go." He drove me to a big house in a new district of the city. "Sir, I don't know him," he said on the way there, shaking his head. "I've done everything for him at Sayyid Jalal's request.

I found an organization that looks after disabled and paralyzed children for him. They might take him to Europe. A doctor told me some medical researchers there are interested in his case. I've been telling my father for ages to stay out of it but he won't give up. Sir, you should know that everything I've done for him has been for the sake of Sayyid Jalal."

After he dropped me off on that hot and dusty day, I never saw him again. Yes, that was the only time I met Sayyid Muzhda-i Shams, the man who had been meant to take Muhammad the Glass-Hearted to meet the Last Saryas. When I spoke to him, however, he knew nothing about Muhammad and was unaware of the story of the other Saryases. He said, "I only have time to manage my own life. For years I've been asking Sayyid Jalal Shams, 'What is this glass pomegranate? Let me throw it away. My safe's not a garbage bin.' Every time he comes to see me, he asks me to open it, looks at the pomegranate, and cries. I ask him every time, 'Dad, what is it? When was it made? It's not an antique. What can I do with it?' It's a waste of space! He always says not to throw it away, that it'll reveal some big secret one day."

He gave me the glass pomegranate outside the house and said, "I've kept this for years and years. Now it's all yours. When you see Sayyid Jalal Shams, tell him I handed it over to you safely so that he knows I didn't let him down."

I said soothingly, "You may rest assured. Don't worry."

He let me out and asked if he should pick me up again later.

"You are kind, but no. I know all the roads in the world."

I don't know why he didn't come in – maybe he couldn't bear to approach the world those children were living in. He wasn't someone who let the

259

world's worries affect him. As he left, he honked his horn somewhat indifferently by way of farewell and soon left me far behind.

A foreign organization had built the house for disabled adolescents. I can't tell you exactly how many rooms it had but it felt like there were an infinite number of winding corridors, large halls, and wards. From the outside, it looked like an ordinary house but inside it seemed to stretch to the end of the universe. My friends, I can tell you that to my dying day I will remember my terrifying journey through its strange corridors, wards, and rooms.

Every ward was full of disabled and deformed youths. Boys without arms, without legs, strange beings you wouldn't see anywhere else. Boys whose mutilated bodies had been put back together without skill. The rooms seemed to be categorized according to their residents' medical conditions. First were many long wards packed with youths who had lost both legs and were walking on their hands. Some lay in blankets made into hammocks, swinging in midair. Others seemed to dangle from their crutches, and still more slept under their iron beds, leaving their plates next to them, peering out at people who passed by.

Next was a section for youths who had lost their hands. It was a bizarre scene: hundreds of youths with no hands, holding their plates in their mouths and balancing their trays on their heads as they proceeded along a corridor as if in a long but silent race.

I walked through the wards one by one, assailed by the smell of a terrifying world. I wondered how all that suffering could exist in that one place: thousands of disabled children and youths coming and going quietly, indifferent to their surroundings. It was one of the quietest places in the world; you could hardly hear a sound. They spoke in nervous whispers, and when you asked them anything, their answer was invariably muted, almost inaudible.

In the section for the blind, a gray calm prevailed as if their inability to see had produced faded pictures and colors. In the section for the deaf, there was a silence I had only experienced in the desert. In another section, I saw young men whose bodies seemed to have been shattered then reassembled, their deformities a collage of body parts attached to one another. It was as if one person's head had been attached to another person's body, one person's eyes placed in someone else's head, or a nose planted on a different face, as if whoever had mutilated them had so mixed them up that the original bodies could not be reconstructed. It was almost like they had been built from thousands of bits of other human beings.

"Does anyone know Saryas-i Subhdam?" I asked as I walked through the corridors, wards, and rooms.

"We don't know him," a quiet voice would whisper, although you could never tell where it came from or to whom it belonged. I'd look back to find out, but no one would be looking at me.

I finally found Saryas-i Subhdam in a ward off the very end of a corridor, in the "Children of the Embers" section, housing boys who had suffered burns in wartime. I stood at the door and said loudly, "Excuse me. Do any of you know Saryas-i Subhdam?"

A slender young boy was wandering around wearing only underpants and an undershirt. His entire body was horribly burned. His blue eyes were set in a shriveled face without eyebrows or eyelashes. Like a ghost escaped from a nightmare, he stood before me quietly and said, "Did Sayyid Jalal Shams send you?"

I whispered into his ear, "Yes, he did. Sayyid Jalal Shams sent me. Are you Saryas-i Subhdam?"

He took my hands and quietly led the way. He told me the rooms were home to the Children of the Embers, to hundreds of young burn victims whose bodies had melted like candle wax. Their bodies spilled over the beds like rubber that had cooled but never been placed in a mold. Some seemed to be still on fire because when you looked into their eyes, they were filled with embers and their breath was like the heat from a blazing furnace. When you walked through the rooms, you felt hot air stronger than a desert wind.

The boy, who seemed in better health than everyone else, said, "My name is Astera Kamil, but they call me Black Star because I am the only one who can go out in the pitch black after midnight and see the dark streets and bazaars. Do you know how I got burned? Of course, you don't. It happened in a green wheat field. I was sleeping under a clear sky with the daughter of a sheikh. Her relatives set both of us on fire. Somehow, I managed to reach water while I was still aflame. She couldn't get away and burned to death in the field." He spoke in an unusually low voice, as if he were in a dangerous prison rather than a hospital and care home. His burns were so bad that you couldn't imagine what he might have looked like before, but there was still a sparkle and a cheerfulness in his eyes.

"Do you know why we speak in such low voices?" he asked.

I replied that I didn't.

"Well, you should. Everyone here screams or groans. If we're too loud, we disturb the rest of the organization's doctors and staff who live on the floor above. One day they came and expelled everyone who was screaming or groaning. If you want to live here, be fed, and have a warm bed to sleep in, you mustn't scream." Suddenly he paused, looked at me with some suspicion, and said, "Who are you? You don't seem like someone who has seen this place before or even lived in this city."

I looked at him unfazed and said, "I am Saryas-i Subhdam's father."

I couldn't read anything in his eyes, as if he didn't want me to look at them too long, as if he knew that the clarity and depth of his gaze would give away the secrets of his heart. He lowered his head and said, "I've never seen you before."

As if startled by something, he abruptly looked back up at me. "They're sending Saryas-i Subhdam to Europe. His selection's already been confirmed. He leaves in a few days. And they'll study him there. Five of them are going. They were chosen by two Englishmen." He lowered his head sadly again. "But they didn't pick me. They wanted someone who'd been burned by heavy weapons. They chose people burned by bombs and chemical gas. One of them touched my skin and said, 'We don't want this one.'" He pointed to his friends. "They call us the Children of the Embers because we've all walked through fire. They used to call this section 'Hell,' but one day a poet came and he gave us the name Children of the Embers. He had written a long poem, which went out on TV. Then he came and read it for us as well. It was a long poem. I can't remember any of it."

He stopped. "Do you know that Saryas-i Subhdam doesn't speak?"

I hadn't asked Sayyid Jalal Shams for details because I wanted to hug

Saryas myself, to touch him and understand his suffering. "No, I didn't know," I said.

In an even lower and sadder voice, he continued, "He can't talk. Not since he got burned. He can say a few words that only exist in his imagination. His bed is next to mine. I wait for days to string his words together, and even then I can only make partial sense of them. I'm the only one who can." He shyly bowed his head. "It's because his bed's next to mine."

The corridors were much longer than I had expected. As we walked along them, Black Star said, "Saryas won't recognize you. He doesn't recognize anyone. One day a blind man came with another young man, but he didn't know who they were. It was only a week later when I'd strung his words together that I realized."

Saryas-i Subhdam was sitting on the last bed in a ward off the last corridor. Black Star pointed him out, and I approached slowly. He was playing with a long string of prayer beads. I hadn't understood why Sayyid Jalal Shams didn't want me to see him until I actually saw him close up. Oh God, what a horror! It seemed as though his eyes had melted onto his cheeks and his cheeks had been raked with claws, exposing the bones. His lips had slipped onto his chin, while his ears curved away, and a powerful wind seemed to have uprooted all his hair. The skin on the right side of his forehead had unfurled like a leaf over his eye so that he could only see if he lifted the flap of skin and held it up with his hand. His right eye was far smaller than his left, which itself was disproportionately elongated. His nose looked like a piece of burnt meat, and when he breathed, you could hear him wheezing. I went over to him, bowed down, and kissed his burnt legs. It was as if I was kneeling to a small god. No one saw what I was doing except Black Star, not even Saryas himself. Life had savaged him so repeatedly that he couldn't sense my small and meaningless kisses. It was then that I remembered what Sayyid Jalal Shams had said: "Love will no longer heal these children's wounds."

My love had come too late, and a love that's too late is always closer to mercy and regret than to love. Standing before those young men, it was as if my life's journey was over, as if nothing in the universe mattered more than the moment I bowed down and kissed my son, who was oblivious to me and immersed in a world of his own.

It seemed he hadn't grown to full maturity. Since being burned, he had spent most of his time enclosed in dark rooms. Before the organization took him in, he had apparently lived for a long time in a dark room in a mosque with a few other vulnerable people. The support of Sayyid Jalal Shams saved him. He couldn't move. His legs had remained unusually small, like a child's. They stopped growing on the day he was burned by the bomb. Only his torso had grown, but even that was crooked.

He knew nothing about his childhood and nothing about the outside world. He could barely see or speak, although Black Star had said that he could understand some things Saryas said.

I stood before him and said, "I am your father."

He looked at me without emotion and said nothing, as if he'd never heard the word before. But then he noticed the glass object in my hand and said, "Pomegranate." He lowered his head again and sadly repeated the word a few times.

I hugged him carefully, put my lips to his wounded forehead, and kissed him. I had never kissed anyone in such a way before, and it seemed he had never been kissed like that either. The hardest thing to imagine was how to find a way into his heart.

When I kissed him, he happily raised his head and said, "Tomorrow. Tomorrow."

Black Star, who was next to us, said, "In a few days' time, you'll be able to work out what he's saying."

There are moments in life when a new chapter begins unexpectedly. The boy who was lying right there, who had emerged from the world of fire, his body traumatized and carrying the scent of all the shadowy rooms he had grown up in, was my son. It was the first time I had been able to hug someone whom I could call "my son," a moment I had thought about so much in the desert. And no, you mustn't assume that seeing him assuaged my grief for the other Saryases. Or that as soon as I hugged him I forgot about the Second Saryas in his dark prison, or that it severed my emotional bond to the grave of the First Saryas, buried among the thorns and weeds of a remote plain. You mustn't assume I forgot about all the vulnerable children who had no relatives or friends or anyone at all to guide them, who were stranded in bazaars, in the countryside, and on battlefields. But the moment I embraced the Last Saryas, I realized I would never become a real father. I opened my eyes, and it dawned on me that there was something missing that I needed to become a real father. I had no more than a grave, a burnt boy's mutilated flesh, a few tapes, and two glass pomegranates. Just as the Saryases never became each other's brothers, so I couldn't become their father. We were a fantasy family that required something more than brotherhood, fatherhood, or ordinary love.

When I embraced the exhausted, barely conscious youth, a light began to shine deep within me. I understood the meaning of the pacts that had once bound Saryas the Great to his friends and the sisters in white, just as I understood the meaning of the oath that connected Lawlaw and Shadarya. At that moment, I understood that these pacts were their only defense against the desert and death, and losing each other.

As I hugged him, my arms around his neck like someone grasping a tree in the midst of a great flood, I felt the heat of his body; I felt the relentless fire inside his soul. And it was then that I realized our lives require a great oath, a promise greater than fatherhood, love, or compassion. During our embrace, as I took in the scent of him, Sayyid Jalal Shams's powerful sentence echoed in my head. I looked into his eyes again and put my arms around him. I kissed him, put his slender, burnt hands against my heart. I wept and laid my head on his chest, through which his blood circulated undisturbed.

"Love will no longer heal these children's wounds" – what a powerful sentence it was. I looked up, saw the long wards of the center and the burnt boys, each playing with something on their bed. I saw their destroyed bodies, wrecked lives, and quiet gazes. I saw Black Star, staring jealously at Saryas-i Subhdam in my arms. Right at that moment, with tears in my eyes and my heart bleeding with sorrow, I decided to bind myself and my life to that boy for ever. A pact with myself that I drafted and signed, then kept in the shrine of my heart.

I would never leave Saryas-i Subhdam again. I would follow him wherever he went on this earth. I would look for and find him whenever we became separated, and whenever I lost him, I would dedicate my whole life to finding him again.

The Last Saryas didn't know why I was kissing him nor what father-hood meant. But I sensed that my embrace was making his heart dance. Maybe his eyes, one longer than the other, saw the world differently from the rest of us. How lonely I felt in the warmth of his body! It had been a lifetime since I myself had been held in anyone's arms. The boy's mutilated body contained a deep and powerful call to life. When I held him, he, like any soul deprived of love, would cling to me even more. He didn't really know who I was, why I was embracing him, or what I wanted from him, but he had some grasp of my intentions.

It was strange; no sooner than finding Saryas-i Subhdam, I had to lose him all over again. Black Star, who was sitting next to Saryas on his bed, looked at us and said, "They're taking him to Europe in a few days' time. They may cure him. They may make him well again. He may even be able to walk." He embraced Saryas, just as I had, and said, "I'll really miss him. We're friends. We eat together every day." To me, he said, "You can take him out with you for a few days. He may be going to Europe, but before they take him, he can spend a few days with you." He gripped my hand. "Take me with you too. I haven't slept outdoors in a long time. I'd like to see the stars – I don't get to see them in here."

I was completely at a loss. I washed my face at the sink outside the ward, and in the mirror, I could see the fear and panic in my eyes. I bent my head over the sink and it felt as if I was vomiting blood. I was angry at the world, the heavens, the universe, anyone who had anything to do with how life is organized on this planet. At anyone who thought of themselves representative of God's kingdom on earth, who had inflicted all this pain on the Saryases. But I didn't know where to direct my anger. I put my head on the sink and tried to calm myself. Seeing all those wounds on one person's body could make anyone doubt their own innocence. These corridors and wards were enough to make every single person in the world feel guilty.

The Last Saryas wasn't the kind of person whose secrets you could understand quickly. I lost all hope that he might open the door to the mysteries of the other Saryases because he himself was such an immense mystery. I felt a great heart lay behind his disfigured face, lost gaze, and deafening silence. Back in his room, I laid my head on his chest and listened to his heartbeats, the regular rhythm of his breathing coming and going through his chest like a butterfly in flight. At one point, when he felt tired, he lay down on his bed, looking at the ceiling with his large eye.

He kept repeating words that didn't mean anything, as if he were talking to himself. Black Star said, "If you want to take him with you, I can teach you what to say."

I put my hands on his shoulders and said, "Come here, Black Star. I do want to take him with me. I want to take you with me too. All three of us will stay together until the day of his departure."

I couldn't tell from his face if Black Star was happy. In burning his skin, the fire had removed his capacity to show his emotions, but in his voice I could detect the secret and profound contentment of his soul, which the fire couldn't reach. He showed me how to take Saryas-i Subhdam out of the ward. He came with me to the floor above, where the organization's staff, doctors, and officials worked. Black Star seemed to wield some special power over everyone working there. He took me to a doctor, who needed to be shown my ID. Black Star had told me, "No matter what happens, you mustn't get angry. You just need to repeat what you want again and again, but calmly. No one's allowed to raise their voice here. If you do, neither Saryas-i Subhdam nor I will be able to come with you."

The doctor sent us off to someone else, a Miss Chiman, a dark-skinned girl who was extremely slender and small. She looked so young she could have finished elementary school that very day. In the tone of one child to another, she said, "What's your problem, please?"

I explained my story to her and said, "I want to take Saryas-i Subhdam and Black Star out somewhere so that we can be together for a few days before Saryas leaves."

Black Star was standing outside the door. Miss Chiman's childlike face peeped out. "Aw, dear Star, are you going out as well?" The sentence perfectly suited her appearance.

Black Star came into the room and said, "I want to go out for a bit to look at the sky, to sleep outdoors, and drink cow's milk."

Miss Chiman said, "What will you do if I say no, Black Star?"

"I'll bite myself," he replied. "I'll bite myself to death."

Miss Chiman brought her head forward, softened her voice, and, as if confiding in a female friend, whispered to me, "He's really nuts this one. If you pester him, he'll bite himself. You'll need to look after him. I'll let you take them out as long as you don't take your eyes off him. They need him here. You must take good care of him."

I filled out a form guaranteeing that I would bring both of them back to the hospital early in the morning in two days' time.

When they granted me permission, I held Black Star's hands and realized that never in my life would there be a repeat of the days ahead. I took both of them to the village in a small jeep. Saryas-i Subhdam seemed not to have seen the outside for a long time. I can't tell you how expressive his cries of astonishment were. But there was also a fear in his eyes that I hadn't seen when he was inside the care home.

Black Star said, "He's never left the hospital. Many of the patients can't because no one can bear looking at them." If the doors of the center were ever left open, the city would fill with thousands of wounded young men, horrifying those who couldn't bear to look at their faces – the real visage of life in this country.

Leaving the hospital, I understood that an invisible army lives deep in the hidden nooks and crannies of our country, a host of people besieged and trapped, whose appearances contain something other than what we see on the streets every day. I had a feeling that if one day those who live in the underworld of our society did emerge, war would break out between those who want to forget the reality of existence and those who wish to see what life really looks like.

Throughout the journey to the village, Black Star chattered about life in the hospital, recounting one by one the tales of people burned in various battles. He talked about a friend, ablaze with a flame that was impossible to extinguish, who had come down a mountain to the city to be admitted to the hospital. No water could douse the flames, although they left his body unscathed. "They poured water over him, but it wouldn't go out, attacked it with blankets but it couldn't be extinguished. They even put him in a pool, but it made no difference. When he walked around the wards, we were all worried that our curtains, bedcovers, and clothes might catch fire. He slept on a metal bed without any covers at all. Even when he was asleep, he was still ablaze. The mullahs said he was burning because he was bound for hell, that he was a miracle sent by God to show us hell. He was in a lot of pain. One night he ran away from the guards and disappeared. No one knows where he is. They called him 'the Fireflower.' He loved Saryas-i Subhdam a lot. Saryas-i Subhdam has been living in that room for seven years. The Fireflower loved me too, but I was afraid of him. I'm not afraid of Saryas. No one is. In seven years, he's only been taken into the back garden once. Otherwise he's never been outside."

Saryas said erratically, "Sunshine, sunshine, sunshine. Night, night, night. Breeze, breeze." I held his head against my shoulder and let him speak. Black Star put his head out the window of the vehicle, gazing at the landscape.

I had no energy to talk to either of them. It was impossible for me to understand the mental impact of a lifetime in a hospital ward, alongside thousands of other wounded people, unable to leave and live independently. I knew what the desert did to the soul but I had no idea what the endless hurricane of fire and the charred life the children lived had done to theirs. There was a dark thread binding the destiny of these broken bodies to the wider destruction of the country. I contemplated the Second Saryas's words about the smashed carts and imagined the bazaars that were normally so full of life, ruined one morning from one end to the other. I imagined the demolished villages of which no trace is left on earth. It was as though the same sinister hand that had destroyed all these things had also led the Second Saryas to smash his glass pomegranate and hurl it into the unknown. The same hand that kept the Last Saryas's inside a dark safe, smashed Kazhal's Chest, and swept things and people away indiscriminately.

I held the Last Saryas in my arms. In him I found the broken glass pomegranate tossed away by the Second Saryas, the pieces of Kazhal's Chest, and the murdered body of the Marshal as if he had risen from the dust of the grave and returned to me. In him I saw the Second Saryas trembling with fear, he who had gone from the dust of the trenches to a remote and impenetrable prison. When the Last Saryas laid his head on my shoulder, I could hear the breath of time in his wheezing lungs. The boy's deep suffering was so bound up with all the pain in the world that, as I took his burnt body in my arms, I was embracing all the fires of the world.

While I was lost in my thoughts, Black Star was rejoicing at the sight of green fields and farms. Even when he was looking at the landscape, something would take him back to the world of the hospital. As if explaining a secret, he said, "They're not all bad, you know. You could see that. Some of them call me their favorite Star. At first, my heart was very delicate. It took very little to break it, as if it were made of glass. One day we got a new nurse. She was very beautiful, with extremely long hair. Pretending to have a headache one night, I went upstairs and said, 'I like you a lot. Can you help me? I really, really, really like you.' She didn't answer me. Instead she held my hands, put me back in bed, and covered me with the blanket, saying, 'Sleep, darling. Don't think about such things.' I visited her every night and told her, 'Will you help me? I love you.' And every night she held my hands, put me in bed, and kissed me as she would a child, saying, 'Darling, sleep.' Our relationship went on like this for two years until one night she came to me, crying, and said, 'Dear Star, I won't be seeing you again.' The following day, she left the hospital for good. She had got into some trouble – a sex scandal – with a doctor and his superior. Then she set herself on fire. One day I saw her being taken to the women's section. Did you know there's a women's section too? I've never seen it. But someone has – a journalist. He visited once to write about us; he told us all about it. He said he'd suggest mixing the two sexes up so we could understand each other better. Yes, that was his idea. He was only with us for a day, but he planted many ideas in our heads. I don't know what happened to him. We never saw him again." As always, when he finished talking, he lowered his head and glanced up at me furtively.

I asked him softly, "And what happened later? What happened to your heart?"

"Oh, my heart. My heart changed. Once she left, it became like a stone." Sometimes he would scratch his head frantically and then suddenly stop, embarrassed. I was surprised when he said it was as if his heart were made of glass, as if he were sending me a strange signal. To stop myself from overthinking, I pressed his hands and said, "A person's heart shouldn't be made of glass. It really shouldn't. Because then he will die too soon and take everything with him." I didn't want to lose someone else whose heart was made of glass, another person who would leave me with a bunch of complicated secrets.

But when I said that, Black Star lowered his head anxiously and said, "But that was the case. Once upon a time, my heart was made of glass." He said nothing else until we reached the house of the sisters in white.

19

One evening, the Last Saryas and I made our way to the last pomegranate tree in the world. I carried him on my back from the foot of the mountain and didn't put him down until we reached the summit. He was so light and small, it was as if I was carrying a soul, a thought, a breath of wind.

The Last Saryas had to make that climb, to see the world from up there just as his brothers had. He was the missing shadow the others had searched for, the part of their past and future they had lost. Only there could I turn back time to bring together the three brothers the war had torn apart. There too I could revive the oaths that death had broken and enter the fray myself, burying my own oath beneath the pomegranate tree at a time when the brothers had become mirages, the father had turned to sand in a desert and the sons to ashes.

From the mountaintop, I could see the world and smell the dreams that rained down from the branches of the tree. A divine breeze began to blow across my skin. I saw all the hopes and aspirations the youths had buried under the tree and wrote my own eternal pact right there: I resolved to follow the Last Saryas wherever he went, to be close to him as long as I lived, and to carry the stories of the Saryases with me always.

The Last Saryas couldn't join me in writing or signing anything. He didn't owe anyone anything. None of them did anymore. We, the living who knew their stories, needed to bring them out of oblivion and dust. It was an oath between me and the sky, between me and the last pomegranate tree in the world, which was the last witness of their dreams still standing, here between earth and sky. It was a dream they themselves couldn't name, that could only be articulated through this tree, a dream of human beings, brothers and enemies, understanding one another.

My friends, all of you who have been listening to this story patiently for so many nights, do you now understand what I am doing here on this ferry, white-bearded old man that I am? I was driven here by that oath, my friends. From this ship, I am hoping to find a path that will lead me back to the Last Saryas.

And so I signed my oath with the tree and left it there, plucking a twig as a memento. If any of you ever happen upon it, you should do the same. People need to introduce themselves to life anew. Under the tree, I felt I was about to embark on a new life, that I had discovered what to live for and the goal I should pursue. I experienced the clearest moments of my life as I descended the summit. After twenty-one years, I could finally put my finger on the secret of the great freedom that comes from finding a path of one's own.

When I boarded the ferry at Patras, all my strength and will were focused: I would not lose the way back to the Last Saryas, who must surely be gazing at the stars from the window of a hospital in England. I had found my way, and don't tell me that here on this boat none of us knows where we are. My friends, this sea is full of such routes; every inch of its water is a pathway. If you know your destination, you won't go astray – no matter how many times you get lost on the journey. I know people can lose their way easily. This is a bitter truth that we find hard to believe. No other creature on earth loses its way as we do; it's the essence of being human. Yes, my friends, you who listen patiently to me, humans are creatures who have no route to take because they do not know their ultimate destinations. They prefer to lock the door themselves to avoid giving in to the adventure of finding their way.

But let me tell you, this is a perilous error. When I was in prison, I had this one recurring dream that always suppressed any other. I saw an endless road in a desert of bronze sand. I knew neither where it came from nor where it went. Always, at the end, a strong wind would blow, wiping out any trace of the road. In the dream, I would keep on walking, carefree. My fear that the road would disappear faded as the years went by. Eventually, I understood that every inch on earth may be the start of another road. Every direction, on land and sea, is potentially the key to an undiscovered path. Look, my friends, the roads take us where they like.

No, fellow refugees of this dark ocean, I am not implying people are stranded without will or agency. What I am getting at is that if only people could overcome the feeling of being lost and thinking that it means the game is up, if they could only believe that even if they are lost, they can resume their journey from wherever they are, they could navigate their ordinary, everyday problems as well. After all, what is life but a great detour from what we think of as "normal" until we look at things from a new perspective?

The last pomegranate tree in the world told me to look for the roads that I needed to find, just as it had told Nadim-i Shazada to search every corner of the earth for his sight, just as it had inspired the Saryases to stay away from war and seek an eternal brotherhood. Under the pomegranate tree, the Last Saryas's heart also seemed to beat differently. Lifting the burnt skin that covered his eye, he looked out at the boundless paradise he had never seen before. As if grasping the magic of the tree, he squeezed my hand, put his head on my lap, and fell asleep.

I don't remember now how long he slept, but I do remember that having his head in my lap made me feel I'd become part of the children's dream world. I held in my arms not only the Last Saryas, but the lives of all the others. For the first time, I could hear the enchanting music Muhammad the Glass-Hearted had heard there and see the wonderful images of the universe and sky that the Saryases had seen. I smelled the days, evenings, and nights when they had made a fire there. The pictures danced before my eyes as if the tree was passing its memory on to me, linking the images in its mind to my own.

Now I'm not sure if it was real or a dream. Was I asleep when I plunged into the shadow of those days or awake with the tree really sharing its secrets with me? In that one moment I lived all the things the Saryases had lived. I touched the Last Saryas's heart and sensed the same excitement.

When he woke up, he was so astonished that all the fires in the world could not have burned the beauty of his amazement. He was full of hopes and fantasies about the sky, the tree, and the sea. He had connected to the energy that united us all. When I put him on my back and descended from the peak, instead of fire he smelled of pomegranates. I set him down at the foot of the mountain and kissed him, and he was still wrapped in the scent of pomegranates, of a land he had stepped into in a dream. It was an ancient world, shared with the other friends of the tree, filled with hope, possibility, and life.

The two days in which I held the Last Saryas in my arms were the shortest of my life. The sisters in white were, as ever, adamant that they didn't want to meet anyone else named Saryas-i Subhdam. They loved people for their uniqueness. I went to their room, kissed their white hands, bent down, and begged them to understand that Saryas-i Subhdam was the name of a being that existed on earth in various colors, that he was more than just one person, more than just a grave. He was a great prism, each facet of which had something to show us. They gave me a cold stare and said nothing.

The sisters in white did not betray the memory of their brother. No angel could adhere to his pact with God as they held to theirs with the First Saryas. There was no way for anyone new to enter their lives. They had moved to the village to hide from any temptation and doubt, focusing on nurturing kids who would not ask them to do the impossible. I pleaded with them to come and smell Saryas, to feel the heat of the fire still blazing in his heart, but they never came. My friends, you who do not tire of listening to me, they didn't want to change anything about the story they had witnessed. They considered all my efforts to be the lies of a father unwilling to believe his son had died, determined to find the child he had lost twenty-one years earlier. The fact that there were three Saryases was just a coincidence to them, nothing more.

During those two days, Black Star walked freely around the plains, near the streams and woods. He entertained himself there, drinking as much milk as he wanted. I was pleased to see him happy. At one point, he asked me, "When Saryas leaves, will you visit me again at the hospital, Muzafar-i Subhdam?"

I told him sadly, "No, Black Star. On the day Saryas leaves, I need to prepare to go too. I have to follow him. I'll take a ferry from Greece and follow him to England."

A deep sorrow spoke from his eyes but I knew there was nothing I could do for him. I was helpless to offer any support to him or to the many other burnt people left in the hospital. The young man was trapped. He couldn't return to the streets of the city, he couldn't travel, and he couldn't stay in the hospital forever.

When we returned, it was as if I had betrayed him. At the door, he turned to me shyly and said with great sadness, "So, you won't be coming back?"

I didn't want to lie or to give him false hope. I didn't want him to wait for someone who would never arrive. I hugged him and said, "Get out of here, Black Star. You can talk. You can speak on behalf of all the burnt men. You're stronger than all of them. Come out and show your real face, don't be afraid. This city must learn to see your faces."

Black Star said fearfully, "If they kick us out of here, we won't survive. If they put us out onto the streets, the stray animals out there will eat us alive."

I shook him. "Tell them to leave. All of you should come out of the hospital and take to the streets. Come out so we can see you. So that people who haven't heard your stories can see you."

Black Star wriggled free of my arms and cried, "They know. They all do. There's no one who doesn't, no one at all."

I called after him, "You've got to get out of there, all of you. Come out and show yourselves to us, to the trees, to the wind and rain. Hold each other's hands and come out."

I know my cry was meaningless, that it died on the quiet street. My friends, it breaks my heart that I didn't really get to know Black Star. His tale had wrapped itself around my own, but my search would separate them again. Black Star knew I couldn't follow him, and he merely passed close by me, the way a ghost passes through a story. Our farewell is a sad shadow over my memory.

I held Saryas's hands then put my arms around him as we walked towards the hospital. At that moment, a car pulled up beside us. Four identical-looking gunmen got out and swiftly surrounded us. The most imposing of them said, "Good day, Muzafar-i Subhdam. Forgive us, but we have our orders, and you have to come with us. Just put the patient down. We'll take Saryas-i Subhdam ourselves, right back to his bed. Don't worry about that. Just get in the car and keep calm. Don't try anything. We all know you. As I said, we have our orders. Please, get in. We've found you at last. God only knows how long we've been looking for you, Muzafar-i Subhdam. Ages, absolutely ages. Where on earth have you been?"

It had been that way since he was a child. Whenever he told a lie, something strange would happen. Either there would be a sudden downpour, trees would fall, or a flock of birds would soar above our heads. When I was arrested outside the hospital, I was sure they would take me to him. All the days I walked around in freedom, I was sure one day I would be taken to him. I have never been afraid of him despite all his sins. He was part of my life, after all. I knew many had left the country for fear of him but I was not afraid.

They took me to him late in the evening. He was lying in a dark room that smelled of death. He had aged in the few months since I'd last seen him. He was wrapped in a blanket on a large, stately bed wearing an expensive robe. It wasn't cold but it seemed he was chilled to the bone. He had locked all the doors and I got the impression that he was terrified even of his own bodyguards.

When he saw me, he sat up, dignified. "You're here, Muzafar-i Subhdam. I was worried you might not come, that they might not find you." Resignation filled his voice, not anger. Although neither of us was very old, we both looked like old men meeting to discuss some important issue.

Neither of us knew where to start. We looked at each other for a while, wordlessly. He had aged so much I hardly recognized the man who, many years ago, had left me alone on that dark night.

I went over to him and said, "Yaqub-i Snawbar, you've aged a great deal."

He squeezed my hands tightly. "I told you a plague was spreading, some sort of fatal disease, didn't I?"

"You did. I remember you telling me that."

He shook his head sadly. "I told you you were pure gold, didn't I?"

"You did, you did indeed," I replied soothingly.

He looked at me through unhappy eyes and said, "I told you not to go back to that world, not to drench yourself in that filth, to keep your soul away from all that. That's right, your soul – the innocent soul God gave you. Why did you go? Why didn't you understand what I was talking about? Why?"

"We're both ill, Yaqub-i Snawbar. We're both getting on. And we have lots of accounts to settle between us. Lots and lots."

His room was regal but he looked like a patient on his deathbed. He frequently coughed and would take a colorful tissue from a beautiful box to wipe his mouth. When I mentioned the unsettled business between us, he beamed, the grin of an old man who has forgotten how to laugh. Then, with his old gaze – that of an indecisive leader, a man who has tasted all the fruits of pleasure, who has understood the secret of death and suffering as well as the joys and delights of living, whose thoughts are fixed solely on death – he said quietly, "You and I don't have friends. No one can adjudicate between us. No one."

"Those who could are either dead, imprisoned, or have no voice."

"That was our last chance. Now we have no hope. You and I could have lived in seclusion together, far from all the corruption and the plague. We could have tried to understand things. But now you know everything. Knowledge stains a person's innocence. A person is innocent only so long as he knows nothing of other people's sins but after that the dirt of this world sticks to him."

I knew what he was getting at. I put my hands on his shoulders and said, "I've seen everything now, understood some secrets, and opened some doors. On my own feet, I entered the filth, and you think I shouldn't have, that I should've waited for you in the green house forever, right?"

"If you hadn't left, there could have been something else between us. We could have talked about what makes a human being, the crux of life, the essence of being, without you giving me that look that makes me feel ashamed. I wanted us to talk about good and evil, beauty and ugliness, to live together and talk about things beyond our narrow existence. Do you understand?"

He rested for a moment. I looked at him but said nothing. I knew we still had a long time to discuss everything. Illness and weakness had done nothing to diminish his sharp mind or the depth of his gaze. When he looked at you, you could tell he could see things you couldn't, feel things you didn't.

He coughed again, slowly rose from his bed, and wrapped the blanket around himself. "It was a green house. I had it built for our old age, for when we were tired of everyday life, somewhere we could meet and dedicate ourselves to bigger issues. We wouldn't have to talk about politics and war but about life without them, without the suffering that humans have added to it. We would have enjoyed the silence of nature. How wonderful to be able to think in deep peace, to think and to die in deep peace. You deprived me of that pleasure. I am scared to think about life alone. I am scared that on my deathbed I will be there, thinking about the meaning of life, all alone."

When he realized I had nothing to say, he carried on, "There's only one type of innocence. Just one. And that comes from not letting people understand one another. Once they do, sin will prevail."

"Yaqub," I replied, "what sort of innocence is born of ignorance? What knowledge makes us enemies, robs us of certainty, prevents us from living and sleeping in peace?"

"I am talking about a knowledge that restores my innocence and keeps me from too much soul-searching. I am fed up with peering into my own psyche, Muzafar. In the end, a person shouldn't be worrying about questions he has failed to answer his whole life. Before I die, I want to have the strength to forget the small questions. I want us both to die at peace, which means not searching for anything as death approaches, not having to dwell on any petty issues. I talked to you about being at peace. Why didn't you understand me then? Why is it that as death approaches, people always think about the past? I want to die without looking back."

"Because you see the Saryases when you look back," I spat, "and you're afraid of that. You want us to form a friendship built on disregarding the past, on ignorance and forgetting. Like all rulers, you want to burn your secrets so nobody can look at them after you die. Like all rulers, like all prophets, you want to banish people from your mind. Yaqub, your path and mine diverge. I'm sorry I couldn't take yours, my friend, but after twenty-one years of imprisonment, I can't ignore human beings. You want us both to wipe people from our memories. You live to forget them but I live to bring their memories to life. We are not on the same path."

He had expected these words. "Whether they are alive or dead, whether or not you remember them, there will be no meeting of minds, no common ground. Their hearts were filled with indifference and contempt, disgust and neglect, apathy and hatred. I had to ignore them. I had no choice." He said this in such a strange tone I couldn't tell what he was feeling. His voice was filled with both arrogance and regret. "I knew you'd follow them. That day, when you asked about Saryas-i Subhdam, I was sure everything between us would be ruined. I knew one day you'd take a path that would lead you to Sayyid Jalal Shams. Damn him for unraveling the secret of this story!"

Once he mentioned Sayyid Jalal Shams, I knew he wanted to tell me the story he had been keeping hidden for years. With the sadness of an old man, he said, "Now you have two glass pomegranates, and I have none." He went over to the windows and opened the curtains wide. The evening's silence permeated the room. He wrapped the blanket more tightly around himself and sat on a black leather sofa by the window.

"There were three glass pomegranates, made by the same hands. A father made them for his three sons. An artisan, a real artist, with remarkable skills. His sons were all Peshmergas, and all three were martyred in a bombardment by the Iraqi regime. I was in a small village up north, gathering our forces. It was in the early days of the revolution. The bodies of all three martyrs were brought and placed beside one another in the village mosque. Their father arrived late in the evening, an old man now, carrying nothing but the three pomegranates. When he saw me, he put his arms around my neck, bowed, and kissed my hands. The killing of his sons had not demoralized him. He was troubled because he hadn't managed to give them the pomegranates. He told me: 'These three brothers were never parted. They were always together: at school, on the playing field, at university. They did everything together, and when they became Peshmergas, they didn't let go of each other's hands. One day, they sent a message to my workshop, saying the leaders of the revolution had ordered them to be separated; the revolution required them to go to separate regions and serve the homeland in separate units. They asked me to make something they could take with them and look at when they missed each other, something that would stir their feelings of brotherhood whenever they held it, something that would bind them together.'

"Muzafar-i Subhdam, after all these years I can still see that old man's face; his voice is still ringing in my ears. He and I walked through the fog. Instead of talking about his sons, he was talking about something that could bind us all together. Even though the fog was thick, I can still remember his eyes. With great sadness, he put his hands on my shoulders and said, 'I made these pomegranates for them.' Then he reached into his pockets and took out three glass pomegranates. 'The pomegranates never reached them. Keep them, Leader, keep these pomegranates, so that there's something that binds everyone together, me to you and my sons to those who are being born now, something that unites today and tomorrow. My sons should have had them but now it's too late. Give them to people who must not forget each other. They are my only gift to the revolution.'

"That same night I hid the three pomegranates somewhere no one could find them. His sons no longer needed them. They were meant for life and for the living. Oh God, Muzafar, I remember it as if it were yesterday, the dark nights at the height of the revolution, when I would go and take the pomegranates out to look at. All our Peshmergas were ready to sacrifice their lives. They had sworn to die. But these were pomegranates of hope from an old man who wanted his sons never to be forgotten. I didn't want to give the pomegranates to someone who was about to die, about to be killed in battle. I wanted to give them to someone with their whole life before them. But I didn't know anyone I was certain would stay alive! I couldn't reveal the importance of the pomegranates: symbols of eternal brotherhood between three people who would never lose one another. Oh, Muzafar-i Subhdam, I know as well as you do that nothing hurts more than losing track of someone. The night the Saryases came into the world, it was as if they'd been born for those three pomegranates. Do you understand? As if they'd been made for them."

I interrupted him: "And yet, you eventually gave the pomegranates to children that you did lose and they lost you; you lost track of them, and they lost track of each other."

"Be quiet!" he said, raising his voice. "Be quiet, Muzafar-i Subhdam. Let me tell you the beginning of the story. I am the only person on this planet who knows it. Don't spoil the moment I have been waiting for my whole life." He paused, drank a little water, took a deep breath, and continued. "You know you are the father of one of the Saryases but only one. I'm sure you have never wondered who fathered the other two. You can't fool me. I have no doubt that you have never questioned what cruel man could abandon two of his sons to the storms of life. You haven't asked because you were sure you could never find the answer, that even if you had a suspicion, you could never be certain. But I'll tell you: the other two are my sons, my illegitimate children. Do you see? Illegitimate children from those dark nights of the revolution that I spent in the arms of different women in the high mountain villages. The revolution would have killed me without those women – what do you think kept me alive in the mountains? I survived because of the nights when I left the base in secret, without anyone knowing where I was going. The nights when no matter where I was in this country, no matter which village, there was always a woman to sleep with me. I would have felt defeated otherwise."

Everything else fell silent as he talked. He was clearly speaking from the heart. Nothing moved; the air was still, the curtains hung motionless, even the flowers and leaves in the vases held their breath. He wasn't lying. It was as if he had decided the world would freeze so that nothing but truth could emerge that evening, a truth that would bestow peace on his soul and his surroundings. Coughing heavily, he raised his hand like a sick pharaoh.

"They were my sons, of my blood, fruit of my dark nights whom only I, God, and my mistress knew about. Until now, no one has known their secret. Listen to me, Muzafar-i Subhdam, and don't be sad: a big part of this secret will go to the grave with me. Without secrets, life would become a great slaughterhouse, families would collapse, armies would be crushed, and people disgraced. I've always worshipped secrets, always. Always. And the two Saryases were among my biggest secrets. I fathered them. Their mother was a farmer's widow. I knew children might be born from our trysts, two illegitimate sons I didn't want to bring into the world. That's how it always is; it's what a revolution's like. There will always be children born from its belly whom no one wants. Their mother died in childbirth. I was the only midwife. I took her to a high cave, close to God and far from earth, so no one would know about the children. If a single person had found out, I would have been forced to give up the revolution, to leave its leadership to those poised to put their hands around my throat. I would have had to give up on the nation, which would have been paralyzed without me. Listen, Muzafar, listen to this twenty-one-year-old secret. At night I took that woman to a remote cave, out of reach of my opponents and the claws of her relatives. Because I loved her. Had I not, I could have left her to die. But I didn't, not until she gave birth to two sons by the light of a smoky kerosene lamp. She died in great pain. Muzafar, my friend, please understand. Understand my fear and pain that night. Imagine having two newborn babies, illegitimate babies at that, and a dead woman on your hands, while you yourself are still soaked in blood and fear. I swaddled the babies and buried their mother in a grave no one will ever find. It will remain a secret no one will uncover, just like this country's great secrets, which we shut the lid on once we've put them in a dark box. I told you, pleaded with you not to pursue things that were lost in a deep ocean, not to look for a myth you'd never find. But you didn't listen. You ignored what I said. That night, I buried my mistress under the stars, and no one on this planet noticed. I bade her farewell and climbed back down the mountains with the two babies. You know which night it was, don't you? One month after the night when the two of us were besieged and we said goodbye to each other. Your name carried a certain weight among supporters of the revolution then. I had left your Saryas in a village with a family who were friends of the Party.

No one could know that the other two were my sons. I carried them through the night, shaking in the dark like the devil that I was. I couldn't just leave them among the rocks. They were my sons, I needed to know them, to see them, to sense their existence. I didn't want to just throw them away, to abandon them outside a mosque. Even though that's how it all unfolded, it wasn't what I intended – I had some ambitions for those illegitimate children, really, I did. Do you see? I can't change life. I'm a leader, not God. Leaders can only change dreams. I am not God, not at all. God changes life. But Subhdam, you don't understand. The boys, my sons, had their own dreams. There's nothing sadder than being unable to interpret the dreams of your own sons."

It was like he was speaking to his own shadow in an empty room. He wiped his mouth and continued. "But let me tell you the story in a different way. Back then, they all knew you'd left behind a son, that when you were captured, you'd just become a father. They knew his name was Saryas – an extraordinary name and an extraordinary father. As I stood trembling in the wind, something deep in my heart told me that the loneliness of that infant without a family was no different than the loneliness of my two babies without theirs. None of them had a mother, none of them could be with their father, and none of them had anyone on earth who would adopt them. Tell me, Muzafar, what could we – a group of mountain men – have done with them?" He took a deep breath and shouted, "Shame on me!"

"The only way I could think of to save them was to give all three the same name so their secret would not be lost among all the other secrets but would disappear altogether. I would lose track of them myself but the thread connecting us all would stay intact. I pitied myself that this was my only choice. Shame on me!"

By this time, he was wailing hysterically.

"I didn't think I'd survive and be able to save them. They had to save themselves. That night when I went to take out the glass pomegranates, saddle the horse, and turn to Sayyid Jalal Shams, I knew that neither you nor I could save them; none of us could." He calmed himself a little. "Don't be frightened by my groans and screams, Muzafar-i Subhdam. It all still seems like a terrifying nightmare. They were all one. They needed to have the same name, and it had to be yours so that if one day they wanted to take pride in something, they would take pride in you. They all needed to be called Saryas, to take three different paths and live in three different regions so they wouldn't be called bastards but the sons of Muzafar-i Subhdam. Their three stories were really one and the same. I had to make sure no one could trace their secret. Damn whoever first went in search of the story's secret. He is cursed and must die. Almighty Lord, I had to split them up lest I be found out so that if someone asked who Saryas was I wouldn't have to talk about my own illegitimate children but could talk instead about the child of a prisoner who was proudly fighting the occupiers of our land from his cell. No one in this world knew there were three Saryases apart from Sayyid Jalal Shams and me. I had a dream, Muzafar-i Subhdam. The glass pomegranates had to be our witnesses, as did the names. They all had the same name so they would understand that they were all the same person, the same being, that they all endured the same suffering and would grow up inside the same inferno with the same problems. They had to know I looked on them all in the same way, as if they were all my sons. I already knew they would grow up without you or me, that we would never be reunited. Muzafar, you were as good as dead, and the three of them would one day know that to me they were all the same, that all three would live, grow up, and die in the world I ruled." He paused briefly then said, "They had similar lives. It would have been a lie to give them different names."

After a long silence, I asked, "Was it a lie, or did you just use the name Saryas to mask your guilt?"

His eyes met mine again and he said, "That does nothing to change the fact that they were brothers. They needed to have something in common, to bind them together. When I separated them, I had to leave them a thread they could follow to find each other in the future. What happened after that wasn't my fault. I couldn't do anything about it. Do you know what would happen if we revealed our illegitimate children? Do you? It would be the end of me and that would be the end of the homeland."

I couldn't bear it. "Tell me, Yaqub-i Snawbar, did you try to find them after the success of the revolution? Were you aware of what happened to them after the uprising?"

"That question is beyond me, out of my reach," he said, shaking his head. "I have tried all my life to find the answer but in vain. You don't know what it was like. You just don't. I lost them at the height of the revolution. I only found them again years later and by then there was so much I had to deal with in my own life. When I found them, they were lost for good. The wall between us was too high to overcome."

He looked at me suspiciously. "These three bastards born during the dark nights of the revolution are neither your sons nor mine. They are the sons of that time, sons of those miserable days." Angry, he stood up and shouted, "I could have raised them like the sons of kings, Muzafar. I could have sent them far, far away, to a happier life in another country, but what an almighty lie it would have been, what a betrayal. Listen, I'm innocent too. An innocent among the innocent!"

His insistence sent a shiver down my spine.

"I am not looking for the guilty, Yaqub," I said softly. "I am looking for Saryas-i Subhdam."

He didn't let me say much, interrupting me as usual. He put his arm around my shoulders and said, "If you'd been in my position, you wouldn't have disturbed their lives or created a fake life for them either. They were born here and had to live in the way imposed by the times. They left us without being able to fulfill their dreams." After a short silence, he went back to the sofa and sat down. He rested his head on his hands and stared out into the distance." I kept an eye on them during their early years. I knew where they were, what their lives were like, who was looking after them. I received news about each of them, but I couldn't interfere with fate. Then the world suddenly changed. Great catastrophes set life on a course you cannot alter. During those years, we failed. We woke up one morning and realized there was only a tiny bit of sky left above us. We fled, leaping over the bones of our friends, and it was then that I lost the Saryases. They were plunged into a life of hardship, like hundreds of thousands of others, and I never found them again. After that, none of us were ever our old selves again, just as the land, the fields, and orchards, never recovered. Once you've left a person, you've left them forever. Once you've left a place, it is forever in your past. Tell me, Muzafar-i Subhdam, what was I supposed to look for? I didn't even recognize the earth under my feet. There was a sea of corpses before me. By the time the new era had set in, their lives had taken on their final forms."

He leaned back, the ghost of a happy memory seeming to brush past him. "When I returned, I found the injured and disfigured Saryas first. Sayyid Jalal Shams had found him in a village. We visited him one night. He was with a group of other burnt children, and didn't know who we were. I didn't tell him I was his father because it would have been pointless. I wasn't his father and neither was anyone else. He was the son of that fire, its embers burning in his heart; the other children who had fallen into a pool of flames were his family. There comes a moment in life when we can no longer support someone else. He and I could do nothing for one another. I was convinced that the closer I got, the farther away the children moved.

The more I stretched out my hand towards them, the more repulsed they were. They were not the only ones. The three of them were just like all the others. There will be no common ground, no meeting of minds, with them."

Dear friends, my fellow refugees with whom I share the ocean tonight, at the very moment he said that he could not tear the Saryases from their worlds and from their peers, I had a strange feeling, one I had experienced before. What I heard wasn't just Yaqub-i Snawbar's voice. The man standing opposite me wasn't just Yaqub; he was another image of myself. His voice was my own, emerging from someone else's mouth. I listened to him in astonishment. My God, he and I were the same, one person torn apart.

Yes, I was sure that had I walked his path, I would have done just as he had. I too would have named each of them Saryas and given each of them a glass pomegranate, set them on three different paths and said to them, "Off you go, and live." I know I might have done many other things, cried in front of them, told them of my love for them. I might have asked them to include me in their pledges but something fundamental would have remained that I couldn't have changed: there would still be a wall between them and the world. It cut them off, this wall that Yaqub-i Snawbar was certain he couldn't climb, that I am stubbornly trying to scale to this day.

My friends, we share the storm, our hopes, and our sadnesses equally. I was overwhelmed by the uncanny resemblance between us; we were a bunch of mixed-up images of one another. The more he talked, the more speechless I became; it was my ownvoice that I was listening to. There was something stronger than the difference between two souls. The resemblance was that of two halves of one person, like two shadows cast by a single body in two different directions. Having taken completely different paths in life, we had both concluded that there was a great distance separating our children from us – a distance that I, despite my weakness, was trying with all my might to close, while he, despite his strength, left it as it was. No, neither of us were fathers.

I stood before him and listened to his screams and groans, and they were the same burdens I had carried all my life. When we embraced, I was sure that I was holding the shadow of myself. I paused for a moment and a terrifying thought raced through my mind. The secluded life he longed for was simply one of the many oaths we could have signed but didn't. It was nothing but a dream, just like those beneath the pomegranate tree. He and I were one person who had been divided, just as the Saryases were one person split into three.

How could a man with such a charismatic authority, so much frightening power, be connected to me, a broken man? We had been severed for good, could not be reattached. He and I were one broken person, one broken father, just as the Saryases were one broken son.

No, I was sure that no secluded retreat, no dream, would bring us back together. He was right, my friends. He was right. We had completely seen through each other's secrets but I could no longer swear an oath with him because I knew he wanted one thing only: that we should part on good terms. I had sworn to follow the story of the Saryases to its end, without stopping my search or absolving myself. He wanted to end our personal journeys in search of ourselves by finding peace of mind; I had promised to dedicate myself to uneasiness of truth, to give the story a different ending.

He had summoned me because he wanted us to reach the end, whereas I believed I was still at the beginning.

As if he knew what I was thinking and wanted to explain his indifference, he said, "They and we – the Saryases and us – we don't recognize each other. A few years ago, at the height of the civil war, I was inspecting our forces on a distant mountain when I heard one Peshmerga calling to another, 'Tell Saryas-i Subhdam to put some provisions in the back of the pickup.' It was a fleeting shout but nevertheless I realized one of my sons was there. A few hours later, a tall, bearded young man came to me and said, 'Leader, my name is Saryas-i Subhdam. I'd like to make a request, sir: transfer me to the frontlines, to wherever the fighting is most ferocious.' He was a handsome young man, but without hope. I, who was known for being hard-hearted and merciless, nearly threw my arms around his neck, nearly kissed him, nearly bowed down to ask his forgiveness. But I didn't. I looked at him calmly and said, 'Why, my son? Why do you want to go to a place where death is?' He replied in astonishment, 'Leader, forgive me, but on the battlefield, at the front, there is life. Death is here. Sir, what am I supposed to live for if not for the war?' I didn't know if he was joking or not. This could be my son, but I couldn't call him that or embrace him, and I was astonished by the words he uttered so casually. He didn't recognize me, of course, but I heard hatred and disgust in his voice. He spoke politely but it was as if he were somehow tricking us. He meant it when he said he wanted to go to the war. However, it wasn't because he liked fighting: it was because he couldn't take life seriously. From the way he looked at me, I understood we would never recognize each other. His eyes were filled with mockery towards us and towards life. If he'd known I was his father, he would've been even more confused. I put my hand on his shoulders and said, 'Go, go wherever you want. But look after yourself.'

"He had no idea who I was to him and, had it not been for his name, I wouldn't have recognized him either. It was as if he'd come to tell me, 'Nothing ties me to you. This is the life you created for us, and I am living it, but in my heart I despise you and this entire world.' Before leaving the room, Muzafar-i Subhdam, in the same polite but sarcastic tone, he said, 'It is a great honor to die for this pure homeland, for your name, for your power. I am absolutely delighted that you've accepted me and feed me as one of your fighters.' All his words served to mock me, Muzafar. He'd come to tell me, 'I am fighting for you because there's nothing else to do.'

"I couldn't sleep that night and I couldn't stand it at the base. Like a madman, I took to the mountains, where I sat and wept beneath a tree until morning. I hadn't cried for fifteen years. Do you know how bad it is for you to have shed no tears for such a long time? Early the next morning, I wrote thousands of letters to my enemies, my close friends, to distant countries. I sent countless letters around the world, suing for peace. But no one answered me, Muzafar. No one at all."

Yaqub-i Snawbar went over to the window, reached out to open it, but changed his mind. To stop our evening from going on too long, I said, "The boy you saw, Yaqub, is the Second Saryas. That's what I call him. He's a prisoner now."

"I know, I know," he said sadly. "I know everything. I've brought you here to beg you not to tell him I'm his father. There's nothing between us now except disgust and regret. Maybe one day I'll arrange a swap of prisoners

298

but I can't imagine sharing my seclusion with him. He's no good for that."
He came closer. "I too am condemned to contemplate my death on my own, utterly alone."

I wanted to reassure him. "Don't be afraid, Yaqub-i Snawbar. If Saryas is released, he'll change his name and migrate to another country."

Sighing, he said, "What about you? What will you do?"

"I'll go to England with the Last Saryas."

"I'll leave all of the Saryases to you, all of them, and go to hell by myself," he said.

It was how we'd been since we were kids: he leaving his duties to me, I leaving mine to him. "Leave them to me and don't worry," I said, putting my hands on his shoulders. "Leave them to me and be at peace. I don't ask anything of them. You demand the impossible. Do you know what I mean? Do you? About fatherhood? You want these boys to acknowledge our fatherhood, to recognize and understand us, for something to exist between us. I don't ask anything of them. Nor will I. I learned from the desert and the silence of the sand not to expect any replies. I won't do anything except dedicate myself to them. You and I are not entitled to ask for anything at all."

He took my hand, as if shaking it in farewell. "That's the one thing I couldn't do. If I were to live my life over again, despite all my regrets, I couldn't dedicate myself to them. But it's not me who loses track of people, who ignores my own children; it's the paths themselves that keep us apart. That's what it is, brother, the paths."

I would have loved to tell him about the last pomegranate tree in the world, to tell him that the boys had found the tree of their dreams, hopes, and inspirations more enchanting than his mansion, but he probably wouldn't have understood. He was so certain nothing was left between him and the Saryases that no connection would ever be possible.

He watched me closely, as if it were the last time he would see me and he was trying to read my final expressions. "I was hoping their paths would cross even without me," he said. "But it was a dark time, Muzafar. Looking in the dark for other people or for something you've never seen is pointless."

I held his hand and slowly led him back to his bed. "But I will look for them," I said. "I have nothing else to do. You, on the other hand, have too much. Yaqub-i Snawbar, you have just enough time to rule the country, let alone search the darkness for something you don't even know."

He coughed so terribly I feared he might die there and then. After the rattle had settled in his lungs and he had wiped his face and mouth, he wheezed, "I have just enough time to rule this hideous world. After all, someone has to do it. And whoever rules will become fed up and take mistresses so that when he starts a revolution, he will father illegitimate children. And he must be able to renounce them, push them aside, and keep them in dark rooms, and it's his right to forbid anyone else from shining a light in. Whoever rules such an ugly world must face the consequences, Muzafar-i Subhdam – great privileges but also a great price to pay. Ruling a country plagued with corruption affords great pleasures and great suffering. I have drunk deep of them both."

After that he wanted to sleep forever but I wanted to wake up. He clutched my hand and said, "I want to sleep and be at peace. He who rules the world must sleep peacefully." He quietly pulled the blanket over himself.

I sat on the edge of the bed and said, "I'm leaving, Yaqub-i Snawbar. Tell your guards not to stop me. I must carry on walking my own path."

"They were your children and mine, the offspring of us both," he said. "No one knows that but me. I kept them away from me to save them from hell. Like leaves, they were blown away by the wind. And that's that."

"Everyone leaves a footprint, the hint of a breath, some mark. I am looking for the traces they left behind. But listen to me, Yaqub. I don't want to run away from you again. Tell your guards to open the door for me."

"You're free, Muzafar-i Subhdam," he said as he settled down to sleep. "You're free. You always have been. You can go; all the guards know you're free. Goodbye. I'll be waiting for you. If you ever come back, we'll talk about death. I hope you and I will die together, Muzafar-i Subhdam. I'll be waiting for you."

I left the room without saying goodbye and found myself in the yard of a large mansion. Another castle, another mansion of illusions. Strange scenes from the early days of the revolution came back to me. I felt a strong wind blowing, a great stirring in the trees. I saw hundreds of confused birds flying in all directions in the yard. I had the same feeling I'd had in the mountains many years ago, when Yaqub used to gather the Peshmergas together in the woods, caves, or foothills and talk to them of freedom and of justice.

Confused, I begged the guards to show me the way out. They opened the door to the exit, and before I crossed the threshold, I said to myself, "Almighty God, I really don't want to die with him."

To this day, when I remember his words, I am gripped by a deep fear and have to tell myself I am not dying. I do not acknowledge my own death or that of the Saryases. Those who do not acknowledge death must search for the living they have lost. My friends, that path is longer and more complicated than mine, set between the desert and the sea. Those who don't acknowledge death are condemned to play a hard game with life, to look for their friends, their fellow humans, and to know for certain that one day they will find them somewhere else.

20

Two weeks later, I was awoken by the voices of the sisters in white. They stood waiting for me in the doorway, like two beacons of light. We had agreed that I would pay my last visit to the graves of the First Saryas and Muhammad the Glass-Hearted, the boy whose journey stirred up the dust I've been living in. I also wanted to spend one last evening with Ikram-i Kew before I set off for Europe early the next day.

The only thing I had in my pocket was the address of a hospital in England where I had heard the Last Saryas was staying, no doubt looking out the windows at the stars.

The two sisters' glow remained with me from morning to evening that day. I couldn't believe such cool eyes were capable of weeping so passionately. My departure marked the end of a period of time that they considered sad but beautiful. They were adamant that I was chasing a mirage, that I was engaged in an endless game.

The sisters read my palm, an old art they hadn't practiced for some time. Leaning over the lines of my hand, they predicted I would be lost at sea.

I just laughed. "Even if I am, I still have to go."

We took flowers, incense, and candles to the First Saryas's grave. On the way, the sisters said over and over again, "Don't go just to be lost at sea. Please, don't. You won't find anything."

Lawlaw, delicate as an angel fallen from heaven, kept saying, "Father of Saryas, what are you chasing after? Fine sand scattered by the wind many years ago cannot be brought back together again."

Shadarya said, "Lala and I will be at your service for ever. As you know, we're never going to get married. We are your loyal daughters; see out your days with us and we'll always be with you. Look how beautiful the plains are, the water, the little children! Your sheep, your chickens, your ducks, aren't they lovely? Don't go. I've dreamed about you being lost at sea. Please, don't go."

Lawlaw locked her arm with mine and said, "Father of Saryas, you can visit Saryas's grave every week. We'll go with you. He is your son, your only son. I'm sure of that. Everything about him was like you. Don't go chasing after anything else."

I put my arms around them and said, "I carried the burnt boy all the way to the last pomegranate tree. Right there beneath it, I swore an oath that I would never leave him. He's the only living person I've got left. You know how much I love you both. You've planted a rare beauty in me that will last forever. You taught me there are tender, big-hearted people who stay loyal to their loved ones. Before I stepped into your house and you told me the stories of the Saryases, I was buried in the sand. It is thanks to your generosity, your light, that I am able to take even a single step towards life, no longer afraid of the leaves and the trees. I am forever in your debt. But I must be loyal to Saryas. A person must repay their debts, don't you agree?"

The sisters began to weep in the middle of the plains. "You don't owe anyone anything. Don't go. You won't reach England. We know this. We've dreamed about it, Sheikh of Sadness, Father of Suffering. You'll never get there."

So it went on, back and forth between us, our hearts torn. I was the only one for whom the story of Saryas wasn't over.

As I bid goodbye to the grave of the Professor of our Dark Nights, I felt the sky tremble above me. "The heart of this dead boy, his life, his breath – they're not here. They are in the heart, life, and breath of the Last Saryas, who lives on behalf of all the Saryases. That's why I have to follow him."

"If you go," they pleaded, "we'll become two sad old women with neither memories nor people to make us happy."

My friends, these two girls lived in the past. You don't find that often anymore but they did. And to them, I was a part of it. I was part of an old story they could neither detach themselves from nor betray.

I saw this same pain in them at the grave of Muhammad the Glass-Hearted. We all three kissed the tombstone and whispered to him, "Muhammad the Glass-Hearted, we love you." As we were about to leave, we felt the clarity of his soul like a cool breeze, a secret stirring of the air.

"We've only thought of ourselves for years," they said sadly. "But now we realize that we love him. Right from the first moment, when he was floating in the rainwater in his sodden clothes, we loved him, had a soft spot for him at least. But a love that can't be realized is useless. It has no future."

I took their hands and led them away from the grave. "Thoughts like that will only leave you hopeless and tormented." From the bottom of my heart, I wanted to save them from the pain of guilt, wanted them to live on without any doubt about their innocence.

Even now, every night when I look out to sea, I say, "Oh great sea, oh stars, help the two sisters, help them live with a clear conscience. In this story that I'm telling you and the lost refugees, there is no guilty party. Oh sleeping waves, I'm not telling a story to find someone to blame, so how could the sisters in white, the angels who lit up my heart, be guilty? People are delicate creatures. Oh God, how vulnerable we are."

When I held the hands of the sisters in white, I could feel their incredible fragility. It was as though they, too, were made of glass and would break if they bumped into anything. God, how terrified I was. You have no idea what fear I felt when I led them away from the grave and said, "Look after yourselves. You're both made of glass."

Ever since I left my homeland and the sisters in white, the worry that they would break during my absence has been eating away at me. It is still with me, that fear that if and when I return, the girls will have shattered, leaving behind two piles of white dust. I can't get the picture out of my head: two girls fading away like mist until they become a fine dust, swept away and scattered by the wind. Two girls who would melt into air, mixing with the evening haze and disappearing, leaving behind only two black handkerchiefs, symbols of their love for Saryas the Great. I bade farewell to the sisters in white with that terrible fear that they'd break and I'd never see them again.

They went out of their way to reassure me they wouldn't break; they had signed a lifelong pledge so it wouldn't happen, rejecting love for the same reason. They needed a brother who would keep them safe forever. They had left the city so they wouldn't be broken, but the fear that it has happened, that they have turned to dust, has stayed with me since my first night at sea.

On the eve of my journey, they packed my bag and sang, their voices becoming more tender as the evening wore on. Despite their own deep sadness, they were trying to make sure my final hours with them were happy. They brought me two white fabric flowers they had made and put them in the bag with my clothes to remember them by.

Lala brought me a silver vase and a glass pomegranate. You all remember the silver vase that Muhammad the Glass-Hearted caught during the flood and gave as a gift to the sisters. It was their biggest memento of him and they gave it to me to accompany me on my voyage. Lala had wrapped the glass pomegranate in a beautiful purple cloth and said, "It's yours. You love him too, just as we do. May it help you on your journey and keep you from being lost at sea."

I put both gifts in the bag, kissed her forehead, and wept.

Ikram-i Kew arrived that evening. As always, he seemed pensive but quiet and sad. I related the recent developments in my story in minute detail: going to see Sayyid Jalal Shams; visiting the dark and harrowing hospital; finding the Last Saryas with his burns; how I was arrested and met with Yaqub-i Snawbar; climbing to the summit of the last pomegranate tree in the world and signing an everlasting oath there. All these things had taken place in a short space of time.

He looked at me reproachfully. "Why didn't you take me with you? It would have been wonderful to experience it all!" We ate our last meal and cleared up together one last time. We both knew this might be our final farewell.

I said, "Great Ikram, I had to do all those things, to do them alone like someone who takes their fate into their own hands and risks death. No one else could have taken this path on my behalf. A man has to know his own paths, the ones no one else can take for him. There are some paths you have to take, even if you need to come back from the dead to do so, because your death will be incomplete otherwise. And I don't want an incomplete death."

Ikram's giant figure cast a large shadow in the light of the kerosene lamp. Slowly, he sipped his tea and said, "Be careful at sea. Take care of yourself. Many people drown there." Just as he had done once before, he produced a bag of money and gave it all to me. "You will have to work when you get to Istanbul. Look out for thieves. Be careful choosing which streets to go down and which ships to take. Let me know when you get there."

"Ikram, my friend, I need to ask some favors of you, difficult tasks, things only you can do."

He said sadly, "I'll do whatever I can but I can't heal all the suffering out there."

"I know, Ikram. I know what a mighty angel you are, I know humans can't face suffering alone and yet the beautiful people of our country are always on their own. The problem is not whether we can or can't do something but that we have to do it quietly. I'm not calling it a war because fighting compounds the suffering of the world. Even when fought against every evil, even when completely just, war ultimately fills the earth with suffering and sadness. No, Ikram, I'm not concerned about justice. Otherwise, I would have gone after the killers of the First Saryas, those who caused the Second Saryas so much pain, and those who burned the Last Saryas. Justice can be even more cruel than its opposite. I am talking about something that doesn't even have a name. Everyone needs to do something, drawing inspiration from their own lives. You were the one who first inspired me to do all this. I'm talking about being someone who dedicates himself to others."

Just as I had on my first night with him, I raised my voice on my last. "I am leaving such a lot behind for you: the sisters in white, the Second Saryas in his remote prison, Nadim-i Shazda, whom I've never met but without whom this story and all the stories in the world are incomplete. I'm also leaving you Black Star, the child someone must get out of that hospital; the patients in the burn unit, whom the world has forgotten; and the graves of Saryas and Muhammad the Glass-Hearted. You must visit them on my behalf. I am also leaving you the last pomegranate tree in the world."

He was looking at me quietly, saying nothing. Finally he said, "I can't promise you anything but I'll do my best."

The next morning, I said goodbye to the sisters in white and kissed their foreheads as tears ran down my cheeks and beard. Ikram held my hand, helped me into his car, and said, "Let's go."

I won't hide it from you that I couldn't bear to look back at the sisters in white. I didn't dare bid them a final farewell. You have to understand that I had to be constantly on the move, that I couldn't settle anywhere. They would be standing, the morning wind playing with their hair, the hair that I still feel upon me, that flutters out here at sea, following the rise and fall of the waves. I didn't look them in the eyes, only saw their wild hair, carried on the wind, as behind them the last shaft of moonlight shone on the early hours of the morning.

The sun had barely risen when I left Ikram's car for the one that would take me to the border. Ikram-i Kew opened the door for me and we embraced and wept in the first light of day. Something deeper and stronger than friendship had grown between us, which I would say was one human coming to understand another. He recognized my winding roads, my dark nights, my emotions and moods that were as changeable as desert sand lifted by the wind.

"I have to be out there, in that jungle, waiting to see what wounded bird lands near me and needs my healing." It was the last thing he said. He wiped his eyes, handed me his handkerchief, said goodbye, and left.

Frozen to the spot, I wept, my vision full of his looming shadow, the only thing in the world I could see. When he left, I felt naked and weak, a loneliness that has remained with me ever since.

But our paths went in different directions. I was heading seaward to finish the journey that was mine and mine alone.

And that's how I, who had come from the desert, set out for the sea, how I left the city that had introduced me to all these people in such a short time. On the night I boarded the ferry in Patras, my bag still contained everything meant to be in it: a few clothes, two glass pomegranates – the third had been lost forever – a silver vase, the Second Saryas's tapes, the address of a hospital in England where Saryas would be looking out the window at the stars, a small twig from the last pomegranate tree that I'll carry with me till I die, a scrap of a newspaper with a photo of the Marshal and his small cart, and two enchanting white flowers, which, during the night, bring the scent of the sisters in white back into my life.

I received the Second Saryas's last tape in Istanbul and sent him my last one from Patras. Even now as I stand on this ship and tell you this story, he remains in prison, awaiting a peace deal that will release him from the fortress, dreaming of the day that he'll change his name, leave the country, and have a child who has never heard the name Saryas-i Subhdam.

My friends, I don't know what I will tell you tomorrow night. My story never ends, this tale of glass boys living in a glass time in a glass country. I could start again tomorrow night from the same place and choose a different route to bring you back to this ferry. Ultimately what matters is that a man should come out of the sand and be lost at sea on a refugee boat. I am that man.

My doubts about this journey have grown night after night. We don't know what we're doing, floating in circles on a perilous sea for many nights without getting anywhere. Every night, I shout out to sea, "Where are you, Saryas-i Subhdam? I am a man made of sand and water. You are a boy made of ash." Every night when you are all sleep, I ask the sea to bring me something from him, to take him something from me. I call out to him, begging him to answer, but only the echo of the waves comes back to me. I cry out, "Child of fire, I am coming to you, speak to me!" But there is no answer.

On many nights I feel that getting lost at sea is the same as getting lost in his endless silence. He went through fire and chose silence because there was nothing else to choose. The silence of this sea and that of the Saryases, my getting lost in both, drowning in both, are one and the same. My friends, you have listened to me so patiently. Come, give me your hands and let's look at these waves that keep us turning, always and forever on the move. See, the stars are gazing down on us and everything is bringing us the same melody. Everything is telling us to pause and take in as much as possible.

I cannot be angry at this vast sea that plays with us mercilessly. Look at those waves, how furiously they roll in to play havoc with our ferry. I smell a threatening storm coming from afar, darkening the skies. Do you think the sea still listens to our cries? Oh God, I see enormous waves crashing in from afar. The black breeze of death sweeps over us, and the waters are dragging us deeper into darkness, but you, Sea, I do not fear you. Listen to me! I will not give up. Even if I die here, I am certain something will carry my voice far away, mixing it with other voices, taking my story to the other side of the sea. Someone else will eventually hear my story, decipher its codes, and share it with others.

Come and look at the sea. Tomorrow night, I will tell you this story again so that even if you don't learn it by heart, the sea and the fish and the stars all will. Tomorrow we will sit here again, and I'll tell it in a different way, the story of the boys for whom I am making this journey.

Don't go! Even if you don't listen, the wind does. Even if you don't hear me, the sleeping birds perched on the rail do. Come, keep your eyes on the sea. We will be lost on it forever. Whoever is lost at sea must be able to look at themselves in the water, as if in a mirror, like someone lost in the desert who looks for himself in the sand.

Here I am, lost here at sea. And yet, from the depth and the darkness of the waters, I cry out, over and over and over again, "Saryas-i Subhdam, where are you? Where are you? Where are you? Where are you?"

Translator's Note

My friend Melanie Moore – an editor who also translates from French and Russian – has been very generous with her time, reading two drafts of the entire book and making a significant number of corrections and suggestions. She also acted as a great sounding board throughout. I can't thank her enough for her contribution. I had the final say over all her edits though because only I speak both languages and therefore was best positioned to make the "right" call.

Special thanks to Marie LaBrosse who refined my translation of two poems that feature in the book.

The translation is also the outcome of close collaboration with the author, Bachtyar Ali, who was always happy to provide detailed answers to our queries.

I dedicate this translation to my family and friends, many of whom have supported me in my literary journey. And more specifically I dedicate it to my mum, who acted as the guardian of the many books in my childhood home – a treasure trove as instrumental to my education as my formal schooling – even though she herself could barely read them.

—Kareem Abdulrahman